McBain's Ladies, Too

MORE WOMEN OF THE 87TH PRECINCT

ALSO BY ED McBAIN

THE 87TH PRECINCT NOVELS

1956 : Cop Hater ★ The Mugger ★ The Pusher
1957 : The Con Man ★ Killer's Choice
1958 : Killer's Payoff ★ Killer's Wedge ★ Lady Killer
1959 : 'Til Death ★ King's Ransom
1960 : Give the Boys a Great Big Hand ★ The Heckler ★ See Them Die
1961 : Lady, Lady, I Did It!
1962 : The Empty Hours ★ Like Love
1963 : Ten Plus One
1964 : Ax
1965 : He Who Hesitates ★ Doll
1966 : Eighty Million Eyes
1968 : Fuzz
1969 : Shotgun
1970 : Jigsaw
1971 : Hail, Hail, the Gang's All Here
1972 : Sadie When She Died ★ Let's Hear It for the Deaf Man
1973 : Hail to the Chief
1974 : Bread
1975 : Blood Relatives
1976 : So Long as You Both Shall Live
1977 : Long Time No See
1979 : Calypso
1980 : Ghosts
1981 : Heat
1983 : Ice
1984 : Lightning
1985 : Eight Black Horses
1987 : Poison ★ Tricks
1989 : Lullaby

THE MATTHEW HOPE NOVELS

1978 : Goldilocks
1981 : Rumpelstiltskin
1982 : Beauty and the Beast
1984 : Jack and the Beanstalk
1985 : Snow White and Rose Red
1986 : Cinderella
1987 : Puss in Boots
1988 : The House That Jack Built

OTHER NOVELS

1965 : The Sentries
1975 : Where There's Smoke ★ Doors
1976 : Guns
1986 : Another Part of the City

McBain's Ladies, Too

MORE WOMEN OF THE 87TH PRECINCT

Ed McBain

THE MYSTERIOUS PRESS
New York • London • Tokyo

The city in these pages is imaginary.
The people, the places are all fictitious.
Only the police routine is based on established
investigatory technique.

Copyright © 1959, 1965, 1983 by Ed McBain
Copyright © 1979, 1980, 1986, 1989 by Hui Corporation.

Pages 3–15 and 243–262 from *Ice*, copyright © 1983 by Ed McBain

Pages 19–42 from *Doll*, copyright © 1965 by Ed McBain

Pages 45–70 from *Calypso*, copyright © 1979 by Hui Corporation

Pages 73–113 from *Ghosts*, copyright © 1980 by Hui Corporation. Used by permission of Bantam Books. All rights reserved.

Pages 117–148 from *Eight Black Horses*, copyright © 1985 by Hui Corporation

Pages 151–163 from *'Til Death*, copyright © 1959 by Ed McBain

Pages 167–239 from *Killer's Wedge*, copyright © 1959 by Ed McBain

 The Mysterious Press, 129 West 56th Street, New York, N.Y. 10019

Printed in the United States of America

First Printing: June 1989

10 9 8 7 6 5 4 3 2 1

Library of Congress Cataloging-in-Publication Data

McBain, Ed. 1926–
    McBain's ladies, too.

    1. Women—Fiction.   2. Detective and mystery stories,
American.   I. Title.
PS3515.U585M344   1989   813'.54   88–34475
ISBN 0–89296–285–2

This is for
Grace and Joe Penner

INTRODUCTION

When my publisher asked me to write an introduction to *McBain's Ladies*, the volume that preceded this one, I wrote to him as follows:

> *For some time now, I've resisted writing the introduction you requested, despite having set aside blocks of time in which to do it. I kept wondering why. I think I now know why.*
>
> *My reluctance has nothing to do with avoiding work. A five-page intro is a leaf on the wind. I have learned over the years, however, to trust my instincts as they regard editorial suggestions, and my instincts tell me this is a bad idea. It would be a bad idea even if someone else wrote it. It is a bad idea because:*
>
> *Readers—this reader at least—tend to equate introductions with works of non-fiction or collections of short stories.* Ladies *and* Ladies, Too *are neither. Readers tend to believe introductions are boring—and they are usually right. Readers tend to skip introductions—as even you and I do. So why does a publisher or an editor feel an introduction is necessary? Either he doesn't trust the book, or he doesn't trust the reader.*

That is what I wrote on August 28, 1987.
As I sit at the keyboard now, it is a bit more than a year later.
And I am writing an introduction.
You may wonder why.
I'll tell you why.
Too many people questioned the motives behind *McBain's Ladies*. One reviewer went so far as to suggest that a venal

publisher decided to take (and I quote) "pecuniary advantage of Joe Public. That's you." Since *McBain's Ladies* did not contain any "new piece of work, essay, glossary, critical piece," or even the boring introduction my publisher had requested, the argument was that we were stealing tons of money from unsuspecting readers by selling them a mere book of excerpts. I would hate to tell that reviewer how little money I received for putting together *both* books; the knowledge would entirely destroy his theory. But in a profit-seeking world, profit-seeking motives are naturally expected. And when they are not there, they are imagined to be there.

Another reviewer suggested that Ed McBain (that's me) had nothing further to say, and was therefore rehashing his old stuff while he sat by the river fishing. This reviewer will be unhappy to learn that a new Matthew Hope novel was published in 1988, several months *after* the publication of *McBain's Ladies*, and a new 87th Precinct novel will be published in January of 1989, a good six months *before* the publication of the book now in your hands. I haven't been fishing. Neither have I been aboard a yacht on the Riviera, spending the ill-gotten gains of the first *Ladies* book.

Several other reviewers wondered why I was taking the risk of exposing to the reader how very little I really know about women. To one reviewer, Teddy Carella was a "Stepford wife" and Bert Kling was a "token sufferer" linked to women who invariably found themselves in trouble not of their own making—as if any woman might prefer being in trouble she *herself* had made. To another reviewer, all of the women were "as numb as bollards except in one throbbing particular." I had to look up bollard. It is a thick post on a ship or wharf, used for securing ropes or hawsers. I did not have to look up "throbbing particular." Well, I plead guilty to knowing almost nothing at *all* about women. But, given my male limitations, I do try to present them as *people*, which is all I try to do for the men in my novels. McBain's ladies are not there, as this same reviewer seemed to think, merely "to warm a policeman's sheets, or wet a tearful pillow, all ravishing or ravaged in the line of duty." Neither are the *men* in my novels there merely to warm a policewoman's sheets, or to shed tears on their own pillows, as they often do. And, while they are not quite ravishing, my men are also ravaged in the line of duty. I might suggest, by the way, that if hearing-impaired Teddy ever read the words "Stepford wife" on *anyone's* lips, male or female, she would hit that person on the head with a hammer, which is a good weapon for a woman to keep beside her bed.

Why then?

If I wasn't doing this for money, and I wasn't doing it because I'd dried up and had nothing further to write about, and I wasn't doing it to show off my regrettable ignorance about the opposite (to me, anyway) sex, why bother to put together two volumes of excerpts that did not contain any new piece of work, essay, glossary, or critical piece? What could my motive or motives possibly have been?

I will tell you.

Both *Ladies* and *Ladies, Too* are labors of love.

I put these books together for the reader and for myself. Not every 87th Precinct reader has read every novel in the series. Over the years, I continued to receive a great many letters asking for details on the prominently featured women in the series. In which book did Teddy learn she was going to have a baby? In which book did Kling meet Augusta Blair? Who killed Claire Townsend? Who did Hawes take on that skiing trip? And so on. Often, I myself did not know the answers to these questions without checking back through the body of work. So it occurred to me that it might be a good idea to track down some of these women chronologically, focusing on the high points of their lives in a way that might be interesting for the reader and, yes, for myself. And since many of the readers expressed a fascination with some of the women who'd put in only brief appearances, most of them less than law-abiding . . .

Who was the woman who kept Carella chained to a radiator?

What was the name of Santo Chadderton's jailer?

Who killed Jeremiah Newman?

. . . why not single out a few of the more interesting ones and lead *them* into the spotlight as well?

There were risks involved, but none of them was the risk of exposing my admitted ignorance about women. The risks were, in fact, twofold. First, the writing would be uneven. I started the 87th Precinct series in 1956, and by the time I began putting together the two volumes of excerpts, I had been writing the books for thirty years. If my writing had not improved in all that time, it would indeed have been a good idea to go fishing. In rereading some of the older books, I found the writing barely adequate to the task. But that was the way I wrote then, and this is the way I write now. *Ice* is a far, far cry from *Cop Hater*. And when I write *Exit*, to be published after my death, I hope that it too will be light years away from *Lullaby*, the most recent novel in the series. So the *biggest* risk was that I would be revealing what an appallingly bad writer I was back then when both the series and I were very young.

The companion risk was that in trimming out most of the pure mystery elements, I would be left with a group of women floundering around looking for a plot. Or worse, by merely *hinting* at the mysteries, I would baffle the reader. The dangers of either boredom or bafflement were stronger in *Ladies*, which traced the women through many different books spanning a good many years, than in the present volume, where each excerpt is taken from a single different novel in the series. In the first volume, I hope I presented the stories of my women in a readable and exciting way. In the present volume, the task was easier.

Both books, by the way, were put together during the same work period. First *Ladies* and then, immediately following it, *Ladies, Too*. In other words, the zillions of dollars my publishers and I made on the *first* collection of excerpts was *not* what prompted us to foist upon "Joe Public" a *second* fraudulent entry. The books were conceived as a pair, and offered to my publisher as a pair, for better or worse, till death do us part.

I put these books together to inform the reader and to inform myself. For as much as the *reader* wanted to know how these women had developed over the years, so did I. As much as the reader wanted a score card telling who were the good guys and who were the bad guys, so did I. In the first volume, we had mostly the good guys. In this one, we've got mostly the bad guys. The word "Ladies" in the first book was not intended to be sexist. When I was growing up in a Manhattan slum, calling a woman a lady wasn't a terrible thing to do. It was, in fact, a sign of enormous respect that had filtered down into the streets from old-world tradition and custom. The word "Ladies" in this second volume is perhaps intended satirically, but satire is what closes on Saturday night. In any event, here are more *women* of the 87th Precinct. I trust the book, and I trust the reader, too.

Ed McBain
Norwalk, Connecticut
September 6, 1988

THE PREGNANT HOOKER

Well, there it is, Carella thought. Same old precinct. Hasn't changed a bit since I first started working here, probably won't change even after I'm dead and gone. Same rotten precinct.

He was walking uptown from the subway kiosk on Grover Avenue, approaching the station house from the west. He normally drove to work, but the streets in Riverhead hadn't yet been plowed when he'd awakened this morning, and he figured the subway would be faster. As it was, a switch had frozen shut somewhere on the track just before the train plunged underground at Lindblad Avenue, and he'd had to wait with another hundred shivering passengers until the trouble on the line was cleared. It was now almost 9:00 A.M. Carella was an hour and fifteen minutes late.

It was bitterly cold. He could understand how a switch could freeze in this weather; his *own* switch felt shrunken and limp in his trousers, even though he was wearing long woolen underwear. Just before Christmas, his wife had suggested that what he needed was a willy-warmer. He had never heard it called a willy before. He asked her where she'd picked up the expres-

3

sion. She said her uncle had always called her cousin's wee apparatus a willy. That figured. She had been Theodora Franklin before he'd married her, four-fifths Irish with (as she was fond of saying) a fifth of Scotch thrown in. So naturally her cousin owned a "wee apparatus" and naturally her uncle called it a "willy" and naturally she'd suggested just before Christmas that what a nice Italian boy like Carella could use in his stocking on Christmas morning was a nice mink willy-warmer. Carella told her he already *had* a willy-warmer, and it was better than mink. Teddy blushed.

He climbed the steps leading to the front door of the station house. A pair of green globes flanked the wooden entrance doors, the numerals 87 painted on each in white. The doorknob on the one operable door was the original brass one that had been installed when the building was new, sometime shortly after the turn of the century. It was polished bright by constant hand-rubbings, like the toes of a bronze saint in St. Peter's Cathedral. Carella grasped the knob, and twisted it, and opened the door, and stepped into the huge ground-floor muster room that was always colder than any place else in the building. This morning, compared with the glacier outside, it felt almost cozy.

The high muster desk was on the right side of the cavernous room, looking almost like a judge's altar of justice except for the waist-high brass railing before it and Sergeant Dave Murchison behind it, framed on one side by a sign that requested all visitors to stop and state their business, and on the other by an open ledger that held the records—in the process known as "booking"—of the various and sundry criminals who passed this way, day and night. Murchison wasn't booking anyone at the moment. Murchison was drinking a cup of coffee. He held the mug in thick fingers, the steam rising in a cloud around his jowly face. Murchison was a man in his fifties, somewhat stout, bundled now in a worn blue cardigan sweater that made him look chubbier than he actually was and that, besides, was nonregulation. He looked up as Carella passed the desk.

"Half a day today?" he asked.

"Morning, Dave," Carella said. "How's it going?"

"Quiet down *here*," Murchison said, "but wait till you get upstairs."

"So what else is new?" Carella said, and sighed heavily, and walked for perhaps the ten-thousandth time past the inconspicuous and dirty white sign nailed to the wall, its black lettering announcing DETECTIVE DIVISION, its pointing, crudely drawn hand signaling any visitors to take the steps up to the second floor. The stairs leading up were metal, and narrow, and scrupulously clean. They went up for a total of sixteen risers, then turned back on themselves and continued on up for another sixteen risers, and there he was, automatically turning to the right in the dimly lighted corridor. He opened the first of the doors labeled with a LOCKERS sign, went directly to his own locker in a row second closest to the door, twisted the dial on the combination lock, opened the locker door, and hung up his coat and his muffler. He debated taking off the long johns. No, on a day like today, the squadroom would be cold.

He went out of the locker room and started down the corridor, passing a wooden bench on his left and wondering for the thousandth time who had carved the initials C.J. in a heart on one arm of the bench, passing a backless bench on the right and set into a narrow alcove before the sealed doors of what had once been an elevator shaft, passing a door also on the right and marked MEN'S LAVATORY, and a door on his left over which a small sign read CLERICAL. The detective squadroom was at the end of the corridor.

He saw first the familiar slatted wooden rail divider. Beyond that, he saw desks and telephones, and a bulletin board with various photographs and notices on it, and a hanging light globe, and beyond that more desks and the grilled windows that opened on the front of the building. He couldn't see very much that went on beyond the railing on his right because two huge metal filing cabinets blocked the desks on that side of the room. But the sounds coming from beyond the cabinets told him the place was a zoo this morning.

Detective Richard Genero's portable radio, sitting on the corner of his desk in miniaturized Japanese splendor, blasted a rock tune into the already dissonant din. Genero's little symphony meant that the lieutenant wasn't in yet. Without a by-your-leave, Carella went directly to Genero's desk, and turned off the radio. It helped, but not much. The sounds in this squadroom were as much a part of his working days as were the look and the feel of it. He sometimes felt he was more at home in this scarred and flaking, resonating apple-green room than he was in his own living room.

Everyone on the squad thought Carella looked short when he wore a turtleneck. He was not short. He was close to six feet tall, with the wide shoulders, narrow hips, and sinewy movements of a natural athlete—which he was not. His eyes, brown

5

and slanted slightly downward, gave his face a somewhat Oriental look that prompted the squadroom wags to claim he was distantly related to Takashi Fujiwara, the only Japanese-American detective on the squad. Tack told them it was true; he and Carella *were*, in fact, cousins—a blatant lie. But Tack was very young, and he admired Carella a great deal, and was really fonder of him than he was of his no-good *real* cousins. Carella knew how to say "Good morning" in Japanese. Whenever Tack came into the squadroom—morning, noon, or night—Carella said, "Oh-hi-oh." Tack answered, "Hello, cousin."

Carella was wearing a turtleneck shirt under his sports jacket that Saturday morning. The first thing Meyer Meyer said to him was, "Those things make you look short."

"They keep me warm," Carella said.

"Is it better to be warm or tall?" Meyer asked philosophically, and went back to his typing.

He did not, even under normal circumstances, enjoy typing. Today, because of the very pregnant lady across the room who was shouting Spanish obscenities at the world in general and at Detective Cotton Hawes and an appreciative chorus of early-morning drunks in particular, Meyer found it even more difficult to concentrate on the keyboard in front of him. Patiently, doggedly, he kept typing, while across the room the pregnant lady was loudly questioning Cotton Hawes's legitimacy.

Meyer's patience was an acquired skill, nurtured over the years until it had reached a finely honed edge of perfection. He had certainly not been born patient. He had, however, been born with all the attributes that would later make a life of patience an absolute necessity if he were to survive. Meyer's father had been a very comical man. At the *bris*, the traditional circumcision ceremony, Meyer's father made his announcement. The announcement concerned the name of his new offspring. The boy was to be called Meyer Meyer. The old man thought this was exceedingly humorous. The *moyle* didn't think it was so humorous. When he heard the announcement, his hand almost slipped. In that moment, he almost deprived Meyer of something more than a normal name. Fortunately, Meyer Meyer emerged unscathed.

But being an Orthodox Jew in a predominantly gentile neighborhood can be trying even if your name isn't Meyer Meyer. As with all things, something had to give. Meyer Meyer had begun losing his hair when he was still rather young. He was now completely bald, a burly man with china blue eyes, slightly taller than Carella—even when Carella *wasn't* wearing a turtleneck. He was smoking a cigar as he typed, and wishing he could have a cigarette. He had begun smoking cigars on Father's Day last year when his daughter presented him with an expensive box in an attempt to break his cigarette habit. He still sneaked a cigarette every now and then, but he was determined to quit entirely and irrevocably. On a day like today, with the squadroom erupting so early in the morning, he found his patience a bit strained, his determination somewhat undermined.

Across the room, the pregnant lady—in a mixture of street-wise English and hooker's Spanish—yelled, "So how comes, *pendego*, you kippin me here when I couldn't make even a *blind* man happy in my condition?"

Her condition was imminent. Perhaps that was why the four drunks in the detention cage in the corner of the room found her so comical. Or perhaps it was because she was wearing nothing but a half-slip under her black cloth coat. The coat was unbuttoned, and the pregnant lady's belly ballooned over the elastic waistband of the peach-colored slip. Above that, her naked breasts, swollen with the threat of parturition, bobbed indignantly and rather perkily in time to her words, which the drunks found hilarious.

"Tell me, *hijo de la gran puta*," she said grandly to Hawes, grinning at the detention cage, pleased with her receptive audience and playing to the house, "would *you* pay for somebody looks like me?" and here she grabbed both frisky breasts and squeezed them in her hands, the nipples popping between her index and middle fingers. "Would you? Hah?"

"Yes!" one of the drunks in the cage shouted.

"The arresting officer says you propositioned him," Hawes said wearily.

"So where *is* this arresting officer, hah?" the woman asked.

"Yeah, where *is* he?" one of the drunks in the cage shouted.

"Down the hall," Hawes said.

The arresting officer was Genero. Genero was a horse's ass. Nobody in his right mind would have arrested a pregnant hooker. Nobody in his right mind would have filled the detention cage with drunks at nine o'clock on a Saturday morning. There would be stale vomit in the cage tonight, when the citizenry began howling and the cage was *really* needed. Genero had first brought in the drunks, one at a time, and then he had brought in the pregnant hooker. Genero was on a crusade. Genero was a one-man Moral Majority. Which, perhaps, the *real* Moral Majority was as well.

"Sit down and shut up," Hawes said to the hooker.

"No, keep *standin'*," one of the drunks in the cage yelled.

"Turn this way, honey!" another one yelled. "Let's see 'em one more time!"

"Muy linda, verdad?" the hooker said, and showed her breasts to the drunks again.

Hawes shook his head. In a squadroom where fairness was an unspoken credo, it rankled that Genero had dragged in a pregnant hooker. He could be forgiven the cageful of drunks—*maybe*—but a pregnant hooker? Even Hawes's father would have looked the other way, and Jeremiah Hawes had been an extremely religious person, a man who'd felt that Cotton Mather was the greatest of the Puritan priests, a man who'd named his own son in honor of the colonial God-seeker who'd hunted witches with the worst of them. Hawes's father had chalked off the Salem witch trials as the personal petty revenges of a town feeding on its own ingrown fears, thereby exonerating Cotton Mather and the role the priest had played in bringing the delusion to its fever pitch. Would his father, if he were still alive, have similarly excused Genero for his zeal? Hawes doubted it.

The woman came back to his desk.

"So what you say?" she said.

"About what?"

"You let me walk, okay?"

"I can't," Hawes said.

"I got somethin' in the oven juss now," the woman said, and spread her hands wide on her belly. "But I pay you back later, okay? When this is all finish, okay?" She winked at him. "Come on, let me walk," she said. "You very cute, you know? We have a nice time together later, okay?"

"Cute?" one of the drunks in the cage yelled, insulted. *"Jesus,* lady!"

"He's *very* cute, this little *muchacho*," the woman said, and chucked Hawes under the chin as though he were a cuddly little ten-year-old dumpling. He was, in fact, six feet two inches tall, and he weighed an even two hundred pounds now that he wasn't watching his diet too closely, and he had somewhat unnervingly clear blue eyes and flaming red hair with a white streak over the left temple—the result of a peculiar accident while he was still working as a Detective/Third out of the 30th Precinct downtown. He had responded to a 10-21, a Burglary

Past, and the victim had been a hysterical woman who came screaming out of her apartment to greet him, and the super of the building had come running up with a knife when he spotted Hawes, mistaking Hawes for the burglar, who was already eighteen blocks away, and lunging at him with the knife and putting a big gash on his head. The doctors shaved the hair to get at the cut, and when it grew back, it grew in white—which had been the exact color of Hawes's terror.

The streak in his hair had accounted for a great many different reactions from a great many different women—but none of them had ever thought he was "cute." Looking at the pregnant hooker's naked breasts and appraising eyes, he began to think that maybe he *was* cute, after all. He also began to think that it wouldn't be such a bad idea to let her walk and to take her up later on her fine proposition. She was a good-looking woman in her mid-thirties, he guessed, who carried her coming infant like a barrage balloon, but who had a good slender body otherwise, with long strong legs and very nice breasts indeed, swollen to bursting now and being flaunted with deliberate coercive intent as she sashayed past Hawes's desk, back and forth, back and forth, black coat open, belly and breasts billowing like the mainsail and jibsail of an oceangoing schooner. The drunks began to applaud.

If he *did* let her walk, of course, Genero would bring departmental charges or do something else stupid. Hawes was pondering the inequity of having to work with someone like Genero when Hal Willis pushed through the slatted rail divider, dragging behind him two people handcuffed to each other. Hawes couldn't tell whether the people were boys or girls because they were both wearing designer jeans and woolen ski masks. The drunks in the cage cheered again, this time in greeting to the masked couple. Willis took a bow, spotted the pregnant hooker with the open coat, said, "Close your coat, lady, you'll freeze those sweet little darlings to death," and then said, "Come in, gentlemen," to the two people in the designer jeans and the ski masks. "Hello, Steve," he said to Carella, "it's starting early today, isn't it? Who's that in the cage? The Mormon Tabernacle Choir?"

The drunks found this almost as amusing as they found the pregnant hooker. The drunks were having the time of their lives. First a topless floor show, and now a stand-up comic with two guys in funny costumes. The drunks *never* wanted to leave this place.

"What've you got?" Carella asked.

"Two masked bandits," Willis said, and turned to them. "Sit down, boys," he said. "You won't believe this," he said to Carella, and then he turned to where Meyer was typing, and said, "You won't believe this, Meyer."

"What won't I believe?" Meyer asked, and his words seemed to command the immediate respect of everyone in the squad-room, as though—like a superb ringmaster—he had cracked a whip to call attention to the morning's star performers, diminutive Hal Willis and the two masked men. The pregnant hooker turned to look at them, and even closed her coat so that her *own* star performers would not detract from the action in the main ring. The drunks put their faces close to the meshed steel of the detention cage as if they were Death Row inmates in a B-movie, watching a fellow prisoner walk that Long Last Mile. Hawes looked, Carella looked, Meyer looked, everybody looked.

Willis, never one to shun the limelight, upstaged the two masked and manacled bandits, and said, "I was heading in to work, you know? Snow tires in the trunk 'cause I planned to have them put on at the garage on Ainsley and Third, okay? So I stop there, and I tell the mechanic to put on the tires for me—don't ask why I waited till February, okay? The *Farmer's Almanac* said it was gonna be a harsh winter. So he starts jackin' up the car, and I take the key to the men's room, and I go out to take a leak—excuse me, lady."

"De nada," the pregnant hooker said.

"And when I come back, these two guys are standin' there with cannons in their hands and yelling at the mechanic, who already crapped his pants, to open the safe. The mechanic is babbling he hasn't got the combination, and *these* two heroes here are yelling that he'd better *find* the combination fast or they'll blow his goddamn brains out, excuse me, lady. That's when I come out of the can zipping up my fly."

"What happened?" one of the drunks asked breathlessly and with sincere interest. This was really turning into a *marvelous* morning! First the topless dancer, then the stand-up comic, who was now becoming a very fine dramatic actor with a good sense of timing and a wonderful supporting cast of actors in masks as in the Japanese traditional No theater.

"Do I need an attempted armed robbery at nine in the morning?" Willis asked the cageful of drunks. "Do I need an armed robbery at *any* time of day?" he asked the pregnant hooker. "I stop in a garage to get my tires changed and to take a leak, and I run into *these* two punks."

"So what'd you *do*?" the drunk insisted. The suspense was unbearable, and all this talk about taking a leak was making *him* want to pee, too.

"I almost ran out of there," Willis said. "What would you have done?" he asked Hawes. "You're zipping up your fly and suddenly there are two punks with forty-fives in their hands?"

"I'd have run," Hawes said, and nodded solemnly.

"Of *course*," Willis said. "Any cop in his right *mind* would've run."

"I'd have run, too," Carella said, nodding.

"Me, too," Meyer said.

"No question," Willis said.

He was beginning to enjoy this. He was hoping the drunk would ask him again about what had happened back there at the garage. Like any good actor, he was beginning to thrive on audience feedback. At five feet eight inches tall, Willis had minimally cleared the height requirement for policemen in this city—at least when *he* had joined the force. Things had changed since; there were now uniformed cops, and even some detectives, who resembled fire hydrants more than they did law enforcers. But until recently, Willis had most certainly been the smallest detective anyone in this city had ever seen, with narrow bones and an alert cocker-spaniel look on his thin face, a sort of younger Fred Astaire look-alike carrying a .38 Detective's Special instead of a cane, and kicking down doors instead of dancing up staircases. Willis knew judo the way he knew the Penal Code, and he could lay a thief on his back faster than any six men using fists. He wondered now if he should toss one of the masked men over his shoulder, just to liven up the action a bit. He decided instead to tell what had happened back there at the garage.

"I pulled my gun," he said, and to demonstrate, pulled the .38 from its shoulder holster and fanned the air with it. "These two heroes here immediately yell, 'Don't shoot!' You want to know why? Because their *own* guns aren't loaded! Can you imagine that? They go in for a stickup, and they're carrying empty guns!"

"That ain't such a good story," the previously interested drunk said.

"So go ask for your money back," Willis said. "Sit down, punks," he said to the masked men.

"We're handcuffed together. How can we sit?" one of them said.

"On two chairs," Willis said, "like Siamese twins. And take off those stupid masks."

"Don't," one of them said to the other.

"Why not?" the other one said.

"We don't have to," the first one said. "We know our constitutional rights," he said to Willis.

"I'll give you *rights*," Willis said. "I could've got *shot*, you realize that?"

"How?" Meyer said. "You just told us the guns—"

"I mean *if* they'd been loaded," he said, and just then Genero came up the hall from the men's room. He said, "Who turned off my radio?" looked around for the pregnant hooker, the only one of his prisoners who wasn't in the detention cage, spotted her sitting on the edge of Hawes's desk, walked swiftly toward her, and was saying, "Okay, sister, let's . . ." when suddenly she began screaming at him. The scream scared Genero half out of his wits. He ducked and covered his head as if he'd suddenly been caught in a mortar attack. The scream scared all the drunks in the cage, too. In defense, *they* all began screaming as well, as if they'd just seen mice coming out of the walls and bats flying across the room to eat them.

The woman's strenuous effort, her penetrating, persistent, high-pitched angry scream—aside from probably breaking every window within an eight-mile radius—also broke something else. As the detectives and the drunks and the two masked men watched in male astonishment, they saw a huge splash of water cascade from between the pregnant hooker's legs. The drunks thought she had wet her pants. Willis and Hawes, both bachelors, thought so, too. Carella and Meyer, who were experienced married men, knew that the woman had broken water, and that she might go into labor at any moment. Genero, his hands over his head, thought he had done something to provoke the lady to pee on the floor, and he was sure he would get sent to his room without dinner.

"*Madre de Dios!*" the woman said, shocked, and clutched her belly.

"Get an ambulance!" Meyer yelled to Hawes.

Hawes picked up the phone receiver and jiggled the hook.

"My baby's comin'," the woman said, very softly, almost reverently, and then very quietly lay down on the floor near Meyer's desk.

"Dave," Hawes said into the phone, "we need a meat wagon, *fast*! We got a pregnant lady up here about to give birth!"

"You know how to do this?" Meyer asked Carella.

12

"No. Do you?"

"Help me," the woman said with quiet dignity.

"For Christ's sake, *help* her!" Hawes said, hanging up the phone.

"*Me?*" Willis said.

"Somebody!" Hawes said.

The woman moaned. Pain shot from her contracting belly into her face.

"Get some hot water or something," Carella said.

"Where?" Willis said.

"The Clerical Office," Carella said. "Steal some of Miscolo's hot water."

"Help me," the woman said again, and Meyer knelt beside her just as the phone on Carella's desk rang. He picked up the receiver.

"Eighty-Seventh Squad, Carella," he said.

"Just a second," the voice on the other end said. "Ralph, will you please pick up that other *phone*, please!"

In the detention cage, the drunks were suddenly very still. They pressed against the mesh. They watched as Meyer leaned over the pregnant woman. They tried to hear his whispered words. The woman screamed again, but this time they did not echo her scream with their own screams. This was not a scream of anger. This was something quite different. They listened to the scream in awe, and were hushed by it.

"Sorry," the voice on the phone said, "they're ringing it off the hook today. This is Levine, Midtown East. We had a shooting around midnight, D.O.A., girl named—"

"Listen," Carella said, "can you call back a little later? We've got a sort of emergency up here."

"This is a *homicide*," Levine said, as if that single word would clear all the decks for action, cause whoever heard it to drop whatever else he was doing and heed the call to arms. Levine was right.

"Shoot," Carella said.

"Girl's name was Sally Anderson," Levine said. "That mean anything to you?"

"Nothing," Carella said, and looked across the room. Willis had come back from the Clerical Office not only with Miscolo's boiling water, but with Miscolo himself. Miscolo was now kneeling on the other side of the woman on the floor. Carella realized all at once that Miscolo and Meyer were going to try delivering the baby.

13

"Reason I'm calling," Levine said, "it looks like this may be related to something you're working."

Carella moved his desk pad into place and picked up a pencil. He could not take his eyes off what was happening across the room.

"I got a call from Ballistics ten minutes ago," Levine said. "Guy named Dorfsman, smart guy, very alert. On the slugs they dug out of the girl's chest and head. You working a case involving a thirty-eight-caliber Smith & Wesson?"

"Yes?" Carella said.

"A homicide this would be. The case you're working. You sent some slugs to Dorfsman, right?"

"Yes?" Carella said. He was still writing. He was still looking across the room.

"They match the ones that iced the girl."

"You're sure about that?"

"Right down the line. Dorfsman doesn't make mistakes. The same gun was used in both killings."

"Uh-huh," Carella said.

Across the room, Miscolo said, "Bear down now."

"Hard," Meyer said.

"However you want to," Miscolo said.

"So what I want to know is who takes this one?" Levine asked.

"You're sure it's the same gun?"

"Positive. Dorfsman put the bullets under the microscope a dozen times. No mistake. The same thirty-eight-caliber Smith & Wesson."

"Midtown East is a long way from home," Carella said.

"I know it is. And I'm not trying to dump anything on you, believe me. I just don't know what the regs say in a case like this."

"If they're related, I would guess—"

"Oh, they're related, all right. But is it yours or mine, that's the question. I mean, you caught the original squeal."

"I'll have to check with the lieutenant," Carella said. "When he comes in."

"I already checked with mine. He thinks I ought to turn it over to you. This has nothing to do with how busy we are down here, Carella. One more stiff ain't gonna kill us. It's that you probably already done a lot of legwork . . ."

"I have," Carella said.

"And I don't know what you come up with so far, if anything . . ."

"Not much," Carella said. "The victim here was a small-time gram dealer."

"Well, this girl's a dancer, the victim here."

"Was she doing drugs?"

"I don't have anything yet, Carella. That's why I'm calling you. If I'm gonna start, I'll start. If it's your case, I'll back off."

"That's the way," Meyer said. "Very good."

"We can see the head," Miscolo said. "Now you can push a little harder."

"That's the way," Meyer said again.

"I'll check with the lieutenant and get back to you," Carella said. "Meanwhile, can you send me the paper on this?"

"Will do. I don't have to tell you—"

"The first twenty-four hours are the most important," Carella said by rote.

"So if I'm gonna move, it's got to be today."

"I've got it," Carella said. "I'll call you back."

"Push!" Miscolo said.

"Push!" Meyer said.

"Oh, my God!" the woman said.

"Here it comes, here it *comes*!" Meyer said.

"Oh, my God, my God, my *God*!" the woman said exultantly.

"That's *some* little buster!" Miscolo said.

Meyer lifted the blood-smeared infant and slapped its buttocks. A triumphant cry pierced the stillness of the squadroom.

"Is it a boy or a girl?" one of the drunks whispered.

Ice, 1983

THE GIRL

The patrolman outside the apartment was startled to see a grown detective rushing by him with a doll under his arm. Carella got into the elevator, hurriedly found what he wanted in Tinka's address book, and debated whether he should call the squad to tell them where he was headed, possibly get Kling to assist him with the arrest. He suddenly remembered that Kling had left the squadroom early. His anger boiled to the surface again. The *hell* with him, he thought, and came out into the street at a trot, running for his car. His thoughts came in a disorderly jumble, one following the next, the brutality of it, the goddamn stalking animal brutality of it, should I try making the collar alone, God that poor kid listening to her mother's murder, maybe I ought to go back to the office first, get Meyer to assist, but suppose my man is getting ready to cut out, why doesn't Kling shape up, oh God, slashed again and again. He started the car. The child's doll was on the seat beside him. He looked again at the name and address in Tinka's book. Well? he thought. Which? Get help or go it alone?

He stepped on the accelerator.

There was an excitement pounding inside him now, coupled with the anger, a high anticipatory clamor that drowned out whatever note of caution whispered automatically in his mind. It did not usually happen this way, there were usually weeks or months of drudgery. The surprise of his windfall, the idea of a sudden culmination to a chase barely begun, unleashed a wild energy inside him, forced his foot onto the gas pedal more firmly. His hands were tight on the wheel. He drove with a recklessness that would have brought a summons to a civilian, weaving in and out of traffic, hitting the horn and the brake, his hands and his feet a part of the machine that hurtled steadily downtown toward the address listed in Tinka's book.

He parked the car, and came out onto the sidewalk, leaving the doll on the front seat. He studied the name plates in the entrance hallway—yes, this was it. He pushed a bell button at random, turned the knob on the locked inside door when the answering buzz sounded. Swiftly he began climbing the steps to the third floor. On the second-floor landing, he drew his service revolver, a .38 Smith & Wesson Police Model 10. The gun had a two-inch barrel that made it virtually impossible to snag on clothing when drawn. It weighed only two ounces and was six and seven-eighths of an inch long, with a blue finish and a checked walnut Magna stock with the familiar S&W monogram. It was capable of firing six shots without reloading.

He reached the third floor and started down the hallway. The mailbox had told him the apartment number was 34. He found it at the end of the hall, and put his ear to the door, listening. He could hear the muted voices of a man and a woman inside the apartment. Kick it in, he thought. You've got enough for an arrest. Kick in the door, and go in shooting if necessary—he's your man. He backed away from the door. He braced himself against the corridor wall opposite the door, lifted his right leg high, pulling back the knee, and then stepped forward and simultaneously unleashed a piston kick, aiming for the lock high on the door.

The wood splintered, the lock ripped from the jamb, the door shot inward. He followed the opening door into the room, the gun leveled in his right hand. He saw only a big beautiful dark-haired woman sitting on a couch facing the door, her legs crossed, a look of startled surprise on her face. But he had heard a man from outside. Where—?

He turned suddenly. He had abruptly realized that the apartment fanned out on both sides of the entrance door, and that the man could easily be to his right or his left, beyond his field of vision. He turned naturally to the right because he was right-handed, because the gun was in his right hand, and made the mistake that could have cost him his life.

The man was on his left.

Carella heard the sound of his approach too late, reversed his direction, caught a single glimpse of straight blond hair like Sonny Tufts, and then felt something hard and heavy smashing into his face.

There was no furniture in the small room, save for a wooden chair to the right of the door. There were two windows on the wall facing the door, and these were covered with drawn green shades. The room was perhaps twelve feet wide by fifteen long, with a radiator in the center of one of the fifteen-foot walls.

Carella blinked his eyes and stared into the semidarkness.

There were nighttime noises outside the windows, and he could see the intermittent flash of neon around the edges of the drawn shades. He wondered what time it was. He started to raise his left hand for a look at his watch, and discovered that it was handcuffed to the radiator. The handcuffs were his own. Whoever had closed the cuff onto his wrist had done so quickly and viciously; the metal was biting sharply into his flesh. The other cuff was clasped shut around the radiator leg. His watch was gone, and he seemed to have been stripped as well of his service revolver, his billet, his cartridges, his wallet and loose change, and even his shoes and socks. The side of his face hurt like hell. He lifted his right hand in exploration and found that his cheek and temple were crusted with dried blood. He looked down again at the radiator leg around which the second cuff was looped. Then he moved to the right of the radiator and looked behind it to see how it was fastened to the wall. If the fittings were loose—

He heard a key being inserted into the door lock. It suddenly occurred to him that he was still alive, and the knowledge filled him with a sense of impending dread rather than elation. *Why* was he still alive? And was someone opening the door right this minute in order to remedy that oversight?

The key turned.

The overhead light snapped on.

A big brunette girl came into the room. She was the same girl who had been sitting on the couch when he'd bravely kicked in the front door. She was carrying a tray in her hands, and he caught the aroma of coffee the moment she entered the room, that and the overriding scent of the heavy perfume the girl was wearing.

"Hello," she said.

"Hello," he answered.

"Have a nice sleep?"

"Lovely."

She was very big, much bigger than she had seemed seated on the couch. She had the bones and body of a showgirl, five feet eight or nine inches tall, with firm, full breasts threatening a low-cut peasant blouse, solid thighs sheathed in a tight black skirt that ended just above her knees. Her legs were long and very white, shaped like a dancer's with full calves and slender ankles. She was wearing black slippers, and she closed the door behind her and came into the room silently, the slippers whispering across the floor.

She moved slowly, almost as though she were sleepwalking. There was a current of sensuality about her, emphasized by her dreamlike motion. She seemed to possess an acute awareness of her lush body, and this in turn seemed coupled with the knowledge that whatever she might be—housewife or whore, slattern or saint—men would try to do things to that body, and succeed, repeatedly and without mercy. She was a victim, and she moved with the cautious tread of someone who had been beaten before and now expected attack from any quarter. Her caution, her awareness, the ripeness of her body, the certain knowledge that it was available, the curious look of inevitability the girl wore, all invited further abuses, encouraged fantasies, drew dark imaginings from hidden corners of the mind. Rinsed raven-black hair framed the girl's white face. It was a face hard with knowledge. Smoky Cleopatra makeup shaded her eyes and lashes, hiding the deeper-toned flesh there. Her nose had been fixed once, a long time ago, but it was beginning to fall out of shape so that it looked now as if someone had broken it, and this too added to the victim's look she wore. Her mouth was brightly painted, a whore's mouth, a doll's mouth. It had said every word ever invented. It had done everything a mouth was ever forced to do.

"I brought you some coffee," she said.

Her voice was almost a whisper. He watched her as she came closer. He had the feeling that she could kill a man as readily as kiss him, and he wondered again why he was still alive.

He noticed for the first time that there was a gun on the tray, alongside the coffeepot. The girl lifted the gun now, and pointed it at his belly, still holding the tray with one hand. "Back," she said.

"Why?"

"Don't fuck around with me," she said. "Do what I tell you to do when I tell you to do it."

Carella moved back as far as his cuffed wrist would allow him. The girl crouched, the tight skirt riding up over her thighs, and pushed the tray toward the radiator. Her face was dead serious. The gun was a super .38-caliber Llama automatic. The girl held it steady in her right hand. The thumb safety on the left side of the gun had been thrown. The automatic was ready for firing.

The girl rose and backed away toward the chair near the entrance door, the gun still trained on him. She sat, lowered the gun, and said, "Go ahead."

Carella poured coffee from the pot into the single mug on the tray. He took a swallow. The coffee was hot and strong.

"How is it?" the girl asked.

"Fine."

"I made it myself."

"Thank you."

"I'll bring you a wet towel later," she said. "So you can wipe off that blood. It looks terrible."

"It doesn't feel so good, either," Carella said.

"Well, who invited you?" the girl asked. She seemed about to smile, and then changed her mind.

"No one, that's true." He took another sip of coffee. The girl watched him steadily.

"Steve Carella," she said. "Is that it?"

"That's right. What's *your* name?"

He asked the question quickly and naturally, but the girl did not step into the trap.

"Detective Second/Grade," she said, "87th Squad." She paused. "Where's that?"

"Across from the park."

"What park?"

"Grover Park."

"Oh, yeah," she said. "That's a nice park. That's the nicest park in this whole damn city."

"Yes," Carella said.

"I saved your life, you know," the girl said conversationally.

"Did you?"

"Yeah. *He* wanted to kill you."

"I'm surprised he didn't."

23

"Cheer up, maybe he will."

"When?"

"You in a hurry?"

"Not particularly."

The room went silent. Carella took another swallow of coffee. The girl kept staring at him. Outside, he could hear the sounds of traffic.

"What time is it?" he asked.

"About nine. Why? You got a date?"

"I'm wondering how long it'll be before I'm missed, that's all," Carella said, and watched the girl.

"Don't try to scare me," she said. "Nothing scares me."

"I wasn't trying to scare you."

The girl scratched her leg idly, and then said, "There're some questions I have to ask you."

"I'm not sure I'll answer them."

"You will," she said. There was something cold and deadly in her voice. "I can guarantee that. Sooner or later, you will."

"Then it'll have to be later."

"You're not being smart, mister."

"I'm being very smart."

"How?"

"I figure I'm alive only because you don't know the answers."

"Maybe you're alive because I *want* you to be alive," the girl said.

"Why?"

"I've never had anything like you before," she said, and for the first time since she'd come into the room, she smiled. The smile was frightening. He could feel the flesh at the back of his neck beginning to crawl. He wet his lips and looked at her, and she returned his gaze steadily, the tiny evil smile lingering on her lips. "I'm life or death to you," she said. "If I tell him to kill you, he will."

"Not until you know all the answers," Carella said.

"Oh, we'll get the answers. We'll have plenty of time to get the answers." The smile dropped from her face. She put one hand inside her blouse and idly scratched her breast, and then looked at him again, and said, "How'd you get here?"

"I took the subway."

"That's a lie," the girl said. There was no rancor in her voice. She accused him matter-of-factly, and then said, "Your car was downstairs. The registration was in the glove compartment. There was also a sign on the sun visor, something about a law officer on a duty call."

"All right, I drove here," Carella said.

"Are you married?"

"Yes."

"Do you have any children?"

"Two."

"Girls?"

"A girl and a boy."

"Then that's who the doll is for," the girl said.

"What doll?"

"The one that was in the car. On the front seat of the car."

"Yes," Carella lied. "It's for my daughter. Tomorrow's her birthday."

"He brought it upstairs. It's outside in the living room." The girl paused. "Would you like to give your daughter that doll?"

"Yes."

"Would you like to see her ever again?"

"Yes."

"Then answer whatever I ask you, without any more lies about the subway or anything."

"What's my guarantee?"

"Of what?"

"That I'll stay alive."

"*I'm* your guarantee."

"Why should I trust you?"

"You have to trust me," the girl said. "You're mine." And again she smiled, and again he could feel the hairs stiffening at the back of his neck.

She got out of the chair. She scratched her belly, and then moved toward him, that same slow and cautious movement, as though she expected someone to strike her and was bracing herself for the blow.

"I haven't got much time," she said. "He'll be back soon."

"Then what?"

The girl shrugged. "Who knows you're here?" she asked suddenly.

Carella did not answer.

"How'd you get to us?"

Again, he did not answer.

"Did somebody see him leaving Tinka's apartment?"

Carella did not answer.

"How did you know where to come?"

Carella shook his head.

"Did someone identify him? How did you trace him?"

Carella kept watching her. She was standing three feet away

from him now, too far to reach, the Llama dangling loosely in her right hand. She raised the gun.

"Do you want me to shoot you?" she asked conversationally.

"No."

"I'll aim for your balls, would you like that?"

"No."

"Then answer my questions."

"You're not going to kill me," Carella said. He did not take his eyes from the girl's face. The gun was pointed at his groin now, but he did not look at her finger curled inside the trigger guard.

The girl took a step closer. Carella crouched near the radiator, unable to get to his feet, his left hand manacled close to the floor. "I'll enjoy this," the girl promised, and struck him suddenly with the butt of the heavy gun, turning the butt up swiftly as her hand lashed out. He felt the numbing shock of metal against bone as the automatic caught him on the jaw and his head jerked back.

"You like?" the girl asked.

He said nothing.

"You *no* like, huh, baby?" She paused. "How'd you find us?"

Again, he did not answer. She moved past him swiftly, so that he could not turn in time to stop the blow that came from behind him, could not kick out at her as he had planned to do the next time she approached. The butt caught him on the ear, and he felt the cartilage tearing as the metal rasped downward. He whirled toward her angrily, grasping at her with his right arm as he turned, but she danced out of his reach and around to the front of him again, and again hit him with the automatic, cutting him over the left eye this time. He felt the blood start down his face from the open gash.

"What do you say?" she asked.

"I say go to hell," Carella said, and the girl swung the gun again. He thought he was ready for her this time. But she was only feinting, and he grabbed out at empty air as she moved swiftly to his right and out of reach. The manacled hand threw him off balance. He fell forward, reaching for support with his free hand, the handcuff biting sharply into his other wrist. The gun butt caught him again just as his hand touched the floor. He felt it colliding with the base of his skull, a two-pound-six-and-a-half-ounce weapon swung with all the force of the girl's substantial body behind it. The pain shot clear to the top of his head. He blinked his eyes against the sudden dizziness. Hold on, he told himself, hold on, and was suddenly nauseous.

The vomit came up into his throat, and he brought his right hand to his mouth just as the girl hit him again. He fell back dizzily against the radiator. He blinked up at the girl. Her lips were pulled back taut over her teeth, she was breathing harshly, the gun hand went back again, he was too weak to turn his head aside. He tried to raise his right arm, but it fell limply into his lap.

"Who saw him?" the girl asked.

"No," he mumbled.

"I'm going to break your nose," she said. Her voice sounded very far away. He tried to hold the floor for support, but he wasn't sure where the floor was any more. The room was spinning. He looked up at the girl and saw her spinning face and breasts, smelled the heavy, cloying perfume and saw the gun in her hand. "I'm going to break your nose, mister."

"No."

"Yes," she said.

"No."

He did not see the gun this time. He felt only the excruciating pain of bones splintering. His head rocked back with the blow, colliding with the cast-iron ribs of the radiator. The pain brought him back to raging consciousness. He lifted his right hand to his nose, and the girl hit him again, at the base of the skull again, and again he felt sensibility slipping away from him. He smiled stupidly. She would not let him die, and she would not let him live. She would not allow him to become unconscious, and she would not allow him to regain enough strength to defend himself.

"I'm going to knock out all of your teeth," the girl said.

He shook his head.

"Who told you where to find us? Was it the elevator operator? Was it that one-eyed bastard?"

He did not answer.

"Do you want to lose all your teeth?"

"No."

"Then tell me."

"No."

"You have to tell me," she said. "You *belong* to me."

"No," he said.

There was a silence. He knew the gun was coming again. He tried to raise his hand to his mouth, to protect his teeth, but there was no strength in his arm. He sat with his left wrist caught in the fierce biting grip of the handcuff, swollen, throbbing, with blood pouring down his face and from his nose, his nose a throbbing mass of splintered bone, and waited for the girl to knock out his teeth as she had promised, helpless to stop her.

He felt her lips upon him.

She kissed him fiercely and with her mouth open, her tongue searching his lips and his teeth. Then she pulled away from him, and he heard her whisper, "In the morning, they'll find you dead."

He lost consciousness again.

On Tuesday morning, they found the automobile at the bottom of a steep cliff some fifty miles across the River Harb, in a sparsely populated area of the adjoining state. Most of the paint had been burned away by what must have been an intensely hot fire, but it was still possible to tell that the car was a green 1961 Pontiac sedan bearing the license plate RI 7–3461.

The body on the front seat of the car had been incinerated. They knew by what remained of the lower portions that the body had once been a man, but the face and torso had been cooked beyond recognition, the hair and clothing gone, the skin black and charred, the arms drawn up into the typical pugilistic attitude caused by post-mortem contracture of burned muscles, the fingers hooked like claws. A gold wedding band was on the third finger of the skeletal left hand. The fire had eaten away the skin and charred the remaining bones and turned the gold of the ring to a dull black. A .38 Smith & Wesson was caught in the exposed springs of the front seat, together with the metal parts that remained of what had once been a holster.

All of the man's teeth were missing from his mouth.

In the cinders of what they supposed had been his wallet, they found a detective's shield with the identifying number 714–5632.

A call to headquarters across the river informed the investigating police that the shield belonged to a Detective/Second Grade named Stephen Louis Carella.

He lay naked on the floor near the radiator.

He could hear rain lashing against the window panes, but the room was warm and he felt no discomfort. Yesterday, the girl had loosened the handcuff a bit, so that it no longer was clamped so tightly on his wrist. His nose was still swollen, but the throbbing pain was gone now, and the girl had washed his cuts and promised to shave him as soon as they were healed.

He was hungry.

He knew that the girl would come with food the moment it grew dark; she always did. There was one meal a day, always at dusk, and the girl brought it to him on a tray and then watched him while he ate, talking to him. Two days ago, she had showed him the newspapers, and he had read them with a peculiar feeling of unreality. The picture in the newspapers had been taken when he was still a patrolman. He looked very young and very innocent. The headline said he was dead.

He listened for the sound of her heels now. He could hear nothing in the other room; the apartment was silent. He wondered if she had gone, and felt a momentary pang. He glanced again at the waning light around the edges of the window shades. The rain drummed steadily against the glass. There was the sound of traffic below, tires hushed on rainswept streets. In the room, the gloom of dusk spread into the corners. Neon suddenly blinked against the drawn shades. He waited, listening, but there was no sound.

He must have dozed again. He was awakened by the sound of the key being inserted in the door lock. He sat upright, his left hand extended behind him and manacled to the radiator, and watched as the girl came into the room. She was wearing a short silk dressing gown belted tightly at the waist. The gown was a bright red, and she wore black high-heeled pumps that added several inches to her height. She closed the door behind her, and put the tray down just inside the door.

"Hello, doll," she whispered.

She did not turn on the overhead light. She went to one of the windows instead and raised the shade. Green neon rainsnakes slithered along the glass pane. The floor was washed with melting green, and then the neon blinked out and the room was dark again. He could hear the girl's breathing. The sign outside flashed again. The girl stood near the window in the red gown, the green neon behind her limning her long legs. The sign went out.

"Are you hungry, doll?" she whispered, and walked to him swiftly and kissed him on the cheek. She laughed deep in her throat, then moved away from him and went to the door. The Llama rested on the tray alongside the coffeepot. A sandwich was on a paper plate to the right of the gun.

"Do I still need this?" she asked, hefting the gun and pointing it at him.

Carella did not answer.

"I guess not," the girl said, and laughed again, that same low, throaty laugh that was somehow not at all mirthful.

"Why am I alive?" he said. He was very hungry, and he could smell the coffee deep and strong in his nostrils, but he had learned not to ask for his food. He had asked for it last night, and the girl had deliberately postponed feeding him, talking to him for more than an hour before she reluctantly brought the tray to him.

"You're not alive," the girl said. "You're dead. I showed you the papers, didn't I? You're dead."

"Why didn't you really kill me?"

"You're too valuable."

"How do you figure that?"

"You know who killed Tinka."

"Then you're better off with me dead."

"No." The girl shook her head. "No, doll. We want to know how you found out."

"What difference does it make?"

"Oh, a lot of difference," the girl said. "He's very concerned about it, really he is. He's getting very impatient. He figures he made a mistake someplace, you see, and he wants to know what it was. Because if *you* found out, chances are somebody else will sooner or later. Unless you tell us what it was, you see. Then we can make sure nobody else finds out. Ever."

"There's nothing to tell you."

"There's plenty to tell," the girl said. She smiled. "You'll tell us. Are you hungry?"

"Yes."

"Tch," the girl said.

"Who was that in the burned car?"

"The elevator operator. Messner." The girl smiled again. "It was my idea. Two birds with one stone."

"What do you mean?"

"Well, I thought it would be a good idea to get rid of Messner just in case he was the one who led you to us. Insurance. And I also figured that if everybody thought you were dead, that'd give us more time to work on you."

"If Messner was my source, why do you have to work on me?"

"Well, there are a lot of unanswered questions," the girl said. "Gee, that coffee smells good, doesn't it?"

"Yes," Carella said.

"Are you cold?"

"No."

"I can get you a blanket if you're cold."

"I'm fine, thanks."

"I thought, with the rain, you might be a little chilly."

"No."

"You look good naked," the girl said.

"Thank you."

"I'll feed you, don't worry," she said.

"I know you will."

"But about those questions, they're really bothering him, you know. He's liable to get bugged completely and just decide the hell with the whole thing. I mean, I like having you and all, but I don't know if I'll be able to control him much longer. If you don't cooperate, I mean."

"Messner was my source," Carella said. "He gave me the description."

"Then it's a good thing we killed him, isn't it?"

"I suppose so."

"Of course, that still doesn't answer those questions I was talking about."

"What questions?"

"For example, how did you get the name? Messner may have given you a description, but where did you get the name? Or the address, for that matter?"

"They were in Tinka's address book. Both the name *and* the address."

"Was the description there, too?"

"I don't know what you mean."

"You know what I mean, doll. Unless Tinka had a *description* in that book of hers, how could you match a name to what Messner had told you?" Carella was silent. The girl smiled again. "I'm *sure* she didn't have descriptions of people in her address book, did she?"

"No."

"Good, I'm glad you're telling the truth. Because we found the address book in your pocket the night you came busting in here, and we know damn well there're no descriptions of people in it. You hungry?"

"Yes, I'm very hungry," Carella said.

"I'll feed you, don't worry," she said again. She paused. "How'd you know the name and address?"

"Just luck. I was checking each and every name in the book. A process of elimination, that's all."

"That's another lie," the girl said. "I wish you wouldn't lie to

31

me." She lifted the gun from the tray. She held the gun loosely in one hand, picked up the tray with the other, and then said, "Back off."

Carella moved as far back as the handcuff would allow. The girl walked to him, crouched, and put the tray on the floor.

"I'm not wearing anything under this robe," she said.

"I can see that."

"I thought you could," the girl said, grinning, and then rose swiftly and backed toward the door. She sat in the chair and crossed her legs, the short robe riding up on her thighs. "Go ahead," she said, and indicated the tray with a wave of the gun.

Carella poured himself a cup of coffee. He took a quick swallow, and then picked up the sandwich and bit into it.

"Good?" the girl asked, watching.

"Yes."

"I made it myself. You have to admit I take good care of you."

"Sure," Carella said.

"I'm going to take even better care of you," she said. "Why'd you lie to me? Do you think it's nice to lie to me?"

"I didn't lie."

"You said you reached us by luck, a process of elimination. That means you didn't know who or what to expect when you got here, right? You were just looking for someone in Tinka's book who would fit Messner's description."

"That's right."

"Then why'd you kick the door in? Why'd you have a gun in your hand? See what I mean? You knew who he was *before* you got here. You knew he was the one. How?"

"I told you. It was just luck."

"Ahh, gee, I wish you wouldn't lie. Are you finished there?"

"Not yet."

"Let me know when."

"All right."

"I have things to do."

"All right."

"To *you*," the girl said.

Carella chewed on the sandwich. He washed it down with a gulp of coffee. He did not look at the girl. She was jiggling her foot now, the gun hand resting in her lap.

"Are you afraid?" she asked.

"Of what?"

"Of what I might do to you."

"No. Should I be?"

"I might break your nose all over again, who knows?"

"That's true, you might."

"Or I might even keep my promise to knock out all your teeth." The girl smiled. "*That* was my idea, too, you know, knocking out Messner's teeth. You people can make identifications from dental charts, can't you?"

"Yes."

"That's what I thought. That's what I told him. *He* thought it was a good idea, too."

"You're just *full* of good ideas."

"Yeah, I have a lot of good ideas," the girl said. "You're not scared, huh?"

"No."

"I would be, if I were you. Really, I would be."

"The worst you can do is kill me," Carella said. "And since I'm already dead, what difference will it make?"

"I like a man with a sense of humor," the girl said, but she did not smile. "I can do worse than kill you."

"What can you do?"

"I can corrupt you."

"I'm incorruptible," Carella said, and smiled.

"Nobody's incorruptible," she said. "I'm going to make you *beg* to tell us what you know. Really. I'm warning you."

"I've told you everything I know."

"Uh-uh," the girl said, shaking her head. "Are you finished there?"

"Yes."

"Shove the tray away from you."

Carella slid the tray across the floor. The girl went to it, stooped again, and picked it up. She walked back to the chair and sat. She crossed her legs. She began jiggling her foot.

"What's your wife's name?" she asked.

"Teddy."

"That's a nice name. But you'll forget it soon enough."

"I don't think so," Carella said evenly.

"You'll forget her name, and you'll forget her, too."

He shook his head.

"I promise," the girl said. "In a week's time, you won't even remember your *own* name."

The room was silent. The girl sat quite still except for the jiggling of her foot. The green neon splashed across the floor, and then blinked out. There were seconds of darkness, and then the light came on again. She was standing now. She had left the gun on the seat of the chair and moved to the center of the

33

room. The neon went out. When it flashed on again, she had moved closer to where he was manacled to the radiator.

"What would you like me to do to you?" she asked.

"Nothing."

"What would you like to do to me?"

"Nothing," he said.

"No?" she smiled. "Look, doll."

She loosened the sash at her waist. The robe parted over her breasts and naked belly. Neon washed the length of her body with green, and then blinked off. In the intermittent flashes, he saw the girl moving—as though in a silent movie—toward the light switch near the door, the open robe flapping loose around her. She snapped on the overhead light, and then walked slowly back to the center of the room and stood under the bulb. She held the front of the robe open, the long pale white sheath of her body exposed, the red silk covering her back and her arms, her fingernails tipped with red as glowing as the silk.

"What do you think?" she asked. Carella did not answer. "You want some of it?"

"No," he said.

"You're lying."

"I'm telling you the absolute truth," he said.

"I could make you forget her in a minute," the girl said. "I know things you never dreamed of. You want it?"

"No."

"Just try and get it," she said, and closed the robe and tightened the sash around her waist. "I don't like it when you lie to me."

"I'm not lying."

"You're naked, mister, don't tell *me* you're not lying." She burst out laughing and walked to the door, opening it, and then turned to face him again. Her voice was very low, her face serious. "Listen to me, doll," she said. "You are *mine*, do you understand that? I can do whatever I want with you, don't you forget it. I'm promising you right here and now that in a week's time you'll be crawling on your hands and knees to me, you'll be licking my feet, you'll be *begging* for the opportunity to tell me what you know. And once you tell me, I'm going to throw you away, doll, I'm going to throw you broken and cracked in the gutter, doll, and you're going to wish, believe me, you are just going to *wish* it was you they found dead in that car, believe me." She paused. "Think about it," she said, and turned out the light and went out of the room.

He heard the key turning in the lock.

He was suddenly very frightened.

She had handcuffed both hands behind his back during one of his periods of unconsciousness, and then had used a leather belt to lash his feet together. He lay naked on the floor now and waited for her arrival, trying to tell himself he did not need her, and knowing that he needed her desperately.

It was very warm in the room, but he was shivering. His skin was beginning to itch but he could not scratch himself because his hands were manacled behind his back. He could smell his own body odors—he had not been bathed or shaved in three days—but he did not care about his smell or his beard, he only cared that she was not here yet, what was keeping her?

He lay in the darkness and tried not to count the minutes.

The girl was naked when she came into the room. She did not put on the light. There was the familiar tray in her hands, but it did not carry food any more. The Llama was on the left-hand side of the tray. Alongside the gun were a small cardboard box, a book of matches, a spoon with its handle bent back toward the bowl, and a glassine envelope.

"Hello, doll," she said. "Did you miss me?"

Carella did not answer.

"Have you been waiting for me?" the girl asked. "What's the matter, don't you feel like talking?" She laughed her mirthless laugh. "Don't worry, baby," she said. "I'm going to fix you."

She put the tray down on the chair near the door, and then walked to him.

"I think I'll play with you awhile," she said. "Would you like me to play with you?"

Carella did not answer.

"Well, if you're not even going to talk to me, I guess I'll just have to leave. After all, I know when I'm not—"

"No, don't go," Carella said.

"Do you want me to stay?"

"Yes."

"Say it."

"I want you to stay."

"That's better. What would you like, baby? Would you like me to play with you a little?"

"No."

"Don't you like being played with?"

"No."

"What do you like, baby?"

He did not answer.

"Well, you have to tell me," she said, "or I just won't give it to you."

"I don't know," he said.

"You don't know what you like?"

"Yes."

"Do you like the way I look without any clothes on?"

"Yes, you look all right."

"But that doesn't interest you, does it?"

"No."

"What *does* interest you?"

Again, he did not answer.

"Well, you *must* know what interests you. Don't you know?"

"No, I don't know."

"Tch," the girl said, and rose and began walking toward the door.

"Where are you going?" he asked quickly.

"Just to put some water in the spoon, doll," she said soothingly. "Don't worry. I'll be back."

She took the spoon from the tray and walked out of the room, leaving the door open. He could hear the water tap running in the kitchen. Hurry up, he thought, and then thought, No, I don't need you, leave me alone, goddamn you, leave me alone!

"Here I am," she said. She took the tray off the seat of the chair and then sat and picked up the glassine envelope. She emptied its contents into the spoon, and then struck a match and held it under the blackened bowl. "Got to cook it up," she said. "Got to cook it up for my baby. You getting itchy for it, baby? Don't worry, I'll take care of you. What's your wife's name?"

"Teddy," he said.

"Oh my," she said, "you still remember. That's a shame." She blew out the match. She opened the small box on the tray, and removed the hypodermic syringe and needle from it. She affixed the needle to the syringe, and depressed the plunger to squeeze any air out of the cylindrical glass tube. From the same cardboard box, which was the original container in which the syringe had been marketed, she took a piece of absorbent cotton, which she placed over the milky white liquid in the bowl of the spoon. Using the cotton as a filter, knowing that even the smallest piece of solid matter would clog the tiny opening in the hypodermic needle, she drew the liquid up into the syringe, and then smiled and said, "There we are, all ready for my doll."

"I don't want it," Carella said suddenly.

"Oh, honey, please don't lie to me," she said calmly. "I *know* you want it, what's your wife's name?"

"Teddy."

"Teddy, tch, tch, well, well," she said. From the cardboard box, she took a loop of string, and then walked to Carella and put the syringe on the floor beside him. She looped the piece of string around his arm, just above the elbow joint.

"What's your wife's name?" she asked.

"Teddy."

"You want this, doll?"

"No."

"Oooh, it's very good," she said. "We had some this afternoon, it was very good stuff. Aren't you just aching all over for it, what's your wife's name?"

"Teddy."

"Has she got tits like mine?"

Carella did not answer.

"Oh, but that doesn't interest you, does it? All that interests you is what's right here in this syringe, isn't that right?"

"No."

"This is a very high-class shooting gallery, baby. No eyedroppers here, oh no. Everything veddy high-tone. Though I don't know how we're going to keep ourselves in junk now that little Sweetass is gone. He shouldn't have killed her, he really shouldn't have."

"Then why did he?"

"I'll ask the questions, doll. Do you remember your wife's name?"

"Yes."

"What is it?"

"Teddy."

"Then I guess I'll go. I can make good use of this myself." She picked up the syringe. "Shall I go?"

"Do what you want to do."

"If I leave this room," the girl said, "I won't come back until tomorrow morning. That'll be a long night, baby. You think you can last the night without a fix?" She paused. "Do you want this or not?"

"Leave me alone," he said.

"No. No, no, we can't leave you alone. In a little while, baby, you are going to tell us everything you know, you are going to tell us exactly how you found us, you are going to tell us because if you don't we'll leave you here to drown in your own vomit. Now what's your wife's name?"

"Teddy."

"No."

"Yes. Her name is Teddy."

"How can I give you this if your memory's so good?"

"Then don't give it to me."

"Okay," the girl said, and walked toward the door. "Goodnight, doll. I'll see you in the morning."

"Wait."

"Yes?" The girl turned. There was no expression on her face.

"You forgot your tourniquet," Carella said.

"So I did," the girl answered. She walked back to him and removed the string from his arm. "Play it cool," she said. "Go ahead. See how far you get by playing it cool. Tomorrow morning you'll be rolling all over the floor when I come in." She kissed him swiftly on the mouth. She sighed deeply. "Ahh," she said, "why do you force me to be mean to you?"

She went back to the door and busied herself with putting the string and cotton back into the box, straightening the book of matches and the spoon, aligning the syringe with the other items.

"Well, good night," she said, and walked out of the room, locking the door behind her.

The girl came back into the room at nine-twenty-five. She was fully clothed. The Llama was in her right hand. She closed the door gently behind her, but did not bother to switch on the overhead light. She watched Carella silently for several moments, the neon blinking around the edges of the drawn shade across the room. Then she said, "You're shivering, baby."

Carella did not answer.

"How tall are you?" she asked. "We'll get some clothes to fit you."

"Why the sudden concern?" Carella asked. He was sweating profusely, and shivering at the same time, wanting to tear his hands free of the cuffs, wanting to kick out with his lashed feet, helpless to do either, feeling desperately ill and knowing the only thing that would cure him.

"No concern at all, baby," she said. "We're dressing you because we've got to take you away from here."

"Where are you taking me?"

"Away."

"Where?"

"Don't worry," she said. "We'll give you a nice big fix first."

He felt suddenly exhilarated. He tried to keep the joy from showing on his face, tried not to smile, hoping against hope that she wasn't just teasing him again. He lay shivering on the floor, and the girl laughed and said, "My, it's rough when a little jolt is overdue, isn't it?"

Carella said nothing.

"Do you know what an overdose of heroin is?" she asked suddenly.

The shivering stopped for just a moment, and then began again more violently. Her words seemed to echo in the room, do you know what an overdose of heroin is, overdose, heroin, do you, do you?

"Do you?" the girl persisted.

"Yes."

"It won't hurt you." She said. "It'll *kill* you, but it won't hurt you." She laughed again. "Think of it, baby. How many addicts would you say there are in this city? Twenty thousand, twenty-one thousand, what's your guess?"

"I don't know," Carella said.

"Let's make it twenty thousand, okay? I like round numbers. Twenty thousand junkies out there, all hustling around and wondering where their next shot is coming from, and here we are about to give you a fix that'd take care of seven or eight of them for a week. How about that? That's real generosity, baby."

"Thanks," Carella said. "What do you think," he started, and stopped because his teeth were chattering. He waited. He took a deep breath and tried again. "What do you think you'll . . . you'll accomplish by killing me?"

"Silence," the girl said.

"How?"

"You're the only one in the world who knows who we are or where we are. Once you're dead, silence."

"No."

"Ah, *yes*, baby."

"I'm telling you no. They'll find you."

"Uh-uh."

"Yes."

"How?"

"The same way I did."

"Uh-uh. Impossible."

"If *I* uncovered your mistake—"

"There *was* no mistake, baby." The girl paused. "There was only a little girl playing with her doll."

The room was silent.

"We've got the doll, honey. We found it in your car, remember? It's a very nice doll. Very expensive, I'll bet."

"It's a present for my daughter," Carella said. "I told you—"

"You weren't going to give your daughter a *used* doll for a present, were you? No, honey." The girl smiled. "I happened to look under the doll's dress a few minutes ago. Baby, it's all over for you, believe me." She turned and opened the door. "Fritz," she yelled to the other room, "come in here and give me a hand."

The mailbox downstairs told them Fritz Schmidt was in apartment 34. They took the steps up two at a time, drawing their revolvers when they were on the third floor, and then scanning the numerals on each door as they moved down the corridor. Meyer put his ear to the door at the end of the hall. He could hear nothing. He moved away from the door, and then nodded to Kling. Kling stepped back several feet, bracing himself, his legs widespread. There was no wall opposite the end door, nothing to use as a launching support for a flat-footed kick at the latch. Meyer used Kling's body as the support he needed, raising his knee high as Kling shoved him out and forward. Meyer's foot connected. The lock sprang and the door swung wide. He followed it into the apartment, gun in hand, Kling not three feet behind him. They fanned out the moment they were inside the room, Kling to the right, Meyer to the left.

A man came running out of the room to the right of the large living room. He was a tall man with straight blond hair and huge shoulders. He looked at the detectives and then thrust one hand inside his jacket and down toward his belt. Neither Meyer nor Kling waited to find out what he was reaching for. They opened fire simultaneously. The bullets caught the man in his enormous chest and flung him back against the wall, which he clung to for just a moment before falling headlong to the floor. A second person appeared in the doorway. The second person was a girl, and she was very big, and she held a pistol in her right hand. A look of panic was riding her face, but it was curiously coupled with a fixed smile, as though she'd been expecting them all along and was ready for them, was in fact welcoming their arrival.

"Watch it, she's loaded!" Meyer yelled, but the girl swung around swiftly, pointing the gun into the other room instead, aiming it at the floor. In the split second it took her to turn and extend her arm, Kling saw the man lying trussed near the radiator. The man was turned away from the door, but Kling knew instinctively it was Carella.

He fired automatically and without hesitation, the first time he had ever shot a human being in the back, placing the shot high between the girl's shoulders. The Llama in her hand went off at almost the same instant, but the impact of Kling's slug sent her falling halfway across the room, her own bullet going wild. She struggled to rise as Kling ran into the room. She turned the gun on Carella again, but Kling's foot struck her extended hand, kicking the gun up as the second shot exploded. The girl would not let go. Her fingers were still tight around the stock of the gun. She swung it back a third time and shouted, "Let me *kill* him, you bastard!" and tightened her finger on the trigger.

Kling fired again.

His bullet entered her forehead just above the right eye. The Llama went off as she fell backward, the bullet spanging against the metal of the radiator and then ricocheting across the room and tearing through the drawn window shade and shattering the glass behind it.

Meyer was at his side.

"Easy," he said.

She sat in the darkness of the hospital room and watched her sedated husband, waiting for him to open his eyes, barely able to believe that he was alive, praying now that he would be well again soon.

The doctors had promised to begin treatment at once. They had explained to her that it was difficult to fix the length of time necessary for anyone to become an addict, primarily because heroin procured illegally varied in its degree of adulteration. But Carella had told them he'd received his first injection sometime late Friday night, which meant he had been on the drug for slightly more than three days. In their opinion, a person psychologically prepared for addiction could undoubtedly become a habitual user in that short a time, if he was using pure heroin of normal strength. But they were working on the assumption that Carella had never used drugs before and had been injected only with narcotics acquired illegally and therefore greatly adulterated. If this was the case, anywhere between two and three weeks would have been necessary to transform him into a confirmed addict. At any rate, they would begin withdrawal (if so strong a word was applicable at all) immediately, and they had no doubt that the cure (and again they apologized for using so strong a word) would be permanent. They had explained that there was none of the addict's usual psychological dependence evident in Carella's case, and then had gone on at great length about personality disturbances, and tolerance levels, and physical dependence—and then one of the doctors suddenly and quietly asked whether or not Carella had ever expressed a prior interest in experimenting with drugs.

Teddy had emphatically shaken her head.

Well, fine then, they said. We're sure everything will work out fine. We're confident of that, Mrs. Carella. As for his nose, we'll have to make a more thorough examination in the morning. We don't know when he sustained the injury, you see, or whether or not the broken bones have already knitted. In any case, we should be able to reset it, though it may involve an operation. Please be assured we'll do everything in our power. Would you like to see him now?

She sat in the darkness.

When at last he opened his eyes, he seemed surprised to see her. He smiled and then said, "Teddy."

She returned the smile. She touched his face tentatively.

"Teddy," he said again, and then—because the room was dark and because she could not see his mouth too clearly—he said something which she was sure she misunderstood.

"That's your name," he said. "I didn't forget."

Doll, 1965

42

CHLOE CHADDERTON

Chloe Chadderton responded to their insistent knocking in a voice still unraveling sleep. When they identified themselves as police officers, she opened the door a crack, and asked that they show her their shields. Only when she was satisfied that these were truly policemen standing there in the hallway, did she take off the night chain and open the door.

She was a tall slender woman in her late twenties, her complexion a flawless beige, her sloe eyes dark and luminous in the narrow oval of her face. Standing in the doorway wearing a long pink robe over a pink nightgown, she looked only sleepy and a trifle annoyed. No anticipation in those eyes or on that face, no expectation of bad news, no sense of alarm. In this neighborhood, visits from the police were common-place. They were always knocking on doors, investigating this or that burglary or mugging, usually in the daytime, but sometimes at night if the crime was more serious.

"Mrs. Chadderton?" Carella asked, and the first faint suspicion flickered on her face. He had called her by name, this was not a routine door-to-door inquiry, they had come here specifically to talk to *her*, to talk to Mrs. *Chadderton*; the time was two in the morning, and her husband wasn't yet home.

"What is it?" she said at once.

"Are you Chloe Chadderton?"

"Yes, what is it?"

"Mrs. Chadderton, I'm sorry to tell you this," Carella said, "but your husband . . ."

"What is it?" she said. "Has he been hurt?"

"He's dead," Carella said.

The woman flinched at his words. She backed away from him, shaking her head as she moved out of the doorway, back into the kitchen, against the refrigerator, shaking her head, staring at him.

"I'm sorry," Carella said. "May we come in?"

"George?" she said. "Is it *George* Chadderton? Are you sure you have the right . . ."

"Ma'am, I'm sorry," Carella said.

She screamed then. She screamed and immediately brought her hand to her mouth, and bit down hard on the knuckle of her bent index finger. She turned her back to them. She stood by the refrigerator, the scream trailing into a choking sob that swelled into a torrent of tears. Carella and Meyer stood just outside the open door. Meyer was looking down at his shoes.

"Mrs. Chadderton?" Carella said.

Weeping, she shook her head, and—still with her back to them—gestured with one hand widespread behind her, the fingers patting the air, silently asking them to wait. They waited. She fumbled in the pocket of the robe for a handkerchief, found none, went to the sink where a roll of paper towels hung over the drainboard, tore one loose, and buried her face in it, sobbing. She blew her nose. She began sobbing again, and again buried her face in the toweling. A door down the hall opened. A woman with her hair tied in rags poked her head out.

"What is it?" she shouted. "Chloe?"

"It's all right," Carella said. "We're the police."

"They're the police," Chloe murmured.

"It's all right, go back to sleep," Carella said, and entered the apartment behind Meyer, and closed the door.

It wasn't all right; there was no going back to sleep for Chloe Chadderton. She wanted to know what had happened, and they told her. She listened, numbed. She cried again. She asked for details. They gave her the details. She asked if they had caught who'd done it. They told her they had just begun working on it. All the formula answers. Strangers bearing witness to a stranger's naked grief. Strangers who had to ask questions now at ten past two in the morning because someone had taken another man's life, and these first twenty-four hours were the most important.

"We can come back in the morning," Carella said, hoping she would not ask them to. He wanted the time edge. The killer had all the time in the world. Only the detectives were working against time.

"What difference will it make?" she said, and began weeping softly again. She went to the kitchen table, took a chair from it, and sat. The flap of the robe fell open, revealing long slender legs and the laced edge of the baby-doll nightgown. "Please sit down," she said.

Carella took a chair at the table. Meyer stood near the refrigerator. He had taken off the Professor Higgins hat. His coat was sopping wet from the rain outside.

"Mrs. Chadderton," Carella said gently, "can you tell me when you last saw your husband alive?"

"When he left the apartment tonight."

"When was that? What time?"

"About seven-thirty. Ame stopped by to pick him up."

"Ame?"

"Ambrose Harding. His manager."

"Did your husband receive any phone calls before he left the apartment?"

"No calls."

"Did anyone try to reach him after he left?"

"No one."

"Were you here all night, Mrs. Chadderton?"

"Yes, all night."

"Then you would have heard the phone—"

"Yes."

"And answered it, if it had rung."

"Yes."

"Mrs. Chadderton, have you ever answered the phone in recent weeks only to have the caller hang up on you?"

"No."

"If your husband had received any threatening calls, would he have mentioned them to you?"

"Yes, I'm sure he would have."

"*Were* there any such calls?"

"No."

"Any hate mail?"

"No."

"Has he had any recent arguments with anyone about money, or—"

"Everybody has arguments," she said.

"*Did* your husband have a recent argument with someone?"

"What kind of argument?"

"About anything at all, however insignificant it might have seemed at the time."

"Well, everybody has arguments," she said again.

Carella was silent for a moment. Then, very gently, he asked, "Did you and he argue about something, is that it?"

"Sometimes."

"What about, Mrs. Chadderton?"

"My job. He wanted me to quit my job."

"What *is* your job?"

"I'm a dancer."

"Where do you dance?"

"At the Flamingo. On Landis Avenue." She hesitated. Her eyes met his. "It's a topless club."

"I see," Carella said.

"My husband didn't like the idea of me dancing there. He asked me to quit the job. But it brings in money," she said. "George wasn't earning all that much with his calypso."

"How much would you say he normally—"

"Two, three hundred a week, *some* weeks. Other weeks, nothing."

"Did he owe anyone money?"

"No. But that's only because of the dancing. That's why I didn't want to quit the job. We wouldn't have been able to make ends meet otherwise."

"But aside from any arguments you had about your job . . ."

"We didn't argue about anything else," she said, and suddenly burst into tears again.

"I'm sorry," Carella said at once. "If this is difficult for you right now, we'll come back in the morning. Would you prefer that?"

"No, that's all right," she said.

"Then . . . can you tell me if your husband argued with anyone *else* recently?"

"Nobody I can think of."

"Mrs. Chadderton, in the past several days have you noticed anyone who seemed particularly interested in your husband's comings and goings? Anyone lurking around outside the building or in the hallway, for example."

"No," she said, shaking her head.

"How about tonight? Notice anyone in the hallway when your husband left?"

"I didn't go out in the hall with him."

"Hear anything in the hall after he was gone? Anyone who might have been listening or watching, trying to find out if he was still home?"

"I didn't hear anything."

"Would anyone else have heard anything?"

"How would I know?"

"I meant, was there anyone here with you? A neighbor? A friend?"

"I was alone."

"Mrs. Chadderton," he said, "I have to ask this next question, I hope you'll forgive me for asking it."

"George wasn't fooling around with any other women," she said at once. "Is that the question?"

"That was the question, yes."

"And *I* wasn't fooling around with any other men."

"The reason he had to ask," Meyer said, "is—"

"I *know* why he had to ask," Chloe said. "But I don't think he'd have asked a *white* woman that same question."

"White *or* black, the questions are the same," Carella said flatly. "If you were having trouble in your marriage—"

"There was no trouble in my marriage," she said, turning to him, her dark eyes blazing.

"Fine then, the matter is closed."

It was not closed, not so far as Carella was concerned. He would come back to it later if only because Chloe's reaction had been so violent. In the meantime, he picked up again on the line of questioning that was mandatory in any homicide.

"Mrs. Chadderton," he said, "at any time during the past few weeks—"

"Because I guess it's *impossible* for two black people to have a good marriage, right?" she said, again coming back to the matter—which apparently was not yet closed for *her*, either.

Carella wondered what to say next. Should he go through the tired "Some of My Best Friends Are Blacks" routine? Should he explain that Arthur Brown, a detective on the 87th Squad, was in fact happily married and that he and his wife, Caroline, had spent hours in the Carellas' house discussing toilet training and school busing and, yes, *even* racial prejudice? Should he defend himself as a white man in a white man's world, when this woman's husband—a black man—had been robbed of his life in a section of the precinct that was at least fifty-percent black? Should he ignore the possibility that Chloe Chadderton, who had immediately flared upon mention of marital infidelity, was as suspect in this damn case as anyone else in the city? *More* suspect, in fact, despite the screaming and the hollering and the tears, despite the numbness as she'd listened to the details.

White or black, they *all* seemed numb, even the ones who'd stuck an icepick in someone's skull an hour earlier; they all seemed numb. The tears were sometimes genuine and sometimes not; sometimes, they were only tears of guilt or relief. In this city where husbands killed wives and lovers killed rivals; in this city where children were starved or beaten to death by their parents, and grandmothers were slain by their junkie grandsons for the few dollars in their purses; in this city any immediate member of the family was not only a *possible* murderer but a *probable* one. The crime statistics here changed as often as did the weather, but the latest ones indicated a swing back to so-called family homicides, as opposed to those involving total strangers, where the victim and the murderer alike were unknown to each other before that final moment of obscene intimacy.

A witness had described George Chadderton's killer as a tall, skinny man, almost a boy. A man who looked like a teen-ager. Chloe Chadderton was perhaps five feet nine inches tall, with the lithe, supple body of a dancer. Given the poor visibility of the rain-drenched night, mightn't she have passed for a teen-age boy? In Shakespeare's time, it was the teen-age boys who'd acted the women's roles in his plays. Chloe had taken offense at a question routinely asked and now chose to cloud the issue with black indignation, perhaps genuine, perhaps intended only to bewilder and confuse. So Carella looked at her, and wondered what he should say next. Get tough? Get apologetic? Ignore the challenge? What? In the silence, rain lashed the single window in the kitchen. Carella had the feeling it would never stop raining.

"Ma'am," he said, "we want to find your husband's murderer. If you'd feel more comfortable with a black cop, we've got plenty of black cops, and we'll send some around. They'll ask the same questions."

She looked at him.

"The same questions," he repeated.

"Ask your questions," she said, and folded her arms across her breasts.

"All right," he said, and nodded. "At any time during the past few weeks did you notice anything strange about your husband's behavior?"

"Strange how?" Chloe said. Her voice was still edged with anger, her arms were still folded defensively across her breasts.

"Anything out of the ordinary, any breaks in his usual routine—I take it you knew most of his friends and business acquaintances."

"Yes, I did."

"*Were* there any such breaks in his usual routine?"

"I don't think so."

"Did your husband keep an appointment calendar?"

"Yes."

"Is it here in the apartment?"

"In the bedroom. On the dresser."

"Could I see it, Mrs. Chadderton?"

"Yes," she said, and rose and left the room. Carella and Meyer waited. Somewhere outside, far below, a drainpipe dripped steadily and noisily. When Chloe came back into the room, she was carrying a black appointment book in her hand. She gave it to Carella, and he immediately opened it to the two facing pages for the month of September.

"Today's the fifteenth," Meyer said.

Carella nodded, and then began scanning the entries of the week beginning September eleventh. On Monday at 3:00 P.M., according to the entry scrawled in black ink in the square for that date, George Chadderton had gone for a haircut. On Tuesday at 12:30 P.M., he'd had lunch with someone identified only as Charlie. Carella looked up.

"Who's Charlie?" he said.

"Charlie?"

"'Lunch 12:30 P.M., Charlie,'" Carella read.

"Oh. That's not a person, it's a place. Restaurant called Charlie down on Granada Street."

"Have any idea who your husband had lunch with that day?"

"No. He was always meeting with people, discussing gigs and contracts and like that."

"Didn't Ambrose Harding handle all his business affairs?"

"Yes, but George liked to meet who he'd be playing for, the promoter or the man who owned the hall or whoever."

Carella nodded and looked down at the calendar again. There were no entries for Wednesday. For Thursday, the fourteenth, there were two entries: "Office, 11:00 A.M." and "Lunch 1:00 P.M. Harry Caine."

"What would 'Office' be?" Carella asked.

"Ame's office."

"And who's Harry Caine?"

"I don't know."

Carella looked at the book again. For tonight, Friday, September fifteenth, Chadderton had written "Graham Palmer Hall, 8:30, Ame pickup 7:30." For tomorrow, Saturday the sixteenth, he had written "C. J. at C. C. 12 noon."

"Who's C. J.?" Carella asked, looking up.

"I don't know," Chloe said.

"How about C. C.? Does that mean anything to you?"

"No."

"Would it be a person or a place?"

"I have no idea."

"But you did know most of his friends and business acquaintances?"

"Yes, I did."

"Were there any recent conversations or meetings with strangers?"

"Strangers?"

"People you didn't know. Like this C. J., for example. Were there people whose names you didn't recognize when they phoned? Or people you saw him with, who—"

"No, there was nobody like that."

"Did anyone named C. J. ever phone here?"

"No."

"Did your husband mention that he had a meeting with this C. J. tomorrow at noon?"

"No."

"Mind if I take this with me?" Carella asked.

"Why do you need it?"

"I want to study it more closely, prepare a list of names, see if you can identify any of them for me. Would that be all right?"

"Yes, fine."

"I'll give you a receipt for the book."

"Fine."

"Mrs. Chadderton, when I spoke to Ambrose Harding earlier tonight, he mentioned that your husband's songs—*some* of his songs—dealt with situations and perhaps personalities here in Diamondback. Is that true?"

"George wrote about anything that bothered him."

"Would he have been associating lately with any of the people he wrote about? To gather material, or to—"

"You don't have to do research to know what's happening in Diamondback," Chloe said. "All you need is eyes in your head."

"When you say he *wrote* these songs—"

"He wrote the songs down before he sang them. I know that's not what calypso *used* to be, people used to make them up right on the spot. But George wrote them all down before hand."

"The words *and* the music?"

"Just the words. In calypso, the melody's almost always the same. There're a dozen melody lines they use over and again. It's the *words* that count."

"Where did he write these words?"

"What do you mean *where*? Here in the apartment."

"No, I meant . . ."

"Oh. In a notebook. A spiral notebook."

"Do you have that notebook?"

"Yes, it's in the bedroom, too."

"Could I see it?"

"I suppose so," she said, and rose wearily.

"I wonder if I could look through his closet, too," Carella said."

"What for?"

"He was dressed distinctively tonight, the red pants and the yellow shirt. I was wondering . . ."

"That was for the gig. He always dressed that way for a gig."

"Same outfit?"

"No, different ones. But always colorful. He was singing calypso, he was trying to make people think of Carnival time."

"Could I see some of those other outfits?"

"I still don't know why."

"I'm trying to figure out whether anyone might have recognized him from the costume alone. It was raining very hard, you know, visibility . . ."

"Well, nobody would've seen the costume. He was wearing a raincoat over it."

"Even so. Would it be all right?"

Chloe shrugged, and walked wordlessly out of the kitchen. The detectives followed her through the living room, and then into a bedroom furnished with a rumpled king-sized bed, a pair of night tables, a large mahogany dresser, and a standing floor lamp beside an easy chair. Chloe opened the top drawer of the dresser, rummaged among the handkerchiefs and socks there, and found a spiral notebook with a battered blue cover. She handed the book to Carella.

"Thank you," he said, and immediately began leafing through the pages. There were penciled lyrics for what appeared to be a dozen or more songs. There were pages of doodles, apparently scrawled while Chadderton was awaiting inspiration. On one of the pages, doodled all across it in block lettering and script lettering alike, overlapping and criss-crossing, were the words "IN THE LIFE."

"What's this?" Carella said, and showed the page to Chloe.

"I don't know. Maybe a song title."

"Did he sing anything called 'In the Life'?"

"No, but maybe it's just the *idea* for a song, just the title."

"Do you know what that expression means?" Carella asked.

"Yes, I think so. It refers to criminals, doesn't it? People in . . . well, in the criminal life."

"Yes," Carella said. "But your husband wasn't associating with any criminals, was he?"

"Not to my knowledge."

"None of the pushers or prostitutes he wrote about?"

"Not to my knowledge."

"That's a common expression among prostitutes," Carella said. "In the life."

Chloe said nothing.

"Is that the closet?" Carella asked.

"Yes, right there," she said, gesturing with her head. Carella handed the spiral notebook to Meyer, and then opened the closet door. Chloe watched him as he began moving hangers and clothing. She watched him intently. He wondered if she realized he was not looking for any of the colorful costumes her husband had worn on his various gigs, but instead was looking for black boots, a black raincoat, and a black hat—preferably wet. "These are what he wore, huh?" he asked.

"Yes. He had them made for him by a woman on St. Sab's."

"Nice," Carella said. Chloe was still watching him. He shoved aside several of the garments on their hangers, looked deeper into the closet.

"Mrs. Chadderton," Meyer said, "can you tell us whether your husband seemed worried or depressed lately? Were there any unexplained absences, did he seem to have any inkling at all that his life was in danger?"

Searching the closet, hoping that his search appeared casual, Carella recognized that Meyer had buried his "unexplained absences" question in a heap of camouflaging debris, circling back to the matter of possible infidelity in a way that might not ruffle Chloe's already substantially ruffled feathers. In the closet, there were several coats, none of them black and none of them wet. On the floor, a row of women's high-heeled pumps, several pairs of men's shoes, some low-heeled women's walking shoes, and a pair of medium-heeled women's boots—tan. Chloe had still not answered Meyer's question. Her attention had focused on Carella again.

"Mrs. Chadderton?" Meyer said.

"No. He seemed the same as always," she said. "What are you looking for?" she asked Carella abruptly. "A gun?"

"No, ma'am," Carella said. "You don't own a gun, do you?"

"This has got to be some kind of comedy act," Chloe said, and stalked out of the bedroom. They followed her into the kitchen. She was standing by the refrigerator, weeping again.

"I didn't kill him," she said.

Neither of the detectives said anything.

"If you're done here, I wish you'd leave," she said.

"May I take the notebook with me?" Carella asked.

"Take it. Just go."

"I'll give you a receipt, ma'am, if you—"

"I don't *need* a receipt," she said, and burst into fresh tears.

"Ma'am . . ."

"Would you please *go*?" she said. "Would you please get the hell out of here?"

They left silently.

In the hallway outside, Meyer said, "We were clumsy."

"We were worse than that," Carella said.

Both plate-glass windows of the Club Flamingo were painted over pink. In the center of the window on the left was a huge hand-lettered sign advertising TOPLESS, BOTTOMLESS, NOON TO 4:00 A.M. The club apparently offered more by way of spectacle than Chloe had revealed to him last night. "It's a topless club," she'd said, the difference between topless and bottomless being somewhat akin to that between Manslaughter and Murder One. In the other window was an equally large sign promising GENEROUS DRINKS, FREE LUNCH. Carella was hungry—he'd had only a glass of orange juice and a cup of coffee for breakfast. He opened one of the two entrance doors and stepped into the club's dim interior. Adjusting his eyes to the gloom, he stood just inside the entrance doors, listening to the canned rock music that blared from speakers all around the room. Dead ahead was a long oval bar. Two girls, one on either side of the bar, were gyrating in time to the rock music. Both girls were wearing sequined, high-heeled, ankle-strapped pumps and fringed G-strings. Both girls were bare-breasted. Neither of them wore anything under the G-strings. Neither of them was Chloe Chadderton.

He noticed now that there were small tables around the

perimeter of the room. The place was not very crowded. He suspected the rain was keeping customers away. But at one of the tables, a blond girl danced—if one could call it that—for the exclusive pleasure of a man who sat there alone, nursing a beer. There were four men sitting at the bar, two on each side of it, three of them white, one of them black. Carella took a seat midway down the bar. One of the bartenders—a young red-headed girl wearing a black leotard and black net stockings—walked to where he was sitting, her high-heeled pumps clicking on the hard wooden floor.

"Something to drink, sir?" she said.

"Have you got anything soft?" Carella asked.

"Oh, yes indeed," she said, and rolled her eyes and took in a deep breath, at once imparting sexual innuendo to his innocuous question. He looked at her. She figured she'd somehow made a mistake and immediately said, "Pepsi, Coke, Seven-Up, or ginger ale. It'll cost you same as the whiskey, though."

"How much is that?"

"Three-fifty. But that includes the lunch bar."

"Coke or Pepsi, either one's fine," Carella said. "Has Chloe Chadderton come in yet?"

"She's taking her break just now," the redhead said, and then casually asked, "You a cop?"

"Yes," Carella said, "I'm a cop."

"Figures. Guy comes in here wanting an ice-cream soda, he's got to be a cop on duty. What do you want with Chloe?"

"That's between her and me, isn't it?"

"This is a clean place, mister."

"Nobody said it wasn't."

"Chloe dances same as the other girls. You won't see nothing here you can't see in any one of the legitimate theaters downtown. They got big stage shows downtown with nude dancers in them, same as here."

"Mm-huh," Carella said.

The redhead turned away, uncapped his soft drink, and poured it into a glass. "Nobody is allowed to touch the girls here. They just dance, period. Same as downtown. If it isn't against the law in a legitimate theater, then it isn't against the law here, either."

"Relax," Carella said. "I'm not looking for a bust."

The girl rolled her eyes again. For a moment, he didn't quite understand her reaction. And then he realized she was deliberately equating the police expression for "arrest"—a term he was certain she'd heard a hundred times before—with what was bursting exuberantly in the black leotard top. He looked at her again. She shrugged elaborately, turned away, and walked to the cash register at the end of the bar. One of the dancers was squatting before the solitary black customer now, her legs widespread, tossing aside the fringe of the G-string to reveal herself completely. The man stared at her exposed genitals. The girl smiled at him. She licked her lips. The man was wearing eyeglasses. The girl took the glasses from his eyes, and wiped them slowly over her opening, a mock expression of shocked propriety on her face. She returned the glasses to the man's head, and then arched herself over backward, supporting herself with her arms, thrusting her open crotch toward his face and pumping at him while he continued staring. Just like the legitimate theaters downtown, Carella thought.

The state's obscenity laws were defined in Article 235, Section 2 of the Criminal Law, wherein "producing, presenting or directing an obscene performance or participating in a portion thereof which is obscene and contributes to its obscenity" was considered a Class-A misdemeanor. A related provision—PL 235.00, Subdivision 1—stated: "Any material or performance is 'obscene' if (a) considered as a whole, its predominant appeal is to prurient, shameful or morbid interest in nudity, sex, excretion, sadism or masochism, AND (b) it goes substantially beyond customary limits of candor in describing or representing such matters, AND (c) it is utterly without redeeming social value."

There was no question in Carella's mind but that the girl down the bar, her back arched, her own hand now toying with her vulva for the obvious pleasure of the man seated before her, was performing an act the predominant appeal of which was to a prurient interest in nudity and sex. But as the redheaded bartender had pointed out to him a moment ago, there wasn't anything you could see here that you couldn't see in some of the legitimate theaters downtown, provided you had a first-row seat. Make the bust, and you found yourself in endless courtroom squabbles about the difference between art and pornography, a thin line Carella himself—and even the Supreme Court of the United States—was quite unready to define.

When you thought about it—and he thought about it often—what the hell was so terrible about pornography, anyway? He had seen motion pictures rated "R" (no one under seventeen admitted unless in the company of an adult) or even "PG" (parental guidance advised) that he had found to be dirtier than any of the "X"-rated porn flicks running in the sleazy theaters along The Stem. The language in these socially acceptable films was identical to what he heard in the squadroom and on the street every single waking day of his life—and he was a man whose job placed him in constant contact with the lowest elements of society. The sex in these approved films was equally candid, sparing an audience only the explicit intercourse, fellatio, and cunnilingus common in "X"-rated films. So where did you draw the line? If it was okay for a big-name male star to make simulated love to a totally naked woman in a multimillion-dollar epic (provided he kept his pants on), then why was it wrong to depict the *actual* sex act in a low-budget film starring unknowns? Put a serious actress up there on the screen, show her simulating the sex act (but, God forbid, never actually performing it), and somehow this became high cinema art, while *Deep Throat* remained cheap porn. He guessed it was all in the camera angles. He guessed he was a cop who shouldn't be wondering so often about the laws he was being paid to enforce.

But what if he walked down the length of the bar right this minute and busted the dancer there for "participating in an obscene performance" (screwing a man's eyeglasses was certainly obscene, wasn't it?) and then busted the owner of the joint for "producing, presenting or directing an obscene performance"—what then? The offense was a Class-A misdemeanor, punishable by not more than a year in jail or more than a thousand-dollar fine. Get your conviction (which was unlikely), and they'd be out on the street again in three months' time. Meanwhile, there were killers, rapists, burglars, muggers, armed robbers, child molesters, and pushers roaming the city and victimizing the populace. So what was an honest cop to do? An honest cop sipped at his Pepsi or his Coca-Cola, whichever the redhead with the inventive pornographic mind had served him, and listened to the blaring rock, and watched the naked backside of the blond dancer across the bar as she leaned over to bring her enormous breasts to within an inch of a customer's lips.

At twenty minutes to one, Chloe Chadderton—naked except for high-heeled shoes and a silvery fringed G-string—stepped up onto the bar at the far end of it. The dancer she was replacing, the one who'd wiped the black man's glasses over what the Vice Squad would have called her "privates," patted Chloe on the behind as she strutted past her and down the ramp leading off the bartop. A new rock record dropped into place on the turntable. Smiling broadly, Chloe began dancing to it, high-stepping down the bar past the black man with the steamy eyeglasses, shaking her naked breasts, thrusting her hips, bumping and grinding to the frantic rhythm of the canned guitars, and finally stopping directly in front of Carella. Still shaking wildly, she began kneeling before him, arms stretched above her head, fingers widespread, breasts quaking, knees opening—and suddenly recognized him. A look of shocked embarrassment crossed her face. The smile dropped from her mouth.

"I'll talk to you during your next break," Carella said.

Chloe nodded. She rose, listened for a moment to recapture the beat, and then swiveled long-leggedly to where the black man sat at the other end of the bar.

She danced for half an hour, and then came to the small table where Carella was eating the sandwich he'd made at the lunch bar. She explained at once that she had only a ten-minute break. Her embarrassment seemed to have passed. She was wearing a flimsy nylon wrapper belted at the waist, but she was still naked beneath it, and when she leaned over to rest her folded arms on the tabletop, he could see her breasts and nipples in the V-necked opening of the gown.

"I want to apologize for last night," he said at once, and she opened her eyes wide in surprise. "I'm sorry. I was trying to touch all the bases, but I guess I slid into second with my cleats flying."

"That's okay," she said.

"I'm sorry. I mean it."

"I said it's okay. Did you look at George's notebook?"

"Yes. I have it here with me," he said, reaching under his chair to where he'd placed the manila envelope. "I didn't find anything I can use. Would you mind if I asked you a few more questions?"

"Go ahead," she said, and turned to look at the wall clock. "Just remember it's a half hour on the bar, and a ten-minute break. They don't pay me for sitting around talking to cops."

"Do they know your husband was killed last night?"

"The boss knows, he read it in the newspaper. I don't think any of the others do."

"I was surprised you came to work today."

"Got to eat," Chloe said, and shrugged. "What did you want to ask me?"

"I'm going to start by getting you sore again," he said, and smiled.

"Go ahead," she said, but she did not return the smile.

"You lied about this place," he said.

"Yes."

"Did you lie about anything else?"

"Nothing."

"Positive about that?"

"Positive."

"Really no trouble between you and your husband? No unexplained absences on his part? No mysterious phone calls?"

"What makes you think there might have been?"

"I'm asking, that's all."

"No trouble between us. None at all," she said.

"How about unexplained absences?"

"He was gone a lot of the time, but that had nothing to do with another woman."

"What did it have to do with?"

"Business."

"I jotted some names down," Carella said, nodding. "Got them from his appointment calendar, people he had lunch with or meetings with in the past month, people he was scheduled to see in the next few weeks ahead. I wonder if you can identify them for me."

"I'll try," Chloe said.

Carella opened his notebook, found the page he wanted, and began reading. "Buster Greerson," he said.

"Saxophone player. He was trying to get George to join a band he's putting together."

"Lester . . . Handey, is it?"

"Hanley. He's George's vocal coach."

"Okay, that explains the regularity. Once every two weeks, right?"

"Yes, on Tuesdays."

"Hawkins. Who's that?"

"I don't know. What's his first name?"

"No first name. Just Hawkins. Appears in the calendar for the first time on August tenth, that was a Thursday. Then again on August twenty-fourth, another Thursday."

"I don't know anybody named Hawkins."

"How about Lou Davis?"

"He's the man who owns Graham Palmer Hall. That's where George—"

"Oh, sure," Carella said, "how dumb." He looked at his notebook again. "Jerri Lincoln."

"Girl singer. Another one of George's album ideas. He wanted to do a double with her. But that was a long time ago."

"Saw her on August thirtieth, according to his calendar."

"Well, maybe she started bugging him again."

"Just business between them."

"You should see her," Chloe said, and smiled. "*Strictly* business, believe me."

"Don Latham," Carella said.

"Head of a company called Latham Records. The label is Black Power."

"C. J.," Carella said. "Your husband saw him—or *her*," he said, with a shrug, "on the thirty-first of August, and again on September seventh, and he was supposed to have lunch with whoever it is today—I *guess* it was going to be lunch—at twelve noon. Mean anything to you?"

"No, you asked me that last night."

"C. J.," Carella said again.

"No, I'm sorry."

"Okay, who's Jimmy Talbot?"

"Don't know him."

"Davey . . . Kennemer, is it?"

"Kennemer, yes, he's a trumpet player."

"And Arthur Spessard?"

"Another musician, I forget what he plays."

"Okay, that's it," Carella said, and closed the notebook. "Tell me about George's brother," he said abruptly.

"Santo? What do you want to know about him?"

"Is is true he ran away seven years ago?"

"Who told you that?"

"Ambrose Harding. Is it true?"

"Yes."

"Ambrose said he may have gone back to Trinidad."

"He didn't go to Trinidad. George went there looking for him, and he wasn't there."

"Have any ideas where he might be?"

Chloe hesitated.

"Yes?" Carella said.

"George thought . . ."

"Yes, what?"

"That somebody killed his brother."

"What made him think that?"

"The way it happened, the way he just disappeared from sight."

"Did George mention any names? Anybody he suspected?"

"No. But he kept at it all the time. Wasn't a day went by he wasn't asking somebody or other about his brother."

"Where'd he do the asking?"

"Everywhere."

"In Diamondback?"

"In Diamondback, yes, but not only there. He was involved in a whole big private investigation. Police wouldn't do nothing, so George went out on his own."

"When you say his brother just disappeared, what do you mean?"

"After a job one night."

"Tell me what happened."

"I don't *know* what happened, exactly. Neither does anyone else, for that matter. It was after a job—they used to play in a band together, George and his brother."

"Yes, I know that."

"George and two other guys in the band were waiting in the van for Santo to come out. He'd gone to the men's room or something, I'm not sure. Anyway, he never *did* come out. George went back inside the place, searched it top to bottom, couldn't find him."

"The other musicians who were there that night—would you know them?"

"I know their names, but I've never met them."

"What are their names?"

"Freddie Bones and Vincent Barragan."

"Bones? Is that his real name?"

"I think so."

"How do you spell the other name?"

"I think it's B-A-R-R-A-G-A-N. It's a Spanish name, he's from Puerto Rico."

"But you've never met either of them?"

"No, they were both before my time. I've only been married to George for four years."

"How do you happen to know the names then?"

"Well, he mentioned them a lot. Because they were there the night his brother disappeared, you know. And he was always talking to them on the phone."

"Recently?"

"No, not recently."

"Four years," Carella said. "Then you never met George's brother, either."

"Never."

"Santo Chadderton, is it?"

"Santo Chadderton, yes."

"Is this your first marriage?"

"Yes."

"Was it George's?"

"No. He was married before." She hesitated. "To a white woman," she said, and looked him straight in the eye.

"Divorce her or what?"

"Divorced her, yes."

"When?"

"Couple of months after we met. They were already separated when we met."

"What's *her* name, would you know?"

"Irene Chadderton. That's if she's still using her married name."

"What was her maiden name?"

"I don't know."

"Does she live here in the city?"

"Used to, I don't know if she still does."

"Would *she* have known Santo?"

"I suppose so."

"Would she know anything about his disappearance?"

"Anybody who ever had anything to do with George knows about his brother's disappearance, believe me. It was like a goddamn obsession with him. That's the *other* thing we argued about, okay? My dancing here, and him talking about his *brother* all the time! *Searching* for him all the time, checking *newspapers*, and *court* records, and *hospitals* and driving everybody *crazy*."

"You told me you had a good marriage," Carella said flatly.

"It was good as most," Chloe answered, and then shrugged. The flap of the gown slid away from one of her breasts with the motion, exposing it almost completely. She made no effort to close the gown. She stared into Carella's eyes and said, "I didn't kill him, Mr. Carella," and then turned to look at the wall clock again. "I got to get back up there, my audience awaits," she said breathlessly and smiled suddenly and radiantly.

"Don't forget this," Carella said, handing her the envelope.

"Thank you," she said. "If you learn anything . . ."

"I have your number."

"Yes," she said, and nodded, and looked at him a moment longer and then turned to walk toward the bar. Carella put on his coat and hat—both still wet—and went to the register to pay his check. As he walked out of the place, he turned to look toward the bar again. Chloe was in the same position the other dancer had assumed less than forty-five minutes ago—back arched, elbows locked, legs widespread, furiously smiling and grinding at a customer sitting not a foot away from her crotch. As Carella pushed open the door to step into the rain, the customer slid a dollar bill into the waistband of her G-string.

After forty-eight hours, you begin to get a little desperate. After seventy-two, you start praying for a break; it is amazing how many cops get religion after putting in seventy-two hours on a cold homicide case. After four days, you're sure you'll *never* solve the damn thing. When you hit the six-day mark, you begin getting desperate all over again. It is a different sort of desperation. It is a desperation bordering on obsession; you begin to see murderers under every rock. If your grandmother looks at you cockeyed, you begin to suspect her. You go over your typed reports again and again, you study your crime-scene drawings, you read homicide reports from other precincts, you search through the files looking for homicide cases in which the weapon was a .38 or the victim was a hooker or a singer or a business manager, you hash over homicide cases involving frauds or semifrauds like Harry Caine's vanity-house caper, you rehash homicide cases involving missing or kidnapped persons—and eventually you become an expert on all such homicides committed in the goddamn city during the past ten years but you *still* don't know who the hell killed three people in the immediate past, never mind ten years ago.

It was now 9:40 A.M. on Friday morning, September 22, only fourteen hours short of 11:40 P.M., when exactly one week ago a concerned citizen dialed Emergency 911 to report two men bleeding on the sidewalk at Culver and South Eleventh. Fourteen hours short of a week. Fourteen short hours short. At twenty minutes to midnight tonight, George C. Chadderton would have been dead a full week. At 3:30 A.M. tomorrow morning, Clara Jean Hawkins would likewise have been dead a full week. Ambrose Harding, who was at present lying in a coffin at the Monroe Funeral Home on St. Sebastian Avenue, would be buried tomorrow morning at 9:00 A.M., by which time *he'd* have been dead almost four days. And the case continued to lie there like a lox without a bagel.

At 9:40 that morning, Carella went to see Chloe Chadderton at her apartment in Diamondback. He had called from home first, and was therefore somewhat surprised to find her wearing the same long pink robe she'd worn on that night almost a week ago, when he and Meyer had knocked on her door at two in the morning. It occurred to him, as she let him into the apartment that he had never seen Chloe in street clothes. She was always either in a nightgown with a robe over it, as she was now, or else strutting half-naked on a bartop, or else sitting at a table and wearing only a flimsy nylon wrapper over her dancing costume. He could understand why George Chadderton wanted his wife to get out of "show biz," considering what she seemed intent on showing day and night to any interested viewer. Sitting opposite her in the living room now, Carella looked across at the long length of leg revealed in the opening of her robe and silently admitted that he himself was an interested viewer. Embarrassed, recalling Chloe's total exposure on the bartop at the Flamingo, he quickly took out his notebook and busied himself leafing through its pages.

"Would you like some coffee?" she asked. "I have some on the stove."

"No, thanks," Carella said. "I just want to ask you some questions, and then I'll be on my way."

"No hurry," she said, and smiled.

"Mrs. Chadderton," he said, "I tried to fill you in a little on the phone about what we believe is the connection between your husband and C. J. Hawkins, the fact that they'd been talking about doing an album together."

"Yes, but George never mentioned that to me," Chloe said.

"Something called 'In the Life.' Do you remember in his notebook . . ."

"Yes . . ."

"The night we were here . . ."

"Yes, I remember."

"That's what we think the title of the album was going to be."

"Mm-huh," Chloe said.

"But he never mentioned this album to you."

"No."

"Or Miss Hawkins. He never mentioned anyone named Clara Jean Hawkins or C. J. Hawkins."

"Never," Chloe said, and shifted her weight on the sofa.

Carella looked at his notebook again. "Mrs. Chadderton . . ." he said.

"I wish you'd call me Chloe," she said.

"Well . . . uh . . . yes, fine," he said, but instead skirted the name the way he might have a puddle on the sidewalk. "In the appointment calendar you let me have, the name Hawkins and the initials C. J. appeared on the following dates: August tenth, August twenty-fourth, August thirty-first, and September seventh. Those are all Thursdays. We know that Miss Hawkins's day off was Thursday—"

"Just like a cleaning woman," Chloe said, and smiled.

"What?" Carella said.

"Thursdays and every other Sunday," Chloe said.

"Oh. Well, I hadn't made that connection," Carella said.

"Don't worry, I'm not about to start another racial hassle," Chloe said.

"I didn't think you were."

"I was wrong about you that night," she said. "That first night."

"Well," he said, "that's—"

"Do you know when I realized you were okay?"

"No, when was that?"

"At the Flamingo. You were checking names and dates in your little notebook, same as you're doing now, and you asked me who Lou Davis was and I told you he was the man who owned the hall my husband . . ."

"Yes, I remember."

"And you said 'How dumb,' or something like that. About your*self*, I mean. You were calling yourself dumb."

"I was *right*, too," Carella said, and smiled.

"So I decided I liked you."

"Well . . . good. I'm glad to hear that."

"In fact, I was very happy when you called this morning," Chloe said.

"Well . . . uh . . . good," he said, and smiled. "I was saying that your husband's meetings with C. J. Hawkins—"

"She was a hooker, is that right?"

"Yes—always took place on Thursdays, which was her day off, Thursday. We've got reason to believe that some sort of beach party took place every *Wednesday* night, however, and I wonder if your husband ever mentioned any such party to you."

"A beach party?"

"Well, we don't know if it was a party *on* the beach. We only know that C. J. went out to the beach someplace—"

"What beach?"

"We don't know—and got paid for her services out there."

"Oh."

"Yes, we think it was, you know, some sort of regular, uh, prostitution she was performing out there someplace."

"With George, are you saying?"

"No, I'm not suggesting that. I know you had a good marriage, I know there was no trouble—"

"Bullshit," Chloe said.

Carella looked at her.

"I know that's what I told you," she said.

"Yes, more than once, Mrs. Chadderton."

"More than *twice*, in fact," she said, and smiled. "And it's Chloe. I wish you'd call me Chloe."

"Are you telling me now that things *weren't* good in your marriage?"

"Things were rotten," she said.

"Other women?"

"I would guess."

"Hookers?"

"I wouldn't put it past him, for all his 'Sister Woman' bullshit."

"Then you're not discounting the possibility of a sexual relationship between your husband and Miss Hawkins."

"I'm not discounting *anything*."

"Was he ever gone from the apartment on a Wednesday night?"

"He was gone from the apartment almost *every* night."

"I'm trying to find out—"

"You're trying to find out whether he and this woman were together on Wednesday nights."

"Yes, Mrs. Chadderton, because—"

"Chloe," she said.

"Chloe, right—because if I can establish that there was something more than this *cockamamie* record album between them, if I can establish that they were seeing each other, and maybe got somebody *angry* about it—"

"Not me," Chloe said at once.

"I wasn't suggesting that."

"Why not? I just told you we were unhappy. I just told you he had other women. Isn't that reason . . ."

"Well, maybe," Carella said, "but the logistics aren't right. We were here until almost three A.M. last Friday night, and C. J. was killed at three-thirty. You couldn't possibly have dressed, traveled all the way downtown, and found her on the street in that short a time."

"Then you *did* consider it?"

"I considered it," Carella said, and smiled. "I've been considering *everything* these past few days. That's why I'd appreciate any help you can give me. What I'm looking for is a connection between the two of them."

"Two of them? What about Ame?"

"No. I think Harding was killed because the murderer was afraid of identification. He was even warned beforehand."

"Warned?"

"Warned. With a pink orchid called *Calypso bulbosa*. I think the killer wants to be caught. I think it's like that guy years ago who scrawled it in lipstick on a mirror. That orchid is the same damn thing. Otherwise why warn the man? Why not just kill him? He wants to be stopped, whoever he is. So if you can remember anything at all about any Wednesday night your husband was out of this apartment . . ."

"I don't think you understand," Chloe said. "He was gone more often than he was here. There were times, this last little while, when I'd be sitting here talking to the four walls. I'd find myself longing to go back to the club. I'd get home sometime around eight-thirty, nine o'clock, and I'd eat here alone in the apartment, George'd be gone, and I'd sit here wondering what the hell I was *doing* here, why didn't I just go on back to the club? Talk to the girls, have someone to talk to. Dance for the men, have someone looking at me as if he knew I was *alive*, do you understand? George was so involved with his own damn self, he never . . . Well, look at me, I'm a pretty woman, at least I *think* I'm a pretty woman, and he was—do you think I'm pretty?"

"Yes," Carella said, "I do."

"Sure, but not to George. George was so much in love with himself, so completely involved in his own projects, his pipe-dream record albums that never got made, his big-shot calypso singer bullshit, his search for his goddamn brother who probably ran off and left him cause he couldn't stand him any more than anyone *else* could! George, George, George, it was all George, George, George, he named himself right, the bastard, King George, that's exactly what he thought he was, a fuckin *king*! You know what he told me when he wanted me to quit the Flamingo? He told me my dancing there reflected badly on his image as a popular singer. *His* image! I was embarrassing *him*, do you understand? It never once occurred to him that maybe I was embarrassing *myself*, too. I mean, man, that's degrading, isn't it? Squatting on a bartop and shoving myself in some man's face? You look nervous," she said suddenly. "Am I making you nervous?"

"A little."

"Why? Because you've seen me naked?"

"Maybe."

"Join the club," she said airily, and waved one arm languidly over her head. "Do you understand what I'm saying though?"

"I think so."

"There was nothing between us anymore is what I'm saying. When you brought me the news that night, when you came here and told me George had got killed, I started crying because . . . because I thought, hell, George got killed a long time ago. The George I loved and married got killed more years ago than I can remember. All that was left was somebody running around trying to be the big star he didn't have a chance in hell of becoming. That's why I began crying that night. I began crying because I suddenly realized how long he'd been dead. How long *we'd* been dead, in fact."

Carella nodded and said nothing.

"I've been lonely a long time," she said. And then softly, so softly that it seemed a part of the whisper of rain against the windows, she said, "Steve."

The room went silent. In the kitchen, he could hear the steady hiss of the gas jet under the coffeepot. Somewhere in the distance, there was the low rumble of thunder. He looked at her, looked at the long length of tan leg and thigh in the opening of the pink gown, looked at the slender ankle and the jiggling foot, and remembered her on the Flamingo bartop.

"If . . . if there's nothing more you can tell me," he said, "I'd better be going."

"Stay," she said.

"Chloe . . ." he said.

"Stay. You liked what you saw that day, didn't you?"

"I liked what I saw, yes," Carella said.

"Then stay," she whispered. "The rain is gentler in the other room."

He looked at her and wished he could tell her he didn't want to make love to her without having to say it straight out. He knew a hundred cops in the department—well, fifty anyway—who claimed they'd been to bed with every burglary, robbery, assault, or what-have-you victim they'd ever met, and maybe they had, Carella guessed maybe they had. He guessed Cotton Hawes had, though he wasn't too sure about that, and he supposed Hal Willis had, and he knew Andy Parker had or else was lying when he boasted in the squadroom about all his bedroom conquests. But he knew Meyer hadn't, and he knew that he himself would rather cut off his right arm than be unfaithful to Teddy, though there were many times—like right this goddamn minute with Chloe Chadderton sitting there opposite him, the smile gone from her face now, her eyes narrowed, her foot jiggling, her robe open clear to Sunday— when he would have liked nothing better than to spend a wet Friday in bed with a warm stranger in another room where the rain was gentler. He looked at her. Their eyes locked.

"Chloe," he said, "you're a beautiful, exciting woman—but I'm a working cop with three homicides to solve."

"Suppose you didn't have all those homicides to solve?" she asked.

"I'm also a married man," he said.

"Does that mean anything nowadays?"

"Yes."

"Okay," she said.

"Please," he said.

"I said okay," she snapped. And then, her voice rising, her words clipped and angry, she said, "I don't know anything about George's Wednesday night parties, or the whore's either. If there's nothing else, I'd like to get dressed now."

She folded her arms defensively across her breasts, and pulled the robe closed around her crossed legs. She was sitting that way when he left the apartment.

Calypso, 1979

HILLARY SCOTT

Hillary Scott called Carella at home at eight-thirty Saturday morning. He was still in bed. He propped himself up on one elbow and lifted the receiver of the phone on the night table.

"Hello," he said.

"Were you trying to reach me?"

"Yes," he said.

"I sensed it," Hillary said. "What is it?"

"How'd you get my home phone number?" he asked.

"From the phone book."

Thank God, he thought. If she'd plucked his home phone number out of thin air, he'd begin believing all *sorts* of things. There was, in fact, something eerie about talking to her on the telephone, visualizing her as she spoke, conjuring the near-duplicate image of his wife, who lay beside him with her arms wrapped around the pillow, her black hair spread against the pillowcase. Teddy Carella was a deaf-mute; she had not heard the ringing telephone; she did not now hear Carella's conversation with the woman who looked so much like her. He

73

wondered, abruptly, whether—if Teddy had a voice—it would sound like Hillary Scott's.

"You tried me at the apartment, didn't you?" she said.

"Yes."

"I'm here now," she said. "I came back to get some clothes. The flux was strongest around the telephone."

"Yes, well, good," he said. "Can you tell me where you're staying now, so in case I need to . . . ?"

"You can reach me at my sister's," she said. "Her name is Denise Scott; the number there is Gardner 4-7706. You'd better write it down, it's unlisted."

He had already written it down. "And the address?" he said.

"Thirty-one-seventeen Laster Drive. What did you want, Detective Carella?"

"The security guard who normally has the noon to six at Harborview called last night. Jerry . . ."

"Jerry Mandel, yes."

"Yes. He said Mr. Craig had a visitor at 5:00 P.M. on the day he was murdered. A man named Daniel Corbett. Does that name mean anything to you?"

There was a silence on the line.

"Miss Scott?"

"Yes. Daniel Corbett was Greg's editor on *Shades*."

"He was described to me as a young man with black hair and brown eyes."

"Yes."

"Miss Scott, when we were in the apartment yesterday . . ."

"Yes, I know what you're about to say. The spirit I described."

"A young male, you said. Black hair and brown eyes." Carella paused. "Did you have any reason for . . . ?"

"The flux was strongest at the desk."

"Aside from the flux."

"Only the flux," she said.

"But you do know Daniel Corbett."

"Yes, I know him."

"Is he, in *fact*, a young man?"

"Thirty-two."

"With black hair and brown eyes?"

"Yes."

"Where do I reach him, Miss Scott?"

"At Harlow House."

"Where's that?"

"That's the name of the publishing firm. Harlow House. It's on Jefferson and Lloyd."

"Today's Saturday. Would you know his home number?"

"I'm sure Greg has it in his book."

"Are you in the bedroom now?"

"No, I'm in the living room."

"Could you go into the bedroom, please, and look up the number for me?"

"Yes, of course. But it wasn't Daniel I was sensing yesterday. It wasn't Daniel at all."

"Even so . . ."

"Yes, just a minute, please."

He waited. Beside him, Teddy rolled over, and stirred, and then sat up and blinked into the room. She was wearing a cream-colored baby doll nightgown he'd given her for her birthday. She stretched, and smiled at him, and then kissed him on the cheek, got swiftly out of bed, and padded across the room to the bathroom. No panties. The twin crescents of her buttocks peeped from below the lace hem of the short gown. He watched her as she crossed the room, forgetting for a moment that she was his own wife.

"Hello?" Hillary said.

"Yes, I'm here."

The bathroom door closed. He turned his full attention back to the medium on the telephone.

"I've got two numbers for him," Hillary said. "One in Isola, and the other in Gracelands, upstate. He has a place up there he goes to on weekends."

"Let me have both numbers, please." In the bathroom, he heard the toilet flushing and then the water tap running. He wrote down the numbers and then said, "Thank you, Miss Scott, I'll be in touch."

"It wasn't Daniel," she said, and hung up.

Teddy came out of the bathroom. Her hair was sleep-tousled, her face was pale without makeup, but her dark eyes were sparkling and clear, and he watched her as she crossed to the bed and for perhaps the thousandth time thanked the phenomenal luck that had brought her into his life more years ago than he cared to remember. She was not the young girl he'd known then, she did not at her age possess the lithe body of a twenty-two-year-old like Hillary Scott, but her breasts were still firm, her legs long and supple, and she watched her weight like a hawk. Cozily she lay down beside him as he dialed the first of the numbers Hillary had given him. Her hand went under the blanket.

"Hello?" a man's voice said.

"Mr. Corbett?"

"Yes?" The voice sounded a trifle annoyed. Carella realized it was still only a little before nine on a Saturday morning—the big Christmas weekend no less. Under the blanket, Teddy's hand roamed familiarly.

"I'm sorry to bother you so early in the morning," Carella said. "This is Detective Carella of the 87th Squad. I'm investigating the murder of Gregory Craig."

"Oh. Yes," Corbett said.

"I was wondering if I might stop by there a little later this morning," Carella said. "There are some questions I'd like to ask you."

"Yes, certainly."

Carella looked at the bedside clock. "Would ten o'clock be all right?"

Beside him, Teddy read his lips and shook her head.

"Or eleven," Carella corrected, "whichever is more convenient for you."

"Eleven would be better," Corbett said.

"May I have the address there, please?"

Corbett gave it to him. As Carella wrote, Teddy's hand became more insistent.

"I'll see you at eleven," he said, "thanks a lot," and hung up, and turned to her.

"I have to call Cotton first," he said.

She rolled her eyes heavenward.

"It'll only take a minute."

She released him as suddenly as she had grasped him and with a sigh lay back against the pillow, her hands behind her head, the bedclothes lowered to her thighs, the baby doll gown carelessly exposing the black triangular patch of hair below the hem.

"Cotton," he said, "I've made an appointment with Daniel Corbett for eleven o'clock. He's down in the Quarter. Can you meet me there?"

"How'd you find him?" Hawes asked.

"The Spook called."

"Out of the blue?"

"Flux. Write this down, will you?" Carella said, and read off the address. "Eleven o'clock."

"See you there," Hawes said, and hung up.

Carella put the receiver back on the cradle and rolled over to

Teddy. Her hands were still behind her head; there was an expression of utter boredom on her face. "Okay," he said.

She sat up suddenly. Her hands fluttered on the air. He watched her fingers, reading the words they formed, and then began grinning.

"What do you *mean*, you've got a headache?" he said.

Her hands moved again, fluidly, fluently.

I always get headaches when people stay on the phone too long, she said.

"I'm off the phone now," he said.

She shrugged airily.

"So what do you say?"

She shrugged again.

"You want to fool around a little?" he asked, grinning.

Her eyes narrowed smokily, in imitation of some bygone silent-movie star. She wet her lips with her tongue. She lowered one strap of the gown from her shoulder, exposing her breast. Her hands moved again. *I want to fool around a* lot, *big boy*, she said, and licked her lips again, and fell greedily into his arms.

The second crank call—or so it seemed at first—came twenty minutes after the first one. He lifted the receiver from its cradle and said, "Eighty-seventh Squad, Carella."

"It has something to do with water," a woman's voice said.

"What?"

"Water," the voice repeated, and suddenly he recognized her. "Miss Scott?" he said.

"Yes. The murder has to do with water. Can I see you this afternoon? You're the source."

"What do you mean?"

"I'm not sure yet. But you're the source. I have to talk to you."

He remembered what Gregory Craig's daughter had told them yesterday: *She drowned. They said it was an accident.* Water, he thought, and said at once, "Where will you be?"

"At my sister's," she said.

"Give me half an hour," he said.

"I'll see you there," she said, and hung up.

When she opened the door for him, she was wearing a short robe belted over either pantyhose or nylons. She wore no makeup; without lipstick, rouge, or liner, she resembled Teddy even more than she had before.

"I'm sorry," she said at once. "I was dressing when my sister called. Come in."

The apartment was in the Stewart City section of Isola. Stewart City was not really a city, or even a town, but merely a collection of swank apartment buildings overlooking the River Dix on the true city's south side. If you could boast of a Stewart City address, you could also boast of a high income, a country place on Sands Spit, and a Mercedes-Benz in the garage under your building. You could give your address with a measure of snobbery and pride. There were few places left in the city—or perhaps the world—where you could do the same. Hillary's sister's apartment, as befitted its location, was decorated expensively but not ostentatiously; it had the effect on Carella of making him feel immediately uncomfortable. The cool white artificial Christmas tree in one corner of the room compounded his sense of ill ease. He was accustomed to the scuzziness of the Eight-Seven, where the Christmas trees were real and the carpeting underfoot—unlike the *lawn* growing in this place—was more often than not tattered and frayed.

"Miss Scott," he said, "on the phone, you . . ."

"Is it still snowing out there?" she asked.

"Yes."

"I'm supposed to be downtown at five for a cocktail party. Are there any cabs on the street?"

"A few."

"Can I get you a drink?" she asked. "What time is it anyway?"

"Four o'clock," he said.

"That's not too early for a drink, is it?"

"I can't," he said.

"Right, you're on duty," she said. "Mind if I have one?"

"Go right ahead."

She went to a tall cabinet on the wall opposite the tree and opened both doors of it to reveal an array of bottles within. She poured generously from one of the bottles, took two ice cubes from a bucket, and dropped them into the glass. Turning to him, she said, "Cheers, happy holidays."

"Cheers," he said.

"Sit down," she said. "Please." Her smile was so similar to Teddy's that he found himself experiencing an odd sense of disorientation. The woman in this apartment should have been in his Riverhead house instead. He should have been telling her about the hard day's work he'd put in, soliciting sympathy for the policeman's lot; he should have been mixing her a scotch and soda and laying a fire for her on the hearth. Instead, he was here to talk about water.

"So," he said, "what about water?"

She looked at him, puzzled, and then said, "Thanks, I prefer it on the rocks."

He looked back at her, equally puzzled. She sat in the chair opposite him, the robe falling away as she crossed her legs. She rearranged the wayward flap at once.

"Are you sure you won't have one?" she asked.

"Positive."

"She may be a while, you know."

"I'm sorry, what . . . ?"

"My sister. I spoke to her half an hour ago."

"Your sister?"

"Yes."

"What's *she* got to do . . . ?"

"Hillary," she said.

"Hillary?" he said, and blinked. The lady, as he'd surmised from the very beginning, was a prime candidate for the loony bin. "Miss Scott," he said, "I'm sorry, but I don't understand what . . ."

"My twin sister," she said.

He looked at her. She was smiling over the rim of her glass. He had the feeling she had done this many times before and enjoyed doing it each and every time.

"I see," he said.

"I'm Denise," she said. "We look a lot alike, don't you think?"

"Yes, you do," he said cautiously, wondering whether there really *was* a twin sister or whether Hillary was just having a little sport with him at the city's expense. "You say you spoke to her . . ."

"Yes, half an hour ago."

"Where was she?"

"At the office. She was just leaving. But with this snow . . ."

"Listen," he said, "are you *really* . . . ?"

"Denise Scott," she said, "yes," and nodded. "Which of us do you think is prettiest?"

"I couldn't say, Miss Scott."

"*I* am," she said, and giggled, and rose suddenly, and went to the liquor cabinet. He watched as she poured herself another drink. "Are you sure?" she asked, and lifted the glass to him.

"I'm sorry, I can't."

"Pity," she said, and went back to her chair and sat again. She crossed her legs more recklessly this time. The flap of the robe fell open again, and he saw the gartered tops of nylon stockings. He glanced away.

"I have twins myself," he said.

"Yes, Hillary told me."

"I never mentioned to her . . ."

"Psychic, you know," Denise said, and tapped her temple with her forefinger.

"How about you?" he said.

"No, no, my talents run in other directions," she said, and smiled at him. "Aren't you glad garter belts are coming back?" she said.

"I've . . . never much thought about it," he said.

"Think about it," she said.

"Miss Scott," he said, "I know you have an appointment, so if you want to get dressed, I'll be perfectly all right here."

"Wouldn't *dream* of leaving you alone," she said, and suddenly bent over the coffee table to spear a cigarette from the container there. The upper half of the robe gapped open over her breasts. She was wearing no bra. She held the pose an instant longer than she needed to, reaching for the cigarette, looking up at him and suddenly smiling.

"Miss Scott," he said, rising, "I'll be back in a little while. When your sister gets here, tell her . . ."

He heard a key turning in the door behind him. The door swung wide, and Hillary Scott came into the room. She was wearing a raccoon coat open over a white blouse and a red skirt. Her dark brown boots were wet. She looked across the room to where Denise was still bent over the coffee table. "Go put on some clothes," she said, "you'll catch cold." To Carella, she said, "I'm sorry I'm late. I had a hell of a time getting a cab." She looked at her sister again. "Denise?"

"Nice meeting you," Denise said, and rose, and tucked one flap of the robe over the other, and tightened the belt. He watched her as she left the room. The door to what he assumed was the bedroom whispered shut behind her.

"Didn't know there were *three* of us, did you?" Hillary said.

"Three of you?"

"Including your wife."

"You've never met my wife," Carella said.

"But we resemble each other."

"Yes."

"You have twins."

"Yes."

"The little girl looks like your wife. She was born in April."

"No, but that's her name."

"Terry. Is it Terry?"

"Teddy."

"Yes, Teddy. Franklin? Was her maiden name Franklin?"

"Yes," he said. He was staring at her unbelievingly. "Miss Scott," he said, "on the phone you told me . . ."

"Yes, water."

"What *about* water?"

"Something to do with water. Did someone mention water to you recently?"

Beyond the bedroom door he heard either a radio or a record player erupting with a rock tune. Hillary turned impatiently toward the door and shouted, "Denise, turn that down!" She waited a moment, the music blaring, and then shouted, *"Denise!"* Just as the music dropped six decibels. Angrily she took a cigarette from the container on the table, put a match to it, and let out a stream of smoke. "We'll wait till she's gone," she said. "It's impossible to achieve any level of concentration with her here. Would you like a drink?"

"No, thank you."

"I think *I'll* have one," she said, and went to the cabinet, and poured a hefty shot of whiskey into a tumbler, and drank it almost in one gulp. Carella suddenly remembered the Craig autopsy report.

"Was Craig a heavy drinker?" he asked.

"Why do you want to know?"

"The autopsy report indicated he'd been drinking before his death."

"I wouldn't say he was a heavy drinker, no."

"Social drinker?"

"Two or three before dinner."

"Did he drink while he was working?"

"Never."

In the next ten minutes, while her sister dressed in the other room, Hillary consumed two more healthy glasses of whiskey, presumably the better to heighten her psychic awareness. Carella wondered what the hell he was doing here. Take a phone call from a crazy lady who claimed to be psychic, link it foolishly to a drowning in Massachusetts that happened three years ago, and then wait around while the clock ticked steadily and the snow kept falling and the whiskey content in the bottle got lower and lower. But she had known his wife's name without being told it, knew they had twins, almost zeroed in on April. He did not for a moment believe she could actually read minds, but he knew that people with extrasensory perception did possibly exist, and he was not about to dismiss her earlier reference to water. Gregory Craig's wife had drowned three years ago—and his daughter could not believe it was an accident.

The bedroom door opened.

Denise Scott was wearing a clinging green jersey dress slit outrageously wide over her breasts and held precariously together at the midriff with a diamond clasp the size of Taiwan. The dress was somewhat shorter than was fashionable these days, giving her legs an extraordinarily long and supple look. She was wearing green high-heeled satin pumps; Carella gave them a life expectancy of thirty seconds in the snow outside. She walked to the hall closet without saying a word, took off the pumps, zipped on a pair of black leather boots, took a long black coat from the closet, picked up a black velvet bag from the hall table, tucked the pumps under her arm, opened the door, grinned at Carella, said, "Another time, *amigo*," and walked out without saying good-bye to Hillary.

"Bitch," Hillary said, and poured herself another drink.

"Go easy on that, okay?" Carella said.

"Tried to take Greg away from me," she said. "Went to the apartment one afternoon while he was working, pulled the twin-sister routine on him. I found her naked in bed with him." She shook her head and took a swift swallow of whiskey.

"When was this?" he asked at once. She had just presented him with the best possible motive for murder. Good old-fashioned slayings were now in vogue again: husbands shooting wives and vice versa, lovers taking axes to rivals, sons stabbing mothers and sisters; your average garden-variety homespun killings. Hillary Scott had found Gregory Craig in bed with her own sister.

"When?" he asked again.

"When what?"

"When did you discover them together?"

"Last month sometime."

"November?"

"November."

"What happened?"

"Little nympho bitch," Hillary said.

"What happened? What did you do?"

"Told her if she ever came near that apartment again . . ." She shook her head. "My own sister. Said it was a joke, said she wanted to see if Greg could tell us apart."

"Could he?"

"He said he thought she was me. He said she fooled him completely."

"What did *you* think?"

"I think he knew."

"But you're here with her now."

"What?"

"You're staying with her. Even after what happened."

"I didn't talk to her for weeks. Then she called one day in tears and . . . she's my sister. We're closer than any two people in the world. We're *twins*. What could I do?"

He understood this completely. Despite their constant bickering, his own twins were inseparable. Listening to their running dialogues was like listening to one person talking out loud to himself. When both of them were engaged in make-believe together, it was sometimes impossible to break in on what amounted to a tandem stream of consciousness. He had read someplace that twins were a gang of miniature; he had understood the writer's allusion at once. He had once scolded Mark for carelessly breaking an expensive vase and had punished him by sending him to his room. When he'd mentioned to her that *she* wasn't the one being punished, April had said, "Well, I just thought I'd help him out." If there was any truth to the adage that blood ran thicker than water, it ran doubly thick between twins. Hillary had found her sister in bed with Gregory Craig, but Craig was the stranger, and Denise was her twin. And now Craig was dead.

"How'd that affect your relationship with him?" Carella asked.

"I trusted him less. But I still loved him. If you love somebody, you're willing to forgive a lapse or two."

Carella nodded. He supposed she was telling the truth, but he wondered at the same time how *he'd* have felt if he'd found Teddy in bed with his twin brother, if he *had* a twin brother or any brother at all, which he didn't have.

"What's this about water?" he said. "You told me on the phone . . ."

"Someone mentioned water to you, am I right?"

"Yes, someone did."

"Something about water. And biting."

She drowned in the Bight, Abigail Craig had told him, *two miles from where my father was renting his famous haunted house.*

"What else?" Carella asked.

"Bite," she said.

"Yes, what about it?"

"Give me your hands."

He held out his hands to her. They stood two feet apart from each other, facing each other, their hands clasped. She closed her eyes.

"Someone swimming," she said. "A woman. Tape. So strong. I feel it pulsing in your hands. Tape. No, I'm *losing* it," she said abruptly, and opened her eyes wide. "Concentrate! You're the source!" She squeezed his hands tightly and closed her eyes again. "Yes," she said, the word coming out like a hiss. She was breathing harshly now; her hands in his own were trembling. "Drowning. Tape. Drowning, drowning," she said, and suddenly released his hands and threw her arms around him, her eyes still closed, her own hands clasping him behind the neck. He tried to back away from her, but her lips found his, and her mouth drew at him as though trying to suck the breath from his body. Hissing, she clamped her teeth onto his lower lip, and he pushed her away at once. She stood there with her eyes closed, her entire body shaking. She seemed unaware of him now. She began to sway, and then suddenly she began talking in a voice quite unlike her own, a hollow sepulchral voice that seemed to rumble up from the depths of some forgotten bog, trailing tatters of mist and a wind as cold as the grave.

"You stole," she said. "I know, I heard, you stole, I know, I'll tell," she said, "you stole, you stole . . ."

Her voice trailed. The room was silent except for the ticking of the clock. She stood there swaying, her eyes still closed, but the trembling was gone now, and at last the swaying stopped, too, and she was utterly motionless for several moments. She opened her eyes then and seemed surprised to find him there.

"I . . . have to rest," she said. "Please go."

She left him alone in the room. The door to the bedroom eased shut behind her. He stood there watching the closed door for a moment, and then he put on his coat and left the apartment.

The way they reconstructed it later, the killer had gone after the wrong person. The mistake was reasonable; even Carella had made the same mistake earlier. The killer must have been watching her for the past several days, and when he saw her—or the person he *assumed* was Hillary Scott—coming out of the Stewart City apartment building at eight-thirty Wednesday morning, he followed her all the way to the subway kiosk and then attempted to stab her with what Denise Scott later described as "the biggest damn knife I've ever seen in my life."

Minutes after Denise rushed into the apartment with the

front of her black cloth coat and her white satin blouse slashed, Hillary called first the local precinct and then Carella at home. He and Hawes got there an hour later. The patrolmen from Midtown South were already there, wondering what they were supposed to do. They asked Carella whether they should report this to their precinct as a 10-24—an "Assault Past"—or would the Eight-Seven take care of it? Carella explained that the attack might have been linked to a homicide they were working, and the patrolmen should forget about it. The patrolmen seemed unconvinced.

"What about the paper?" one of them asked. "Who'll take care of the paper?"

"I will," Carella said.

"So then maybe *we* get in a jam," the second patrolman said.

"If you want to file, go ahead and file," Carella said.

"As what? A 10-24?"

"That's what it was."

"Where do we *say* it was?"

"What do you mean?"

"The guy tried to stab her outside the subway on Masters. But she didn't call us till she got back here. So what do we put down as the scene?"

"Here," Carella said. "This is where you responded, isn't it?"

"Yeah, but this ain't where it happened."

"So let *me* file, okay?" Carella said. "Don't worry about it."

"You ain't got a sergeant like we got," the first patrolman said.

"Look, I want to talk to the victim," Carella said. "I told you this is a homicide we're working, so how about letting *me* file, and then you won't have to worry about it?"

"Get his name and shield number," the second patrolman advised.

"Detective/Second Grade Stephen Louis Carella," Carella said patiently, "87th Squad. My shield number is seven-one-four, five-six-three-two."

"You got that?" the second patrolman asked his partner.

"I got it," the first patrolman said, and they both left the apartment, still concerned about what their sergeant might say.

Denise Scott was in a state of numbed shock. Her face was pale, her lips were trembling, she had not taken off her coat—as if somehow it still afforded her protection against the assailant's knife. Hillary brought her a whopping snifter of brandy, and when she had taken several swallows of it and the color had returned to her cheeks, she seemed ready to talk about what had happened. What had happened was really quite simple. Someone had grabbed her from behind as she was starting down the steps to the subway station, pulled her over backward, and then slashed at the front of her coat with the biggest damn knife she'd ever seen in her life. She'd hit out at him with her bag, and she'd begun screaming, and the man had turned and begun running when someone started up the steps from below.

"It was a man, you're sure of that?" Carella said.

"Positive."

"What did he look like?" Hawes asked.

"Black hair and brown eyes. A very narrow face," Denise said.

"How old?"

"Late twenties, I'd say."

"Would you recognize him if you saw him again?"

"In a minute."

"Did he say anything to you?"

"Not a word. He just pulled me around and tried to stab me. Look what he did to my coat and blouse," she said, and eased the torn blouse aside to study the sloping top of her left breast. Hawes seemed very interested in whether or not the knife had penetrated her flesh. He stared at the V opening of her blouse with all the scrutiny of an assistant medical examiner. "I was just lucky, that's all," Denise said, and let the blouse fall back into place.

"He was after *me*," Hillary said.

Carella did not ask her why she thought so; he was thinking exactly the same thing.

"Let me have the coat," she said.

"What?" her sister said.

"Your coat. Let me have it."

Denise took off the coat. The knife thrust had torn the blouse over her left breast. Beneath the gaping satiny slash, Hawes could glimpse a promise of Denise's flesh, a milkier white against the off white of the satin. Hillary held the black coat against her own breasts like a phantom lover. Closing her eyes, she began to sway the way she had after she'd kissed Carella. Hawes looked at her and then looked at her sister and decided he would rather go to bed with Denise than with Hillary. Then he decided the exact opposite. Then he decided both of them wouldn't be bad together, at the same time, in the king-sized bed in his apartment. Carella, not being psychic, didn't know that everybody in the world had threesomes in mind this holiday season. Hillary, claiming to be what Carella knew he wasn't, began intoning in a voice reminiscent of the one she'd used after she'd kissed him, "Tape, you stole, tape," the same old routine.

Befuddled, Hawes watched her; he had never caught her act before. Denise, used to the ways of mediums, yawned. The brandy was reaching her. She seemed to have forgotten that less than an hour ago someone had tried to dispatch her to that great beyond her sister was now presumably tapping—Hillary had said it was a ghost who'd killed Gregory Craig, and now the same ghost had tried to kill her sister, and her black overcoat was giving off emanations that seemed to indicate either something or nothing at all.

"Hemp," she said.

Carella wasn't sure whether or not she was clearing her throat.

"Hemp," she said again. "Stay."

He hadn't planned on leaving, so he didn't know what the hell she meant.

"Hemp, stay," she said. "Hempstead. Hampstead."

Carella distinctively felt the hair on the back of his neck bristling. Hawes, watching Denise—who now crossed her legs recklessly and grinned at him in brandy-inspired abandon— felt only a bristling somewhere in the area of his groin.

"Mass," Hillary intoned, her eyes still closed, her body swaying, the black overcoat clutched in her hands. "Mass. Massachusetts. Hampstead, Massachusetts," and Carella's mouth dropped open.

Hillary opened her eyes and stared blankly at him. His own stare was equally blank. Like a pair of blind idiot savants sharing the same mysterious knowledge, they stared at each other across an abyss no wider than three feet, but writhing with whispering demons and restless corpses. His feet were suddenly cold. He stared at her unblinkingly, and she stared back, and he could swear her eyes were on fire, the deep brown lighted from within with all the reds and yellows of glittering opals.

"Someone drowned in Hampstead, Massachusetts," she said.

She said this directly to him, ignoring Hawes and her sister. And Carella, knowing full well that she had lived with Craig for the past year and more, knowing, too, that he might have told her all about the drowning of his former wife two miles from where he was renting the haunted house he made famous in

Deadly Shades, nonetheless believed that the knowledge had come to her from the black overcoat she held in her hands.

When she said, "We'll go to Massachusetts, you and I," he knew that they would because Craig's wife had drowned up there three summers ago, and now three more people were dead, and another murder attempt had been made—and maybe there *were* ghosts involved after all.

They had hoped to get there by one in the afternoon, a not unrealistic estimate in that they left the city at a little after ten and Hampstead—by the map— was no more than 200 miles to the northeast. The roads outside the city were bone-dry; the storm that had blanketed Isola had left the surrounding areas untouched. It was only when they entered Massachusetts that they encountered difficulty. Whereas earlier Carella had maintained a steady fifty-five miles an hour in keeping with the federal energy-saving speed limit, he now eased off on the accelerator and hoped he would average thirty. Snow was not the problem; any state hoping for skiers during the winter months made certain the roads were plowed and scraped the instant the first snowflake fell. But the temperature had dropped to eighteen degrees Fahrenheit, and the roadside snow that had been melting during the midmorning hours had now frozen into a thin slick that covered the asphalt from median divider to shoulder and made driving treacherous and exhausting.

They reached Hampstead at two-twenty-five that afternoon. The sky was overcast, and a harsh wind blew in over the ocean, rattling the wooden shutters on the seaside buildings. The town seemed to have crawled up out of the Atlantic like some prehistoric thing seeking the sun, finding instead a rocky, inhospitable coastline and collapsing upon it in disappointment and exhaustion. The ramshackle buildings on the waterfront were uniformly gray, their weather-beaten shingles evoking a time when Hampstead was a small fishing village and men went down to the sea in ships. There were still nets and lobster pots in evidence, but the inevitable crush of progress had threaded through the town a gaudy string of motels and fast-food joints that thoroughly blighted what could not have been a particularly cheerful place to begin with.

The Common, such as it was, consisted of a sere rectangle of untended lawn surrounded by the town's municipal buildings and a four-story brick hotel that called itself the Hampstead Arms. The tawdry tinsel of the season encompassed the square like a squadron of dancing girls in sequins and spangles. An unlighted Christmas tree was in the center of the Common, looking rather like a sodden sea gull that had lost its bearings. Carella parked the car, and together he and Hillary walked to the Town Hall, where he hoped to find the Coroner's Office and the records pertaining to the death of Gregory Craig's former wife. Hillary was wearing a bulky raccoon coat, a brown woolen hat pulled down over her ears, brown gloves, brown boots, and the same outfit she'd been wearing in her sister's apartment that morning: a tweedy beige skirt flecked with threads of green and brown, a turtleneck the color of bitter chocolate, and a green cardigan sweater with leather buttons. Carella was wearing much of the finery that had been given to him two days earlier: a pair of dark gray flannel slacks from Fanny, a red plaid flannel shirt from April, a tweed sports jacket the color of smoked herring from Teddy, a dark blue car coat with a fleece lining and a fake fur collar, also from Teddy, and a pair of fur-lined gloves from Mark. His feet were cold; he had put on loafers this morning, not expecting to be trodding the streets of an oceanfront town in Massachusetts, where the temperature lurked somewhere just above zero and the wind came in off the Atlantic like the revenge of every seaman ever lost in those dark waters offshore. As they crossed the Common, Hillary nodded and said, "Yes, I knew it would look like this."

Hampstead's Town Hall was a white clapboard building with a gray shingled roof. It faced westward, away from the ocean, shielding the sidewalk outside from the fierce Atlantic blasts. All the lights were on in defense against the afternoon gloom; they beckoned like beacons to lost mariners. Inside, the building was as toasty warm as a general store with a potbellied stove. Carella studied the information board in the lobby, a black rectangle with white plastic letters and numbers on it, announcing the various departments and the rooms in which they might be found. There was no listing for a Coroner's Office. He settled for the Town Clerk's Office and spoke there to a woman who sounded a lot like the late President Kennedy. She told him that the Coroner's Office was located in Hampstead General Hospital, which was about two miles to the northeast, just the other side of the Bight. Reluctant to face the frozen waste yet another time, Carella nonetheless walked with Hillary to where he'd parked the car and then drove due north along an oceanfront road that curved past what appeared to be a large saltwater pond, but which was identified by a roadside sign as HAMPSTEAD BIGHT.

"That's where she drowned," Hillary said. "Stop the car."

"No," Carella said. "First let's find out *how* she drowned."

The coroner was a man in his late sixties, as pale and as thin as a cadaver, with a fringe of graying hair around his flaking bald pate. He was wearing a threadbare brown sweater, rumpled brown slacks, a white shirt with a frayed collar, and a tie the color of cow dung. His desk was cluttered with a sheaf of loosely scattered file folders and a black plastic sign that announced his name in white letters: MR. HIRAM HOLLISTER. Carella spoke to him alone; it was one thing to bring your medium with you when you went calling on ghosts; it was quite another to conduct official business in the presence of a startlingly beautiful twenty-two-year-old wearing a raccoon coat that made her look cozily cuddlesome. Hillary waited on a bench in the corridor outside.

"I'm investigating three possibly linked homicides in Isola," Carella said, showing his shield. "One of the victims was a man named Gregory Craig, who . . ."

"What's that say there?" Hollister asked, peering at the gold shield with its blue enameling and its embossed city seal.

"Detective," Carella said.

"Oh, detective, yup," Hollister said.

"One of the victims was a man named Gregory Craig. His former wife, Stephanie Craig, drowned in Hampstead Bight three summers ago. Your office concluded that the death was accidental. I wonder if I might . . ."

"Three summers ago, yup," Hollister said.

"Do you remember the case?"

"No, but I remember three summers ago, all right. That was the year we got all that rain."

"Would you have a record of what happened? I'm assuming there was an inquest . . ."

"Oh, yes, there woulda been in a drowning."

"Stephanie Craig," Carella said. "Does that name mean anything to you?"

"Not offhand. We get tourists here, you know, they don't know how tricky the currents can be. We get our share of drownings, I'll tell you, same as any other coastal community."

"How about Gregory Craig?"

"Don't recollect him either."

"He wrote a book called *Deadly Shades*."

"Haven't read it."

"About a house in this town."

"Nope, don't know it."

Carella thought briefly about the illusiveness of fame. Behind his desk Hollister was nodding as though he had suddenly remembered something he had not earlier revealed.

"Yup," he said.

Carella waited.

"Lots of rain that summer. Washed away the dock outside Logan's Pier."

"Mr. Hollister," Carella said, "where would I find a record of the inquest?"

"Right down the hall," Hollister said, and looked at his watch. "But it's getting on three o'clock, and I want to start home before the storm hits. Supposed to be getting at least six inches, did you know that?"

"No, I didn't," Carella said, and looked at his own watch. "If you'll pull the folder for me," he said, "I can take a look at it and then leave it on your desk, if that would be all right with you."

"Well," Hollister said.

"I can sign a receipt for it in my official capacity as . . ."

"Nope, don't need a receipt," Hollister said. "Just don't want it getting all messed up and out of place."

"I'll be very careful with it," Carella said.

"Get out-of-state police in here every so often," Hollister said, "they don't know about neatness and orderliness."

"I can understand that, sir," Carella said, figuring a "sir" wouldn't hurt at this uneasy juncture. "But I'm used to handling files, and I promise I'll return the folder in exactly the condition I receive it. Sir," he added.

"Suppose it'd be all right," Hollister said, and eased himself out of his swivel chair, surprising Carella with a six-foot-four frame that should have belonged to a basketball player. He followed Hollister down the corridor, past Hillary, who sat on the bench and looked up at him inquiringly, and then into an office succinctly marked RECORDS on the frosted glass panel of its door. The office was lined with dusty wooden file cabinets that would have fetched handsome prices in any of Isola's antique shops.

"How do you spell that last name?" Hollister asked.

"C-R-A-I-G," Carella said, and thought again about fame, and wondered if somewhere in America there was at this very moment someone asking how you spelled Hemingway or Faulkner or even Harold Robbins.

"C-R-A-I-G," Hollister said, and then went to one of the file cabinets, and opened the drawer, and kept spelling the name over and over to himself as he leafed through the folders.

"Stephanie?" he asked.

"Stephanie," Carella said.

"Here it is," Hollister said, and yanked out an inch-thick folder, and studied the name on it again before handing it to Carella. "Just put it here on top the cabinet when you're through with it. I don't want you trying to file it again, hear?"

"Yes, sir," Carella said.

"Mess up the files that way," Hollister said.

"Yes, sir."

"You can use the desk over there near the windows if you like, take off your coat, make yourself comfortable. Who's that lady outside looks like a grizzly bear?"

"She's helping me with the case," Carella said.

"You can bring her in, too, if that suits you; no sense her freezing her butt off in the hallway. Terrible draft in that hallway."

"Yes, sir, thank you," Carella said.

"Well, that's it, I guess," Hollister said, and shrugged and left Carella alone in the room. Carella poked his head outside the door. Hillary was still cooling her heels on the bench, impatiently jiggling one of her crossed legs.

"Come on in," he said, and she rose instantly and came down the corridor, the heels of her boots clicking on the wooden floor.

"What've you got?" she asked.

"Record of the inquest."

"We'd learn more at the Bight," she said.

Carella turned on the desk's gooseneck lamp and then pulled up a chair for Hillary. She did not take off the raccoon coat. Outside, it was already beginning to snow. The clock on the wall ticked off the time: seven minutes to three.

"I want to make this fast," Carella said, "and get out of here before the storm hits."

"We have to go to the Bight," Hillary said. "I'm here because I want to see the Bight. And the house Greg rented."

"If there's time," he said.

"We won't get out in any event," she said. "They've already closed Route 44."

"How do you know that?" he asked, and she gave him a weary look. "Well . . . let's hurry, anyway," he said. "Did you want to look at this with me? Is there anything here that . . ."

"I want to touch the papers," she said.

After her performance with her sister's coat, he knew better than to scoff at her request. In the car on the drive to Massachusetts, she had tried to explain to him the powers she and others like her possessed. He had listened intently as she told him about extrasensory perception and psychometry in particular. She defined this as the ability to measure with the sixth sense the flux—or electromagnetic radiation—from another person, most often by touching an object owned or worn by that person. People blessed—"Or sometimes cursed," she said—with this gift were capable of garnering information about the past and the present and sometimes, in the case of particularly talented psychometrists, even the future. She explained that one might consider time, from the psychic point of view, as a huge phonograph record with millions upon millions of ridges and grooves, containing millennia of recorded data. The psychic, in a sense, was someone with the extraordinary power of being able to lift the metaphoric arm of a record player and drop the needle into any of the grooves, thereby reproducing in the mind any of the preserved information on the disc. She was not quite certain how this worked concerning future events; she had never been able to prophesy with any amount of accuracy something that was *about* to happen. Clairvoyance, clairaudience, and clairsentience all were talents beyond her meager capabilities. But she was entirely certain of her power to intuit correctly, from any object's electromagnetic leak of energy, the events—past or present—identified with that object. She had been able to do this with her sister's coat yesterday because the coat had come into contact with the killer's knife, and the knife had been held in the killer's hand, and the flux had been strong enough to transfer itself from human being to object to yet another object. Her dissertation, soberly delivered, did much to convince Carella even further that she *did* possess powers he was incapable of reasoning away.

Sitting at the desk beside her now, he opened the case folder and began reading. She did not read along with him. She simply touched the upper right-hand corner of each page, the way one might have if attempting to dog-ear it, holding the page between her thumb and index finger, feeling it as she might have felt a fabric sample, her eyes closed, her body slightly swaying on the chair beside him. She was wearing a heady perfume he had not noticed on the car ride up. He assumed her psychometric concentration was creating emanations of her own by way of body heat that hyped the scent of the perfume.

According to the Coroner's Inquest held on the sixteenth day of September, three weeks after the fatal drowning three summers ago, Stephanie Craig had been swimming alone in Hampstead Bight between three and three-fifty in the afternoon, when, according to observers on the shore, she suddenly disappeared below the surface. She came up twice, struggling and gasping for breath each time, but when she went under for the third time, she did not surface again. One of the eyewitnesses suggested at the inquest that Mrs. Craig (apparently she still used the "Mrs." form of address four years after her divorce from Craig) may have been seized from below by a shark "or some other kind of fish," but the Board rejected this at once, citing the fact that there had been no blood in the water and perhaps mindful of the many recent books and motion pictures that had done little to encourage the flow of tourists to oceanside communities; the last thing on earth Hampstead needed was a shark scare—or any *other* kind of fish scare.

The Board had conducted its inquiry meticulously, eliciting from Mrs. Craig's handyman the information that she'd left for the beach at two-thirty that afternoon, taking with her a towel and a shoulder-slung handbag and telling him she planned to "walk on over to the Bight for a little swim." She was wearing, as he clearly recalled, a blue bikini bathing suit and sandals. Witnesses at the beach recalled seeing her walking to the water's edge, testing the water with her toes, and then coming back from the shoreline to put down her sandals, her towel, and her handbag. One of the witnesses mentioned that it was the "first darn sunny day we'd had in weeks," a comment that must have done little to gladden the hearts of the two Chamber of Commerce members on the Board.

Stephanie Craig went into the water for her swim at 3:00 P.M. The Bight was even calmer that day than it normally was. Protected by a natural-rock breakwater that crashed with ocean waves on its eastern side, fringed with a white sand beach rare in these parts, it was a safe, current-free place for swimming and a favorite among locals and tourists alike. There were sixty-four people on the beach that day. Only a dozen of them witnessed the drowning. Each and every one of them told exactly the same story. She suddenly went under, and she drowned. Period. The Medical Examiner's report stated that there were no contusions, lacerations, or bruises anywhere on the body, dismissing once and for all the notion that a shark "or some other kind of fish" had seized her from below. The report further stated that the body had been delivered to the morgue clad only in the panties of the bikini bathing suit, the bra top apparently having been lost in Mrs. Craig's struggle to save herself from drowning. Findings for drugs or alcohol had been negative. The physician conducting the examination could not state whether a cramp had been the cause of her sudden inability to stay afloat, but the board nonetheless decided that the probable cause of the accident was "a severe cramp or series of cramps that rendered Mrs. Craig powerless in water estimated on that day to have been twenty feet deep where she was swimming." An eyewitness on the beach said that she went under for the last time at ten minutes to four; that meant she'd been swimming for close to an hour in waters not known for their cordial temperatures. But Stephanie Craig had been the winner of three gold medals on Holman University's swimming team, and the Board's report made no mention of this fact.

Carella closed the folder. Hillary passed her hands over the binder and then opened her eyes and said, "It wasn't an accident. Whoever typed this report *knows* it wasn't an accident."

Carella checked the report's first and last pages to see if there was a typist's name or initials anywhere on them. There was not. He made a mental note to call Hollister and find out who had done the typing.

"I want to go to the Bight now," Hillary said. "May we go, please? Before it gets too dark?"

It was almost too dark when they got there. Whatever light still lingered on the horizon was diffused by the falling snow, which made visibility and footing equally uncertain. They stood on the beach and looked out over the water. Stephanie Craig had drowned some fifty feet from shore, just ten yards within the breakwater protection afforded by the curving natural rock ledge. At Hillary's insistence, they walked out onto the breakwater now. It was shaped like a fishhook, the shank jutting out from the shore at a northeasterly angle, the rocks at the farthest end curving back upon themselves to form a natural cove. On the ocean side, waves crashed in against the ledge as if determined to pound it to rubble. But the cove on the bay side was as protected as the larger crescent of beach had been, and here only spume and spray intimidated the flying snowflakes. A rusting iron ladder was fastened to the ledge above the cove. Hillary turned her back to it, and Carella

95

realized all at once that she was planning to go down to the stony beach below. He grabbed her arm and said, "Hey, no."

"It's safe down there," she said. "The ocean's on the other side."

He looked below. The cove did seem safe enough. On the ocean side, towering waves furiously pounded the ledge, but in the protected little cove below he would have trusted his ten-year-old daughter with a rubber duck. He preceded Hillary down the ladder and then turned away circumspectly when she climbed down after him, her skirt whipping about her legs and thighs. There was no wind below. A small cave yawned behind the stony beach, eroded into the ledge. Inside it, they could dimly perceive a beached dinghy painted a green that was flaking and stained red and yellow below its rusting oarlocks. Hillary stopped stock-still just outside the opening cave.

"What is it?" Carella said.

"He was out here," she said.

"Who?"

The light was fading rapidly; he should have taken his flashlight from the glove compartment of the car, but he hadn't. The cave seemed not in the least bit inviting. He had always considered spelunkers the choicest sorts of maniacs, and he feared ever being trapped in a small space, unable to move either forward or backward. But he followed Hillary into the cave, ducking his head to avoid banging it on the low ceiling, squinting into the darkness beyond the dinghy. The cave was shallow; it ended abruptly several feet beyond the boat. Its sloping walls were wet. Hillary touched one of the rusting oarlocks and then pulled her hand back as if she'd received an electric shock.

"No," she said.

"What is it?"

"No," she said backing away from the boat. "Oh, no, God, please, no."

"What the hell is it?"

She did not answer. She shook her head and backed out of the cave. She was climbing the ladder when he came out onto the stone-strewn beach behind her. When she reached the ledge above, the wind caught at her skirt, whipping it about her long legs. He climbed up after her. She was running along the breakwater now, the waves crashing in on her left, heading for the crescent beach beyond which he'd parked the car. He ran after her, out of breath, almost losing his footing on the rocks, almost realizing his second wildest fear, that of drowning. When he got to the car, she was already inside it, her arms folded over the front of the raccoon coat, her body trembling.

"What happened back there?" he said.

"Nothing."

"When you touched that boat . . ."

"Nothing," she said.

He started the car. There were at least two inches of snow in the parking lot. The dashboard clock read 4:00 P.M. He turned on the radio at once, hoping to catch the local news, and listened first to a report on the president's new plan for fighting inflation, then to a report on the latest trouble in the Middle East, and finally to a report on the weather. The storm that had inundated the city had finally reached Massachusetts and was expected to dump somewhere between eight and ten inches of snow before morning. Route 44 was closed, and the turnpike south and west was treacherous. Travelers' advisories were in effect; the state's Highway Department had asked that all vehicles be kept off the roads to allow the plows free access.

"We'd better get back to town," he said, "see if we can't get a couple of rooms for the night."

"No," she said. She was still shivering. "I want to see the house Greg rented that summer."

"I don't want to get stuck out here in the middle of no—"

"It's on the way," she said. "Two miles from the Bight. Isn't that what she told you? Isn't that what his daughter told you?"

Abigail Craig had said, *She drowned in the Bight, two miles from where my father was renting his famous haunted house.* Partial believer that he was, Carella was willing to accept the fact that Hillary could not have known of his conversation with Craig's daughter and had therefore divined it through her psychic powers. But skeptic that he *still* was, he realized Hillary was no doubt familiar with the book Craig had written about the house, so wasn't it now reasonable to assume he'd described it in detail, right down to its geographical location?

"Two miles from the Bight could be two miles in either direction," he said. "I don't want to be driving out into the Atlantic Ocean."

"No, it's on the way to town," she said.

"Did he say so in his book?"

"I recognized it when we passed it," she said.

"You didn't answer my question."

"No, he did not give its exact location in the book."

"Why didn't you say something when we passed it?"

"Because the field was so strong."

"What field?"

"The electromagnetic field."

"So strong that it silenced you?"

"So strong that it *frightened* me."

"But the Bight didn't, huh? When we passed the Bight . . ."

"The Bight was only where she drowned. The house . . ." She shivered again and hunkered down inside her coat. He had never really heard a person's teeth chattering; he'd always thought that was for fiction. But her teeth were truly chattering now; he could hear the tiny click of them above the hum of the car heater.

"What *about* the house?" he said.

"I have to see it. The house was the beginning. The house was where it all started."

"Where all *what* started?"

"The four murders."

"Four?" he said. "There've only been three."

"Four," she repeated.

"Gregory Craig, Marian Esposito, Daniel Corbett . . ."

"And Stephanie Craig," she said.

The house was on the edge of the ocean, 1.8 miles from the Bight, according to the odometer. He parked the car in a rutted sand driveway covered with snow and flanked by withered beach grass and plum. A solitary pine, its branches weighted by the snow upon them, stood to the left of the entrance door like a giant Napoleonic soldier outside Moscow. The house was almost entirely gray: weathered gray shingles on all of its sides; gray shingles of a darker hue on its roof; the door, the shutters, and the window trim all painted a gray that was flaking and faded. A brick chimney climbed the two stories on its northern end, contributing a column of color as red as blood, a piercing vertical shriek against the gray of the house and the white of the whirling snow. This time he had remembered to take along the flashlight. He played it first on a small sign in the window closet to the entrance door. The sign advised that the house was for rent or for sale and provided the name and address of the real estate agent to be contacted. He moved the light to the tarnished doorknob and then tried the knob. The door was locked.

"That's that," he said.

Hillary put her hand on the knob. She closed her eyes. He waited, never knowing *what* the hell to expect when she touched something. A snowflake landed on the back of his neck and melted down his collar.

"There's a back door," she said.

They trudged through the snow around the side of the house, past a thorny patch of brambles, and then onto a gray wooden porch on the ocean side. The wind here had banked the snow against the storm door. He kicked the snow away with the side of his shoe, yanked open the storm door, and then tried the knob on the inner door.

"Locked," he said. "Let's get back to town."

Hillary reached for the knob. Carella sighed. She held the knob for what seemed an inordinately long time, the wind whistling in over the ocean and lashing the small porch, the storm door banging against the side of the house. When she released the knob, she said, "There's a key behind the drain-pipe."

Carella played the light over the drainpipe. The spout was perhaps eight inches above the ground. He felt behind it with his hand. Fastened to the back of the spout was one of those little magnetic key holders designed to make entrance by burglars even easier than it had to be. He slid open the lid on the metal container, took out a key, and tried it on the lock. It slid easily into the keyway; when he twisted it, he heard the tumblers fall with a small oiled click. He tried the knob again, and the door opened. Fumbling on the wall to the right of the door, he found a light switch and flicked it on. He took a step into the room; Hillary, behind him, closed the door.

They were standing in a living room furnished in what might have been termed Beach House Haphazard. A sofa covered with floral-patterned slipcovers was on the window wall overlooking the ocean. Two mismatched upholstered easy chairs faced the sofa like ugly suitors petitioning for the hand of a princess. A stained oval braided rug was on the floor between the sofa and the chairs, and a cobbler's bench coffee table rested on it slightly off center. An upright piano was on a wall bearing two doors, one leading to the kitchen, the other to a pantry. A flight of steps at the far end of the room led to the upper story of the house.

"This isn't it," Hillary said.

"What do you mean?"

"This isn't the house Greg wrote about."

"I thought you said . . ."

"I said it *started* here. But this isn't the house in *Deadly Shades*."

"How do you know?"

"There are no ghosts in this house," she said flatly. "There never *were* any ghosts in this house."

They went through it top to bottom nonetheless. Hillary's manner was calm, almost detached. She went through the place like a disinterested buyer whose husband was trying to force upon her an unwanted purchase—until they reached the basement. In the basement, and Carella was becoming used to these sudden shifts of psychic mood, she bristled at the sight of a closed door. Her hands began flailing the air, the fingers on each widespread like those of a blind person searching for obstacles. Trembling, she approached the door. She lifted the primitive latch and entered a shelf-lined room that contained the house's furnace. Carella was aware all at once that the house was frighteningly cold. His feet were leaden, his hands were numb. On one of the shelves were a diver's mask, a pair of rubber fins, and an oxygen tank. Hillary approached the shelf, but she did not touch anything on it. Again, as she had with the dinghy in the cave, she backed away and said, "No, oh, God, no."

He felt something almost palpable in that room, but he knew better than to believe he was intuiting whatever Hillary was. His response was hard-nosed, that of a detective in one of the world's largest cities, compounded of years of experience and miles of empirical deduction, seasoned with a pinch of guesswork and a heaping tablespoon of hope—but hope was the thing with feathers. Stephanie Craig, an expert swimmer, had drowned in the Bight in a calmer sea than anyone could remember that summer. At least one of the witnesses had suggested that she'd been seized from below by a shark or some other kind of fish. In the basement room of the house her former husband, Gregory, had rented for the summer, they had just stumbled upon a diver's gear. Wasn't it possible . . . ?

"It was Greg," Hillary said. "Greg drowned her."

She came into his room now without knocking. Her face was flushed, her eyes were glowing.

"I've just been on the phone with a woman named Elise Blair," she said. "She's the real estate agent whose sign was in the window of the house Greg rented."

"What about her?" Carella asked.

"I described the house that was in Greg's book. I described it down to the last nail. She knows the house. It was rented three summers ago to a man from Boston. She wasn't the agent on the deal, but she can check with the realtor who was and get the man's name and address from the lease—if you want it."

"Why would I want it?" Carella asked.

"It was the house in *Shades*, don't you understand?"

"No, I don't."

"It was the house Greg wrote about."

"So?"

"*He* wasn't living in that house, someone *else* was," Hillary said. "I want to see for myself if there are ghosts in that house."

The real estate agent who had rented the house three summers ago worked out of the back bedroom of her own house on Main Street. They trudged through the snow at a quarter past six, walking past the lighted Christmas tree on the Common, ducking their heads against the snow and the fierce wind. The woman's name was Sally Barton, and she seemed enormously pleased to be playing detective. She had known all along, she told them, that the house Craig wrote about was really the old Loomis house out on the Spit. He had never pinpointed the location, had never even mentioned the town of Hampstead for that matter—something she supposed they should all be grateful for. But she knew it was the Loomis house. "The house isn't your typical beach house, but it looks right at home on the Spit. Frank Loomis fell in love with it when he was still living in Salem, had it brought down there stick by stick, put it on the beachfront land he owned."

"Salem?" Carella said. "Here in Massachusetts?"

"Yes," Mrs. Barton said. "Where they hanged the witches in 1692."

She offered them the key to the house, which she said she'd been unable to rent the summer before, but that had nothing to do with Gregory Craig's ghosts. Not many people outside the town knew that this was the house he'd made famous in his book.

"Don't know how he got away with it," she said. "Claimed it was a true story and then didn't tell anybody where the house actual *was*. Said it was to protect the innocent. What innocent? Frank Loomis has been dead for fifty years, and his two sons are living in California and couldn't care *less* whether there are ghosts in the house. All they're interested in is renting it each summer. Still, I guess he might've been afraid of legal complications. You'd know more about that than I would," she said and smiled at Carella.

"Well, I'm not a lawyer, ma'am," Carella said, and returned

the smile, aware that he'd just been flattered. "I wonder if you can tell me who rented the house three summers ago."

"Yes, I looked for the lease right after you called. It was a man named Jack Rawles."

"What'd he look like?"

"A pleasant-looking person."

"Young, old?"

"In his late twenties, I'd say."

"What color hair?"

"Black."

"Eyes?"

"Brown."

"And his address?"

She gave him the slip of paper on which she had copied Rawles's Commonwealth Avenue address from the lease, and then she said, "It's not an easy house to rent, you know. Frank never did modernize it. There's electricity, of course, but the only heat's from the fireplaces. There're three of them, one in the living room, one in the kitchen, and another in one of the upstairs bedrooms. It's not bad during the summer, but it's an icebox in the wintertime. Are you sure you want to go out there just now?"

"Yes, we're positive," Hillary said.

"I'd go with you, but I haven't fixed my husband's supper yet."

"We'll return the key to you as soon as we've looked the place over," Carella said.

"There's supposed to be a dead woman there, searching for her husband," Mrs. Barton said.

At a local garage Carella bought a pair of skid chains and asked the attendant to put them on the car while he and Hillary got something to eat at the diner up the street. It was still snowing when they left the town at seven o'clock. The plows were working the streets and the main roads, but he was grateful for the chains when they hit the cutoff that led to the strand of land jutting out into the Atlantic. A sign crusted with snow informed them that this was Albright's Spit, and a sign under it warned that this was a dead-end road. The car struggled through the thick snow, skidding and lurching up what Carella guessed was a packed sand road below. He almost got stuck twice, and when he finally spotted the old house looming on the edge of the sea, he heaved a sigh of relief and parked the car on a relatively level stretch of ground below the sloping driveway. Together, the flashlight lighting their way, he and Hillary made their way to the front door.

"Yes, this is it," Hillary said. "This is the house."

The front door opened into a small entryway facing a flight of stairs that led to the upper story. He found a light switch on the wall to the right of the door and flicked it several times. Nothing happened.

"Wind must've knocked down the power lines," he said, and played the flashlight first on the steps leading upstairs and then around the small entryway. To the right was a door leading to a beamed kitchen. To the left was the living room— what would have been called the "best room" in the days when the house was built. A single thick beam ran the length of the room. There were two windows in the room, one overlooking the ocean, the other on the wall diagonally opposite. The fireplace was not in the exact center of the wall bearing it; the boxed stairwell occupied that space. It was, instead, tucked into the wall beyond, a huge walk-in fireplace with a black iron kettle hanging on a hinge, logs and kindling stacked on the hearth, big black andirons buckled out of shape from the heat of innumerable fires. On the mantel above the fireplace opening, Carella found a pair of candles in pewter candlesticks. He did not smoke; he asked Hillary for a match and lighted both candles.

The room, he now saw, was beautifully furnished in old American antiques, the likes of which could hardly be found for sale anywhere these days, except at exorbitant prices. There were several hurricane lamps around the room, and he lighted these now, and the richly burnished wood of the paneling and the furniture came to flickering life everywhere around him. If there were ghosts in this house, they could not have found a more hospitable place to inhabit. In a brass bucket by the fireplace he found several faded copies of the Hampstead *News*. The dates went back two years, the last time the house had been rented for the summer. He tore the newspapers to shreds, laid a bed of kindling over them, and stacked three hefty logs on top of that. The fire dispelled the lingering chill in the room and, with it, any possible notion that poltergeists might pop out of the woodwork at any moment. Outside, the wind howled in over the ocean and the shutters rattled, but the fire was crackling now, and the lamps and candles were lighted, and the only ghosts visible were the fire devils dancing on the grate. Carella went out into the kitchen, lighted the candles and lamps there, and then started another fire in the second fireplace. Neither he nor Hillary had yet gone up to the second story of the house.

In one of the kitchen cupboards he found an almost full bottle of scotch. The ice-cube trays in the refrigerator were empty, and the tap water had been turned off. He was starting out of the room with the bottle and two glasses when he noticed the kitchen door was ajar. He put down the glasses and the bottle, went to the door, and opened it all the way. The storm door outside was closed, but the simple slip bolt was unlatched. He threw the bolt and then studied the lock on the inner door. It was a Mickey Mouse lock with a spring latch that any burglar could open in seconds with a strip of celluloid, a knife blade, or a credit card. He locked it nonetheless, yanked on the knob to make certain the door was secure, and then went back into the living room, carrying the bottle of scotch and the two glasses. Hillary was standing at the fireplace. She had taken off the raccoon coat and also the green cardigan sweater. She stood with her legs slightly spread, her booted feet on the stone hearth, her hands extended toward the fire.

"Want some of this?" he said.

"Yes, please."

"Only spirits in the place," he said, intending a joke and surprised when she didn't even smile in response. "We'll have to drink it neat," he said.

He poured generously into both glasses, put the bottle down on the mantel, raised his own glass, said, "Cheers," and took a swallow of whiskey that burned its way clear down to his toes.

"See any ghosts yet?" he asked.

"Not yet."

"Would you know one if you saw one?"

"I'd know one."

"Have you *ever* seen one?"

"No. But I understand the phenomenon."

"How about explaining it to me?"

"You're a skeptic," she said. "I'd be wasting my time."

"Try me."

"No. I'd rather not."

"Okay," he said, and shrugged. "Want to tell me about Craig's working habits instead?"

"What do you mean?"

"How did he work? There was a sheet of paper in his typewriter on the day he was killed. Did he normally type his stuff?"

"Yes."

"Always? Did he ever write in longhand, for example?"

"Never."

"Did he ever *dictate*?"

"To a secretary, do you mean? No."

"Or into a machine?"

"A recorder?"

"Yes. Did he put anything on *tape*?"

The word seemed to resonate in the room. He had not yet told her that Maude Jenkins had typed a portion of Craig's book from a two-hour cassette he'd delivered near the end of the summer three years ago. Hillary did not immediately answer. A log shifted on the grate; the fire crackled and spit.

"Did he?" Carella said.

"Not that I know of."

"What was his voice like?"

"Greg's voice?"

"Yes, I understand he was a heavy smoker. Was his voice hoarse or . . . ?" He searched for another word and finally used the one Maude Jenkins had used in describing the voice on the tape. "Rasping? Would you call it rasping?"

"No."

"At least a portion of *Deadly Shades* was on tape," he said. "About a hundred pages of it. Were there . . . ?"

"How do you know that?"

"I spoke to the woman who typed it. Were there any other tapes? The published book ran something like three hundred pages, didn't it?"

"Close to four hundred."

"So where are the tapes? If the first part of it was on tape . . ."

"I never saw any tapes," Hillary said.

"Who typed the final manuscript?"

"I don't know. I didn't know Greg while he was working on *Shades*."

"Who *normally* types his stuff? In the city, I mean."

"He hasn't had anything typed recently. He was still working on the new book, he had no reason to have it typed clean till he finished it."

"Would Daniel Corbett have known anything about the existence of any tapes?"

"I have no idea," Hillary said, and the candles on the mantelpiece went out.

Carella felt a sudden draft in the room and turned abruptly toward the front door, thinking it might have been blown open by the raging wind. He could see past the edge of the boxed stairwell to the small entryway. The door was closed. He went to it anyway and studied the lock—the same as the one on the kitchen door but securely latched nonetheless. He went out into the kitchen. The hurricane lamps were still burning on the fireplace mantel and the drainboard, but the candles he had lighted on the kitchen table were out—and the kitchen door was open.

He stood looking at the door. He was alone in the room. The extinguished candles sent wisps of trailing smoke up toward the ceiling beams. He put his glass down on the kitchen table, went to the door, and looked at the lock. The thumb bolt had been turned; the spring latch was recessed into the locking mechanism. As earlier, the storm door was closed—but the slip bolt had been thrown back. He heard a sound behind him and whirled instantly. Hillary was standing in the doorway to the kitchen.

"They're here," she whispered.

He did not answer her. He locked both doors again and was turning to relight the candles when the hurricane lamp on the drainboard suddenly leaped into the air and fell to the floor, the chimney shattering, kerosene spilling from the base and bursting into flame. He stomped out the flames, and then felt another draft, and knew without question that something had passed this way.

He would never in his life tell a single soul about what happened next. He would not tell any of the men in the squadroom because he knew they would never again trust a certified lunatic in a shoot-out. He would not tell Teddy because he knew that she, too, would never completely trust him afterward. He was turning toward where Hillary stood in the doorway when he saw the figure behind her. The figure was a woman. She was wearing a long dress with an apron over it. A sort of granny hat was on her head. Her eyes were mournful, her hands were clasped over her breasts. She would have been frightening in any event, appearing as suddenly as she had, but the terrifying thing about her was that Carella could see through her body and into the small entryway of the house. Hillary turned in the same instant, either sensing the figure behind her or judging it to be there from the look on Carella's face. The woman vanished at once or, rather, seemed swept away by a fierce wind that sucked her shapelessly into the hall and up the stairs to the second floor of the house. A keening moan trailed behind her; the whispered name "John" echoed up the stairwell and then dissipated on the air.

"Let's follow her," Hillary said.

"Listen," Carella said, "I think we should . . ."

"Come," she said, and started up the stairwell.

Carella was in no mood for a confrontation with a restless spirit looking for a John. What did one do when staring down a ghost? He had not held a crucifix in his hands for more years than he cared to remember, and the last time he'd had a clove of garlic around his neck was when he'd had pneumonia as a child and his grandmother had tied one there on a string to ward off the Evil Eye. Besides, were you *supposed* to treat ghosts like vampires, driving stakes into their hearts and returning them to their truly dead states? Did they even *have* hearts? Or livers? Or kidneys? What the hell *was* a ghost? And besides, who believed in them?

Carella did.

He had never been so frightened since the day he'd walked in on a raving lunatic wielding a hatchet, the man's eyes wide, his mouth dripping spittle, someone's severed hand in his own left hand, dripping blood onto the floor as he charged across the room to where Carella stood frozen in his tracks. He had shot the man six times in the chest, finally dropping him an instant before the hatchet would have taken off his nose and part of his face. But how could you shoot a ghost? Carella did not want to go up to the second story of this house. Hillary was already halfway up the stairs, though, and neither did he want to be called chickenshit. Why not? he thought. *Call* me chickenshit, go ahead. I'm afraid of ghosts. This goddamn house was carried here stick by stick from Salem, where they hanged witches, and I just saw somebody dressed like Rebecca Nurse or Sarah Osborne or Goody Proctor or *whoever* the hell, and she was wailing for a man named John, and there ain't nobody here but us chickens, boss. *Adios*, he thought, and saw Hillary disappear around the corner at the top of the stairs, and suddenly heard her screaming. He pulled his gun and took the steps up two at a time.

Hillary, courageous ghost hunter that she was, had collapsed in a dead faint on the floor. An eerie blue light bathed the second-story hallway. The hallway was icy cold; it raised the hackles at the back of his neck even before he saw the women standing there. There were four of them. They all were dressed in what looked like late-seventeenth-century garments. He could see through them and beyond them to the window at the end of the hallway where snow lashed the ancient leaded panes. They began advancing toward him. They were grinning. One of them had blood on her hands. And then, suddenly, a sound intruded itself from someplace above—the attic, he guessed. He could not make out the sound at first. It was a steady throbbing sound, like the beat of a muffled heart. The women stopped when they heard the sound. Their heads moved in unison, tilting up toward the beamed ceiling. The sound grew louder, but he still could not identify it. The women shrank from the sound, huddling closer together in the corridor, seeming to melt one into the other, their bodies overlapping and then disappearing entirely, sucked away by the same strong wind that had banished the specter below.

He squinted his eyes against the wind. It died as suddenly as it had started. He stood trembling in the corridor, Hillary on the floor behind him, snowlight piercing the window at the farthest end, the steady throbbing sound above him. No, it was more like a thumping, the slow, steady thump of—

He recognized the sound all at once.

Someone was bouncing a ball in the attic.

He stood just outside the door to the story above, debating whether he should go up there, thinking maybe somebody was working tricks with lights and wind machines, causing apparitions to appear, a theater of the supernatural, designed to cause a psychic to faint dead away and an experienced detective to stand shaking in his sodden loafers. He told himself there couldn't be anything like ghosts—but he had already seen five of them. He told himself there was nothing to fear, but he was terrified. Fanning the air with his pistol, he made his way up the steps to the attic. The stairs creaked under his cautious tread. The ball kept bouncing somewhere above him.

She was standing at the top of the stairs. She was no older than his daughter April, wearing a long gray dress and a faded sunbonnet. She was grinning at him. She was bouncing a ball, and grinning, and chanting in tempo with the bouncing ball. The chant echoed down the stairwell. It took him a moment to realize that she was repeating over and over again the words "Hang them." The ball bounced, and the child grinned, and the words "Hang them, hang them" floated down the stairwell to where he stood with the pistol shaking in his fist. The air around her shimmered, the ball took on an iridescent hue. She took a step down the staircase, the ball clutched in her fist now. He backed away, and suddenly lost his footing, and went tumbling down the stairs to the floor below. Above him, he heard her laughter. And then, suddenly, the sound of the ball bouncing again.

He got to his feet and turned the pistol up the steps. She was no longer there. On the floor above he could see a blue luminous glow. His elbow hurt where he had landed on it in his fall. He dragged Hillary to her feet, held her limply against him, hefted her painfully into his arms, and went down the steps to the first floor. Above he could still hear the bouncing ball. Outside the house he carried Hillary to where he'd parked the car, the snowflakes covering her clothes till she resembled a shrouded corpse. He heaved her in onto the front seat and then went back to the house—but only to pick up their coats. The ball was still bouncing in the attic.

He heard it when he went outside again, stumbling through the deep snow toward the car. He heard it over the whine of the starter and the sudden roar of the engine. He heard it over the savage wind and the crash of the ocean. And he knew that whenever in the future anything frightened him, whenever any unknown dark terror seized his mind or clutched his heart, he would hear again the sound of that little girl bouncing the ball in the attic—bouncing it, bouncing it, bouncing it.

"Come in," Hillary said.

She was sitting dejectedly in an easy chair, the two cups of Irish coffee on a low table before her. She was still wearing the raccoon coat, huddled inside it.

"You okay?" he asked.

"I guess."

He took one of the cups from the table, sipped at it, and licked whipped cream from his lips. "Why don't you drink it before it gets cold?" he said.

She lifted the other cup, but she did not drink from it.

"What's the matter?"

"Nothing."

"Drink your coffee."

She sipped at it, her eyes lowered.

"Want to tell me?"

"No."

"Okay," he said.

"It's just . . . I'm so damn ashamed of myself."

"Why?"

"Fainting like that."

"Well, it *was* pretty scary back there," Carella said, and sat on the edge of the bed.

"I'm *still* scared," Hillary said.

"So am I."

"I don't believe that."

"Believe it."

"My first real manifestation," she said, "and I . . ." She shook her head.

"The first time I faced a man with a gun, I went blind," Carella said.

"Blind?"

"With fear. I saw the gun in his hand, and then I didn't see anything else. Everything went white."

"What happened?" Hillary asked.

"He shot me, and I died."

She smiled and sipped her coffee.

"What happened was I came to my senses about three seconds before it would have been too late."

"Did you shoot him?"

"Yes."

"Did you kill him?"

"No."

"Have you *ever* killed anyone?"

"Yes."

"Have you ever been shot yourself?"

"Yes."

"Why do you keep doing it?"

"Doing what?"

"Police work."

"I like it," he said simply, and shrugged.

"I've been wondering how I can ever . . ." She shook her head again and put down the coffee cup.

"Ever what?"

"Go on doing what I'm doing. After tonight I wonder if I shouldn't simply get a job as a *ribbon* clerk or something."

"You wouldn't be good at it."

"I'm not so good at this either."

"Come on, you're *very* good," he said.

"Sure. Fainting like a . . ."

"I almost didn't come up those stairs after you," Carella said.

"Sure."

"It's the truth. I almost ran out of that damn house."

"Yet you're willing to face men with guns in their hands."

"A gun is a gun. A ghost . . ." He shrugged.

"I suppose I'm glad I saw them," she said.

"So am I."

"I wet my pants, you know."

"No, I didn't know that."

"I did."

"I almost wet mine."

"Fine pair," she said, and smiled again.

The room went silent.

"Do I really look like your wife?" she asked.

"Yes. You know that."

"I'm not sure of anything anymore."

Again the room went silent.

"Well," Carella said, and got to his feet.

"No, don't go yet," she said.

He looked at her.

"Please," she said.

"Well, okay, few minutes," he said, and sat on the edge of the bed again.

"Is your wife anything at all like me?" Hillary asked. "Or is the resemblance purely physical?"

"Purely physical."

"Is she prettier than I am?"

"Well . . . you really look a lot alike."

"I always thought my sister was prettier than I am," Hillary said, and shrugged.

"She thinks so, too."

"She told you that?"

"Yes."

"Bitch," Hillary said, but she was smiling. "Shall we order another round of these?"

"No, I don't think so. We've got a long drive back tomorrow. We'd better get some sleep."

"Yes, we'd better," Hillary said.

"So," he said, and rose again. "I'll leave a call for . . ."

"No, don't go," she said. "I'm still frightened."

"It's really getting late," he said. "We . . ."

"Every time I think of them I shudder."

"There's nothing to be afraid of," he said. "You're here, and our lady friends are miles from . . ."

"Stay with me," she said.

Her eyes met his. He looked into her face.

"Sleep here," she said. "With me."

"Hillary," he said, "thank you, but . . ."

"Just to hold me," she said. "In the night."

111

"Just to hold you, huh?" he said, and smiled.

"Well, whatever," she said and returned the smile. "Okay?"

"No," he said. "Not okay."

"I think you'd like to," she said. She was still smiling.

He hesitated. "Yes, I'd like to," he said.

"So what's . . . ?"

"But I won't."

"We're stranded here . . ."

"Yes . . ."

"No one would ever know."

"*I* would know."

"You'd forgive yourself," she said, and her smile widened.

"Hillary, come on, let's quit it, okay?"

"No," she said. "Not okay."

"Look, I . . . come on, really."

"Do you know how my sister would handle this?" she asked. "She'd tell you she washed out her panties the minute she got back here to the room. She'd tell you her panties were hanging on the shower rod in the bathroom. She'd tell you she wasn't wearing any panties under her skirt. Do you think *that* would interest you?"

"Only if I were in the lingerie business," Carella said, and to his great surprise and enormous relief, Hillary burst out laughing.

"You really *mean* it, don't you?" she said.

"Yeah, what can you do?" Carella said, and shrugged.

"Well, okay then," Hillary said, "I *guess*." She rose, shrugged out of the coat, laughed gently again, murmured, "The *lingerie* business," shook her head, and said, "I'll see you in the morning."

"Good night, Hillary," he said.

"Good night, Steve," she said, and sighed and went into the bathroom.

He stood looking at the closed bathroom door for a moment, and then he went into his own room and locked the door behind him.

He dreamed that night that the door between their rooms opened as mysteriously as the doors at the Loomis house had. He dreamed that Hillary stood in the doorway naked, the light from her own room limning the curves of her young body for an instant before she closed the door again behind her. She stood silently just inside the door, her eyes adjusting to the darkness, and then she came softly and silently to the bed and slipped under the covers beside him. Her hand found him. In the darkness she whispered, "I don't care *what* you think," and her mouth descended.

In the morning, when he awoke, the snow had stopped.

He went to the door between the rooms and tried the knob. The door was locked. But in the bathroom he smelled the lingering scent of her perfume and saw a long black hair curled like a question mark against the white tile of the sink.

He would not tell Teddy about *this* encounter either. Seven ghosts in one night was one more ghost than anybody needed or wanted.

Ghosts, 1980

NAOMI SCHNEIDER

The rain lashed the windows of the bar on Jefferson Avenue, some three and a half miles southwest of the station house. The tall blond man with the hearing aid in his right ear had just told Naomi he was a cop. A police *detective*, no less. She didn't know the police department was hiring deaf people nowadays. Antidiscrimination laws, she supposed. They allowed you to hire *anybody*. Next you'd have detectives who were midgets. Not that a hearing aid necessarily meant you were deaf. Not stone *cold* deaf anyway. Still she guessed any degree of hearing loss could be considered an infirmity, and she was far too polite to ask him how a man wearing a hearing aid had passed the physical examinations she supposed the police department required. Some people were sensitive about such things.

He was good-looking.

For a cop.

"So what's your name?" she asked.

"Steve," he said.

"Steve what?"

"Carella," he said. "Steve Carella."

"Really?" she said. "Italian?"

"Yes," he said.

"Me too," Naomi said. "Half."

"What's the other half?"

"Wildcat," she said, and grinned, and then lifted her glass. She was drinking C.C. and soda, which she thought was sophisticated. She looked up at him seductively over the rim of her glass, which she had learned to do from one of her women's magazines, where she had also learned how to have multiple orgasms, occasionally.

Actually she was half-Italian and half-Jewish, which she guessed accounted for the black hair and blue eyes. The tip-tilted nose was Irish, not that her parents could claim any credit for that. The nose's true father was Dr. Stanley Horowitz, who had done the job for her three years ago, when she was twenty-two years old. She'd asked him at the time if he didn't think she should get a little something done to her boobs as well, but he'd smiled and said she didn't need any help in *that* department, which she supposed was true.

She was wearing a low-cut blue nylon blouse that showed her breasts to good advantage and also echoed the color of her eyes. She noticed that the deaf man's eyes—what'd he say his name was?—kept wandering down to the front of her blouse, though occasionally he checked out her legs, too. She had good legs. That's why she was wearing very high-heeled, ankle-strapped shoes, to emphasize the curve of the leg. Lifted the ass, too, the high heels did, though you couldn't tell that when she was sitting. Dark blue shoes and smoky blue nylons. Sexy. She felt sexy. Her legs were crossed now, her navy blue skirt riding up over one knee.

"I'm sorry, *what* was your name again?" she asked.

"Steve Carella," he said.

"I got so carried away with your being *Italian*," she said, rolling her eyes, "that I . . ."

"A lot of people forget Italian names," he said.

"Well, *I* certainly shouldn't," Naomi said. "My mother's maiden name was Giamboglio."

"And your name?" he said.

"Naomi Schneider." She paused and then said, "That's what the other half is . . . Jewish." She waited for a reaction. Not a flicker on his face. Good. Actually she enjoyed being a Big City Jewish Girl. There was something special about the Jewish girls who lived in this city—a sharpness of attitude, a quickness of tongue, an intelligence, an awareness that came across as sophisticated and witty and hip. If anybody didn't like her being Jewish—well, *half* Jewish—then so long, it was nice knowing you. He seemed to like it, though. At least he kept staring into her blouse. And checking out the sexy legs in the smoky blue nylons.

"So, Steve," she said, "where do you work?"

"Uptown," he said, "At the Eight-Seven. Right across the street from Grover Park."

"Rotten neighborhood up there, isn't it?"

"Not the best," he said, and smiled.

"You must have your hands full."

"Occasionally," he said.

"What do you get up there? A lot of murders and such?"

"Murders, armed robberies, burglaries, rapes, arsons, muggings . . . you name it, we've got it."

"Must be exciting, though," Naomi said. She had learned in one of her women's magazines to show an intense interest in a man's work. This got difficult when you were talking to a dentist, for example. But police work really *was* interesting, so right now she didn't have to fake any deep emotional involvement with a left lateral molar, for example.

"Are you working on anything interesting just now?" she asked.

"We caught a homicide on the twenty-fifth," he said. "Dead woman in the park, about your age."

"Oh my," Naomi said.

"Shot in the back of the head. Totally naked, not a stitch on her."

"Oh my," Naomi said again.

"Not much to go on yet," he said, "but we're working on it."

"I guess you see a lot of that."

"We do."

She lifted her glass, sipped at her C.C. and soda, looking at him over the rim, and then put the glass down on the bartop again, empty. The bar at five-thirty in the afternoon was just beginning to get crowded. She'd come over directly from work, the long weekend ahead, hoping she might meet someone interesting. *This* one was certainly interesting; she'd never met a detective before. Good-looking, too. A naked dead girl in the park, how about that?

"Would you care for another one?" he asked.

"Oh, thank you," she said. "It's C.C. and soda." She waited for a reaction. Usually you said C.C. and soda to a wimp, he asked, "What's that, C.C.?" *This* one didn't even bat an eyelash.

Either he knew what C.C. was, or he was smart enough to pretend he knew. She liked smart men. She liked handsome men, too. Some men, you woke up the next morning, it wasn't even worth the shower.

He signaled to the bartender, indicated another round, and then turned to her again, smiling. He had a nice smile. The jukebox was playing the new McCartney single. The rain beat against the plate glass windows of the bar. It felt cozy and warm and comfortably crowded in here, the hum of conversation, the tinkle of ice cubes in glasses, the music from the juke, the brittle laughter of Big City women like herself.

"What sort of work do *you* do, Naomi?" he asked.

"I work for CBS," she said.

It usually impressed people when she said she worked for CBS. Actually what she did, she was a receptionist there, but still it was impressive, a network. Again nothing registered on his face. He was a very cool one, this one, well-dressed, handsome, a feeling of . . . absolute certainty about him. Well, he'd probably seen it all and done it all, this one. She found that exciting.

Well, maybe she was looking for a little excitement.

This morning, when she was dressing for work, she'd put on the lingerie she'd ordered from *Victoria's Secret*. Blue, like the blouse. A demicup underwire bra designed for low necklines, a lace-front string bikini with a cotton panel at the crotch, a garter belt with V-shaped lace panels. Sat at the desk in the lobby with the sexy underwear under her skirt and blouse, thinking she'd hit one of the bars after work, find some excitement. "CBS, good morning." And under her clothes, secret lace.

"Actually I'm just a receptionist there," she said, and wondered why she'd admitted this. "But I do get to meet a lot of performers and such. Who come up to do shows, you know."

"Uh-huh," he said.

"It's a fairly boring job," she said, and again wondered why she was telling him this.

"Uh-huh," he said.

"I plan to get into publishing eventually."

"I plan to get into *you* eventually," he said.

Normally she would have said, "Hey, get lost, creep, huh?" But he was looking at her so intently, not a smile on his face, and he appeared so . . . *confident* that for a moment she didn't know *what* to say. She had the sudden feeling that if she told him to disappear, he might arrest her or something. For what, she couldn't imagine. She also had the feeling that he knew exactly what she was wearing under her skirt and blouse. It was uncanny. As if he had X-ray vision, like Superman. She was nodding before she even realized it. She kept nodding. She hoped her face was saying, "Oh, yeah, wise guy?" She didn't know what her face was saying. She just kept nodding.

"You're pretty sure of yourself, aren't you?" she asked.

"Yes," he said.

"Walk into a bar, sit down next to a pretty girl . . ."

"You are," he said.

"Think all you have to do . . ."

"Yes," he said.

"Man of few words," she said. Her heart was pounding.

"Yes," he said.

"Mmm," she said, still nodding.

The record on the juke changed. Something by the Stones. There was a hush for a moment, one of those sudden silences, all conversation seeming to stop everywhere around them, as though E. F. Hutton were talking. And then a woman laughed someplace down the bar, and Mick Jagger's voice cut through the renewed din, and Naomi idly twirled her finger in her drink, turning the ice cubes, turning them. She wondered if he liked sexy underwear. Most men liked sexy underwear. She visualized him tearing off her blouse and bra, getting on his knees before her to kiss her where the cotton panel covered her crotch, his big hands twisted in the garters against her thighs. She could feel the garters against her thighs.

"So . . . uh . . . where do you live, Steve?" she asked. "Near the precinct?"

"It doesn't matter where I live," he said. "We're going to *your* place."

"Oh, *are* we?" she said, and arched one eyebrow. She was jiggling her foot, she realized. She sipped at the drink, this time looking into the glass and not over the rim of it.

"Naomi," he said, "we are . . ."

"Bet you can't even spell it," she said. "Naomi."

Her magazines had said it was a good idea to get a man to spell your name out loud. That way, he would remember it. But it was as if he hadn't even heard her, as if her statement had been too ridiculous to dignify with a reply.

"We *are*," he repeated, giving the word emphasis because she'd interrupted him, "going to your apartment, *wherever* it is, and we are going to spend the weekend there."

"That's what . . . what you think," she said.

She was suddenly aware of the fact that her panties were damp.

"How do you know I'm not married?" she said.

"Are you?"

"No," she said. "How do you know I'm not living with someone?"

"Are you?"

"No, but . . ."

"Finish your drink, Naomi."

"Listen, I don't like men who come on so strong, I mean it."

"Don't you?" he said. He was smiling.

"No, I don't."

"You do," he said.

"Do all detectives come on so strong?" she said.

"I don't know what *all* detectives do," he said.

"'Cause, you know, you really *are* coming on very strong, Steve. I don't usually like that, you know. A man coming on so strong."

"I'm giving you sixty seconds to finish that drink," he said.

God, I'm soaking *wet*, she thought, and wondered if she'd suddenly got her period.

"Are *you* married?" she asked.

"No," he said, and pushed back the cuff on his jacket. He was wearing a gold Rolex. She wondered briefly how come a detective could afford a gold Rolex.

"Sixty seconds," he said. "Starting *now*."

"What if I *don't* finish it in sixty seconds?"

"You lose," he said simply.

She did not pick up her glass.

"Fifty-five seconds," he said.

She looked into his face and then reached for her glass. "I'm drinking this because I *want* to," she said. "Not because you're looking at your watch."

"Fifty seconds," he said.

Deliberately, she sipped at the drink very slowly, and then suddenly wondered if she could really *finish* the damn thing in whatever time was left. She also wondered if she'd made the bed this morning.

"Forty seconds," he said.

"You're really something, you know that?" she said, and took a longer swallow this time.

"In exactly thirty-eight seconds . . ." he said.

"Do you carry a gun?" she asked.

"Thirty-five seconds now . . ."

"'Cause I'm a little afraid of guns."

"Thirty seconds . . ."

"What is this, a countdown?" she asked, but she took another hasty swallow of the drink.

"Twenty-six seconds . . ."

"You're making me very nervous, you know that?" she said.

"Twenty seconds . . ."

"Forcing me to . . ."

"Fifteen . . ."

"Slow *down*, will . . . ?"

"In exactly twelve seconds . . ."

"I'm gonna *choke* on this," she said.

"Ten seconds . . ."

"Jesus!"

"You and I . . . eight seconds . . . are going to . . . five seconds . . . walk out of here . . . two seconds . . ."

"All *right*, already!" she said and plunked the empty glass down on the bartop.

Their eyes met.

"Good," he said, and smiled.

She had found the ribbons for him in her sewing box. He had asked her for the ribbons. By then she would have given him the moon. Silk ribbons. A red one on her right wrist. A blue one on her left wrist. Pink ribbons on her ankles. She was spread-eagled on her king-size bed, her wrists and ankles tied to the bars of the brass headboard and footboard. She was still wearing the smoky blue nylons, the high-heeled, ankle-strapped shoes, and the garter belt. He had taken off her panties and her bra. She lay there open and exposed, waiting for whatever he chose to do next, *wanting* whatever he chose to do next.

He had put his shoulder holster and gun on the seat of the armchair across the room. That was when he was undressing. Jokingly she had said, "Let me see your badge," which is what anybody in this city said when somebody knocked on your door in the middle of the night and claimed to be a cop. He had looked at her without a smile. "*Here's* my badge, baby," he'd said, and unzipped his fly. She knew she was in trouble right that minute. She just didn't know how *much* trouble. She had looked down at him and said, "Oh, boy, I'm in trouble," and had giggled nervously, like a schoolgirl, and suddenly she was in his arms, and his lips were on hers, and she was lost, she knew she was lost.

That had been four hours ago, before he'd tied her to the bed. The clock on the dresser now read ten o'clock.

He had insisted that they leave the shades on the windows up, even though she protested that people in the building across the way might see them. There were lights on in the building across the way. Above the building the night was black. She wondered if anyone across the way could see her tied to the bed with silk ribbons. She was oozing below again, dizzy with wanting him again. She visualized someone across the way looking at her. Somehow it made her even more excited.

She watched him as he went to the armchair, picked up the holster, and took the pistol from it. Broad, tanned shoulders, a narrow waist, her fingernail marks still on his ass from where she'd clawed at him. She'd described herself to him, back there in the bar, as half-wildcat, but that was something she'd never believed of herself, even after she'd learned all about multiple orgasms. Tonight . . . Jesus! Afloat on her own ocean. Still wet with his juices and her own, still wanting more.

He approached the bed with the gun in his hand.

"Is there a burglar in the house?" she asked, smiling.

He did not smile back.

"A lesson," he said.

"Is that loaded?" she said. She was looking at his cock, not the gun, though in truth the gun did frighten her. She had never liked guns. But she was still smiling, seductively she thought. She writhed on the bed, twisting against the tight silken ribbons.

"Empty," he said, and snapped open the cylinder to show her. "A Colt Detective Special," he said. "Snub-nosed."

"Like me," she said. "Do you like my nose?"

"Are you ready for the lesson?" he asked.

"Oh my," she said, opening her eyes and her bound hands in mock fright. "*Another* lesson?" The gun was empty, she wasn't afraid of it now. And she was ready to play any game he invented.

"If you're ready for one," he said.

"I'm ready for anything you've got," she said.

"A lesson in combinations and permutations," he said, and suddenly opened his left hand. A bullet was in it. "Voilà," he said. "Six empty chambers in the . . ."

"There's an empty chamber right here," she said.

". . . cylinder of the pistol."

"Come fill it," she said.

"And one bullet in my left hand."

He showed her the bullet.

"I insert this into the cylinder . . ."

"Insert something in *me*, will you, please?"

". . . and we now have one full chamber and five empty ones. Question: What are the odds against the shell being in firing position when I stop twirling the cylinder?" he started twirling the cylinder, slowly, idly. "Any idea?" he said.

"Five to one," she said. "Come fuck me."

"Five to one, correct," he said, and sat on the edge of the bed, resting the barrel of the gun against the inside of her thigh.

"Careful with that," she said.

He smiled. His finger was inside the trigger guard.

"Really," she said. "There's a bullet in it now."

"Yes, I know."

"So . . . you know . . . move it away from there, okay?" She twisted on the bed. The cold barrel of the gun touched her thigh again. "Come on, Steve."

"We're going to play a little Russian roulette," he said, smiling.

"Like hell we are," she said.

But she was tied to the bed.

He rose suddenly. Standing beside the bed, looking down at her, he began twirling the cylinder. He kept twirling it. Twirling it. Smiling.

"Come, Steve," she said, "you're scaring me."

"Nothing to be scared of," he said. "The odds are five to one."

He stopped twirling the cylinder.

He sat on the edge of the bed again.

He looked at her.

He looked at the gun.

And then, gently, he placed the barrel of the gun into the hollow of her throat.

She recoiled, terrified, twisting her head. The metal was cold against her flesh.

"Hey, listen," she said, and he pulled the trigger.

The silence was deafening.

She lay there sweating, breathing harshly, certain he would pull the trigger yet another time. The odds were five to one. How many times could he . . . ?

"It's made of wood," he said. "The bullet in the gun. You weren't in any danger."

He moved the barrel of the gun away from her throat.

She heaved a sigh of relief.

125

And realized how wet she was.

And looked at him.

His erection was enormous.

"You . . . shouldn't have scared me that way," she said.

She was throbbing everywhere.

"I can do whatever I *want* with you," he said.

"No, you can't."

"I own you," he said.

"No, you don't," she whispered.

But she struggled against the restraining ribbons to open wider for him as he mounted her again.

They did not budge from that apartment all weekend.

She did not know what was happening to her; nothing like this had ever happened to her in her life.

He left early Monday morning, promising to call her soon.

As soon as he was gone, she dressed as he had ordered her to.

Sitting behind the reception desk at CBS later that morning, she wore no panties under her skirt and no bra under her blouse.

"CBS, good morning," she said into the phone.

And ached for him.

"Eighty-seventh Squad, Brown," he said.

"Hello, yes," the voice on the other end said. A young woman. Slightly nervous. "May I speak to Detective Carella, please?"

"I'm sorry, he's not here just now," Brown said. "Should be in any minute, though." He looked up at the wall clock. Five minutes to eight. "Can I take a message for him?"

"Yes," the woman said. "Would you tell him Naomi called?"

"Yes, Miss, Naomi who?" Brown said. O'Brien was on his way out of the squadroom. He waved to Brown, and Brown waved back.

"Just tell him Naomi. He'll know who it is."

"Well, Miss, we like to . . ."

"He'll know," she said, and hung up.

Brown looked at the telephone receiver.

He shrugged and put it back on its cradle.

Carella walked into the squadroom not three minutes later.

"Your girlfriend called," Brown said.

"I told her never to call me at the office," Carella said.

He looked like an Eskimo. He was wearing a short woolen car coat with a hood pulled up over his head. The hood was lined with some kind of fur, probably rabbit, Brown thought.

He was wearing leather fur-lined gloves. His nose was red, and his eyes were tearing.

"Where'd summer go?" he asked.

"Naomi," Brown said, and winked. "She said you'd know who."

The phone rang again.

Brown picked up the receiver.

"Eighty-seventh Squad, Brown," he said.

"Hello, it's Naomi again," the voice said, still sounding nervous. "I'm sorry to bother you, but I'll be leaving for work in a few minutes, and I'm not sure he has the number there."

"Hold on, he just came in," Brown said, and held the phone out to Carella. "Naomi," he said.

Carella looked at him.

"Naomi," Brown said again, and shrugged.

"You kidding?" Carella asked.

"It's Naomi," Brown said. "Would I kid you about Naomi?"

Carella walked to his own desk.

"What extension is she on?" he asked.

"Six. You want a little privacy? Shall I go down the hall?"

Carella pushed the six button on the base of his phone and lifted the receiver. "Detective Carella," he said.

"Steve?" a woman's voice said. "It's Naomi."

"Uh-huh," he said, and looked at Brown.

Brown rolled his eyes.

"You promised you'd call," she said.

"Uh-huh," Carella said, and looked at Brown again. The way he figured it, there were only two possible explanations for the youngish-sounding lady on the phone. One: She was someone he'd dealt with before in the course of a working day, an honest citizen with one complaint or another, and he'd simply forgotten her name. Or two, and he considered this more likely: The witty gents of the Eight-Seven had concocted a little gag, and he was the butt of it. He remembered back to last April, when they'd asked a friendly neighborhood hooker to come up here and tell Genero she was pregnant with his child. Now there was Naomi. City-honed voice calling him "Steve" and telling him he'd promised to call. And Brown sitting across the room, watching him expectantly. Okay, he thought, let's play the string out.

"Steve?" she said. "Are you still there?"

"Yep," he said. "Still here. What's this in reference to, Miss?"

"It's in reference to your pistol."

"Oh, I see, my pistol," he said.

"Yes, your big pistol."

"Uh-huh," he said.

"When am I going to see you again, Steve?"

"Well, that all depends," he said, and smiled at Brown. *"Who'd* you say this was?"

"What is it?" she said. "Can't you talk just now?"

"Yes, Miss, certainly," he said. "But police regulations require that we get the name and address of anyone calling the squadroom. Didn't they tell you that?"

"Didn't *who* tell me that?"

"Whoever put you up to calling me."

There was a long silence on the line.

"What is it?" she said. "Don't you *want* to talk to me?"

"Miss," Carella said, "I would *love* to talk to you, truly. I would love to talk to you for hours on end. It's just that these jackasses up here"—he looked meaningfully at Brown—"don't seem to understand that a dedicated and hardworking policeman has better things to do at eight o'clock in the morning than . . ."

"Why are you acting so peculiarly?" she said.

"Would you like to talk to Artie again?" Carella said.

"Who's Artie?"

"Or did Meyer set this up?"

"I don't know what you're talking about," she said.

"Cotton, right? It was Cotton."

"Am I talking to the right person?" she asked.

"You are talking to the person they asked you to talk to," he said, and winked at Brown. Brown did not wink back. Carella felt suddenly uneasy.

"Is this Detective Steve Carella?" she asked.

"Yes," he said cautiously, beginning to think he'd made a terrible mistake. If this *was* an honest citizen calling on legitimate police business . . .

"Who ties girls to beds and plays Russian roulette," she said. "With a wooden bullet."

Uh-oh, he thought, a bedbug. He signaled to Brown to pick up the extension, and then he put his forefinger to his temple and twirled it clockwise in the universal sign language for someone who'd lost his marbles.

"Can you let me have your last name, please?" he said. He was all business now. This was someone out there who might need help. Brown had picked up the phone on his desk. Both men heard a heavy sigh on the other end of the line.

"Okay," she said, "if you want to play games, we'll play games. This is Naomi Schneider."

"And your address, please?"

"You know my address," she said. "You spent a whole goddamn weekend with me."

"Yes, but can you give it to me again, Miss?"

"No, I won't give it to you again. If you've forgotten where I *live*, for Christ's sake . . ."

"Are you alone there, Miss?" he asked. They sometimes called in desperation. They sometimes asked the desk sergeant to put them through to the detectives, and sometimes the sergeant said, "Just a moment, I'll connect you to Detective Kling," or Brown or whoever the hell—Detective *Carella* in this case—but how did she know his first name?

"Yes, I'm alone," she said. "But you can't come over just now, I'm about to leave for work."

"And where's that, Miss? Where do you work?"

"I'm wearing what you told me to wear," she said. "I've been wearing it every day."

"Yes, Miss, where do you work?"

"The garter belt and stockings," she said.

"Can you tell me where you work, Miss?"

"No panties," she said seductively. "No bra."

"If you'll tell me where you work . . ."

"You know where I work," she said.

"I guess I've forgotten."

"Maybe you weren't listening."

"I was listening, but I guess I . . ."

"Maybe you should have turned up your hearing aid," she said.

"My *what*?" Carella asked at once.

"What?" Naomi said.

"What makes you mention a hearing aid?" Carella said. There was a long silence on the line.

"Miss?" he said.

"Are you *sure* this is Steve Carella?" she said.

"Yes, this is . . ."

"Because you sound strange as hell, I've got to tell you."

"Listen, I'd like to see you," Carella said, "really. If you'll give me your address . . ."

"I told you I'm leaving for work in a few minutes . . ."

"And where's that? I'd like to talk to you, Naomi . . ."

"Is that all you'd like to do?"

"Well, I . . ."

"I thought you might want to fuck me again."

Brown raised his eyebrows. Jesus, Carella thought, he thinks I really *know* this girl! But she had mentioned a hearing aid, and right now he didn't give a damn *what* Brown thought.

"Yes, I'd like to do that, too," he said.

"At *last*," she said, and sighed again. "It's like pulling teeth with you, isn't it?"

"Tell me where you work," he said.

"You already know where I work. Anyway, why would you want to come *there*?"

"Well, I thought . . ."

"We couldn't *do* anything there, could we, Steve?" she said, and giggled. "We'd get arrested."

"Well, what time do you get off tonight?" he asked.

"Five."

"Okay, let me have your address, I'll come by as soon as . . ."

"No," she said.

"Naomi . . ."

"You try to *remember* my address, okay? " she said. "I'll be waiting for you. I'll be wide open and waiting for you."

There was a click on the line.

"Miss?" he said

The line was dead.

"Shit," he said.

Brown was staring at him.

Carella put the receiver back on its cradle. "Listen," he said, "if you're thinking . . ."

"No, I'm, not," Brown said. "I'm thinking the Deaf Man."

The Carella house in Riverhead was a huge white elephant they'd picked up for a song shortly after Teddy Carella gave birth to the twins. At about the same time, Teddy's father presented them with a registered nurse as a month-long gift while Teddy was getting her act together, and Fanny Knowles had elected to stay on with them at a salary they could afford, telling them she was tired of carrying bedpans for sick old men.

A lot of cops ribbed Carella about Fanny. They told him they didn't know any other cop on the force who was rich enough to have a housekeeper, even one who had blue hair and wore a pince-nez. They said he had to be on the take. Carella admitted that being able to afford live-in help was decidedly difficult these days; the numbers boys in Riverhead were always so late paying off. Actually Fanny was worth her weight—a hundred and fifty pounds—in pure gold. She ran the house with all the tenderness of a Marine Corps drill sergeant, and she was fond of saying, "I take no shit from man nor beast," an expression the ten-year-old twins had picked up when they were learning to talk and which Mark now used with more frequency than April. In fact, the twins' speech patterns—much to Carella's consternation—were more closely modeled after Fanny's than anyone else's; Teddy Carella was a deaf mute, and it was *Fanny's* voice the twins heard around the house whenever Carella wasn't home.

When the phone rang at three o'clock that Thanksgiving Day, Fanny was washing dishes in the kitchen. Her hands were soapy but she answered the phone anyway. Whenever she and Teddy were alone in the house, she *had* to answer the phone, of course. But even when Carella was home, she normally picked up because she wanted to make sure it wasn't some idiot detective calling about something that could easily wait till morning.

"Carella residence," she said.

"Yes, hello?" a woman's voice said.

"Hello?" Fanny said.

"Yes, I'm trying to get in touch with Detective Steve Carella. Have I got the right number?"

"This is the Carella residence, yes," Fanny said.

"Is there a Detective Steve Carella there?"

"Who's this, please?" Fanny said.

"Naomi Schneider."

"Is this police business, Miss Schneider?"

"Well . . . uh . . . yes."

"Are you a police officer, Miss Schneider?"

"No."

"Then what's this in reference to, please?"

It wasn't often that a civilian called here at the house, but sometimes they did, even though the number was listed in the book as "Carella, T. F.," for Theodora Franklin Carella. Not too many cops listed their home numbers in the telephone directories; this was because not too many crooks enjoyed being sent up the river, and some of them came out looking for revenge. The way things were nowadays, most of them got out ten minutes after you locked them up. These days, when you threw away the key, it came back at you like a boomerang.

"I'd rather discuss it with him personally," Naomi said.

"Well, he's finishing his dinner just now," Fanny said. "May I take a message?"

"I wonder if you could interrupt him, please," Naomi said.

"I'd rather not do that," Fanny said. "They're just having their coffee. If you'll give me your number . . ."

"They?" Naomi said.

"Him and Mrs. Carella, yes."

There was a long silence on the line.

"His mother, do you mean?" Naomi asked.

"No, his wife. Miss Schneider, he'll be back in the office tomorrow if you'd like to . . ."

"Are you sure I have the right number?" Naomi said. "The Detective Carella I have in mind isn't married."

"Well, this one is," Fanny said. She was beginning to get a bit irritated.

"Detective *Steve* Carella, right?" Naomi said.

"Yes, Miss, that's who lives here," Fanny said. "If you'd like to give me a number where he can reach you . . ."

"No, never mind," Naomi said. "Thank you."

And hung up.

Fanny frowned. She replaced the receiver on the wall hook, dried her hands on a dish towel, and went out into the dining room. She could hear the television set down the hallway turned up full blast, the twins giggling at yet another animated cartoon: Thanksgiving Day and all you got was animated cats chasing animated mice. Carella and Teddy were sitting at the dining room table, finishing their second cups of coffee.

"Who was that?" Carella asked.

"Somebody wanting a Detective Steve Carella," Fanny said.

"Well, who?"

"A woman named Naomi Schneider."

"What?" Carella said.

"Got the wrong Carella," Fanny said, and looked at him. "The one she wanted ain't married."

Teddy was reading her lips. She looked at Carella questioningly.

"Did you get a number?" he asked. "Did she leave a number?"

"She hung up," Fanny said, and looked at Carella again. "You ought to tell people not to bring police business into your home," she said, and went out into the kitchen again.

It was beginning to snow lightly.

Naomi stood under the lamppost across the street from the old house and wondered for perhaps the tenth time whether she should go in or not. Her shrink, whom she used to see three years ago, would have said she was conflicted. That had been one of Dr. Hammerstein's favorite words, "conflicted." If she couldn't decide between the vanilla or the chocolate ice cream, that was because she was conflicted. She once protested about his use of the word "conflicted," and he said, "Good, ve are making progress." That wasn't what he'd really said, he didn't even have a German accent. But Naomi always *thought* of him as having a German accent.

The house across the street looked cozy and warm.

Well, Thanksgiving.

The reason Naomi felt conflicted was because she didn't want to lay this heavy stuff on this bastard Carella's wife, but at the same time nobody should have the right to do to her what he'd done to her, which she wouldn't have let him do if she'd known he was married, which he'd lied about. A cop, no less! A *detective*! Lying to her, taking advantage of her, doing disgusting things to her, and then not even calling her again. She'd called every damn Carella in the Isola phone book and had come down six Carellas in the Riverhead directory before she'd struck pay dirt earlier today with T. F. Carella. Who the hell was T. F. Carella? Was Steve even his right name? She'd never have gone to bed with somebody who didn't even give a person his right name. A married man. She'd never have gone to bed with a married man who'd picked her up in a bar. Well, maybe she would have. Isadora Wing went to bed with married men, didn't she? That wasn't the point. This wasn't a question of her *own* morality here, this was a question of whether a man sworn to uphold the laws of the city, state, and nation should be allowed to get away with not calling up a person after the person had allowed him to do such things to her. You weren't even supposed to take your gun out of your *holster* without justification, were you? No less what *he* had done with it.

She could imagine telling that to Hammerstein.

Ja? Dot is very inner-estink. Are you avare vot a symbol der gun is?

She wondered what Hammerstein was doing these days, the crazy old bastard.

Conflicted, she thought, and started across the street toward the house.

The snow was sticking. She shouldn't have come all the way up here. If the snow got really bad, it would raise hell with mass transit. Well, some things simply had to be done. One thing she'd learned about being conflicted was that if you took action, the confliction disappeared. Better you than me, Steve, she thought, and knocked on the door.

A short fat lady with blue hair answered it.

Is *this* his wife? Naomi thought. No wonder he picks up girls in bars.

"Yes?" the woman said.

"I'm looking for Steve Carella," Naomi said.

"I'm sorry, he's not here just now," the woman said.

"He was here an hour and a half ago," Naomi said. "He was here having coffee with his wife."

The woman studied her more closely.

"Are you the person who called here?" she asked.

"I'm the person who called here," Naomi said. "I'm Naomi Schneider. Are you his wife?"

"No, I'm not his . . ."

Another woman appeared suddenly behind her. Dark eyes and hair the color of a raven's wing, good breasts and legs, an inquisitive look on her face. God, she's *gorgeous*! Naomi thought. Why is that son of a bitch fooling around?

"Mrs. Carella?" she asked.

The woman nodded.

"I'm Naomi Schneider," she said. "I'd like to talk to you about your husband. May I come in?"

The other woman was studying her mouth as she spoke. All at once, Naomi realized she was deaf. Oh God, she thought, what am I doing here? But the woman was gesturing her into the house.

She stepped inside.

I'm going to bring this house down around your ears, Steve, she thought, and followed the woman into the living room.

Teddy listened motionless as Naomi told her all about the man she'd met in a bar some three weeks ago, a man she claimed was Steve Carella. Detective Carella had told her he was not married. They had gone to her apartment afterward. Naomi detailed all the things they had done together in her apartment, her eyes unflinching, the words spilling soundlessly from her lips. They had spent the entire weekend together. He had told her he wanted her to go to work on Monday morning without anything under her . . .

Teddy held up her hand. Not *quite* like a traffic cop, but with much the same effect. She rose, crossed the room to a rolltop desk standing near a Tiffany-type floor lamp, and took from it a pencil and pad. She walked back to where Naomi was sitting.

On the pad she wrote: *Are you sure the name was Detective Stephen Louis Carella?*

"He didn't give me his full name," Naomi said. "He just said Steve Carella."

Did he say where he worked? Teddy wrote.

Naomi began talking again.

Teddy watched her lips.

The man—she kept referring to him as "your *husband*"—had told her he worked uptown at the Eight-Seven, right across the street from Grover Park. He'd told her he was working a homicide he'd caught on the twenty-fifth of October. Dead woman in the park, about your age, he'd said.

"I'm twenty-five," Naomi said, a challenging look on her face.

Told her the woman had been shot in the back of the head. Totally naked, not a stitch on her. Not much to go on, he'd told her, but we're working on it.

How can she know all this? Teddy wondered.

On the pad she wrote: *When was this?*

"November fourth," Naomi said. "A Friday night. He left on Monday morning, the seventh. When I went to work that morning—does your husband ask *you* to run around naked under your dress? Does he tie *you* to the bed and stick his goddamn . . ."

Teddy held up the traffic-cop hand again. She rose and went to the desk again. She picked up her appointment calendar. On Friday night, November 4, she and Carella had had dinner with Bert Kling and his girlfriend, Eileen. They had talked about the plastic surgery Eileen was considering. It had been painful for Eileen to discuss the scar a rapist had put on her left cheek. On Saturday, November 5, she and Carella had taken the kids to see a magic show downtown. On, Sunday, November 6, they had gone to visit Carella's parents. She went back to where Naomi was sitting. On the pad she wrote, *Please wait,* and then went down the hall to fetch Fanny.

"Mrs. Carella would like me to translate for her," Fanny said. She looked at Naomi sternly, her arms folded across her ample bosom. "Save a lot of time that way."

"Fine," Naomi said, looking just as stern.

Teddy's fingers moved.

Fanny watched them and then said, "This man who picked you up wasn't my husband."

"*Your* husband?" Naomi said, looking suddenly puzzled.

"Mrs. *Carella's* husband," Fanny said. "I'm translating exactly what she signs."

Teddy's fingers were moving again.

"My husband and I were together on the weekend you're talking about," Fanny said.

"You're trying to protect him," Naomi said directly to Teddy. Teddy's fingers moved.

"What did this man look like?" Fanny asked.

"He was tall and blond . . ."

Watching Teddy's hands, Fanny said, "My husband has brown hair."

"What color eyes does he have?" Naomi asked.

"Brown," Fanny said, ahead of Teddy's fingers.

Naomi blinked. She realized all at once that she couldn't remember what color his eyes were. Damn it, what color were his *eyes*? "Does he wear a hearing aid?" she asked in desperation.

This time Teddy blinked.

"No, he doesn't wear no damn hearing aid," Fanny said, though Teddy hadn't signed a thing. "You've got the wrong man. Now what I suggest you do is get out of here before I . . ."

Teddy was signing again. Very rapidly. Fanny could hardly keep up.

"This man you met is a criminal," Fanny said, translating. "My husband will want to talk to you. Will you please wait here for him? We'll call him at once."

Naomi nodded.

She suddenly felt as if she were in a spy novel.

Carella did not get back to the house until six that night.

Naomi Schneider was still waiting there for him. Fanny had brought her a cup of tea, and she was sitting in the living room, her legs crossed, chatting with Teddy as Fanny translated, the two of them behaving like old college roommates, Teddy's hands and eyes flashing, her face animated.

Naomi thought Carella was very good-looking, and wondered immediately if he fooled around. She was happy when Teddy excused herself to see how the children were doing. Twins, she explained with her hands as Carella translated. A boy and a girl. Mark and April. Ten years old. Naomi listened with great interest, thinking a good-looking man like this, burdened with a handicapped wife and a set of twins, probably *did* play around a little on the side. She waited for Fanny to leave the room, grateful when she did. She was going to enjoy telling the *real* Steve Carella all about what the *fake* Steve Carella had done to her. She wanted to see the expression on his face when she told him.

The real Steve Carella didn't want to know what the fake Steve Carella had done to her.

Instead he started questioning her like a detective.

Which he was, of course, but even so.

"Tell me exactly what he looked like," he said.

"He was tall and . . ."

"*How* tall?"

"Six-one, six-two?"

"Weight?"

"A hundred and eighty?"

"Color of his eyes?"

"Well, actually I don't remember. But he did terrible things to . . ."

"Any scars or tattoos?"

"I didn't see any." Naomi said. "Not anywhere on his body." She lowered her eyes like a maiden, the way she had learned in her magazines.

"Did he say where he lived?"

"No."

"What was he wearing?"

"Nothing."

"Nothing?"

"Oh, I thought you meant when he was doing all those . . ."

"When you met him."

"A gray suit," she said. "Sort of a nubby fabric. An off-white shirt, a dark blue tie. Black shoes. A gold Rolex watch, *all* gold, not the steel and gold one. A gun in a shoulder holster. He used the gun to . . ."

"What kind of gun?"

"A Colt Detective Special."

"You know guns, do you?"

"That's what he told me it was. This was just before he . . ."

"And you met him where?"

"In a bar near where I work. I work for CBS. On Monday morning, when I went to work, he forced me to . . ."

"What's the name of the bar?"

"The Corners."

"Where is it?"

"On Detavoner and Ash. On the corner there."

"Do you go there a lot?"

"Oh, every now and then. I'll probably drop by there tomorrow after work." She raised one eyebrow. "You ought to check it out," she said.

"Had you ever seen him in that bar before?"

"Never."

"Sure about that?"

"Well, I would have noticed. He was very good-looking."

"Did he seem familiar with the neighborhood?"

"Well, we didn't discuss the neighborhood. What we talked about mostly, he gave me sixty seconds to finish my drink, you see, because he was in such a hurry to . . ."

"Did you get the impression he knew the neighborhood well?"

"I got the feeling he knew his way around, yes."

"Around that particular neighborhood?"

"Well, the city. I got the feeling he knew the city. When we were driving toward my apartment later, he knew exactly how to get there."

"You drove there in his car?"

"Yes."

"What kind of car?"

"A Jaguar."

"He was driving a Jaguar?"

"Yes."

"You didn't find that surprising? A detective driving a Jaguar?"

"Well, I don't know any detectives," she said. "You're only my second detective. My *first*, as a matter of fact, since he wasn't a real detective, was he?"

"What year was it?"

"What?"

"The Jag."

"Oh. I don't know."

"What color?"

"Gray. A four-door sedan. Gray with red leather upholstery."

"I don't suppose you noticed the license plate number."

"No, I'm sorry, I didn't. I was sort of excited, you see. He was a very exciting man. Of course, later, when he started doing all those things to me . . ."

"And you say he knew how to get there? From the bar on Detavoner and Ash to where you live?"

"Oh, yes."

"Where *do* you live, Miss Schneider?"

"On Colby and Radner. Near the circle there. If you'd like to come over later, I can show you . . ."

"Did you ask him for any sort of identification? A shield? An ID card?"

"Well, when he was undressing, I said, 'Let me see your badge.' But I was just kidding around, you know. It never occurred to me that he might not be a real detective."

"*Did* he show you a badge?"

"Well, what he said was, '*Here's* my badge, baby.' And showed me his . . . you know."

"You simply accepted him as a cop, is that right?"

"Well . . . yeah. I'd never met a cop before. Not socially. Of course, *you* must meet a lot of young, attractive women in your line of work, but I've never had the opportunity to . . ."

"Did he say anything about coming *back* to that bar? The Corners?"

"No, he just said he'd call me."

"But he never did."

"No. Actually I'm glad he didn't. Now that I know he wasn't a real detective. And, also, I might never have got to meet you, you know?"

"Miss Schneider," Carella said, "if he *does* call you, I want you to contact me at once. Here's my card," he said, and reached into his wallet. "I'll jot down my home number, too, so you'll have it . . ."

"Well, I already know your home number," she said, but he had begun writing.

"Just so you'll have it handy," he said, and gave the card to her.

"Well, I doubt if he'll call me," she said. "It's already three weeks, almost."

"Well, in case he does."

He looked suddenly very weary. She had an almost uncontrollable urge to reach out and touch his hair, smooth it back, comfort him. She was certain he would be very different in bed than the *fake* Steve Carella had been. She suddenly wondered what it would be like to be in bed with both of them at the same time.

"How are you getting home?" he asked.

End of interview, she thought.

Or was he making his move?

"By subway," she said, and smiled at him. "Unless someone offers to drive me home."

"I'll call the local precinct," he said. "See if I can't get a car to take you down."

"Oh," she said.

"Thanksgiving Day, they might not be too busy."

He rose and started for the phone.

"Miss Schneider," he said, dialing. "I really appreciate the information you've given me."

Yeah, she thought, so why the fuck don't you come home with me?

The next break in the case—if in retrospect it could be considered that—came on the third day of December, a Saturday. It came with a phone call from Naomi Schneider at twenty minutes past three.

"Did you just call me?" she asked Carella.

"No," he said. And then at once, "Have you heard from him again?"

"Well, somebody named Steve Carella just called me," she said.

"Did it sound like him?"

"I guess so. I've never heard his voice on the phone."

"What'd he want?"

"He said he wants to see me again."

"Did he say when?"

"Today."

"Where? Is he coming there?"

"Well, we didn't arrange anything actually. I thought I'd better call you first."

"How'd you leave it?"

"I told him I'd call him back."

"He gave you a number?"

"Yes."

"What is it?"

Naomi gave him the number.

"Stay right there," Carella said. "If he calls again, tell him you're still thinking it over. Tell him you're hurt because you haven't heard from him in such a long time."

"Well, I already told him that," Naomi said.

"You told him . . . ?"

"Well, I really *was* hurt," Naomi said.

"Naomi," Carella said, "this man is a very dangerous criminal. Don't play games with him, do you hear me? If he calls again, tell him you're still considering whether you want to see him again, and then call me here right away. If I'm not here, leave a message with one of the other detectives. Have you got that?"

"Yes, of course, I've got it. I'm not a child," Naomi said.

"I'll get back to you later," he said, and hung up. He checked his personal directory, dialed a number at Headquarters, identified himself to the clerk who answered the phone, and told her he needed an address for a telephone number in his possession. The new hotline at Headquarters had been installed because policemen all over the city had been having trouble getting information from the telephone company, whose policy was not to give out the addresses of subscribers, even if a detective said he was working a homicide. Carella sometimes felt the telephone company was run by either the Mafia or the KGB. The clerk was back on the line three minutes later.

"That number is for a phone booth," she said.

"On the street or where?" Carella asked.

"Got it listed for something called The Corners on Detavoner and Ash."

"Thank you," Carella said, and hung up. "Artie!" he yelled. "Get your hat!"

When the knock sounded on the door to Naomi's apartment, she thought it might be Carella. He had told her he'd get back to her later, hadn't he? She went to the door.

"Who is it?" she asked.

"Me," the voice said. "Steve."

It did not sound like the *real* Carella. It sounded like the *fake* Carella. And the *real* Carella had told her the *fake* Carella was a very dangerous man. As if she didn't know.

"Just a second," she said, and unlocked the door and took off the night chain.

There he was.

Tall, blond, handsome, head cocked to one side, smile on his face.

"Hi," he said.

"Long time no see," she said. She felt suddenly weak. Just the sight of him made her weak.

"Okay to come in?"

"Sure," she said, and let him into the apartment.

The Corners at three-thirty that Saturday afternoon was—thanks to the football game on the television set over the bar—actually more crowded than it would have been at the

141

same time on a weekday. Carella and Brown immediately
checked out the place for anyone who might remotely resemble
the Deaf Man. There was only one blond man sitting at the bar,
and he was short and fat. They went at once to the men's room.
Empty. They knocked on the door to the ladies' room, got no
answer, opened the door, and checked that out, too. Empty.
They went back outside to the bar. Carella showed the bartender his shield. The bartender nodded.

"Tall blond man," Carella said. "Would have used the phone
booth about forty minutes ago."

"What about him?" the bartender said.

"Did you see him?"

"I saw him. Guy with a hearing aid?"

"Yes."

"I saw him."

"He's been in here before, hasn't he?"

"Coupla times."

"Would you know his name?"

"I think it's Dennis, I'm not sure."

"Dennis what?"

"I don't know. He was in here with a guy one night, I heard
the guy calling him Dennis."

"There's just this one room, huh?" Brown said.

"Just this one."

"No little side rooms or anything."

"Just this."

"Any other toilets? Besides the rest rooms back there?"

"That's all," the bartender said. "If you're lookin' for him, he
already left."

"Any idea where he went?"

"Nope."

"Did he leave right after he made his phone call?"

"Nope. Sat at the bar for ten minutes or so, finishing his
drink."

"What was he drinking?" Carella asked.

"Jim Beam and water."

Carella looked at Brown. Brown shrugged. Carella went to
the phone booth and dialed Naomi Schneider's number.

"Let it ring," the Deaf Man said.

She was naked. They were on her bed. She would have let it
ring even if it was the fire department calling to say the
building was on fire. The phone kept ringing. Spread wide
beneath him, her eyes closed, she heard the ringing only

distantly, a faraway sound over the pounding of her own heart, the raging of her blood. At last the phone stopped.

All at once *he* stopped too.

"Hey," she said, "don't . . ."

"I want to talk," he said.

"Put it back in," she said.

"Later."

"Come on," she said.

"No."

"Please, baby, I'm almost there," she said. "Put it back in. Please."

He got off the bed. She watched him as he walked to the dresser, watched him as he shook a cigarette free from the package on the dresser top. He thumbed a gold lighter into flame, blew out a wreath of smoke. Everything was golden about him. Gold watch, gold lighter, golden hair, big magnificent golden . . .

"There's something we have to discuss," he said. "Something I'd like you to do for me."

"Bring it here, I'll show you what I can do for you."

"Later," he said, and smiled.

They were in the unmarked sedan, heading back toward the precinct. The heater, as usual, wasn't working. The windows were frost-rimed. Brown kept rubbing at the windshield with his gloved hand, trying to free it of ice.

"I told her to stay home," Carella said. "I specifically told her to . . ."

"We don't own her," Brown said.

"Who owns you?" the Deaf Man said.

"You do."

"Say it."

"You own me."

"Again."

"You own me."

"And you'll do anything I want you to do, won't you?"

"Anything."

"You think we ought to stop by there?" Brown asked. "It's on the way back."

"What for?" Carella said.

"Maybe she just went down for a newspaper or something."

"Pull over to that phone booth," Carella said. "I'll try her again."

The phone was ringing again.
"You're a busy little lady," the Deaf Man said.
"Shall I answer it?"
"No."
The phone kept ringing.

Carella came out of the booth and walked back to the car. Brown was banging on the heater with the heel of his hand.
"Any luck?"
"No."
"So what do you want to do?"
"Let's take a spin by there," Carella said.

"I need you on Christmas Eve," the Deaf Man said.
"I need you right now," Naomi said.
"I want you to be a very good little girl on Christmas Eve."
"I promise I'll be a very good little girl," she said, and folded her hands in her lap like an eight-year-old. "But you really owe me an apology, you know."
"I owe you nothing," he said flatly.
"I mean for not calling me all this . . ."
"For *nothing*," he said. "Don't ever forget that."
She looked at him. She nodded. She would do whatever he asked her to do, she would wait forever for his phone calls, she would never ask him for explanations or apologies. She had never met anyone like him in her life. She almost said out loud, "I'll bet you've got girls all over this city who'll do anything you want them to do," but she caught herself in time. She did not want him walking out on her. She did not want him disappearing from her life again.
"I want you to dress up for me," he said. "On Christmas Eve."
"Like a good little girl?" she said. "In a short skirt? And knee socks? And Buster Brown shoes? And white cotton panties?"
"No."
"Well, whatever," she said. "Sure."
"A Salvation Army uniform," he said.
"Okay, sure."
That might be kicks, she thought, a Salvation Army uniform. Nothing at all under the skirt. Sort of kinky. Little Goodie-Two-Shoes tambourine-beating virgin with her skirt up around her naked ass.

"Where am I supposed to get a Salvation Army uniform?" she asked.

"I'll get it for you. You don't have to worry about that."

"Sure," she said. "You know my size?"

"You can give me that before I leave."

"Leave?" she said, alarmed. "I'll *kill* you if you walk out of here without . . ."

"I'm not walking out of here. Not until we discuss this fully."

"And not until you . . ."

"Be quiet," he said.

She nodded. She had to be very careful with him. She didn't want to lose him, not ever again.

"Where do you want me to wear this uniform?" she said. "Will you be coming here?"

"No."

"Then where? Your place?"

"Uptown," he said. "Near the precinct."

"Uh-huh," she said, and looked at him. "Is that where you live? Near the precinct?"

"No, that's not where I live. That's where you'll be wearing the uniform. On the street up there. A few blocks from where I work."

"We're gonna do it on the street?" she asked, and smiled.

"You have a very evil mind," he said, and kissed her. She felt the kiss clear down to her toes. "This is a stakeout," he said. "Police work. Both of us in Salvation Army uniforms."

"Oh, *you're* gonna be wearing one, too."

"Yes."

"Sounds like fun," she said. "But what do you *really* have in mind?"

"That's what I have in mind," he said.

"A stakeout, huh?"

"Yes, a stakeout."

"Even though you're not a cop, huh?"

"What do you mean?"

"I mean, I know you're not a cop."

"I'm not, huh?"

"I know you're not Steve Carella."

He looked at her.

"And how do you know that?" he said.

"'Cause I know the *real* Steve Carella," she said.

He kept looking at her.

"I do," she said, and nodded. "I called the station house," she said. "I called the 87th Precinct."

"Why'd you do that?"

"'Cause you told me you worked there."

"You spoke to someone named Carella?"

"Steve Carella, yes. In fact, I met him. Later."

"You met him," he said.

"Yes."

"And?"

"He told me you're not him. As if I didn't know. I mean, the minute I saw him I knew he wasn't . . ."

"What else did he tell you?"

"He said you're very dangerous," Naomi said, and giggled.

"I am," he said.

"Oh, I *know*," she said, and giggled again.

"And what'd you tell him?"

"Oh . . . how we met . . . and what we did . . . and like that."

"Did you tell him *where* we met?"

"Oh, sure, The Corners," she said.

He was very silent.

"What else did you tell him?" he asked at last.

A good way for a statistician to discover how many policemen are on duty in any sector of the city is to put a 10–13 call on the radio. Every cop in the vicinity will immediately respond. Sometimes even cops from other precincts will respond. That is because the 10–13 radio code means ASSIST POLICE OFFICER, and there is no higher priority.

Carella and Brown were a block from Naomi's apartment when the 10–13 erupted from the walkie-talkie on the seat between them. Neither of the men discussed or debated it. The cop in trouble was ten blocks from where they were, in the opposite direction from the one they were traveling. But Brown immediately swung the car around in a sharp U-turn, and Carella hit the siren switch.

The Deaf Man sat up straight the moment he heard the siren. Like an animal sensing danger, Naomi thought. God, he is *so* beautiful. But the siren was moving away from her street, and as it faded into the distance, he seemed to relax.

"What else did you tell him?" he asked again.

"Well . . . nothing," she said.

"Are you sure?"

"Well . . . I told him what you looked like and what you were wearing . . . he was asking me questions, you see."

"Yes, I'm sure he was. How did he react to all this information?"

"He seemed interested."

"Oh, yes, I'm sure."

"He told me to keep in touch."

"And have you kept in touch?"

"Well . . ."

"Have you?"

"Look, don't you think you should tell me who you *really* are?" she said.

"I want to know whether you and Steve Carella have kept in touch."

"He said you're a dangerous *criminal* is what he actually said. *Are* you a criminal?"

"Yes," he said. "Tell me whether you've stayed in touch."

"What kind of criminal are you?"

"A very good one."

"I mean . . . like a burglar . . . or a robber . . . or . . ." She arched her eyebrows, the way her magazines had taught her. "A rapist?"

"When did he tell you I was a criminal?" he asked.

"Well, when I saw him, I guess. At his house."

"Oh, you went to his house, did you?"

"Well, yeah."

"When was that?"

"On Thanksgiving Day."

"And that was when he told you I was a criminal?"

"Yes. And again today. A *dangerous* criminal is what he . . ."

"Today?" the Deaf Man said. "You spoke to him today?"

"Well, yes, I did."

"When?"

"Right after you called."

Four patrol cars were already angled into the curb when Carella and Brown got to the scene. A least a dozen patrolmen with drawn guns were crouched behind the cover of the cars, and more patrolmen were approaching on foot, at a run, their guns magically appearing in their hands the moment they saw what the situation was. Again neither Carella nor Brown discussed anything. They immediately drew their guns and stepped out of the car.

A sergeant told them a cop was inside there. "Inside there" was a doctor's office. The cop and his partner had responded to a simple 10–10—INVESTIGATE SUSPICIOUS PERSON—and had walked into the waiting room to find a man holding a .357 Magnum in his hand. The man opened fire immediately, missing both cops, but knocking a big chunk of plaster out of the waiting room wall and scaring the patients half to death. The point-cop had thrown himself flat on the floor. The backup-cop had managed to get out the door and radio the 10–13. The sergeant figured the man inside there was a junkie looking for dope. Doctors' offices were prime targets for junkies. Carella asked the sergeant if he thought he needed them there. The sergeant said, "No, what I think I need here is the hostage team."

Carella and Brown holstered their guns and went back to the car.

The Deaf Man was putting on his clothes. Naomi watched him from the bed.

"I didn't tell him you were coming here, if that's what's bothering you," she said.

"Nothing's bothering me," he said.

But he was tucking the flaps of his shirt into his trousers. He sat again, put on his socks and shoes, and then went to the dresser for his cuff links. He put on the cuff links and then picked up the gun in its holster. He slipped into the harness and then came back to the chair for his jacket.

She kept watching him, afraid to say anything more. A man like this one, you could lose him if you said too much. Instead, she opened her legs a little wider, give him a better look at her, he was only human, wasn't he? He went to the closet, took his coat from a hanger, and shrugged into it.

He walked back to the bed.

He smiled and reached under his coat, and under his jacket, and pulled the gun from its holster.

Naomi returned his smile and spread her legs a little wider. "Another game with the gun?" she asked.

It took Carella and Brown five minutes to clear the immediate area around the doctor's office. The police had cordoned off the scene, so they had to stop at the barricade to identify themselves. It took them another ten minutes to get uptown to Naomi's apartment.

They were twelve minutes too late.

The door to Naomi's apartment was wide open.

Naomi was lying on the bed with a bullet hole between her eyes.

Eight Black Horses, 1985

148

OONA BLAKE

There was the strong smell of cigar smoke.

There was a long shaft of light far away, and a silhouette filling the piercing beam.

There was pain, excruciating pain that throbbed and vibrated and sang with a thousand shrill voices.

There was warmth, a warmth that was thick and liquidy, oozing, oozing.

Cotton Hawes fought unconsciousness.

He felt as if his body was quivering. He felt as if every part of him was swinging in a wild circle of nauseating blackness. Some inner sense told him he was lying flat on his back, and yet he had the feeling that his hands were clutching, grasping, trying to reach something in the blackness, as if his legs and feet were twitching uncontrollably. The pain at the side of his face was unbearable. It was the pain, finally, that forced away the unconsciousness, needling him with persistent fire, forcing sensibility into his mind, and then his body. He blinked.

The cigar smell was overpowering. It filled his newly alert nostrils with the stink of a thousand saloons. The shaft of light

151

was penetrating and merciless, flowing steadily through an open window at the end of the room, impaling him with sunshine. A man stood at the window, his back to Hawes.

Hawes tried to get to his feet, and the nausea came back with frightening suddenness, swimming into his head and then dropping like a swirling stone to the pit of his stomach. He lay still, not daring to move, aware now that the side of his face was bleeding, remembering now the sudden blinding blow that had knocked him to the floor unconscious. The nausea passed. He could feel the steady seeping of the blood as it traveled past his jawbone and onto his neck. He could almost feel each separate drop of blood rolling over his flesh to be sopped up instantly by the white collar of his shirt. He felt as if he were being born, hypersensitive to every nuance of smell, and sight, and touch. And, newborn, he was also weak. He knew he could not stand without falling flat on his face.

He turned his head slightly to the left. He could see the man at the window clearly, each part of the man combining with the next to form a sharply defined portrait of power as he crouched by the window, the late afternoon sunshine enveloping the silhouette in whitish licking flames of light.

The man's hair was black, worn close to his skull in a tight-fitting woolly cap. The man's brow was immense in profile, a hooked nose jutting out from bushy eyebrows pulled into a frown. A small scar stood out in painful relief against the taut skin of the man's face, close to the right eye. The man's mouth was a tight, almost lipless line that gashed deep into the face above a jaw cleft like a horse's buttocks. His neck was thick, and his shoulders bulged beneath the blue tee shirt he wore, biceps rolling hugely into thick forearms covered with black hair that resembled steel wool. One huge hand was clutched around the barrel of a rifle. The rifle, Hawes noticed, was mounted with a telescopic sight. An open box of cartridges rested near the man's right shoe.

This is no one to tangle with in my present condition, Hawes thought. This may be no one to tangle with in any condition. He looks like a man who tears telephone books in sixteenths. He looks like a man who allows automobiles to drive over his inflated chest. He looks like the meanest son of a bitch I have ever seen in my life, and I am not anxious to tangle with him. Now, or maybe ever.

But that's a rifle he's holding, and it has a telescopic sight, and he sure as hell doesn't plan to pick his teeth with it.

Do I still have my gun? Or has he disarmed me?

Hawes looked down the length of his nose. He could see the white throat of his shirt stained with blood. He could see his shoulder holster strapped to his chest beneath his open coat.

The holster was empty.

There's nothing I can do but lie here, he thought, and wait for my strength to come back.

And pray, meanwhile, that he doesn't take a pot shot at anybody across the yard at the reception.

In the attic of the Birnbaum house, Cotton Hawes felt his strength returning. For the past ten minutes, he had lain silently, his eyes flicking from one corner of the attic to another, and then back to the patiently waiting powerhouse squatting on the floor near the window. The attic was filled with the discarded paraphernalia of living: bundles of old magazines, a green trunk marked "CAMP IDLEMERE" in white paint, a dressmaker's dummy, a lawn mower without blades, a hammer, an Army duffel bag, a radio with a smashed face, three albums marked PHOTOGRAPHS and numerous other items that had undoubtedly cluttered the busy life of a family.

The only item which interested Hawes was the hammer.

It rested on top of the trunk some four feet from where he lay.

If he could get the hammer without being heard or seen, he would promptly use it on the sniper's skull. Provided the sniper didn't turn first and shoot him. It would not be too pleasant to get shot at close range with a rifle.

Well, when? Hawes asked himself.

Not now. I'm not strong enough yet.

You're never going to get any stronger, Hawes thought. *Are you afraid of that big bastard crouched by the window?*

Yes.

What?

Yes, I'm afraid of him. He can break me in half even without using his rifle. And he may use it. So I'm afraid of him, and the hell with you.

Let's go, coward, Hawes thought. *Let's make our play for the hammer. There's no time like the present, the man said.*

The man didn't have to face Neanderthal.

Look, are we . . . ?

All right, all right, let's go.

Silently, he rolled over onto his side. The sniper did not turn. He rolled again, completing a full turn this time, coming to rest a foot away from the trunk. Swallowing hard, he reached out for the hammer. Soundlessly, he slid it off the trunk and gripped it tightly in his right hand.

He swallowed again and got to his knees.

Okay, he thought, we rush him now, hammer raised. We crease his skull before he knows what hit him.

Ready?

He got to a crouching position.

Set?

He stood up and raised the hammer high.

Go!

He took a step forward.

The door behind him opened suddenly.

"Hold it, mister!" a voice said, and he whirled to face a big blonde in a red silk dress. She was reaching into her purse as he leaped at her.

It cannot be said of Cotton Hawes that he did not ordinarily enjoy wrestling with blondes whose proportions matched this one's. For here was truly a blonde. Here was a handful, and an armful, and an eyeful; here was the image that automatically came to mind whenever anyone muttered the magic words "big blonde."

Standing on a runway in Union City, this girl would have caused heart stoppage. Third-row bald heads would have turned pale with trembling.

On the legitimate Broadway stage, this girl would have set the theater on fire, set the customers on their ears, and set the critics rushing back to their typewriters to pound out ecstatic notices.

In a bedroom—Hawes's imagination reeled with the thought.

But unfortunately, this girl was not on a runway or a stage or a bed. This girl was standing in the doorway to a room no bigger than an upper berth in a Pullman. This girl was obviously not planning to set anyone but Hawes on his ear. She reached into her purse with all the determination of a desert rat digging for water, and then her hand stopped, and a surprised look came over her lovely features. In clear, crystal-pure, ladylike tones, she yelled, "Where's my goddamn gun?" and Hawes leaped on her.

The sniper turned from the window at the same moment.

The girl was all flesh and a yard wide. She was also all teeth and all nails. She clamped two rows of teeth into Hawes's hand as he struggled for a grip, and then her nails flashed out wildly, raking the uninjured half of his face. The sniper circled closer, shouting, "Get away from him, Oona! I can't do anything with you . . ."

Hawes did not want to hit the girl. He especially did not want to hit her with the hammer. But the hammer was the only weapon he possessed and he reasoned correctly that if this girl got away from him, Neanderthal would either club him into the floorboards with the stock of the rifle or, worse, plunk a few slugs into his chest. Neither prospect seemed particularly entertaining. The blonde herself was not entertaining in the slightest. Wiggling in his arms, she delivered a roundhouse punch that almost knocked out his right eye. He winced in pain and swung at her with the hammer, but she ducked inside the blow and brought her knee to his groin in an old trick she'd probably learned in grammar school, so expertly did she execute it. Hawes had been kicked before. His reactions, he discovered, were always the same. He always doubled over in pain. But this time, as he doubled, he clutched at the blonde because the blonde was insurance. As long as her hot little body remained close to his, the sniper was helpless. He clutched at her, and he caught the front of her dress and it gave under his hand, tearing in a long rip that exposed the blonde's white brassiere and three-quarters of her left breast.

The material kept ripping, with the blonde at the end of it like an unraveling ball of wool in the paws of a playful kitten. He swung the hammer again, catching flesh this time, his fingers closing tightly as he pulled her toward him. The blonde's dress was torn to the waist now, but Hawes wasn't interested in anatomy. Hawes was interested in clubbing her with the hammer. He swung her around and her backside came up hard against him, a solid muscular backside. He swung one arm around her neck, his elbow cushioned between the fleshy mounds of the girl's breasts, and he brought back the hand with the hammer again, and the girl pulled another old grammar-school trick.

She bent suddenly from the knees, and then shot upward with the force of a piston, the top of her skull slamming into Hawes's jaw. His arm dropped. The girl swung around and leaped at him, a nearly barebreasted fury, clawing at his eyes. He swung the hammer. It struck her right arm, and she clutched at it in pain, her face distorted. "You son of a bitch!" she said, and she reached down, her knee coming up, her skirt pulling back over legs which would have been magnificent on the French Riviera stemming from a bikini, and then she pulled off one high-heeled pump and came at Hawes with the shoe clutched like a mace.

"Get the hell away from him!" the sniper yelled, but the girl would not give up the fight. Circling like wrestlers, the girl's chest heaving in the barely restraining brassiere, Hawes panting breathlessly, one holding a hammer, the other a spiked-heel shoe, they searched for an opening. The girl's lips were skinned back over teeth that looked as if they could bite Hawes in two.

She feinted with the shoe, and he brought up his left arm to ward off the blow, and then she moved swiftly to the side, and he saw only the blur of the red shoe coming at his face, felt only the crashing pain as the stiletto-like spike hit his temple. He felt his fingers loosen from the handle of the hammer. He felt himself pitching forward. He held out his arms to stop his fall, and the girl caught him as he came toward her and his head bounced against her shoulder, slid, and he felt the warm cushion of her breast for an instant before she viciously pushed him away from her.

He struck the floor and the last shamed thought he had was, *A girl. Jesus, a girl* . . .

Oona Blake crouched on the floor over him, her skirt pulled back over powerfully beautiful legs, the top of her dress torn to the waist. Darkness had invaded the small attic room of the Birnbaum house. The vanishing light of daytime filtered feebly through the attic window, catching her blonde hair and then the white exposed flank of her thigh as she knotted the ropes securely around Hawes's body and then went through his pockets.

Marty Sokolin, chewing on his cigar, one huge hand around the rifle barrel, watched her. She scared him somewhat. She was the most beautiful girl he'd ever known in his life, but she moved with the power of a Nike rocket, and she scared him sometimes; but she excited him, too. Watching her flip open the man's wallet, watching her hands as they quickly went through the contents, he was frightened and excited.

"A cop," she said.

"How do you know?"

"A badge, and an ID card. Why didn't you search him before?"

"I was too busy. What's a cop doing here? How'd a cop . . . ?"

"They're crawling all over the place," Oona said.

"Why?" His eyes blinked. He bit down more fiercely on the cigar.

"I shot a man," she answered, and he felt a tiny lurch of fear.

"You . . . ?"

"I shot a man, an old fart who was heading for this house. You told me to keep people away from here, didn't you?"

"Yes, but to *shoot* a man! Oona, why'd you . . . ?"

"Aren't you *here* to shoot a man?"

"Yes, but . . ."

"Did you want someone coming up here?"

"No, Oona, but it's brought cops. I've got a record, for Christ's sake. I can't . . ."

"So have I," she snapped, and he watched the sudden fury in her eyes, and again he was frightened. Sweat erupted on his upper lip. In the gathering gloom, he watched her, frightened, excited.

"Do you want to kill Giordano?" she said.

"Yes. I . . . I do."

"Do you or don't you?"

"I don't know. Jesus, Oona, I don't know. I don't want cops. I don't want to go to jail again."

"That's not what you told me."

"I know, I know."

"You said you wanted him dead."

"Yes."

"You said you'd never be able to rest until he was dead."

"Yes."

"You asked for my help. I gave it to you. Without me, you wouldn't know how to wipe your nose. Who got the apartment near the photography shop? Me. Who suggested this house? Me. Without me, you'd be carrying your goddamn grudge to the grave. Is that what you want? To carry the grudge to your grave?"

"No, Oona, but . . ."

"Are you a man . . . or what are you?"

"I'm a man."

"You're nothing. You're afraid to shoot him, aren't you?"

"No."

"I've already killed for you, do you know that? I've already killed a man to protect you. And now you're chickening out. What are you? A man or what?"

"I'm a man!" Sokolin said.

"You're nothing. I don't know why I took up with you. I could have had men, real men. You're not a man."

"I'm a man!"

"Then kill him!"

"Oona! It's just . . . there are cops now. There's a cop *here*, right with us . . ."

"There'll be fireworks at eight o'clock . . ."

"Oona, if I kill him, what do I accomplish? I know I said I . . ."

". . . a lot of noise, a lot of explosions. If you fire then, the shot won't even be heard. No one will hear it."

". . . wanted him dead, but now I don't know. Maybe he wasn't responsible for Artie's getting shot. Maybe he didn't know . . ."

"You go to the window, Marty. You pick him up in your sights."

". . . there was a sniper in the trees. I'm clean now. I'm out of jail. Why should I fool around with something like this?"

"You wait for the fireworks to start. You squeeze the trigger. He's dead, and we take off."

"And the cop laying there on the floor? He's seen both of us."

"I'll take care of him," Oona said, and grinned. "It'll be a real pleasure to take care of him." Her voice dropped to a whisper. "Get to the window, Marty."

"Oona . . ."

"Get to the window and get it over with. As soon as the fireworks start. Get it over and done with. And then come with me, Marty, come with me, baby, come to Oona baby. Marty, get it over with, get it over with, *get it out of your system!*"

"Yes," he said. "Yes, Oona."

"Can you see him?"

Him, him, him, him, him . . .

"Yes. I've got him in the sights."

Sights, sights, sights, sights, sights . . .

Don't miss this time, I won't, take careful aim, I will, they're starting the fireworks now, the little ones, I don't like the sound of fireworks, reminds me of guns going off, I hate guns going off, Marty, shut up, concentrate on what you're doing, I am, look they're setting off the pinwheels, can you still see him, yes, don't fire until the big ones go off, we need the cover of the explosions, don't fire yet, Marty, I won't, I won't.

Won't, won't, words, words, people talking, jumble of words, thunder in the distance, gunshots, fire, don't won't . . .

Cotton Hawes climbed the echoing tunnel of unconsciousness, voices and sounds blurred meaninglessly, reverberating inside his head as blackness gave way to brightness, pinwheeling brightness outside, fireworks, yes, fireworks going off outside in the . . .

He blinked his eyes.

He tried to move.

He was trussed like Aunt Sadie's roast; his hands tied to his feet behind him, he sprawled on the floor like the base of a big rocking horse. By turning his head, he could see the window. Beyond the window, the bright dizzy gleam of the fireworks split the night air. Silhouetted in the window was Neanderthal, squatting over the rifle, and standing above him, one hand on his shoulder, leaning over slightly, the red silk stretched taut over her magnificent buttocks, was the girl who'd clonked him with the shoe.

"Take careful aim, Marty," she whispered.

"I am, I am, I've got him. Don't worry."

"Wait for the big ones. The noisy ones."

"Yes. Yes."

"You can do it, Marty."

"I know."

"You're a man, Marty. You're my man."

"I know. Shhh. Shhh. Don't make me nervous."

"When it's over, Marty. You and me. Take careful aim."

"Yes, yes."

He's going to shoot Tommy, Hawes thought helplessly. *Oh my God, he's going to shoot Tommy, and I can't do a goddamn thing to stop him.*

The pinwheels had sputtered out, and the Roman candles had filled the night with red. And now, standing behind the platform, the caterers from Weddings–Fetes, Incorporated, stood at the ready, anxious to light the fuses for the grand finale. Tommy Giordano stood alongside his father-in-law and his bride, bathed in the light from the bandstand, waiting for the medley of explosion and light which would come in the next few moments. He did not know that the crosshairs of a telescopic sight were fixed at a point just above his left eye. He smiled pleasantly as the caterers rushed around behind the platform, squeezed Angela's hand when he saw the first fuse being touched.

The fuse burned shorter, shorter, and then touched the powder. The first of the rockets sailed skyward, exploding in a shower of blue and green stars, followed by the second rocket almost instantly afterward, silver fishes darting against the velvet night. Explosions rocked the peaceful suburb of River-head, shockingly loud explosions that threatened to rip the night to shreds.

In the attic room, Oona Blake dug her fingers into Sokolin's shoulder.

"Now," she said. "Now, Marty."

The men worked together as a highly efficient team, and perhaps everything would have gone smoothly, bloodlessly, had not Bob O'Brien been a part of the team. It was certain that once the men returned to the squadroom, legend and superstition would prevail to single out O'Brien as the culprit.

They had drawn their service revolvers on the front porch of the Birnbaum house. O'Brien stood to one side of the door, and Meyer turned the knob and eased the door open. The living room on the ground floor of the house was dark and silent. Cautiously, both men entered the room.

"If he's here and plans to use a rifle," Meyer whispered, "he must be upstairs."

They waited until their eyes grew accustomed to the dark-ness. They found the staircase then and began climbing it, hesitating when their weight caused the treads to creak. On the second floor, they checked the two bedrooms and found them empty.

"An attic?" O'Brien whispered, and they continued climbing.

They were in the hallway outside the attic room when the fireworks started in the Carella back yard. At first they thought it was gunfire, and then they recognized it for what it was, and both instantly formed the conclusion that their sniper—if he were indeed in the house—had undoubtedly been waiting for the fireworks before opening up with his rifle. They did not speak to each other. There was no need to speak. The operation they were about to perform had been acted out by them hundreds of times before, either together, or as part of other teams. The fireworks in the yard across the way simply added urgency to the operation but they moved swiftly and without panic, Meyer flattening himself against the wall to the right of the door, O'Brien bracing himself against the corridor wall opposite the door. O'Brien glanced at Meyer, and Meyer nod-ded soundlessly.

From inside the room, they heard a woman's voice say, "Now. Now, Marty."

O'Brien shoved himself off the wall, his left leg coming up, the left foot colliding with the door in a powerful, flat-footed kick that splintered the lock and shot the door inward. Like a fullback following a line plunge, O'Brien followed the door into the room, Meyer crossing in behind him like a quarterback ready to take a lateral pass.

O'Brien was not anxious to fire.

His gun was in his hand as he entered the room, following the jet-catapult of the door, his eyes sweeping first to the window where the man crouched over the rifle, then to the floor where Cotton Hawes lay tied in a neat bundle, and then back to the window again as the blonde in the red silk dress whirled to face him.

"Drop the piece!" he shouted, and the man at the window swung around with the rifle in his hands, the rockets exploding behind him in the back yard illuminating his eyes, pinpointing his eyes with fiery lights, and O'Brien's eyes locked with his, and in that moment he weighed the necessity for firing.

"Drop it!" he shouted, his eyes locked with the other man's, and he studied those eyes for the space of three seconds that seemed like three thousand years, studied the fright in them, and then the sudden awakening to the situation, and the rapid calculation. And then the eyes began to narrow and O'Brien had seen the instantaneous narrowing of the eyes of a man with a gun before, and he knew the eyes were telegraphing the action of the trigger finger, and he knew that if he did not fire instantly, he would drop to the floor bleeding in the next split second.

Meyer Meyer had seen the eyes tightening, too, and he shouted, "Watch it, Bob!" and O'Brien fired.

He fired only once, from the hip, fired with a calmness that gave lie to the lurching beat of his heart and the trembling of his legs. His slug took Sokolin in the shoulder at close range, spinning him around and slamming him up against the wall, the rifle dropping from his hands. And all O'Brien could think was *Don't let him die, Dear God don't let him die!*

The blonde hesitated for a fraction of an instant. With Sokolin slowly crumpling from the wall to the floor, with Meyer rushing into the room, with the world outside disintegrating in a shower of sparks and cacophonous welter of explosions, she made her decision and acted upon it, dropping instantly to her knees, pulling her skirt back in a completely feminine gesture as she stooped with masculine purposefulness to pick up the rifle.

Meyer kicked her twice. He kicked her once to knock the rifle upward before her finger found the trigger, and then he kicked

out at her legs, knocking her backward to the floor in a jumble
of white flesh and sliding red silk. She came off the floor like a
banshee out of hell, lips skinned back, fingers curled to rake.
She wasn't looking for conversation, and Meyer didn't give her
any. He swung his .38 up so that the barrel was nested in his
curled fingers, the butt protruding below. Then he brought the
gun around in a side-swinging arc that clipped the girl on the
side of the jaw. She threw her arms and her head back, and she
let out a slight whimper, and then she went down slowly,
slowly, like the *Queen Mary* sinking in the River Harb, dropping to the floor in a curious mixture of titanic collapse and
fragile gracefulness.

O'Brien was already crouched over Sokolin in the corner.
Meyer wiped his brow.

"How is he?"

"He's hurt," O'Brien answered. "But he isn't dead."

"I knew there'd be shooting," Meyer said simply. He turned
to where Cotton Hawes lay on the floor in his rocking-horse
position. "Well, well," he said, "what have we here? Take a look
at this, Bob."

"Get me out of these ropes," Hawes said.

"It talks, Bob," Meyer said. "Why, I do believe it's a talking
dog. Now isn't that a curiosity!"

"Come on, Meyer," Hawes pleaded, and Meyer saw his
battered face for the first time, and quickly stooped to cut the
binding ropes. Hawes rose. Massaging his wrists and ankles, he
said, "You got here just in the nick."

"The Marines always arrive on time," Meyer said.

"And the U.S. Cavalry," O'Brien answered. He glanced at the
blonde. "She's got crazy legs," he said.

The men studied her appreciatively for a moment.

"So," Meyer said at last, "I guess this is it. We'll need the
meat wagon for that joker, won't we?"

"Yeah," O'Brien said listlessly.

"You want to make the call, Bob?"

"Yeah, okay."

He left the room. Meyer walked to the blonde and clamped
his handcuffs onto her wrists. With a married man's dispas-
sionate aloofness, he studied her exposed legs for the last time,
and then pulled down her skirt. "There," he said. "Decency and
morality prevail once more. She had a wild look in her eye,
that one. I wouldn't have wanted to mess with her."

"I *did*," Hawes said.

"Mmm." Meyer looked at his face. "I think maybe we got

another passenger for the meat wagon. You don't look exactly beautiful, dear lad."

"I don't feel exactly beautiful," Hawes said.

Meyer holstered his revolver. "Nothing like a little excitement on a Sunday, is there?"

"What the hell are *you* kicking about?" Hawes asked. "This is *my* day off."

'Til Death, 1959

VIRGINIA DODGE

It was a normal everyday afternoon at the beginning of October.

Outside the grilled windows of the 87th's squadroom, Grover Park was aflame with color. Indian summer, like a Choctaw princess, strutted her feathers, wiggled her bright reds and oranges and yellows on the mild October air. The sun was dazzling in a flawlessly blue sky, its rays pushing at the grilled windows, creating shafts of golden light which dust motes tirelessly climbed. The sounds of the street outside slithered over the window sills and through the open windows, joining with the sounds of the squadroom to create a melody unique and somehow satisfying.

Like a well-constructed symphony, there was an immediately identifiable theme to the sounds inside the squadroom. This theme was built on a three-part harmony of telephone rings, typewriter clackings, and profanities. Upon this theme, the symphony was pyramided into its many variations. The variations ranged from the splendid *wooshy* sound of a bull's fist crashing into a thief's belly, to the shouted roar of a bull wanting to know where the hell his ballpoint pen had gone, to the quietly persistent verbal bludgeoning of an interrogation session, to the muted honey tones of a phone conversation with a Hall Avenue debutante, to the whistling of a rookie delivering a message from Headquarters, to the romantic bellow of a woman filing a complaint against her wife-beating husband, to the gurgle of the water cooler, to the uninhibited laughter following a dirty story.

Such laughter, accompanied by the outside street sounds of October, greeted the punch line of Meyer Meyer's joke on that Friday afternoon.

"He really knows how to tell them," Bert Kling said. "That's the one thing I can't do. Tell a story."

"There are *many* things you can't do," Meyer answered, his blue eyes twinkling, "but we'll excuse the slight inaccuracy. Storytelling, Bert, is an art acquired with age. A young snot like you could never hope to tell a good story. It takes years and years of experience."

Cotton Hawes sipped at his coffee and grinned. His red hair was lighted now by the lazy October sunshine that played with particular intensity on the streak of white over his left temple.

He turned suddenly.

The woman who stood just outside the slatted-rail divider that separated the squadroom from the corridor had entered so silently that none of the men had heard her approach. She had just cleared her throat, and the sound was shockingly loud, so that Kling and Meyer turned to face her at almost the same moment Hawes did.

She looked for a moment like Death personified.

She had deep black hair pulled into a bun at the back of her head. She had brown eyes set in a face without makeup, without lipstick, a face so chalky white that it seemed she had just come from a sickbed somewhere. She wore a black overcoat and black shoes with no stockings. Her bare legs were as white as her face, thin legs that seemed incapable of supporting her. She carried a large black tote bag, and she clung to the black leather handles with thin, bony fingers.

"Yes?" Hawes said.

"Is Detective Carella here?" she asked. Her voice was toneless.

"No," Hawes said. "I'm Detective Hawes. May I hel—"

"When will he be back?" she interrupted.

"That's difficult to say. He had something personal to take care of, and then he was going directly to an outside assignment. Perhaps one of us—"

"I'll wait," the woman said.

"It may take quite a while."

"I have all the time in the world," she answered.

Hawes shrugged. "Well, all right. There's a bench outside. If you'll just—"

"I'll wait inside," she said, and before Hawes could stop her she had pushed open the gate in the railing and started walking toward one of the empty desks in the center of the room. Hawes started after her immediately.

"Miss, I'm sorry," he said, "but visitors are not permitt—"

"*Mrs.*," she corrected. "Mrs. Frank Dodge." She sat. She placed the heavy black bag on her lap, both hands resting firmly on its open top.

"Well, Mrs. Dodge, we don't allow visitors inside the squad-room except on business. I'm sure you can appreciate—"

"I'm here on business," she said and pressed her unpainted lips together into a thin line.

"Well then, can you tell me . . . ?"

"I'm waiting for Detective Carella," she said. "Detective Steve Carella," and she said the last words with surprising bitterness.

"If you're waiting for him," Hawes said patiently, "you'll have to wait on the bench outside. I'm sorry, but that's—"

"I'll wait right here," she said firmly. "And you'll wait, too."

Hawes glanced at Meyer and Kling.

"Lady," Meyer started, "we don't want to seem rude . . ."

"Shut up!" the woman said.

There was the unmistakable ring of command in her voice. The detectives stared at her.

Her hand slipped into the pocket on the right-hand side of her coat. When it emerged, it was holding something cold and hard.

"This is a .38," the woman said.

The street noises outside the squadroom seemed to magnify the silence that followed her simple declaration. The three detectives looked first at each other and then back to the woman and the unwavering .38.

"Give me your guns," she said.

The detectives did not move.

"Give me your guns, or I'll fire."

"Look, lady," Meyer said, "put up the piece. We're all friends here. You're only going to get yourself in trouble."

"I don't care," she said. "Put your guns on the desk here in front of me. Don't try to take them out of the holsters or I'll shoot. This gun is pointed right at the redheaded one's belly. Now move!"

Again, the detectives hesitated.

"All right, redhead," she said. "Say your prayers."

There was not a man in that room who did not realize that once he relinquished his weapon he would be at the mercy of the woman holding the gun. There was not a man in that room, too, who had not faced a gun at one time or another in his career. The men in that room were cops, but they were also human beings who did not particularly relish the thought of an early grave. The men in that room were human beings, but they were also cops who knew the destructive power of a .38, who also knew that women were as capable of squeezing triggers as were men, who realized that this woman holding the gun could cut down all three of them in one hasty volley. And yet, they hesitated.

"Damnit!" she shouted. "I'm not kidding!"

Kling was the first to move, and then only because he saw the knuckle-white tension of the woman's trigger finger. Staring at her all the while, he unstrapped his shoulder rig and dropped holster and Police Special to the desk top. Meyer unclipped his holster from his right hip pocket and deposited it alongside Kling's gun. Hawes was carrying his .38 just off his right hipbone. He unclipped the holster and put it on the desk.

"Which of these desk drawers lock?" the woman asked.

"The top one," Hawes said.

"Where's the key?"

"In the drawer."

She opened the drawer, found the key, and then shoved the guns into the drawer. She locked the desk then, removed the key, and put it into her coat pocket. The big black purse was still on her lap.

"Okay, now you got our guns," Meyer said. "Now what? What is this, lady?"

"I'm going to kill Steve Carella," the woman said.

"Why?"

"Never mind why. Who else is in this place right now?"

Meyer hesitated. From where the woman was sitting, she had a clear view of both the lieutenant's office and the corridor outside the squadroom . . .

"Answer me!" she snapped.

"Just Lieutenant Byrnes," Meyer lied. In the Clerical Office, just outside the slatted-rail divider, Miscolo was busily working on his records. There was the possibility that they could maneuver her so that her back was to the corridor. And then, if Miscolo decided to enter the squadroom on one of his frequent trips, perhaps he would grasp the situation and . . .

"Get the lieutenant," she said.

Meyer began to move.

"Before you go, remember this. The gun is on you. One phony move, and I shoot. And I keep shooting until every man in this place is dead. Now go ahead. Knock on the lieutenant's door and tell him to get out here."

Meyer crossed the silent squadroom. The lieutenant's door was closed. He rapped on the wooden frame alongside the frosted glass.

"Come!" Byrnes called from behind the door.

"Pete, it's me. Meyer."

"The door's unlocked," Byrnes answered.

"Pete, you better come out here."

"What the hell is it?"

"Come on out, Pete."

There was the sound of footsteps behind the door. The door opened. Lieutenant Peter Byrnes, as compact as a rivet, thrust his muscular neck and shoulders into the opening.

"What is it, Meyer? I'm busy."

"There's a woman wants to see you."

"A woman? Where . . . ?" His eyes flicked past Meyer to where the woman sat. Instant recognition crossed his face. "Hello, Virginia," he said, and then he saw the gun.

"Get in here, Lieutenant," Virginia Dodge said.

A frown had come over Byrnes's face. His brows pulled down tightly over scrutinizing blue eyes. Intelligence flashed on his craggy face. Lumberingly, like a man about to lift a heavy log, he crossed the squadroom, walking directly to where Virginia Dodge sat. He seemed ready to pick her up and hurl her into the corridor.

"What is this, Virginia?" he said, and there was the tone of a father in his voice, a rather angry father speaking to a fifteen-year-old daughter who'd come home too late after a dance.

"What does it look like, Lieutenant?"

"It looks like you've blown your wig, that's what it looks like. What the hell's the gun for? What are you doing in here with . . ."

"I'm going to kill Steve Carella," Virginia said.

"Oh, for Christ's sake," Byrnes said in exasperation. "Do you think that's going to help your husband any?"

"Nothing's going to help Frank any more."

171

"What do you mean?"

"Frank died yesterday. In the hospital at Castleview Prison."

Byrnes did not speak for a long while, and then he said slowly, "You can't blame Carella for that."

"Carella sent him up."

"Your husband was a criminal."

"Carella sent him up."

"Carella only arrested him. You can't—"

"*And* pressed the D.A. for a conviction, *and* testified at the trial, *and* did everything in his power to make sure Frank went to jail!"

"Virginia, he—"

"Frank was sick! Carella knew that! He knew that when he put him away!"

"Virginia, for Christ's sake, our job is to—"

"Carella killed him as sure as if he'd shot him. And now I'm going to kill Carella. The minute he steps into this squadroom, I'm going to kill him."

"And then what? How do you expect to get out of here, Virginia? You haven't got a chance."

Virginia smiled thinly. "I'll get out, all right."

"Will you? You fire a gun in here, and every cop in ten miles will come barging upstairs."

"I'm not worried about that, Lieutenant."

"No, huh? Talk sense, Virginia. You want to get the electric chair? Is that what you want?"

"I don't care. I don't want to live without Frank."

Byrnes paused for a long time. Then he said, "I don't believe you, Virginia."

"What don't you believe? That I'm going to kill Carella? That I'll shoot the first one who does anything to stop me?"

"I don't believe you're fool enough to use that gun. I'm walking out of here, Virginia. I'm walking back to my office . . ."

"No, you're not!"

"Yes, I am. I'm walking back to my office, and here's why. There are four men in this room, counting me. You can shoot me, maybe, and maybe another one after me . . . but you'll have to be pretty fast and pretty accurate to get all of us."

"I'll get all of you, Lieutenant," Virginia said, and the thin smile reappeared on her mouth.

"Yeah, well I'm willing to bet on that. Jump her the minute she fires, men." He paused. "I'm going to my office, Virginia, and I'm going to sit in there for five minutes. When I come out, you'd better be gone, and we'll forget all about this. Otherwise I'm going to slap you silly and take that gun away from you and dump you into a detention cell downstairs. Now is that clear, Virginia?"

"It's very clear."

"Five minutes," Byrnes said curtly, and he wheeled and started toward his office.

With supreme confidence in her voice, Virginia said, "I don't have to shoot you, Lieutenant."

Byrnes did not break his stride.

"I don't have to shoot *any* of you."

He continued walking.

"I've got a bottle of nitroglycerin in my purse."

Her words came like an explosion. Byrnes stopped in his tracks and turned slowly to face her, his eyes dropping to the big black bag in her lap. She had turned the barrel of the gun so that it pointed at the bag now, so that its muzzle was thrust into the opening at the top of the bag.

"I don't believe you, Virginia," Byrnes said, and he turned and reached for the doorknob again.

"Don't open the door, Lieutenant," Virginia shouted, "or I'll fire into this purse and we can *all* go to Hell!"

He thought in that moment before twisting the doorknob, *She's lying. She hasn't got any soup in that purse, where would she get any?*

And then he remembered that among her husband's many criminal offenses had been a conviction for safe-blowing.

But she hasn't got any soup, he thought, *Jesus, that's crazy. But suppose she does? But she won't explode it. She's waiting for Carella. She wouldn't . . .*

And then he thought simply, *Meyer Meyer has a wife and three children.*

Slowly, he let his hand drop. Wearily, he turned to Virginia Dodge.

"That's better," she said. "Now let's wait for Carella."

* * *

There were ninety thousand people living in the 87th Precinct.

The streets of the precinct ran south from the River Harb to Grover Park, which was across the way from the station house. The River Highway paralleled the river's course, and beyond that was the first precinct street, fancy Silvermine Road, which still sported elevator operators and doormen in its tall apartment buildings. Continuing south, the precinct ran

173

through the gaudy commercialism of The Stem, and then Ainsley Avenue, and then Culver with its dowdy tenements, its unfrequented churches, and its overflowing bars. Mason Avenue, familiarly known as "La Via de Putas" to the Puerto Ricans, "Whore Street" to the cops, was south of Culver and then came Grover Avenue and the park. The precinct stretch, like a dubious immy-span in muddy water, was a short one from north to south. Actually, it extended into Grover Park but only on a basis of professional courtesy; the park territory was officially under the joint command of the neighboring 88th and 89th. The stretch from east to west, however, was a longer one consisting of thirty-five tightly packed side streets. Even so, the entire territory of the precinct did not cover very much ground. It seemed even smaller when considering the vast number of people who lived there.

The immigration pattern of America, and, as a consequence, the integration pattern were clearly evident in the streets of the 87th. The population was composed almost entirely of third-generation Irish, Italians, and Jews, and first-generation Puerto Ricans. The immigrant groups did not make the slum. Conversely, it was the slum with its ghetto atmosphere of acceptance that attracted the immigrant groups. The rents, contrary to popular belief, were not low. They were as high as many to be found anywhere else in the city and, considering the services rendered for the money, they were exorbitant. Nonetheless, even a slum can become home. Once settled into it, the inhabitants of the 87th put up pictures on chipped plaster walls, threw down scatter rugs on splintered wooden floors. They learned good American tenement occupations like banging on the radiators for heat, stamping on the cockroaches that skittered across the kitchen floor whenever a light was turned on, setting traps for the mice and rats that paraded through the apartment like the *Wehrmacht* through Poland, adjusting the unbending steel bar of a police lock against the entrance door to the flat.

It was the job of the policemen of the 87th to keep the inhabitants from engaging in another popular form of slum activity: the pursuit of a life of criminal adventure.

Virginia Dodge wanted to know how many men were doing this job.

"We've got sixteen detectives on the squad," Byrnes told her.

"Where are they now?"

"Three are right here."

"And the rest?"

"Some are off duty, some are answering squeals, and some are on plants."

"Which?"

"You want a complete rundown, for Christ's sake?"

"Yes."

"Look, Virginia . . ." The pistol moved a fraction of an inch deeper into the purse. "Okay. Cotton, get the duty chart."

Hawes looked at the woman. "Is it okay to move?" he asked.

"Go ahead. Don't open any desk drawers. Where's *your* gun, Lieutenant?"

"I don't carry one."

"You're lying to me. Where is it? In your office?"

Byrnes hesitated.

"Goddamnit," Virginia shouted, "let's get something straight here! I'm dead serious, and the next person who lies to me, or who doesn't do what I tell him to do when I—"

"All right, all right, take it easy," Byrnes said. "It's in my desk drawer." He turned and started for his office.

"Just a minute," Virginia said. "We'll *all* go with you." She picked up her bag gingerly and then swung her gun at the other men in the room. "Move," she said. "Follow the lieutenant."

Like a small herd of cattle, the men followed Byrnes into the office. Virginia crowded into the small room after them. Byrnes walked to his desk.

"Take it out of the drawer and put it on the desk," Virginia said. "Grab it by the muzzle. If your finger comes anywhere near the trigger, the nitro . . ."

"All right, all right," Byrnes said impatiently.

He hefted the revolver by its barrel and placed it on the desk top. Virginia quickly picked up the gun and put it into the left-hand pocket of her coat.

"Outside now," she said.

Again they filed into the squadroom. Virginia sat at the desk she had taken as her command post. She placed the purse on the desk before her, and then leveled the .38 at it. "Get me the duty chart," she said.

"Get it, Cotton," Byrnes said.

Hawes went for the chart. It hung on the wall near one of the rear windows, a simple black rectangle into which white celluloid letters were inserted. It was a detective's responsibility to replace the name of the cop he'd relieved with his own whenever his tour of duty started. Unlike patrolmen, who worked five eight-hour shifts and then swung for the next fifty-six hours, the detectives chose their own duty teams. Since there were sixteen of them attached to the squad, their teams automatically broke down into groups of five, five, and five—with a loose man kicking around from shift to shift. On this bright everyday afternoon in October, six detectives were listed on the duty chart. Three of them—Hawes, Kling, and Meyer—were in the squadroom.

"Where are the other three?" Virginia asked.

"Carella took his wife to the doctor," Byrnes said.

"How sweet," Virginia said bitterly.

"And then he's got a suicide he's working on."

"When will he be back?"

"I don't know."

"You must have some idea."

"I have no idea. He'll be back when he's ready to come back."

"What about the other two men?"

"Brown's on a plant. The back of a tailor shop."

"A what?"

"A plant. A stakeout, call it what you want to. He's sitting there waiting for the place to be held up."

"Don't kid me, Lieutenant."

"I'm not kidding, damnit. Four tailor shops in the neighborhood have been held up during the daylight hours. We expect this one to get hit soon. Brown's waiting for the thief to show."

"When will he come back to the squadroom?"

"A little after dark, I imagine. Unless the thief hits. What time is it now?" Byrnes looked up at the clock on the wall. "Four thirty-eight. I imagine he'll be back by six or so."

"And the last one? Willis?"

Byrnes shrugged. "He was here a half-hour ago. Who's catching?"

"I am," Meyer said.

"Well, where'd Willis go?"

"He's out on a squeal, Pete. A knifing on Mason."

"That's where he is then," Byrnes said to Virginia.

"And when will *he* be back?"

"I don't know."

"Soon?"

"I imagine so."

"Who else is in the building?"

"The desk sergeant and the desk lieutenant. You passed them on your way in."

"Yes?"

"Captain Frick, who commands the entire precinct in a sense."

"What do you mean?"

"I control the squad, but officially . . ."

"Where's he?"

"His office is downstairs."

"Who else?"

"There are a hundred and eighty-six patrolmen attached to this precinct," Byrnes said. "A third of them are on duty now. Some of them are roaming around the building. The rest are out on their beats."

"What are they doing in the building?"

"Twenty-fours mostly." Byrnes paused and then translated. "Duty as records clerks."

"When does the shift change again?"

"At a quarter to midnight."

"Then they won't be back until then? The ones on beats?"

"Most of them'll be relieved on post. But they usually come back to change into their street clothes before going home."

"Will any detectives be coming up here? Besides the ones listed on the duty chart?"

"Possibly."

"We're not supposed to be relieved until midnight Pete," Meyer said.

"But Carella will be back long before then, won't he?" Virginia asked.

"Probably."

"Yes or no?"

"I can't say for sure. I'm playing this straight with you, Virginia. Carella may get a lead that'll keep him out of the office. I don't know."

"Will he call in?"

"Maybe."

"If he does, tell him to come right back here. Do you understand?"

"Yes. I understand."

The telephone rang. It cut the conversation and then shrilled persistently into the silence of the squadroom.

"Answer it," Virginia said. "No funny stuff."

Meyer picked up the receiver. "Eighty-seventh Squad," he said, "Detective Meyer speaking." He paused. "Yes, Dave. Go ahead, I'm listening." He was aware all at once of the fact that Virginia Dodge was hearing only one-half of the telephone conversation with the desk sergeant. Casually, patiently, he listened.

"Meyer, we got a call a little while back from some guy who heard shots and a scream from the apartment next door to his. I sent a car over, and they just reported back. A dame got shot

in the arm, and her boyfriend claims the gun went off accidentally while he was cleaning it. You want to send one of the boys
over?"

"Sure, what's the address?" Meyer said, patiently watching
Virginia.

"2379 Culver. That's next door to the Easy Bar. You know it?"

"I know it. Thanks, Dave."

"Okay." Meyer put up the phone. "That was a lady calling,"
Meyer said. "Dave thought we ought to take it."

"Who's Dave?" Virginia asked.

"Murchison. The desk sergeant," Byrnes said. "What is it,
Meyer?"

"This lady says somebody's trying to break into her apartment. She wants us to send a detective over right away."

Byrnes and Meyer exchanged a long, knowing glance. Such a
call would have been handled by the desk sergeant directly,
and he would not have annoyed the Detective Division with it.
He'd have dispatched a radio motor patrol car immediately.

"Either that or he wants you to contact the captain and see
what he can do about it," Meyer said.

"All right, I'll do that," Byrnes said. "Is that all right with
you, Virginia?"

"No one's leaving this room," Virginia said.

"I know that. Which is why I'm passing the call on to Captain
Frick. Is that all right?"

"Go ahead," she said. "No tricks."

"The address is 2379 Culver," Meyer said.

"Thanks." Byrnes dialed three numbers and waited. Captain
Frick picked up the phone on the second ring.

"Yop?" he said.

"John, this is Pete."

"Oh, hello, Pete. How goes it?"

"So-so. John, I've got a special favor I'd like you to do."

"What's that?" Frick asked.

"Some woman at 2379 Culver is complaining that someone's
trying to get into her apartment. I can't spare a man right now.
Could you get a patrolman over there?"

"What?" Frick said.

"I know it's an unusual request. We'd ordinarily handle it
ourselves, but we're kind of busy."

"What?" Frick said again.

"Can you do it, John?" Standing with the receiver to his ear,
Byrnes watched the shrewdly calculating eyes of Virginia
Dodge. *Come on, John,* he thought. *Wake up, for Christ's sake!*

"You'd ordinarily handle it?" Frick asked. "Boy, that's a laugh. I've got to kill myself to get you to take a *legitimate* squeal. Why bother me with this, Pete? Why don't you just give it to the desk sergeant?" Frick paused. "How the hell'd you get a hold of it anyway? Who's on the desk?"

"Will you take care of it, John?"

"Are you kidding me, Pete? What is this?" Frick began laughing. "Your joke for today, huh? Okay, I bit. How's everything upstairs?"

Byrnes hesitated for a moment, phrasing his next words carefully. Then, watching Virginia, he said, "Not so hot."

"What's the matter? Headaches?"

"Plenty. Why don't you go up and see for yourself?"

"Up? Up where?"

Come on, Byrnes thought. *Think! For just one lousy minute of your life, think!*

"It's part of your job, isn't it?" Byrnes said.

"What's part of my job? Hey, what's the matter with you, Pete? You flipped or something?"

"Well, I think you ought to find out," Byrnes said.

"Find out *what*? Holy Jesus, you have flipped."

"I'll be expecting you to do that then," Byrnes said, aware of a frown starting on Virginia's forehead.

"Do what?"

"Go up there to check on it. Thanks a lot, John."

"You know, I don't understand a damn thing you're—" and Byrnes hung up.

"All settled?" Virginia asked.

"Yes."

She stared at Byrnes thoughtfully. "There are extensions on all these phones, aren't there?" she said.

"Yes," Byrnes said.

"Fine. I'll be listening to any other call that goes in or out of this place."

The problem, Byrnes thought, is that we cannot communicate with each other. This, surely, has been the problem of the human race since the beginning of time, but it's especially aggravated right here and right now. I'm in my own squadroom with three capable detectives, and we can't sit down together to discuss the ways and means of getting that gun and that nitro—if the nitro exists—away from the menacing little bitch. Four intelligent men with a nut cruncher of a problem, and we have no way of talking it out. Not with her sitting there. Not with that .38 in her fist.

And so, lacking communication, I also lack command. In effect, Virginia Dodge now commands the 87th Squad.

She'll continue to command it until one of two things happens:

a) We disarm her.

b) Steve Carella arrives and she shoots him.

There is, of course, a third possibility. There is the possibility that she'll get rattled and put a bullet into that purse with its alleged jar of nitro, and there we go. No more waiting for next week's chapter. It'll be over in a mighty big way. They will probably hear the blast away the hell over in the 88th. The blast might even knock the commissioner out of bed. Assuming, of course, that there really *is* a jar of nitro in that bag. Unfortunately, we cannot proceed as if there isn't. We have to assume, along with Virginia Dodge, that the jar of nitro is as real as the .38. In which case, another interesting possibility presents itself. We can't fool around here. We can't go playing grab-ass because nitroglycerin is very potent stuff which can explode at the slightest provocation. Where the hell did she get a jar of nitro? From her safecracker husband's hope chest?

But even safecrackers—except in Scandinavia—don't use it any more. It's too damn unpredictable. I've known safecrackers who, when using nitro, carried it in a hot-water bottle.

So there she sits with a jar full of the stuff in her purse.

I wonder if she rode the subway with it in her purse? Byrnes thought, and he smiled grimly.

Okay, the nitro is real. We play it as if it's real. It's the only way we *can* play it. And this means no sudden moves, no grabs for the purse.

So what *do* we do?

Wait for Carella? And what time will he be back? What time is it now?

He looked up at the wall clock—5:07.

Still broad daylight outside—well, maybe a hint of dusk—but still a golden afternoon, really. Does anyone out there know we're playing footsie with a bottle of soup?

No one, Byrnes thought. Not even meatheaded Captain Frick. How do you set a fire under that man, how do you get the wall of bricks to fall on his head?

How the hell do we get out of this mess?

I wonder if she smokes, Byrnes thought.

If she smokes . . . Now wait a minute . . . now, let's work this out sensibly. Let's say she smokes. Okay. Okay, we've got that much. Now . . . if we can get her to put the purse on the desk, get it off her lap. That shouldn't be too hard . . . Where's the purse now? . . . Still in her lap . . . Virginia Dodge's goddamn lap dog, a bottle of nitro . . . Okay, let's say I can get her to put the purse on the desk, out of the way . . . Then let's say I offer her a cigarette and then start to light it for her.

If I drop the lighted match in her lap, she'll jump a mile.

And when she jumps, I'll hit her.

I'm not worried about that .38—well, I'm worried, who the hell wants to get shot—but I'm not really worried about it so long as that soup is out of the way. I don't want to have a scuffle anywhere near that explosive. I've faced guns before, but nitro is another thing and I don't want them blotting me off the wall.

I wonder if she smokes.

"How have you been, Virginia?" he asked.

"You can cut it right now, Lieutenant."

"Cut what?"

"The sweet talk. I didn't come here to listen to any of your crap. I heard enough of that last time I was here."

"That was a long time ago, Virginia."

"Five years, three months, and seventeen days. That's how long it was."

"We don't make the laws, Virginia," Byrnes said gently. "We only enforce them. And when a person breaks . . ."

"I don't want a lecture. My husband is dead. Steve Carella sent him up. That's good enough for me."

"Steve only arrested him. A jury tried him, and a judge sentenced him."

"But Carella . . ."

"Virginia, you're forgetting something, aren't you?"

"What?"

"Your husband blinded a man."

"That was an accident."

"Your husband fired a gun at a man during a holdup and deprived that man of his eyesight. And he didn't fire the gun by accident."

"He fired because the man began yelling cop. What would you have done?"

"I wouldn't have been holding up a gas station to begin with."

"No, huh? Big simon-pure Lieutenant Byrnes. I heard all

181

about your junkie son, Lieutenant. The big-shot cop with the drug-addict son."

"That was a long time ago, too, Virginia. My son is all right now."

He could never think back to that time in his life without some pain. Oh, not as much as in the beginning, no, there would never again be that much pain for him, the pain of discovering that his only son was a tried-and-true drug addict, hooked through the bag and back again. A drug addict possibly involved in a homicide. Those had been days of black pain for Peter Byrnes, days when he had withheld information from the men of his own squad, until finally he had told everything to Steve Carella. Carella had almost lost his life working on that case. It had been touch and go after he'd been shot, and no man ever had prayed the way Byrnes did for any other man's recovery. But it was all over now, except for the slight twinge of pain whenever he thought of it. The habit had been kicked, the household was in order. And now, Steve Carella, a man Byrnes considered as almost another son, had a rendezvous with a woman in black. And the woman in black spelled death.

"I'm glad your son is all right now," Virginia said sarcastically. "My husband isn't. My husband is dead. And the way I read it, Carella killed him. Now let's cut the crap, shall we?"

"I'd rather talk awhile."

"Then talk to yourself. I'm not interested." Byrnes sat on the corner of the desk. Virginia shifted the purse in her lap, the revolver pointing into the opening. "Don't come any closer, Lieutenant. I'm warning you."

"What are your plans, exactly, Virginia?"

"I've already told you. When Carella gets here, I'm going to kill him. And then I'm going to leave. And if anyone tries to stop me, I drop the bag with the nitro."

"Suppose I try to get that gun away from you right this minute?"

"I wouldn't if I were you."

"Suppose I tried?"

"I'm banking on something, Lieutenant."

"What's that?"

"The fact that no man is really a hero. Whose life is more important to you—yours or Carella's? You make a try for the gun, and there's a chance the nitro will go off in your face. *Your* face, not his. All right, you'll have saved Carella. But you'll have destroyed yourself."

"Carella may mean a lot to me, Virginia. I might be willing to die for him."

"Yeah? And how much does he mean to the other men in this room? Would they be willing to die for him, too? Or for the crumby salary they're getting from the city? Why don't you take a vote, Lieutenant, and find out how many of your men are ready to lay down their lives right now? Go ahead. Take a vote."

He did not want to take a vote. He was not that familiar with courage or heroics. He knew that each of the men in the room had acted heroically and courageously on many an occasion. But bravery in action was a thing dictated by the demands of the moment. Faced with certain death, would these men be willing to take an impossible gamble? He was not sure. But he felt fairly certain that given the choice "Your life or Carella's?" they would most probably choose to let Carella die. Selfish? Perhaps. Inhuman? Perhaps. But life was not something you could walk into a dime store to buy again if you happened to use one up or wear it out. Life was a thing you clung to and cherished. And even knowing Carella as he did, even (and the word was hard coming for a man like Byrnes) loving Carella, he dared not ask himself the question "Your life or Carella's?" He was too afraid of the answer he might give.

"How old are you, Virginia?"

"What difference does it make?"

"I'd like to know."

"Thirty-two."

Byrnes nodded.

"I look older, don't I?"

"A little."

"A lot. You can thank Carella for that, too. Have you ever seen Castleview Prison, Lieutenant? Have you ever seen the place Carella sent my Frank to? It's for animals, not men. And I had to live alone, waiting, knowing what Frank was going through. How long do you think youth lasts? How long do you think good looks hang around when you've got sorrow and worry inside you like a . . . like a *thing* that's eating your guts?"

"Castleview isn't the best prison in the world, but . . ."

"It's a torture chamber!" Virginia shouted. "Have you ever been inside it? It's dirty, filthy. And hot, and cramped, and rusting. It smells, Lieutenant. You can smell it for blocks before you approach it. And they crowd men into that hot, filthy stench. Did my Frank cause trouble? Yes, of course he did.

Frank was a man, not an animal—and he refused to be treated like an animal, and so they labeled him a troublemaker."

"Well, you can't . . ."

"Do you know you're not allowed to talk to anyone during work hours at Castleview? Do you know they still have buckets in each cell—*buckets*—no toilet facilities! Do you know what the stink is like in those sufferingly hot cubicles? And my Frank was sick! Did Carella think about that, when he became a hero by arresting him?"

"He wasn't thinking of becoming a hero. He was doing his job. Can't you understand that, Virginia? Carella is a cop. *He was only doing his job.*"

"And I'm doing mine," Virginia said flatly.

"How? Do you know what you're carrying in your goddamn purse? Do you realize that it might go up in your face when you fire that gun? Nitroglycerin isn't toothpaste!"

"I don't care."

"Thirty-two years old, and you're ready to kill a man and maybe take your own life in the bargain."

"I don't care."

"Talk sense, Virginia!"

"I don't have to talk sense with you or anyone. I don't have to talk at all." Virginia moved violently, and the purse jiggled in her lap. "I'm doing you a goddamn *favor* by talking to you."

"All right, relax," Byrnes said, nervously eying the purse. "Just relax, willya? Why don't you put that purse on the desk, huh?"

"What for?"

"You're bouncing around like a rubber ball. If you don't care about it going off, I do."

Virginia smiled. Gingerly, she lifted the purse from her lap, and gingerly she placed it on the desk top before her, swinging the .38 around at the same time, as if .38 and nitroglycerin were newlyweds who couldn't bear to be parted for a moment.

"That's better," Byrnes said, and he sighed in relief. "Relax. Don't get upset." He paused. "Why don't we have a smoke?"

"I don't want one," Virginia said.

Byrnes took a package of cigarettes from his pocket. Casually, he moved to her side of the desk, conscious of the .38 against the fabric of the purse. He gauged the distance between himself and Virginia, gauged how close he would be to her when he lighted her cigarette, with which hand he should slug her so that she would not go flying over against the purse. Would her instant reaction to the dropped match be a tightening of her trigger finger? He did not think so. She would pull back. And then he would hit her.

He shook the cigarette loose. "Here," he said. "Have one."

"No."

"Don't you smoke?"

"I smoke. I don't feel like one now."

"Come on. Nothing like a cigarette for relaxation. Here."

He thrust the package toward her.

"Oh, all right," she said. She shifted the .38 to her left hand. The muzzle of the gun was an inch from the bag. With her right hand, she took the cigarette Byrnes offered. Standing at her right, he figured he would extend the match with his left hand, let it fall into her lap, and then clip her with a roundhouse right when she pulled back in fright. Oddly, his heart was pounding furiously.

Suppose the gun went off when she pulled back?

He reached into his pocket for the matches. His hand was trembling. The cigarette dangled from Virginia's lips. Her left hand, holding the gun against the purse, was steady.

Byrnes struck the match.

And the telephone rang.

Virginia whipped the cigarette from her mouth and dropped it into the ashtray on her desk. She switched the gun back to her right hand and then whirled on Bert Kling, who was moving to answer the telephone.

"Hold it, sonny!" she snapped. "What line is that?"

"Extension 31," Kling answered.

"Get away from this desk, Lieutenant," Virginia said. She gestured at him with the gun, and Byrnes backed away. Then, with her free hand, she pulled the telephone to her, studied its face for a moment, and then pushed a button in its base. "All right, answer it," she said, and she lifted her receiver the moment Kling did.

"Eighty-seventh Squad, Detective Kling."

He was very conscious of Virginia Dodge sitting at the next desk, the extension phone to her ear, the snout of the .38 pointed at the center of the big black purse.

"Detective Kling? This is Marcie Snyder."

"Who?"

"Marcie." The voice paused. "Snyder." Intimately, it whispered, "Marcie Snyder. Don't you remember me, Detective Kling?"

"Oh, yes. How are you, Miss Snyder?"

"I'm just fine, thanks. And how's the big blond cop?"

"I'm . . . uh . . . fine. Thanks."

He looked across at Virginia Dodge. Her lips were pressed into a bloodless smile. She seemed sexless, genderless, sitting opposite him with the lethal .38 pointed at the black hulk of the bag. And, in contrast to the thin shadow of death she presented, Marcie Snyder began to ooze life in bucketfuls. Marcie Snyder began to gyrate with her voice, undulate with her whispers so that Kling could visualize the big redhead lying on a chaise lounge in a gossamer negligee, cuddling up to the ivory telephone in her hand.

"It's nice talking to you again," she said. "You were in such a hurry last time you were here."

"I had a date with my fiancée," Kling said flatly.

"Yes. I know. You told me. Repeatedly." She paused. Her voice dropped slightly. "You seemed nervous. What were you nervous about, Detective Kling?"

"Get rid of her," Virginia Dodge whispered.

"What?" Marcie said.

"I didn't say anything," Kling answered.

"I was sure I heard . . ."

"No, I didn't say anything. I'm rather busy, Miss Snyder. How can I help you?"

Marcie Snyder laughed the dirtiest laugh Bert Kling had ever heard in his life. For a moment, he felt as if he were sixteen years old and entering a whorehouse on La Vía de Putas. He almost blushed.

"Come on," he said harshly. "What is it?"

"Nothing. We've recovered the jewels."

"Oh, yeah? How?"

"It turns out they weren't burglarized at all. My sister took them with her when she went to Las Vegas."

"Are you withdrawing the complaint then, Miss Snyder?"

"Why, yes. If there was no burglary, what have I got to complain about?"

"Nothing. I'm glad you located the jewels. If you'll drop us a letter to that effect, stating that your sister—"

"Why don't you come by and pick it up, Detective Kling?"

"I'd do that, Miss Snyder," Kling said, "but there's an awful lot of crime going on in this city, and I'm just about damn near indispensable. Thanks for calling. We'll be waiting for your letter."

He hung up abruptly, and then turned away from the phone.

"You're a regular lover boy, aren't you?" Virginia Dodge said, putting her receiver down.

"Yeah, sure. A regular lover boy," Kling answered.

He walked over to the desk where she sat. The black purse made him nervous. Suppose someone fell against it? Jesus, you had to be absolutely nuts to go around carrying a bottle of nitroglycerin.

"About that girl," he said.

"Yes?"

"Don't get the wrong idea."

"Why, what idea would that be?" Virginia Dodge said.

"Well, I mean . . . I was investigating a burglary, that's all."

"Why, what else *would* you be investigating, honey lamb?" Virginia asked.

"Nothing. Oh, forget it. I don't know why I'm bothering explaining it to you anyway."

"What's the matter with me?" Virginia said.

"Well, I wouldn't say you were exactly a stable person, would you? No offense meant, Mrs. Dodge, but the run-of-the-mill citizen doesn't run around waving a gun and a bottle of soup."

"Don't they?" Virginia was smiling now, enjoying herself immensely.

"Well, it's a slightly crazy stunt. I mean, even you have to admit that. I can see the gun, okay. You want to kill Steve, that's your business. Listen, am I going to fight City Hall? But the nitro's a little dramatic, don't you think? How'd you manage to get it over here without blowing up half the city?"

"I managed," Virginia said. "I walked gently. I didn't sway my hips."

"Yeah, well, that's a good way to walk, I guess. Especially when you've got a high explosive in your bag, huh?" Kling smiled disarmingly. The clock on the wall read 5:33. It was beginning to get dark outside. Dusk spread across the sky, washing a deeper blue behind the color-riot trees in the park. You could hear the kids shouting for a last inning of stickball before real darkness descended. You could hear mothers shouting from windows. You could hear men greeting each other as they entered bars for their before-dinner beers. You could hear all the sounds of life outside the grilled windows and you could hear, too—a sound as real as any of the others—the silence inside the squadroom.

"I like this time of day," Kling said.

"Do you?"

"Yes. Always did. Even when I was a kid. Something nice

about it. Quiet." He paused. "Are you really going to shoot
Steve?"

"Yes," Virginia said.

"I wouldn't," Kling said.

"Why not?"

"Well . . ."

"Is it all right to turn on some lights in here, Virginia?"
Byrnes asked.

"Yes. Go ahead."

"Cotton, snap on the overheads. And can my men get back to
work?"

"What kind of work?" Virginia asked.

"Answering complaints, typing up reports, making calls
to . . ."

"Nobody makes any calls. And nobody picks up a phone
unless I'm on the extension."

"All right. Can they type? Or will that disturb you?"

"They can type. At separate desks."

"All right, men," Byrnes said, "then let's do it. And listen to
everything she tells you, and let's not have any heroics. I'm
playing ball with you, Virginia, because I'm hoping you'll see
reason before it's too late."

"Don't hold your breath," Virginia said.

"He's right, you know," Kling said softly, boyishly.

"Is he?"

"Sure. You're not doing yourself any good, Mrs. Dodge."

"No?"

"No. Your husband's dead. You're not going to help him by
killing a lot of innocent people. And yourself, too, if that soup
should go off."

"I loved my husband," Virginia said tightly.

"Sure. I mean, Jesus, I should hope so. But what's the good of
it? I mean, what are you accomplishing?"

"I'll be getting the man who killed him."

"Steve? Come on, Mrs. Dodge. You know he didn't kill your
husband."

"I know nothing of the sort!"

"Okay, let's say he *did* kill him. I know that's not true, and
you know it too—but we'll say it if it makes you happy, okay?
So what do you accomplish by revenge?" Kling shrugged
boyishly. "Nothing. I'll tell you something, Mrs. Dodge."

"I don't want to hear any more," Virginia snapped.

"You think Frank would want you to do this? Get in all this
trouble over him?"

"Yes! Frank wanted Carella dead. He said so. He hated Carella!"

"And you? Do you hate Carella, too? Do you even know him?"

"I don't care about him. I loved my husband. That's enough for me."

"But your husband was breaking the law when he got arrested. He *shot* a man! Now you couldn't expect Steve to give him a medal, could you? Now come on, Mrs. Dodge, be sensible."

"I loved my husband," Virginia said flatly.

"Mrs. Dodge, I'll tell you something else. You've got to make up your mind. Either you're a woman who really knows what love is all about, or else you're a cold-blooded bitch who's ready to blow this dump to hell and gone. You can't play both sides of the fence. Now which one is it?"

"I'm a woman. I'm here *because* I'm a woman."

"Then act like one. Put the gun up, and get the hell out of here before you get more trouble than you've had in all your life."

"No. No."

"Come on, Mrs. Dodge . . ."

Virginia stiffened in her chair. "All right, sonny," she said, "you can knock it off now."

"Wha . . . ?" Kling started.

"The big blue-eyed baby routine. You can just cut it. It didn't work."

"I wasn't trying to . . ."

"Enough," she said, "damnit, that's enough! Go find somebody else's tit to suck!"

"Mrs. Dodge, I . . ."

"Are you finished?"

The squadroom went silent. The clock on the squadroom wall, white-faced and leering, threw minutes onto the floor where they lay like the ghosts of dead policemen. It was dark outside the grilled windows now. The windows, halfway open to let in the October mildness, also let in the night sounds of early traffic. A typewriter started. Kling glanced toward the desk near one of the windows where Meyer had inserted a blue D.D. report together with two sheets of carbon and two duplicate report sheets into the machine. The hanging globe of light over Meyer cast a dull sheen onto his bald head as he hunched over the typewriter, pecking at the keys. Cotton Hawes walked to the filing cabinet and pulled open a drawer.

The drawer squeaked on its rollers. He opened a folder and began leafing through it. Then he went to sit at the desk near the other window. The water cooler suddenly belched into the silence.

"I'm sorry I bothered you," Kling said to Virginia. "I should have known a person can't talk to a corpse."

There was a sudden commotion in the corridor outside. Virginia tensed where she sat at the desk. For an instant, Kling thought her finger would involuntarily tighten around the trigger of the .38.

"All right, inside, inside," a man's voice said, and Kling recognized it instantly as belonging to Hal Willis. He looked past the desk and into the corridor as Willis and his prisoner came into view.

The prisoner, to be more accurate, *burst* into view. Like the aurora borealis. She was a tall Puerto Rican girl with bleached blond hair. She wore a purple topcoat open over a red peasant blouse which swooped low over a threatening display of bosom. Her waist was narrow, the straight black skirt swelling out tightly over sinuously padded hips. She wore high-heeled pumps, red, with black ankle straps. A gold tooth flashed in the corner of an otherwise dazzlingly white set of teeth. And, in contrast to her holiday garb, she wore no makeup on her face, which was a perfect oval set with rich brown eyes and a full mouth and a clean sweeping aristocratic nose. She was possibly one of the prettiest, if flashiest, prisoners ever to be dragged into the squadroom.

And dragged she was. Holding one wristlet of a pair of handcuffs in his right hand, Willis pulled the girl to the slatted-rail divider while she struggled to retrieve her manacled wrist, cursing in Spanish every inch of the way.

"Come on, *cara mia*," Willis said. "Come on, *tsotzkuluh*. You'd think somebody was trying to hurt you, for Christ's sake. Come on, *Liebchen*. Right through this gate. Hi, Bert! something, huh? Hello, Pete, you like my prisoner? She just ripped open a guy's throat with a razor bl—"

Willis stopped talking.

There was a strange silence in the squadroom.

He looked first at the lieutenant, and then at Kling, and then his eyes flicked to the two rear desks where Hawes and Meyer were silently working. And then he saw Virginia Dodge and the .38 in her hand pointed into the mouth of the black purse.

His first instinct was to drop the wristlet he was holding and draw his gun. The instinct was squelched when Virginia said, 'Get in here. Don't reach for your gun!"

Willis and the girl came into the squadroom.

"*Bruta!*" the girl screamed. "*Pendega! Hijo de la gran puta!*"

"Oh, shut the hell up," Willis said wearily.

"*Pinga!*" she screamed. "Dirtee ro'n cop bastard!"

"Shut up, shut up, shut *up!*" Willis pleaded.

He was, as he surveyed the gun in Virginia Dodge's hand, already figuring on how he could disarm her.

"What's up?" he asked the assembly at large.

"The lady with the gun has a bottle of nitro in her purse," Byrnes said. "She's ready to use it."

"Well, well," Willis said. "Never a dull moment, huh?" He paused and looked at Virginia. "Okay to take off my coat and hat, lady?"

"Put your gun on the desk here first."

"Thorough, huh?" Willis said. "Lady, you give me the chills. You really got a bottle of soup in that bag?"

"I've really got it."

"I'm from Missouri," Willis said, and he took a step closer to the desk.

For an instant, Kling thought the jig was up. He saw only Virginia Dodge's sudden thrust into the bag, and he tensed himself for the explosion he was certain would follow. And then her free hand emerged from the purse, and there was a bottle of colorless fluid in that hand. She put it down on the desk top gently, and Willis eyed it and said, "That could be tap water, lady."

"Would you like to find out whether it is or not?" Virginia said.

"Me? Now, lady, do I look like a hero?"

He walked closer to the desk. Virginia put her purse on the floor. The bottle, pint-sized, gleamed under the glow of the hanging light globes.

"Okay," Willis said, "first we check the gat." He pulled gun and holster off his belt and placed them very carefully on the desk top, his eyes never leaving the pint bottle of fluid. "This plays a little like Dodge City, doesn't it?" he said. "What's the soup for, lady? If I'd known you were having a blowout, I'd have dressed." He tried a laugh that died the moment he saw Virginia's face. "Excuse *me*," he said. "I didn't know the undertakers were holding a convention. What do I do with my prisoner, Pete?"

"Ask Virginia."

"Virginia, huh?" Willis burst out laughing. "Oh, brother, are we getting them today. You know what this one's name is? Angelica! Virginia and Angelica. The Virgin and the Angel!" He burst out laughing again. "Well, how about it, Virginia? What do I do with my angel here?"

"Bring her in. Tell her to sit down."

"Come in, Angelica," Willis said, "have a chair. Angelica! Oh, Jesus, that breaks me up. She just slit a guy from ear to ear. A regular little angel. Sit down, angel. That bottle on the desk there is nitroglycerin."

"What you minn?" Angelica asked.

"The bottle. Nitro."

"Nitro? You mean like in a bom'?"

"You said it, doll," Willis answered.

"A bom'?" Angelica said. "*Madre de los santos!*"

"Yeah," Willis said, and there was something close to awe in his voice.

From where Meyer Meyer sat near the window typing his D.D. report, he could see Willis lead the Puerto Rican girl deeper into the squadroom to offer her one of the straight-backed chairs. He watched as Willis unlocked the handcuffs and then draped both wristlets over his belt. The skipper walked over and exchanged a few words with Willis and then, hands on hips, turned to face the girl. Apparently Virginia Dodge was going to allow them to question the prisoner. How kind of Virginia Dodge!

Patiently, Meyer Meyer turned back to his typing.

He was reasonably certain that Virginia would not walk over to his desk to examine his masterpiece of English composition. He was also reasonably certain that he could do what he had to do unobserved especially now that the Puerto Rican bombshell had exploded into the room. Virginia Dodge seemed completely absorbed with the girl's movements, with the girl's string of colorful epithets. He was sure, then, that he could carry out the first part of his plan without detection.

"What's your name?" Byrnes asked the girl.

"What?" she said.

"Your name! *Cuál es su nombre?*"

"Angelica Gomez."

"She speaks English," Willis said.

"I don' speak Een-glés," the girl said.

"She's full of crap. The only thing she does in Spanish is

192

curse. Come on, Angelica. You play ball with us, and we'll play ball with you."

"I don't know what means thees play ball."

"Oh, we've got a lalapalooza this time," Willis said. "Look, you little slut, cut the Marine Tiger bit, will you? We know you didn't just get off the boat." He turned to Byrnes. "She's been in the city for almost a year, Pete. Hooking mostly."

"I'm no hooker," the girl said.

"Yeah, she's no hooker," Willis said. "Excuse me. I forgot. She worked in the garment district for a month."

"I'm a seamstress, that's what I am. No hooker."

"Okay, you're not a hooker, okay? You lay for money, okay? That's different. That makes it all right, okay? Now, why'd you slit that guy's throat?"

"What guy you speaking abou'?"

"Was there more than one?" Byrnes asked.

"I don' sleet nobody's thro'."

"No? Then who did it?" Willis asked. "Santa Claus? What'd you do with the razor blade?" Again, he turned to Byrnes. "A patrolman broke it up, Pete. Couldn't find the blade, though, thinks she dumped it down the sewer. Is that what you did with it?"

"I don' have no erazor blay." Angelica paused. "I don' cut nobody."

"You've still got blood all over your hands, you little bitch! Who the hell are you trying to snow?"

"That's from d'hanncuffs," Angelica said.

"Oh, Jesus, this one is the absolute end," Willis said.

The trouble, Meyer Meyer thought, is that it's hard to get the right words. It mustn't sound too melodramatic or it'll be dismissed as either a joke or the work of a crank. It has to sound sincere, and yet it has to sound desperate. If it doesn't sound desperate nobody'll believe it, and we're right back where we started. But if it sounds too desperate, nobody'll believe it anyway. So I've got to be careful.

He looked across the room to where Virginia Dodge was watching the interrogation of the Puerto Rican girl.

I've also got to hurry, he thought. She may just take it in her mind to amble over here and see what I'm doing.

"You know whose throat you slit?" Willis asked.

"I don' know nothin'."

"Then I'm gonna let you in on a little secret. You ever hear of a street gang called the Arabian Knights?"

"No."

"It's one of the biggest gangs in the precinct," Willis said. "Teen-age kids mostly. Except the guy who's leader of the gang is twenty-five years old. In fact, he's married and he's got a baby daughter. They call him Kassim. You ever hear of anybody called Kassim?"

"No."

"In fiction, he's Ali Baba's brother. In real life, he's leader of this gang called the Arabian Knights. His real name is José Dorena. Does that ring a bell?"

"No."

"He's a very big man in the streets, Kassim is. He's really a punk—but not in the streets. There's a gang called the Latin Paraders and the shit has been on between them and the Knights for years. And do you know what price the Paraders have set for a truce?"

"No. What?"

"An Arabian Knights jacket as a trophy—and Kassim *dead*."

"So who cares?"

"*You* ought to care, baby. The guy whose throat you slit is Kassim. José Dorena."

Angelica blinked.

"Yeah," Willis said.

"Is this legit?" Byrnes asked.

"You said it, Pete. So you see, Angelica, if Kassim dies, the Latin Paraders'll erect a statue of you in the park. But the Arabian Knights won't like you one damn bit. They're a bunch of mean bastards, sweetie, and they're not even gonna like the fact that you cut him—whether it leads to his untimely demise or not."

"What?" Angelica said.

"Whether he croaks or not, you're on their list, baby."

"I di'n know who he wass," Angelica said.

"Then you did do the cutting?"

"*Sí.* But I di'n know who he wass."

"Then why'd you cut him?"

"He wass bodderin' me."

"How?"

"He wass try to feel me up," Angelica said.

"Oh, come on!" Willis moaned.

"He wass!"

"Dig the virgin, Pete," Willis said. "Why'd you cut him, baby? And let's not have the hearts and flowers this trip."

"He wass grab my bosom," Angelica said. "On the steps. In fron' the stoop. So I cut him."

Willis sighed.

Virginia Dodge seemed to be tiring of the inquisition. Nervously, she sat at the desk commanding a view of both squadroom and corridor beyond, the .38 in her hand, the clear bottle of nitroglycerin resting on the desk before her.

I have to hurry, Meyer thought. Get it all down once and for all with no mistakes, and then start moving. Because if she comes over here and sees this, she is just liable to pull the trigger and blow off the back of my head, and Sarah will be sitting *shivah* for a week. They'll have to cover every mirror in the house and turn all the pictures to the wall. God, it'll be ghastly. So get it done. October ain't a time for dying.

"He grabbed your bosom, huh?" Willis said. "Which one? The right one or the left one?"

"Iss not funny," Angelica said. "For a man he feels you up in public, iss not funny."

"So you slashed him?"

"*Sí.*"

"'Cause he grabbed for your tit, right?"

"*Sí.*"

"What do you think, Pete?"

"Dignity doesn't choose its professions," Byrnes said. "I believe her."

"I think she's lying in her teeth," Willis said. "We check around, we'll probably find out she's been making it with Kassim for the past year. She probably saw him looking at another girl, and so she put the blade to him. That's more like it, isn't it, baby?"

"No. I don' know thees Kassim. He jus' come over an' get fresh. My body iss my body. An' I give it where I want. An' not to peegs with dirty hans."

"Hooray," Willis said. "They're really gonna put a statue of you in the park." He turned to Byrnes. "What do we make it, Pete? Felonious assault?"

"What condition is this Kassim in?"

"They carted him off to the hospital. Who knows? He was bleeding all over the goddamn sidewalk. You know what killed me, Pete? A bunch of young kids were standing around in a circle. You could see they didn't know whether to cry or laugh or just scream. They were kind of hopping up and down, do you know what I mean? Jesus, imagine growing up with this every day of your life? Can you imagine it?"

"Keep in touch with the hospital, Hal," Byrnes said. "Let's

hold the booking until later. We can't do much with . . ." He gestured with his head to where Virginia Dodge sat.

"Yeah. All right, Angelica. Keep your legs crossed. Maybe Kassim won't die. Maybe he's got a charmed life."

"I hope the son a bitch rots in his gray," Angelica said.

"Nice girl," Willis said, and patted her shoulder.

Meyer pulled the report from the typewriter. He separated the carbon from the three blue sheets, and then he read the top sheet. He read it carefully because he was a patient man, and he wanted it to be right the first time. There might not be another chance after this one.

DETECTIVE DIVISION REPORT

PLACE OF OCCURRENCE

THE DETECTIVES OF THE 87th SQUAD ARE

STREET

NAME OF PERSON REPORTING

BEING HELD PRISONER BY A WOMAN WITH

A GUN AND A BOTTLE OF NITROGLYCERIN.

GIVEN NAME   INITIALS

ADDRESS OF PERSON REPORTING

IF YOU FIND THIS NOTE, CALL HEADQUARTERS

AT ONCE! THE NUMBER IS CENTER 6-0800.

STREET

UNIFORM MEMBER ASSIGNED

HURRY!

DETECTIVE 2nd/GR MEYER

SURNAME   INITIALS   SHIELD NUMBER

ARRESTS

The window near the desk was open. The meshed grill outside the window—which protected the glass from the hurled brickbats of the 87th's inhabitants—would present only a small problem. Quickly, with one eye on Virginia Dodge, Meyer rolled the first report sheet into a long cylinder. Hastily, he thrust the cylinder through one of the diamond-shaped openings on the mesh and then shoved it out onto the air. He looked across the room.

Virginia Dodge was not watching him.

He rolled the second sheet and repeated the action.

He was shoving the third and final sheet through the opening when he heard Virginia Dodge shout, "Stop or I'll shoot!"

Meyer whirled from the open window.

He fully expected a bullet to come crashing into him, and then he realized Virginia Dodge was not looking at him, was not even facing in his direction. Hunched over, the .38 thrust out ahead of her, she had left the desk and the bottle of nitroglycerin and was standing a foot inside the slatted-rail divider.

On the other side of the divider was Alf Miscolo.

He stood undecided, his curly black hair matted to his forehead, his blue suspenders taut against his slumped shoulders, his shirt sleeves rolled up over muscular forearms. Total surprise was on his face. He had come out of the Clerical Office, where he'd been sweating over his records all afternoon. He had walked to the railing and shouted, "Hey, anybody ready for chow?" and then had seen the woman leap from the desk with the gun in her hand.

He had turned to run, and she'd yelled, "Stop, or I'll shoot!" and he'd stopped and turned to face her, but now he wondered whether or not he'd done the right thing. Miscolo was not a coward. He was a trained policeman who happened to be a desk jockey, but he'd learned to shoot at the academy and he wished now his gun was in his hand instead of in one of the filing cabinet drawers in the Clerical Office. The woman standing at the railing had the look of a crazy bitch on her face. Miscolo had seen that look before, and so he thought he'd been wise to stop when she yelled at him, and yet there were a lot of other men in that room and Jesus how long had she been here and was she going to shoot up the whole damn joint?

He stood in indecision for a moment longer.

He had a wife and a grown son who was in the Air Force. He did not want his wife to become a cop's widow, he did not want her making up beds in precincts, but, Jesus, that bitch had a crazy look on her face, suppose she shot everyone, suppose she went berserk?

He turned and started to run down the corridor.

Virginia Dodge took careful aim and fired.

She fired only once.

The bullet entered Miscolo's back just a little to the left of his spinal column. It spun him around in a complete circle and then slammed him up against the door to the men's room. He clung to the door for an instant and then slowly slid to the floor.

The bottle of nitroglycerin on the desk did not explode.

The stench of cordite hung on the air with the blue-gray aftersmoke of the explosion. Virginia Dodge, in clear silhouette against the gray of the smoke, seemed suddenly a very real and definite threat. She whirled from the railing just as Cotton Hawes broke from his desk in the corner.

"Get back!" she said.

"There's a hurt man out there," Hawes said, and he pushed through the gate.

"Come back here or you're next!" Virginia shouted.

"The hell with you!" Hawes said, and he ran to where Miscolo lay against the closed door.

The bullet had ripped through Miscolo's back with the clean precision of a needle passing through a piece of linen. Then, erupting at its point of exit, it had torn a hole the size of a baseball just below his collarbone. The front of his shirt was drenched with blood. Miscolo was unconscious, gasping for breath.

"Get him in here," Virginia said.

"He shouldn't be moved," Hawes answered. "For God's sake, he . . ."

"All right, hero," Virginia said tightly, "the nitro goes up!" She turned back toward the desk, swinging the gun so that it was dangerously close to the bottle of clear liquid.

"Bring him in, Cotton!" Byrnes said.

"If we move him, Pete, he's liable to . . ."

"Goddamnit, that's an order! Do as I say!"

Hawes turned toward Byrnes, his eyes narrowed. "Yes, *sir*," he said, and there was barely concealed vehemence in his voice. He reached down for a grip on the prostrate Miscolo. The man was heavy, heavier now with unconsciousness. He could feel Miscolo's bulk as he lifted him from the floor, his muscular arms straining against the man's weight. He braced himself and then shoved Miscolo higher into his arms with a supporting knee. He could feel Miscolo's hot blood rushing against his naked forearm. Staggering with his load, he carried Miscolo through the gate and into the squadroom.

"Put him back there," Virginia said. "On the floor. Out of sight." She turned to Byrnes. "If anybody comes up here, it was an accident, do you hear me? A gun went off accidentally. Nobody was hurt."

"We're going to have to get a doctor for him," Hawes said.

"We're going to have to get *nothing* for him," Virginia snapped.

"The man's been . . ."

"Put him down, redhead! Behind the filing cabinets. And fast."

Hawes carried Miscolo to a point beyond the filing cabinets where the area of squadroom was hidden from the corridor outside. Gently, he lowered Miscolo to the floor. He was rising when he heard footsteps in the hallway beyond. Virginia sat at the desk quietly, putting her purse up in front of the bottle of nitro as a shield, and then quickly moving the pistol directly behind the bottle so that it too was hidden by the bag.

"Remember, Lieutenant," she whispered, and Dave Murchison, the desk sergeant, came puffing down the hallway. Dave was in his fifties, a stout man who didn't like to climb steps and who visited the Detective Division upstairs only when it was absolutely necessary. He stopped just outside the railing, and then waited before speaking while he caught his breath.

"Hey, Lieutenant," he said, "what the hell was that? Sounded like a shot up here."

"Yes," Byrnes said hesitantly. "It was. A shot."

"Anything the . . . ?"

"Just a gun went off. By accident," Byrnes said. "Nothing to worry about. Nobody . . . nobody hurt."

"Jesus, it scared the living bejabbers out of me," Murchison said. "You sure everything's okay?"

"Yes. Yes, everything's okay."

Murchison looked at his superior curiously, and then his eyes wandered into the squadron, pausing on Virginia Dodge, and then passing to where Angelica Gomez sat with her shapely legs crossed.

"Sure got a full house, huh, Loot?" he said.

"Yes. Yes, we're sort of crowded, Dave."

Murchison continued to look at Byrnes curiously. "Well," he

said, shrugging, "long as everything's okay. I'll be seeing you, Pete."

He was turning to go when Byrnes said, "Forthwith."

"Huh?" Murchison said.

Byrnes was smiling thinly. He did not repeat the word.

"Well, I'll be seeing you," Murchison said, puzzled, and he walked off down the corridor. The squadroom was silent. They could hear Murchison's heavy tread on the metal steps leading to the floor below.

"Have we got any Sulfapaks?" Hawes asked from where he was crouched over Miscolo.

"The junk desk," Willis answered. "There should be one in there."

He moved quickly to the desk in the corner of the room, a desk that served as a catchall for the men of the squad, a desk piled high with Wanted circulars, and notices from Headquarters, and pamphlets put out by the department, and two empty holsters, and a spilled box of paper clips, and an empty Thermos bottle, a fingerprint roller, an unfinished game of Dots, the scattered tiles of a Scrabble setup and numerous other such unfilable materials. Willis opened one of the drawers, found a first-aid kit and hurried to Hawes, who had ripped open Miscolo's shirt.

"God," Willis said, "he's bleeding like a stuck pig."

"That bitch," Hawes said, and he hoped Virginia Dodge heard him. As gently as he knew how, he applied the Sulfapak to Miscolo's wound. "Can you get something for his head?" he asked.

"Here, take my jacket," Willis answered. He removed it, rolled it into a makeshift pillow, and then—almost tenderly— put it beneath Miscolo's head.

Byrnes walked over to the men. "What do you think?"

"It isn't good," Hawes said. "He needs a doctor."

"How can I get a doctor?"

"Talk to her."

"What good will that do?"

"For Christ's sake, you're in command here!"

"Am I?"

"Aren't you?"

"Virginia Dodge has pounded a wedge into my command, Cotton, and split it wide open. As long as she sits there with her wedge—that damn bottle of soup—I can't do a thing. Do you want me to kill everyone in this room? Is that what you want?"

"I want you to get a doctor for a man who's been shot," Hawes answered.

"No doctor!" Virginia called across the room. "Forget it. *No doctor!*"

"Does that answer you?" Byrnes wanted to know.

"It answers me," Hawes said.

"Don't be a hero, Cotton. There're more lives in this than your own."

"I'm not particularly dense, Pete," Hawes said. "But what guarantee do we have that she won't fling that bottle when Steve arrives anyway? And even if she doesn't, what gives us the goddamn right to sacrifice Steve Carella on our own petty selfish altars?"

"Would it be better to sacrifice every man in this room on Steve's altar?"

"Stop that talking over there," Virginia said. "Get on the other side of the room, Lieutenant! You, Shorty, over here! And you get in the corner, Redhead."

The men split up. Angelica Gomez watched them with an amused smile on her face. She rose then, her skirt sliding back over a ripe thigh as she did. Swiveling hip against hip socket, she walked over to where Virginia Dodge sat chastely with her gun and her bottle of nitroglycerin. Hawes watched them. He watched partially because he was mad as hell at the Skipper and he wanted to figure out a way of putting Virginia Dodge out of commission. But he watched, too, because the Puerto Rican girl was the most delicious-looking female he had seen in a dog's age.

In his own mind, he didn't know whether Angelica's buttocks interested him more than did the bottle of nitro on the desk. As he toyed with various plans for the bottle of nitro, he also toyed with various fantasies concerning the blonde's explosiveness, and as he fantasized he found that Angelica Gomez was more and more delightful to watch. The girl moved with contradictory economy and fluidity, slender ankle flowing into shapely calf and knee, hip grinding, flat simplicity of belly, firm rounded thrust of breast, sweeping curve of throat and jaw, aristocratic tilt of nose. She seemed absolutely at home within the specified confines of her body. It was a distinct pleasure to watch her. She was perhaps the most unselfconscious female he had ever met. At the same time, he reminded himself, she had slit a man's throat. A nice girl.

"Hey, ees that really a bom'?" Angelica asked Virginia.

"Sit down and don't bother me," Virginia answered.

"Don' be so touchy. I only ask a question."

"It's a bottle of nitroglycerin, yes," Virginia said.

"You gon' essplode it?"

"If I have any trouble, yes."

"Why?"

"Oh, shut up. Stop asking stupid questions."

"You got a gun, too, hah?"

"I've got *two* guns," Virginia said. "One in my hand, and another in my coat pocket. And a desk drawer full of them right here." She indicated the drawer to which she had earlier added Willis's gun.

"You minn business, I guess, hah?"

"I mean business."

"Hey, listen. Why you don' let me go, hah?"

"What are you talking about?"

"Why you don' let me walk out of here? You run the place, no? You hear the cop before, don' you? He say you put a wedge here, no? Okay. I walk out. Okay?"

"You stay put, sweetie," Virginia said.

"*Por qué?* What for?"

"Because if you walk out of here, you talk. And if you talk to the wrong person, all my careful planning is shot to hell."

"Who I'm gon' talk to, hah? I'm gon' talk to nobody. I'm gon' get the hell out the city. Go back Puerto Rico maybe. Take a plane. Hell, I slit a man's throat, you hear? All thees snotnose kids, they be after me now. I wake up dead one morning, no? So come on, Carmen, let me go."

"You stay," Virginia said.

"Carmen, don' be . . ."

"You stay!"

"Suppose I walk out, hah? Suppose I jus' do that?"

"You get what the cop got."

"Argh, you jus' mean," Angelica said, and she walked back to her chair and crossed her legs. She saw Hawes's eyes on her, smiled at him, and then immediately pulled her skirt lower.

Hawes was not really studying her legs. Hawes had just had an idea. The idea was a two-parter, and the first part of the idea—if the plan was to be at all successful—had to be executed in the vicinity where the Puerto Rican girl was sitting. The idea had as its core the functioning of two mechanical appliances, one of which Hawes was reasonably certain would work immediately, the other of which he thought might take quite some time to work if it worked at all. The idea seemed stunning in concept to Hawes and, fascinated with it, he had stared captured into space and the focus of his stare seemed to be Angelica's legs.

If the phone rings, Hawes thought, Virginia will pick it up. She's listening in on conversations now, and she sure as hell won't let one get by her, not with the possibility that it might be Steve calling. And if her attention is diverted by a phone call, that'd be all the time I'd need to do what I have to do, to get this thing rolling so that the big chance can be prepared for later on. Assuming she acts impulsively, the way people will when they're . . . well, we're assuming a lot. Still, it's a chance. So come on, telephone, ring!

His eyes were glued to the telephone. It seemed to him that during the course of the day, the telephone usually rang with malicious insistence every thirty seconds. Someone was always calling in to report a mugging or a beating or a knifing or a robbery or a burglary or any one of a thousand offenses committed daily in the 87th. So why didn't it ring now? Who had declared the holiday on crime? We can't stand a holiday right now—not with Steve waiting to walk into a booby trap, not with Miscolo bleeding from a hole the size of my head, not with that bitch sitting with her bottle of nitro and her neat little .38.

The sound startled Hawes. He almost turned automatically to reach for the wall, and then he remembered that he had to wait until Virginia picked up the phone. He saw Byrnes start across toward the instrument on the desk nearest him. He saw Byrnes waiting for Virginia's nod before he picked up the receiver.

The phone kept shrilling into the squadroom.

Virginia shifted the gun to her left hand. With her right hand, she picked up the receiver and nodded toward Byrnes. Byrnes lifted his phone.

"Eighty-seventh Squad, Lieutenant Byrnes."

"Well, well, how come they've got the big cheese answering telephones?" the voice said.

Hawes edged toward the wall, backing toward it. Virginia Dodge was still partially facing him, so that he could not raise his hand. Then, slowly, she swiveled in the chair so that her back was to him. Swiftly, Hawes lifted his hand.

"Who is this?" Byrnes asked into the mouthpiece.

"This is Sam Grossman at the lab. Who the hell did you think it was?"

The thermostat was secured tightly to the wall. Hawes

grasped it in one hand, and with a quick snap of his wrist raised the setting to its outermost reading.

On one of the mildest days in October, the temperature in the squadroom was now set for ninety-eight degrees.

Hawes unobtrusively closed first one window and then the other. Outside, the sultry night pressed its blackness against the windowpanes, filtered by the triangular mesh beyond the glass. The six hanging light globes, operated by a single switch inside the railing near the coat rack, feebly defended the room against the onslaught of darkness. A determined silence settled over the squadroom, the silence of waiting.

Angelica Gomez sat with her crossed legs and high-heeled pumps, jiggling one foot impatiently. Her coat was draped over the back of her chair. Her peasant blouse swooped low over her confessedly unrestricted bosom. She sat with her own thoughts—thoughts perhaps of the man whose throat she'd cut, a man named Kassim whose friends had behind them the power of the vendetta; thoughts perhaps of the uncompromising arm of the law; thoughts perhaps of an uncomplicated island in the Caribbean where the sun had always shone and where she had helped cut sugar cane in season and drunk deeply of rum at night with the guitars going in the velvet black hills.

At the desk beside her sat Virginia Dodge, solemnly dressed in black—black dress and black overcoat and black shoes and black leather tote bag. Thin white legs and a thin white face. The blue-black steel of a revolver in her fist. The colorless oil of a high explosive on the desk before her. Nervously, the fingers of her left hand rapped a tattoo on the desk top. Her eyes, so brown that they too appeared black, darted about the room, wild birds searching for a roost, settling always on the corridor beyond the railing, waiting for the appearance of a detective who had sent her man to prison.

Behind her, on the floor near the huge green bulk of the metal filing cabinets, lay Alf Miscolo, police clerk. Unconscious, gasping for breath, his chest and head on fire, Miscolo did not know he might be dying. Miscolo knew nothing. In the void of his unconsciousness, he dreamt he was a boy again. He dreamt that it was Halloween, dreamt that he was carrying bundles of paper to be tossed into the huge bonfire set in the middle of the city street. He dreamt he was happy.

Cotton Hawes wondered if the room were getting any hotter. He looked across the room and saw that Willis had unloosened his tie. He hoped desperately that—if the room were truly getting hotter—none of the men would mention the heat, none of them would go to the thermostat and lower it to a normal setting.

Leaning against the bulletin boards near the coat rack, Lieutenant Byrnes watched Hawes with narrowed eyes.

Of all the people in the room, Byrnes had been the only one to see Hawes raise the thermostat setting. Talking with Grossman on the telephone, he had watched Hawes as he stepped swiftly to the wall and twisted the dial on the instrument. Later, he had seen Hawes when he closed both windows, and he knew then that Hawes had something on his mind, that both actions were linked and not the idle movements of a thoughtless man.

He wondered now what the plan was.

He also wondered who or what would screw it up.

He had seen the action, but he was reasonably certain no one else in the room had followed it. And if Hawes was banking on heat, who would soon comment on the heat? Anyone might. Bert Kling had already taken off his jacket and was now mopping his brow. Willis had pulled down his tie. Angelica Gomez had pulled her skirt up over her knees like a girl sitting on a park bench trying to get a breeze from the river. Who would be the first to say, "It's hot as hell in here?"

And why did Hawes want heat to begin with?

He knew that Hawes had misunderstood him. He felt somewhat like a man falsely accused of racial prejudice because of a misunderstood remark. Hawes, of course, had not been attached to the 87th at the time of the Hernandez kill. Hawes did not know that Carella had risked his life for Byrnes's son, had come very close to losing that life. Hawes did not know how strong the bond was between Byrnes and Carella, did not know that Byrnes would gladly face a cannon if he thought it would help Steve.

But Byrnes was faced with the problem of command. And using the timeless logic of generals in battle, he knew that he could not be concerned over the welfare of a single man when the lives of many others were at stake. If Virginia Dodge's single weapon were that .38, he'd have gladly sacrificed himself on its muzzle. But she also held a bottle of high explosive.

And if she fired at the bottle, the squadroom would go up and with it every man in the room. He owed a lot to Carella, but he could not—as commanding officer of the squad—try a gamble that would endanger every life for a single life.

He hoped now that Hawes's plan was not a foolhardy one.

And, sourly, he thought, *Any* plan is a foolhardy one with that bottle of nitro staring at us.

Bert Kling was beginning to sweat.

He almost walked over to the windows and then he remembered something.

Hadn't Cotton just walked over there to *close* them?

Hadn't he just seen Cotton . . . ?

And wasn't the temperature in the room controlled by thermostat? Had someone raised the thermostat? Cotton?

Did Cotton have a plan?

Maybe, maybe not. In any case, Bert Kling would melt right down into a puddle on the wooden floor before he opened a window in the joint. Curiously, he waited. Profusely, he sweated.

Hal Willis was about to comment on the rising temperature in the room when he noticed that Bert Kling's shirt was stained with sweat. Their eyes locked for a moment. Kling wiped a hand across his brow and shook perspiration to the floor.

In an instant of mute understanding, Hal Willis realized that it was *supposed* to be getting hotter in the room.

He searched Kling's eyes, but there was no further clue in them.

Patiently, his underwear shorts beginning to stick to him, he wiggled on his chair and tried to make himself more comfortable.

* * *

Meyer Meyer wiped the beaded sweat from his upper lip.

It's hot as hell in here, he thought. *I wonder if anybody found my notes.*

Why doesn't somebody turn down the goddamn heat? he thought. He glanced over at the thermostat. Cotton Hawes was standing near the wall, his eyes fastened to Virginia Dodge. He looked for all the world like a sentry guarding something. What the hell was he guarding?

Hey, Cotton, he thought, *reach over and lower that damn thermostat, will you?*

The words almost reached his tongue.

And then he wondered again if anyone had found his notes.

And, wondering this, his mind drifted away from thoughts of

the heat in the room and—oddly for a man who had not been inside a synagogue for twenty years—he began to pray silently in Hebrew.

Angelica Gomez spread her legs and closed her eyes.

It was very hot in the room, and with her eyes closed she imagined she was lying on a rock in the mountains with the sun beating down flatly on her browned body. In Puerto Rico, she would climb trails as old as time, trails hidden by lush tropical growth. And then she would find a hidden glade, a glade wild with ferns. And in that glade, there would be a level rock, and she would take off all her clothes and tilt her breasts to be kissed by the sun.

Idly, she wondered why there was no sun in the streets of the city.

Lazily, she kept her eyes closed and allowed the heat to surround her. Suspended, her mind in the Caribbean, she relished the heat and hoped no one would open a window.

Sitting behind the high desk downstairs in the muster room, the desk which looked almost like a judge's altar of justice, the desk which had a sign requesting all visitors to stop there and state their business, Dave Murchison looked through the open doors of the station house to the street outside.

It was a beautiful night, and he wondered what ordinary citizens were doing on a night like this. Walking through the park with their lovers? Screwing with the windows open? Playing bingo or mah-jongg or footsie?

They certainly weren't sitting behind a desk answering telephones.

Now what the hell had the lieutenant meant?

Murchison tried to reconstruct the dialogue in his own mind. He had gone upstairs to see what the hell the noise had been about, and the loot had said it was just an accident, and he had said something about well, so long as everything's okay, and the loot had said yes, everything's fine or something like that and then . . . now here was the important part, so let's get it straight.

He had said to the loot, "Well, long as everything's okay. I'll be seeing you, Pete."

And Byrnes had answered, "Forthwith."

Now that was a very strange answer for the loot to give him because in police jargon "Forthwith" meant "Report immediately."

Now how could he report immediately if he was already standing there in front of the lieutenant?

So, naturally, he had said, "Huh?"

And the loot hadn't said anything in answer, he had just stood there with a kind of sick smile on his face.

Forthwith.

Report immediately.

Had the loot meant something? Or was he just clowning around?

And if he meant something, what did he mean? Report immediately. Report to *whom* immediately? Or maybe report *something* immediately. Report *what*?

The gun going off?

But the loot said that was an accident, and everything sure as hell looked copacetic upstairs. Did he want him to report the accident? Was that it?

No, that didn't make sense. A gun going off by accident wouldn't make the loot look too good, and he certainly wouldn't want that reported.

Argh, I'm making too much of this, Murchison thought. The loot was having his little joke, and here I'm trying to figure out what he meant by a gag. I should be upstairs working with the bulls, that's what. I should have been a detective, trying to figure out the meaning of a stupid little thing the loot tells me. It must be this Indian summer. I should be back in Ireland kissing Irish lasses.

Forthwith.

Report immediately.

A light on Murchison's switchboard exploded into green. One of the patrolmen was calling in. He plugged in his socket and said, "Eighty-seventh Precinct, Sergeant Murchison. Oh, hello, Baldy. Yep. Okay, glad to hear it. Keep on your toes."

All quiet on the Western front, Murchison thought. He pulled the wire from the board.

Forthwith, he thought.

Virginia Dodge rose suddenly.

"Everybody over there," she said. "That side of the room. Hurry up. Lieutenant, get away from that coat rack."

Angelica stirred, rose, smoothed her skirt over her hips, and walked toward the grilled windows. Hawes left his post by the thermostat to join the other men who began drifting toward the windows. Byrnes moved away from the coat rack.

"This gun stays trained on the nitro," Virginia said, "so no funny stuff."

Good! Hawes thought. *She's not only thinking of the heat, she's also worried about the nitro. It's going to work. Jesus, the first part of it is going to work.*

I hope.

Virginia backed toward the coat rack. Quickly, she slipped the coat off her left shoulder, the gun in her right hand aimed at the nitro on the desk. Then she shifted the gun to her left hand, slipped the coat off her right shoulder and, without turning, hung it on one of the pegs on the rack.

"It's hot as hell in here," she said. "Can't someone lower the heat?"

"I will," Hawes said, and went immediately to the thermostat.

There was a grin on his face. He looked across the room to where Virginia Dodge's shapeless black coat hung alongside Willis's hat and coat on the rack.

In the lefthand pocket of Virginia's black garment was the pistol she had taken from Lieutenant Byrnes's office.

It was remarkable how simply it had worked. If everything in life worked as easily as the first part of his plan had, everyone in the world would have his own private pink cloud upon which to float around. But the very ease with which Virginia had taken off her coat and parted with the pistol gave Hawes his first twinge of doubt. He was not a superstitious man, but he regarded simplicity of action with some skepticism. Was the success of the first part an ill omen for the second part?

Anxiously, he began to review the plan in his mind.

The gun was now where he wanted it, in the pocket of a coat hanging on the rack near the bulletin board. Between the coat rack and the bulletin board, on the short stretch of wall inside the slatted railing, was the light switch that controlled the overhead globes. It was Hawes's idea to amble over to the bulletin board, busy himself with taking down some notes from the Wanted circulars and then—when and if the opportunity presented itself—snap out the lights and reach for Byrnes's pistol in the coat. He would not use the pistol immediately because he did not want a long-distance shooting duel, not with that bottle of nitro on the desk in front of Virginia. He would hold the pistol until it was safe to fire it without the attendant possibility of a greater explosion.

He did not see how the plan could fail. The switch controlled every light in the room. One flick, and the lights would go out. It would take him no more than three seconds to snatch the gun, hide it, and flick on the lights again.

Would Virginia Dodge fire at the nitro in those three seconds? He did not believe so.

In the first place, even if she did fire, the room would be in total darkness and she probably wouldn't be able to hit the bottle.

Well, that's a hell of a gamble to be taking, he told himself. She doesn't even have to fire at it, you know. All she has to do is sweep it off the desk with her arm, and there goes eternity.

But he was banking on something else, a person's normal reaction to a suddenly darkened room. Wouldn't Virginia, in the confusion of the moment, assume there'd been a power failure or something? Wouldn't she hold her fire, hold the sweeping motion of her arm at least long enough to be certain one way or the other? And by that time, the lights would be on again and Hawes could invent some excuse about having turned them off by accident.

It had better be a damn good excuse, he told himself.

Or did it really have to be a good one? If, when the lights went on again, everything was apparently as it had been before the darkness, wouldn't she accept any alibi? Or would she remember the gun in the coat pocket? Well, if she did, they'd have it out then and there, nitro or no nitro. And at least they'd be evenly matched, a pistol for a pistol.

Again, he went over the steps in his mind. Get to the bulletin board, busy myself there, flick out the lights, grab the gun . . .

Now wait a minute.

There was an alternate switch at the far end of the corridor, just at the head of the metal steps. This switch, too, controlled the lights in the corridor and the squadroom so that it wasn't necessary to walk the entire length of the hall in complete darkness when coming onto the second floor of the building. But Hawes wondered if he had to do anything to that second switch in order to ensure darkness in the squadroom when he made his play. He did not think so. Each switch, he hoped, worked independently of the other, both capable of either turning on or extinguishing all the lights. In any case, it had better work that way. Virginia Dodge had already used her gun once, and she showed no signs of reticence about pulling the trigger again.

Well, he thought, let's get it over with.

He started across the room.

"Hey."

He stopped. Angelica Gomez had laid a hand on his arm.

"You got a *cigarillo*?" she asked.

"Sure," Hawes said. He took out his pack and shook one free. Angelica accepted it, hung it on her full lower lip, and waited. Hawes struck a match and lighted the cigarette.

"*Muchas gracias*," she said. "You got good manners. Tha's importan'."

"Yeah," Hawes said, and he started away from the girl, and again she caught his sleeve.

"You know something?"

"What?"

"I hate thees city. You know why?"

"No. Why?"

"No manners. Tha's the troo."

"Well, things are rough all over," Hawes said impatiently.

He started away again, and Angelica said, "Wha's your hurry?" and this time Virginia Dodge turned from the desk and looked at Hawes suspiciously.

"No hurry," he said to Angelica. He could feel Virginia's eyes on his back. Like two relentless drills, they bored at his spinal column.

"So sit down," Angelica said. "Talk to me. Nobody thees city ever have time to talk. Iss diff'ren' on the islan'. On the islan', ever'body got time for everytin.'"

Hawes hesitated. Virginia Dodge was still watching him. Trying to appear unhurried, he pulled up a chair and sat. Casually, perhaps too casually, he shook another cigarette from the package and lighted it. His hand, he noticed, was shaking. He pretended to ignore Virginia completely, pretended to be interested only in the lively company of Angelica Gomez. But as he drew on his cigarette, he was wondering, *How long will it be before she remembers she's left a gun in that coat?*

"Where you get that white in your hair?" Angelica asked.

His hand wandered unconsciously to the white smear above his left temple. "I was knifed once," he said. "It grew back this way."

"Where you got knifed?"

"It's a long story."

"I got time."

I haven't, he thought, and then he realized that Virginia was still watching him, and he wondered if she knew he was up to something, and he felt nervousness settle in his stomach like a heavy black brew. He wanted to let out his breath in a giant sigh, wanted to shout something, wanted to pound his fist against the wall. Instead, he forced himself to continue talking in a normal conversational voice, thinking about the pistol all the while, thinking about it so hard he could almost feel his fingers curling around the checked walnut stock.

"I was investigating a burglary," he said. "The woman was pretty hysterical when I got there. I guess she was still in shock. She was terrified when I started to leave. I heard her begin screaming as I was going down the stairwell, these high hysterical screams. I was going to send a patrolman up as soon as I reached the street, but I never got that far. This guy came rushing at me with a knife in his hand."

"This was the burglar?"

"No. No, that's the funny part of it. He was the super of the building. He'd heard her screams, and came running upstairs because he thought it was the burglar returning. The hallway was dark and when he saw me he jumped me. And he cut me. I didn't know he was the super, either. I got mad as hell, and I just kept hitting him until he went limp. But he'd already put the gash in my head."

"So what happened?"

"So they shaved the hair off to get at the cut. And when it grew back, it was white. End of story."

"Did the super go to jail?"

"No. He honestly thought I was the burglar."

There was a pause.

"Will I go to jail?"

"Yes. Probably."

There was another pause. He wondered if he should leave now, but Virginia was still watching him. Angelica Gomez sat with her hands folded in her lap. There was sadness on her face, mingled with a hardness that made her seem older than she actually was.

In a thrust at further conversation, Hawes said, "What brought you to the mainland?"

Without hesitation, she answered, "Pan-American Airlines."

"No, no, I meant . . ."

"Oh. You meant . . ." and she burst out laughing, and suddenly there was no hardness to her face. She threw back her head, and the bleached blond hair seemed, for a moment, as natural as her laughter. She was carefree for an instant, all thought of spontaneous mayhem and violent gang retaliation washed from her mind. Her face relaxed, leaving only the natural beauty that was her birthright and which the city could never rob from her. The laughter trailed off. The relaxation dropped from her face like a gossamer veil drifting to the dust. There was only the hardness again, covering the beauty with the glitter of shellac.

"I come here because I am hungry," she said. "Very poor in Puerto Rico." She pronounced the name of the island with Spanish grandeur, rhyming "Puer" with "prayer," discarding the harsh "Porto" of the native mainlander. And, never having been to the island, Hawes listened to her pronunciation of the words and visualized it immediately as a place of rare beauty.

Angelica shrugged. "I get letters from my cousins. Come the city, come the city. So I come. Very easy. The plane fare is loan you, there are people who loan you *dinero*. Later on, you pay them back. With in'ress. So I come. I get here January. Very cold here, I don' expec' thees. I knew would be winter here, but not so cold I don' expec'."

"Where'd you go, Angelica?"

"I go first what they call a hot bed place. You know what thees minns?"

"No. What?"

"It sounds dirtee, but hot bed is not thees. Hot bed is where people come to sleep in shifts, *comprende*? Like they renn the apartment to three diff'ren' people. You come sleep, you leave. Nex' one comes sleep, he leaves. Then nex' one comes sleep, he leaves. One apartment, three renns. Very smott, much *dinero* in this. For the landlord. Not for the sleeper." She smiled grimly. Hawes smiled with her.

"So," Angelica said, "I stay there a while 'til all my money is gone, an' then I go live with my cousins for a while. An' then I figure I am become—how you say—burn. Burn. When is too much for someone to carry?"

"Burden," Hawes supplied.

"*Sí*. Burd'n. So I find a man an' go live with him."

"Who?"

"Oh, jus' a man. Pretty good man, no police trouble. But I don' live with him now because he beat me once, an' thees I don' like. So I leave. An' sometimes I sleep around now, but only when I need bad the money." She paused. "I tell you something."

"What?"

"In Puerto Rico," and again the "Puer" was a prayer, "I am pretty girl. Here, too, I am also pretty—but I am also cheap.

213

You know? I am look at here, an' men think, 'I sleep with her.' In Puerto Rico, there is respect. Very diff'ren'."

"How do you mean?"

"In Puerto Rico, a girl walks don the stritt, men look an' watch, it is a pretty thing to see. I minn, iss all right a girl could wiggle a little, is nice to see, appreciated. An' also a little comical. I minn, good-natured. Here . . . no. Here, always there is the thinking, 'Cheap. Slut. *Puta.*' I hate thees city."

"Well, you . . ."

"Iss not my fault I don' speak such good English. I learn Spanish. I know *real* Spanish, very high Spanish, very good school Spanish. But Spanish iss no good here. You speak Spanish here, you are a foreigner. But thees is my country, too, no? I am American also, no? Puerto Rico is American, *no es verdad*? But Spanish no good. Spanish here minns *puta*. I hate thees city."

"Angelica . . ."

"You know something? I wann to go back the islan'. I wann to go back there an' never leave. Because I tell you. There I am poor, but there I am me. Angelica Gomez. *Me.* An' there is nobody else the whole worl' who iss also Angelica Gomez. Only me. An' here, I am not me, I am only dirtee Spanish Puerto Rican spic!"

"To *some* people," Hawes said.

Angelica shook her head. "I am in big trouble now, no?" she said.

"Yes. You're in very big trouble."

"*Sí.* So what happens to me now? I go to prison, hah? Maybe worse if thees Kassim dies, hah? An' why do I cut him? You want to know why I cut him? I do it because he forgets one thing. He forgets what everybody else in thees city forgets. He forgets that I am me, Angelica Gomez, an' that what is me is *private* an' nobody can touch unless I say touch. Me. Private." She paused. "Why they cann let a person be private? God-damn, why they cann leave you alone?"

She seemed suddenly on the verge of tears. He reached out to touch her hand, and she shook her head instantly and violently. He pulled back his fingers.

"I am sorree," she said. "I will not cry. One learns fast in thees city that it does no good to cry, no good at all." She shook her head. "I am sorree. Leave me alone. *Por favor.* Leave me alone. Please. Please."

He rose. Virginia Dodge had turned her attention back to the desk. She sat quite silently, staring at the bottle in front of her.

Casually, Hawes walked to the bulletin board near the light switch. Casually, he took a pad from his back pocket and began writing aimlessly into it, waiting for the precise moment of attack. Ideally that moment should be when Virginia Dodge was at the other end of the room. Unfortunately, she showed no signs of moving from the desk behind which she sat in deadly earnestness, staring at the bottle of colorless fluid.

Well then, Hawes thought, the hell with the ideal. Let's just hope she turns her back for a minute, just to give me enough time to snap off the lights.

That's all I need. Just a moment while she turns away, and then the lights go off, and I reach for the gun, lefthand pocket of the coat, mustn't grab for the right-hand pocket by mistake, Jesus, suppose one of the boys thinks there's been a power failure, suppose somebody strikes a match or turns on one of those damn battery-powered emergency lights, is there one in the squadroom? sure under the kneehole of the junk desk, oh Jesus, don't anybody get any bright ideas, please, pun unintentional, don't anybody throw any light on the subject, pun intentional, don't foul me up by being heroes.

Just let the lights go out, and sit tight, and let me get my mitts on that pistol. Just three seconds. Stick my hand in the pocket, close it around the butt, pull it out, and shove the gun into the side pocket of my pants. That's all I need.

Now if she'd only turn her head.

I'm six inches from the light switch. All she has to do is turn her head, and I make my move.

Come on, Virginia darling, turn that deadly little skull of yours.

Virginia darling did not move a muscle. Virginia seemed hypnotized by the bottle of nitro.

Suppose she whacks it off the desk the minute the lights go out?

No, she won't do that.

Suppose she does?

If she does, I'll get a demerit, and never get to make Detective/First Grade.

Come on, you bitch, turn your head. Turn it!

There must be a God, Hawes thought. He watched in fascination as Virginia Dodge slowly but surely turned to look across the room toward the grilled windows.

Hawes moved instantly. His hand darted for the light panel, shoved downwards on the protruding plastic switch.

There was blackness, instant blackness that filled the room like a negative explosion.

"What the hell . . . ?" Virginia started, and then her voice went dead, and there was only silence in the room.

The coat, Hawes thought.

Fast!

He felt the coarse material under his fingers, slid his hands down the side of the garment, felt the heavy bulk of the weapon in the pocket, and then thrust his hand into the slit, reaching for the gun.

And then suddenly, blindingly, unimaginably—the lights went on.

He felt like a kid caught with his hand in the cookie jar.

For a moment, he couldn't imagine what had caused the sudden blinding illumination. And then he realized the lights were on again, and here he was reaching into the pocket of Virginia's coat, his fingers not an inch from the gun. Oddly, time seemed to lose all meaning as soon as the lights went on. He knew that time was speeding by at a remarkable clip, knew that whatever he did in the next few seconds could very well mean the life or death of everyone in the room, and yet time seemed to stop.

He decided, in what seemed to take three years, to whirl on Virginia with the revolver in his hand.

He closed his fingers around the butt of the gun in the warmth of the dark pocket, and the closing of his hand took twelve years. He was ready to draw the gun when he saw Arthur Brown, a puzzled look on his face, striding rapidly up the corridor. He decided then—the decision was a century coming— to yell, "Get out, Brown! Run!" and then the time for yelling was gone because Arthur was pushing through the gate and entering the squadroom. And then, too, the time for pulling the revolver was gone, all the time in the world had suddenly dwindled down to its proper perspective, perhaps twenty seconds in all had gone by since the lights went on, and now there was no time at all, time had gone down the drain, now there was only Virginia Dodge's cold lethal voice cutting through the time-rushing silence of the squadroom.

"Don't pull it, redhead! I'm aiming at the nitro!"

He hesitated. A thought flashed into his head: Is there *really* nitroglycerin in that bottle?

And then the thought blinked out as suddenly as it had come.

He could not chance it. He released his grip on the pistol and turned to face her.

Thunderstruck, Arthur Brown stood just inside the gate.

"What . . . ?" he said.

"Shut up," Virginia snapped. "Get in here!"

"What . . . ?" Brown said again, and there was complete puzzlement on his face. He knew only that he'd returned to the precinct after sitting in the back room of a tailor shop all afternoon. He had climbed the metal steps leading to the second story as he'd done perhaps ten thousand times since joining the 87th Squad. He had found the upstairs corridor in darkness, and had automatically reached for the light switch at the top of the steps, turning on the lights. The first person he'd seen was Cotton Hawes reaching into the pocket of a coat hanging on the rack. And now . . . a woman with a gun.

"Get over here, redhead," Virginia said.

Silently, Hawes walked to her.

"You're a pretty smart bastard, aren't you?" she said.

"I . . ."

The gun in her hand moved upwards blurringly, came down again in a violent sweeping motion of wrist and arm. He felt the fixed sight at the barrel's end ripping into his cheek. He covered his face with his hands because he expected more. But more did not come. He looked at his fingers. They were covered with fresh blood.

"No more stunts, redhead," she said coldly. "Understand?"

"I understand."

"Now get out of my way. Over there on the other side of the room. You!" She turned to Brown. "Inside. Hurry up!"

Brown moved deeper into the room. The puzzlement on his face was slowly giving way to awareness. And fast on the heels of this came a look of shrewd calculation.

Virginia picked up the bottle of nitroglycerin, and then began walking toward the coat rack, the bottle in one hand, the gun in the other. Her walk was a jerky, nervous movement of shoulders, hips, and legs, devoid of all femininity, a sharp, quick perambulation that propelled her across the room. And watching her erratic walk, Hawes was certain that the liquid in her left hand was not the high explosive she claimed it was. And yet, nitro was funny. Sometimes it went if you breathed on it. And other times . . .

He wondered.

Nitro? Or water?

Step into the isolation booth, sir, and answer the question.

Quickly, Virginia removed Byrnes's pistol from her coat. She walked back to the desk, put the bottle of nitro down on its top, unlocked the desk drawer, and tossed the revolver in with the others.

"All right, you," she said to Brown. "Give me your gun."

Brown hesitated.

"The bottle here is full of nitroglycerin," Virginia said calmly. "Give me your gun."

Brown looked to Byrnes.

"Give it to her, Artie," Byrnes said. "She's calling all the shots."

"What's her game?" Brown wanted to know.

"Never mind my game," Virginia said heatedly. "Just shut your mouth and bring me your gun."

"You sure are a tough lady," Brown said. He walked to the desk, watching her. He watched her while he unclipped his gun and holster. He was trying, in his own mind, to determine whether or not Virginia Dodge was a hater. He could usually spot hatred at a thousand paces, could know with instant certainty that the person he was looking at or talking to would allow the color of Brown's skin to determine the course of their relationship. Arthur Brown was a black man. He was also a very impatient man. He had learned early in the game that the chance similarity of his pigmentation and his name—was it chance, or had some long-ago slave owner chosen the name for simplicity?—only added to his black man's burden. Impatiently, he waited for the inevitable slur, the thoughtless comment. Usually, it came—though not always. Now, as he put his gun and holster on the desk, his impatience reached unprecedented heights. He could read nothing on the face of Virginia Dodge. And, too, though he had newly entered the situation in the squadroom, he was impatiently itchy to have it done and over with.

Virginia pushed Brown's gun into the top drawer.

"Now get over there," she said. "The other side of the room."

"Is it okay to report to the lieutenant first?" he asked.

"Lieutenant!" she called. "Come here."

Byrnes walked over.

"He's got a report for you. Give it here, mister, where I can hear it all."

"How'd it go?" Byrnes said.

"No dice. And it isn't *going* to work either, Pete."

"Why not?"

"I stopped off in a candy store when I left the tailor shop. To get a pack of cigarettes."

"Yeah?"

"I got to talking with the owner. He told me there's been a lot of holdups in the neighborhood. Tailor shops mostly."

"Yeah?"

"But he told me the holdups would be stopping soon. You know why?"

"Why?"

"Because—and this is just what he told me—there's a bull sitting in the back room of the tailor shop right up the street, just waiting for the crook to show up. That's what the guy in the candy store told me."

"I see."

"So if *he* knows, every other merchant on the street knows. And if they know, their customers know. And you can bet your ass the thief knows, too. So it won't work, Pete. We'll have to dope out something else."

"Mmm," Byrnes said.

"You finished?" Virginia asked.

"I'm finished."

"All right, get over on the other side of the room."

Byrnes walked away from the desk. Brown hesitated.

"Did you hear me?"

"I heard you."

"Then move!"

"What's the gun and the nitro for, lady?" Brown asked. "I mean, what do you want here? What's your purpose?"

"I'm here to kill Steve Carella."

"With a bottle of soup?"

"With a gun. The nitro is my insurance."

Brown nodded. "Is it real?"

"It's real."

"How do I know?"

"You don't. Would you like to try belling the cat?" Virginia said and smiled.

Brown returned the smile. "No, thank you, lady. I was just asking. Gonna kill Steve, huh? Why, what'd he do to you? Give you a traffic ticket?"

"This isn't funny," Virginia said, the smile leaving her mouth.

"I didn't think it was. Who's the floozy? Your partner?"

"I have no partner," Virginia said, and Brown thought her eyes clouded for a moment. "She's a prisoner."

"Aren't we all?" Brown said, and again he smiled, and Virginia did not return the smile.

Hal Willis walked over to the desk. "Listen," he said, "Miscolo's in a bad way. Will you let us get a doctor in here?"

"No," Virginia said.

"For Christ's sake, he may be dying! Look, you want Carella, don't you? What's the sense in letting an innocent guy . . ."

"No doctor," Virginia said.

"Why not?" Byrnes asked, walking over. "You can keep him here after he treats Miscolo. Same as all of us. What the hell difference will it make?"

"No doctor," she said again.

Hawes drifted over to the desk. Unconsciously, the four men assumed the position they would ordinarily use in interrogating a suspect. Hawes, Byrnes, and Brown were in front of the desk. Willis was standing to the right of it. Virginia sat in her chair, the bottle of nitro within easy reach of her left hand, the .38 in her right hand.

"Suppose I picked up a phone and called a doctor?" Hawes asked.

"I'd shoot you."

"Aren't you afraid of another explosion?" Willis said.

"No."

"You got a little nervous when Murchison came up here last time, didn't you?" Hawes said.

"Shut up, redhead. I've had enough from you."

"Enough to shoot me?" Hawes said.

"Yes."

"And chance the explosion?" Brown put in.

"And another visit from downstairs?"

"You can't chance that, Virginia, can you?"

"I can! Because if anyone else comes up, the nitro goes, goddamnit!"

"But what about Carella? You blow us up, and you don't get Carella. You want Carella, don't you?"

"Yes, but . . ."

"Then how can you explode that nitro?"

"How can you chance another gunshot?"

"You can't shoot any of us, can you? It's too risky."

"Get back," she said. "All of you."

"What are you afraid of, Virginia?"

"You've got the gun, not us."

"Can't you fire it?"

"Are you afraid of firing it?"

Hawes came around to the left side of the desk, moving closer to her.

"Get back!" she said.

Willis moved closer on the right, and Virginia whirled, thrusting the gun at him. In that instant, Hawes stepped between her and the bottle of nitroglycerin. She was out of the chair in the space of a heartbeat, pushing the chair out from beneath her, and starting to rise. And as she started the rise, Willis—seeing that her hand was away from the bottle, knowing she was off balance as she rose—kicked out with his left foot, swinging it in a backward arc that caught her at the ankles. Hawes shoved at her simultaneously, completing the imbalance, sending Virginia sprawling to the right, toppling toward the floor. She hit the floor with resounding force, and her right hand opened as Hawes scuttled around the desk.

The gun fell from her fingers, slid across the floor, whirled in a series of dizzying circles and then came to a sudden stop.

Willis dove for it.

He extended his hand, and Hawes held his breath because they were getting rid of the crazy bitch at last.

And then Willis shrieked in pain as a three-inch dagger of leather and metal stamped his hand into the floor.

The black skirt was taut over the extended leg of Angelica Gomez. It tightened around a fleshy thigh, pulled back over the knee, ended there in sudden revelation of shapely calf and slender ankle. A black strap circled the ankle and beneath that was a red leather pump with a heel like a stiletto. That heel was buried in the back of Willis's hand.

And then Angelica pulled back her leg and stooped immediately to pick up the gun. From the floor, her skirt pulled back over both knees, her eyes flashing, she whirled on Lieutenant Byrnes, who was reaching for the bottle of nitro on the desk top.

"Don' touch it!" she shouted.

Byrnes stopped cold.

"Away from the desk," she said. "Ever'body! Back! Back!"

They moved from the desk, fanning away from it, backing away from a new menace that seemed more deadly than the first. Angelica Gomez had stabbed a man and, for all they knew, that man might now be dead. She had the law to face, and she also had the street gang to face, and so the look on her face was one of desperate resignation. Angelica Gomez was making her pitch for better or worse, and Christ help whoever stepped into her path.

She rose, the pistol unwavering in her fist.

"I'm ge'n out of here," she said. "Don' nobody try to stop me."

Virginia Dodge was on her feet now. She turned to Angelica, and there was a smile on her face. "Good girl," she said. "Give me the gun."

For a moment, Angelica did not understand. She looked at Virginia curiously and then said, "You crazy? I'm leavin'. Now!"

"I know. Give me the gun. I'll cover them for you. While you go."

"Why I should give you the gun?" Angelica said.

"For Christ's sake, are you on their side? The ones who want to send you to jail? Give me the gun!"

"I don' have to do you no favors. I ask before you let me go, an' you say no. Now you want the gun. You crazy."

"All right, I'll put it in black and white. If you take that gun with you, I'm jumped the minute you leave this room. And that means they'll be on the phone in four seconds and the whole damn police force will be after you. If you give me the gun, I hold them. I keep them here. No phone calls. No radio cars looking for you. You're free."

Angelica thought about this for a moment.

"Give me the gun!" Virginia said, and she took a step closer to Angelica. The Puerto Rican girl stood poised like a tigress, her back arched over into a C, her legs widespread, the gun trembling in her hand. Virginia came closer.

"Give it to me," she said.

"You hol' them back?" Angelica asked. "You keep them here?"

"Yes."

"Come then. Come close."

Virginia moved to her side.

"Your hand," Angelica said.

Virginia held out her hand, and Angelica put the gun into it.

"I go now," she said. "You keep them here. I get away. Free," she said, "free."

She started to move. She took one step away from Virginia, her back to the woman. Quickly, Virginia raised the gun. Brutally, she brought it crashing down on the skull of Angelica Gomez. The girl collapsed to the floor, and Virginia stepped over her and moved rapidly to the desk.

"Does anybody still think I'm kidding?" she asked quietly.

Alf Miscolo lay in delirium, and in his tortured sleep he cried out, "Mary! Mary!"

His wife's name was Katherine.

He was not a handsome man, Miscolo. He lay on the floor now with his head propped against Willis's jacket. His forehead was drenched with sweat that rolled down the uneven planes of his face. His nose was massive, and his eyebrows were bushy, and there was a thickness about his neck which created the impression of head sitting directly on shoulders. He was not a handsome man, Miscolo, less handsome now in his pain and his delirium. Blood was seeping through the sulfanilamide bandage, and his life was leaking out of his body drop by precious drop, and he cried out again "Mary!" sharply, because he once had been in love.

Bert Kling put a wet cloth on Miscolo's forehead.

He was used to death and dying. He was a young man, but he had been through a war in which death and dying had been a matter of course, an everyday occurrence like waking up to brush your teeth. And he had held the heads of closer friends on his lap, men he knew far better than Miscolo. And yet, hearing the word *Mary* erupt from Miscolo's lips in a hoarse scream, he felt a chill start at the base of his spine, rocketing into his brain where it exploded in cold fury. In that moment, he wanted to rush across the room and strangle Virginia Dodge.

In that moment, he wondered whether the liquid in that bottle was really nitroglycerin.

Angelica Gomez sat up and shook her head.

Her skirt was pulled back over her knees, and she propped her elbows on both knees and shook her head again, and then looked around the room with a puzzled expression on her face, like a person waking in a hotel.

And then, of course, she remembered.

She touched the back of her head. A huge knob had risen where Virginia had hit her with the gun. She felt the knob and the area around it, all sensitive to her probing fingers. And as the tentacles of pain spread out from the bruise, she felt with each stab a new rush of outraged anger. She rose from the floor and dusted off her black skirt, and the look she threw at Virginia Dodge could have slain the entire Russian Army.

And in that moment, she wondered whether the liquid in that bottle was really nitroglycerin.

Cotton Hawes touched his cheek where the gun sight had ripped open a flap of flesh. The cheek was raw to the touch. He dabbed at it with a cold wet handkerchief, a cloth no colder than his fury.

And he wondered for the tenth time whether the liquid in that bottle was really nitroglycerin.

Steve Carella, she thought.

I will kill Steve Carella. I will shoot the rotten bastard and watch him die, and they won't touch me because they're afraid of what's in this bottle.

I am doing the right thing.

This is the only thing to do.

There is a simple equation here, she thought: A life for a life. Carella's life for my Frank's life. And that is justice.

The concept of justice had never truly entered the thoughts of Virginia Dodge before. She had been born Virginia MacCauley, of an Irish mother and a Scotch father. The family had lived in Calm's Point at the foot of the famous bridge that joined that part of the city with Isola. Even now, she looked upon the bridge with fond remembrance. She had played in its shadow as a little girl, and the bridge to her had been a wondrous structure leading to all the far corners of the earth. One day, she had dreamt, she would cross that bridge and it would take her to lands brimming with spices and rubies. One day, she would cross that bridge into the sky, and there would be men in turbans, and camels in caravans, and temples glowing with gold leaf.

She had crossed the bridge into the arms of Frank Dodge.

Frank Dodge, to the police, was a punk. He'd been arrested at the age of fourteen for mugging an old man in Grover Park. He'd been considered a juvenile offender by the law, and got off with nothing more serious than a reprimand and a J.D. card. Between the ages of fourteen and seventeen, he'd been pulled in on a series of minor offenses—and always his age, his lawyer, and his innocent baby-blue-eyed looks had saved him from incarceration. At nineteen, he committed his first holdup.

This time he was beyond the maximum age limit for a juvenile offender. This time, his innocent baby-blue-eyed looks had lengthened into the severity of near-manhood. This time, they dumped him into the clink on Bailey's Island. Virginia met him shortly after his release.

To Virginia, Frank Dodge was not a punk.

He was the man with the turban astride the long-legged camel, he was the gateway to enchanted lands, rubies trickled from his fingertips, he was her man.

His B-card listed a series of offenses as long as Virginia's right arm—but Frank Dodge was her man, and you can't argue with love.

When he held up that gas station, the attendant yelled for help and it happened that a detective named Steve Carella, who was off-duty and driving toward his apartment in River-head, heard the calls and drove into the station—but not before Dodge had shot the attendant and blinded him. Carella made the collar. Frank Dodge went to prison—Castleview this time, where nobody played games with thieves. It was discovered during his first week of imprisonment that Frank Dodge was anything but an ideal prisoner. He caused trouble with keepers and fellow-prisoners alike. He constantly flouted the rules—as archaic as they were. He tried to obtain his release, but each attempt failed. His letters to his wife, read by prison authorities before they left the prison, grew more and more bitter.

In the second year of his term, it was discovered that Frank Dodge was suffering from tuberculosis. He was transferred to the prison hospital. It was in the prison hospital that he had died yesterday.

Today, Virginia Dodge sat with a pistol and a bottle, and she waited for the man who had killed him. In her mind, there was no doubt that Steve Carella was the man responsible for her husband's death. If she had not believed this with all her heart, she'd never have had the courage to come up here with such an audacious plan.

The amazing part of it was that the plan was working so far. They were all afraid of her, actually afraid of her. Their fear gave her great satisfaction. She could not have explained the satisfaction if she'd wanted to, could not have explained her retaliation against all society in the person of Steve Carella, her flouting of the law in such a flamboyant manner. Could she not, in all truth, in all fairness simply have waited for Carella downstairs and put a bullet in his back when he arrived?

Yes.

In all fairness, she could have. There was no need for a melodramatic declaration of what she was about to do, no need to sit in judgment over the law enforcers as they had sat in

225

judgment over her husband, no need to hold life or death in the palms of her hands, no need to play God to the men who had robbed her of everything she loved.

Or was there a very deep need?

She sat now with her private thoughts. The gun in her hand was steady. The bottle on the table before her caught the slanting rays of the overhead light.

She smiled grimly.

They're wondering, she thought, whether the liquid in this bottle is really nitroglycerin.

The telephone in the squadroom rang at 6:55.

Hal Willis waited for Virginia's signal, and then picked up the receiver.

"Eighty-seventh Squad," he said. "Detective Willis speaking."

"Just a second," a voice on the other end said. The voice retreated from the phone, obviously talking to someone else in the room. "How the hell do I know?" it said. "Turn it over to the Bunco Squad. No, for Christ's sake, what would we be doing with a pickpocket file? Oh, Riley, you're the stupidest sonofabitch I've ever had to work with. I'm on the phone, can you wait just one goddamn minute?" The voice came back onto the line. "Hello?"

"Hello?" Willis said. At the desk opposite him, Virginia Dodge watched and listened.

"Who'm I speaking to?" the voice asked.

"Hal Willis."

"You're a detective, did you say?"

"Yes."

"This the 87th Squad?"

"Yes."

"Yeah. Well then I guess it's a crank."

"Huh?"

"This is Mike Sullivan down Headquarters. We got a call a little while ago, clocked in at . . . ah . . . just a second . . ." Sullivan rattled some papers on the other end of the line. ". . . six forty-nine. Yeah."

"What kind of a call?" Willis said.

"Some college kid. Said he picked up a D.D. report in the street. Had a message typed on it. Something about a broad with a bottle of nitro. Know anything about it?"

At her desk, Virginia Dodge stiffened visibly. The revolver

came up close to the neck of the bottle. From where Willis stood, he could see her trembling.

"Nitro?" he said into the phone, and he watched her hand, and he was certain the barrel of the gun would collide with the bottle at any moment.

"Yeah. Nitroglycerin. How about that?"

"No," Willis said. "There's . . . there's nothing like that up here."

"Yeah, that's what I figured. But the kid gave his name and all, so it sounded like it might be a real squeal. Well, that's the way it goes. Thought I'd check anyway, though. No harm in checking, huh?" Sullivan laughed heartily.

"No," Willis said, desperately trying to think of some way to tell Sullivan that the message was real; whoever had sent it, the damn thing was real. "There's certainly no harm checking." He watched Virginia, watched the trembling gun in her hand.

Sullivan continued laughing. "Never know when there'll really be some nut up there with a bomb, huh, Willis?" he said, and burst into louder laughter.

"No, you . . . you never know," Willis said.

"Sure." Sullivan's laughter trailed off. "Incidentally, is there a cop up there by the name of Meyer?"

Willis hesitated. Had Meyer sent the message? Was it signed? If he said "Yes," would that be the end of it, and would Sullivan make the connection? If he said "No," would Sullivan investigate further, check to see which cops manned the 87th? And would Meyer . . .

"You with me?" Sullivan asked.

"What? Oh, yes."

"Answer him!" Virginia whispered.

"We sometimes get a lousy connection," Sullivan said, "I thought maybe we'd got cut off."

"No, I'm still here," Willis said.

"Yeah. Well, how about it? Any Meyer there?"

"Yes. We have a Meyer."

"Second Grade?"

"Yes."

"That's funny," Sullivan said. "This kid said the note was signed by a Second Grade named Meyer. That's funny, all right."

"Yes," Willis said.

"And you got a Meyer up there, huh?"

"Yes."

"Boy, that sure is funny." Sullivan said. "Well, no harm in checking, huh? What? For God's sake, Riley, can't you see I'm on the phone? I gotta go, Willis. Take it easy, huh? Nice talking to you."

And he hung up.

Willis put the phone back onto the cradle.

Virginia Dodge put down her receiver, picked up the bottle of nitro and slowly walked to where Meyer Meyer was sitting at the desk near the window.

She did not say a word.

She put the bottle down on the desk before him and then she brought her arm across her body and swung the gun in a backhanded swipe that ripped open Meyer's lip. Meyer put up his hands to cover his face, and again the gun came across, again, again, numbing his wrists, forcing his hands down until there was only the vicious metal swiping at his eyes and his bald head and his nose and his mouth.

Virginia's eyes were bright and hard.

Viciously, cruelly, brutally, she kept the pistol going like a whipsaw until, bleeding and dazed, Meyer collapsed on the desk top, almost overturning the bottle of nitroglycerin.

She picked up the bottle and looked at Meyer coldly.

Then she walked back to her own desk.

When Teddy Carella walked into the squadroom at two minutes past seven, Peter Byrnes thought he would have a heart attack. He saw her coming down the corridor and at first he couldn't believe he was seeing correctly and then he recognized the trim figure and proud walk of Steve's wife, and he walked quickly to the railing.

"What are you doing?" Virginia said.

"Somebody coming," Byrnes answered, and he waited. He did not want Virginia to know this was Carella's wife. He had watched the woman grow increasingly more tense and jumpy since the pistol whipping of Meyer, and he did not know what action she might conceivably take against Teddy were she to realize her identity. In the corner of the room, he could see Hawes administering to Meyer. Badly cut, Meyer tried to peer out of his swollen eyes. His lip hung loose, split down the center by the unyielding steel of the revolver. Hawes, working patiently with iodine, kept mumbling over and over again, "Easy, Meyer, easy," and there was a deadly control to his voice as if he—as much as the nitro—were ready to explode into the squadroom.

"Yes, Miss?" Byrnes said.

Teddy stopped dead outside the railing, a surprised look on her face. If she had read the lieutenant's lips correctly . . .

"Can I help you, Miss?" he said.

Teddy blinked.

"Get in here, you," Virginia barked from her desk. Teddy could not see the woman from where she stood. And, not seeing her, she could not "hear" her. She waited now for Byrnes to spring the punch line of whatever gag he was playing, but his face remained set and serious, and then he said, "Won't you come in, Miss?" and—puzzled even more now—Teddy entered the squadroom.

She saw Virginia Dodge immediately and knew intuitively that Byrnes was trying to protect her.

"Sit down," Virginia said. "Do as I tell you and you won't get hurt. What do you want here?"

Teddy did not, could not answer.

"Did you hear me? What are you doing here?"

Teddy shook her head helplessly.

"What's the matter with her?" Virginia asked impatiently. "Damnit, answer me."

"Don't be frightened, Miss," Byrnes said. "Nothing will happen to you if . . ." He stopped dead, feigning discovery, and then turned to Virginia. "I think . . . I think she's a deaf mute," he said.

"Come here," Virginia said, and Teddy walked to her. Their eyes locked over the desk. "Can you hear?"

Teddy touched her lips.

"You can read my lips?"

Teddy nodded.

"But you can't speak?"

Teddy shook her head.

Virginia shoved a sheet of paper across the desk. She took a pencil from the tray and tossed it to Teddy. "There's paper and pencil. Write down what you want here."

In a quick hand, Teddy wrote "Burglary" on the sheet and handed it to Virginia.

"Mmm," Virginia said. "Well, you're getting a lot more than you're bargaining for, honey. Sit down." She turned to Byrnes and, in the first kind words she'd uttered since coming into the squadroom, she said, "She's a pretty little thing, isn't she?"

Teddy sat.

"What's your name?" Virginia asked. "Come over here and write down your name."

Byrnes almost leaped forward to intercept Teddy as she walked to the desk again. Teddy picked up the pencil and rapidly wrote "Marcia . . ." She hesitated. A last name would not come. In desperation, she finally wrote her maiden name— "Franklin."

"Marcia Franklin," Virginia said. "Pretty name. You're a pretty girl, Marcia, do you know that? Can you read my lips?"

Teddy nodded.

"Do you know what I'm saying?"

Again, Teddy nodded.

"You're very pretty. Don't worry, I won't hurt you. I'm only after one person, and I won't hurt anybody unless they try to stop me. Have you ever loved anyone, Marcia?"

Yes, Teddy said with her head.

"Then you know what it's like. Being in love. Well, someone killed the man I loved, Marcia. And now I'm going to kill him. Wouldn't you do that, too?"

Teddy stood motionless.

"You would. I know you would. You're very pretty, Marcia. I was pretty once—until they took my man away from me. A woman needs a man. Life's no good without a man. And mine is dead. And I'm going to kill the man who's responsible. I'm going to kill a rotten bastard named Steve Carella."

The words hit Teddy with the force of a pitched baseball. She flinched visibly, and then she caught her lips between her teeth, and Virginia watched her in puzzlement and then said, "I'm sorry, honey, I didn't mean to swear. But I . . . this has been . . ." She shook her head.

Teddy had gone pale. She stood with her lip caught between her teeth, and she bit it hard, and she looked at the revolver in the hand of the woman at the desk, and her first impulse was to fling herself at the gun. She looked at the wall clock. It was 7:08. She turned toward Virginia and took a step forward.

"Miss," Byrnes said, "that's a bottle of nitroglycerin on the desk there." He paused. "What I mean is, any sudden movement might set it off. And hurt a lot of people."

Their eyes met. Teddy nodded.

She turned away from Virginia and Byrnes, crossing to sit in the chair facing the slatted railing, hoping the lieutenant had not seen the sudden tears in her eyes.

* * *

The clock read 7:10.

Teddy thought only, *I must warn him.*

Methodically, mechanically, the clock chewed time, swallowed it, spat digested seconds into the room. The clock was an old one, and its mechanism was audible to everyone but Teddy, *whirrr, whirrr,* and the old clock digested second after second until they piled into minutes and the hands moved with a sudden click in the stillness of the room.

7:11 . . .

7:12 . . .

I must warn him, she thought. She had given up the thought of jumping Virginia and thought only of warning Steve now. I can see the length of the corridor from here, she thought, can see the top step of the metal stairway leading from below. If I could hear I would recognize his tread even before he came into view because I know his walk, I have imagined the sound of his walk a thousand times. A masculine sound, but light-footed, he moves with animal grace, I would recognize the sound of his walk the moment he entered the building—if only I could hear.

But I cannot hear, and I cannot speak. I cannot shout a warning to him when he enters this second floor corridor. I can only run to him. She will not use the nitro, not if she knows Steve is in the building where she can shoot him. She needs the nitro for her escape. So I'll run to him and be his shield, *he must not die.*

And the baby?

The baby, she thought. Hardly a baby yet, a life just begun, but Steve must not die. Myself, yes. The baby, yes. But not Steve. I will run to him. The moment I see him, I will run to him, and then let her shoot. But not Steve.

She had almost lost him once, she could remember that Christmas as if it were yesterday, the painfully white hospital room, and her man gasping for breath. She had hated his occupation then, detested police work and criminals, abhorred the chance circumstances that had allowed her husband to be shot by a narcotics peddler in a city park. And then she had allowed her hatred to dissolve, and she had prayed, simply and sincerely, and all the while she knew that he would die and that her silent world would truly become silent. With Steve, there was no silence. With Steve, she was surrounded by the noise of life.

This was not a time for prayer.

All the prayers in the world would not save Steve now.

When he comes, she thought, I will run to him and I will take the bullet.

When he comes . . .

231

The clock read 7:13.

That isn't nitroglycerin, Hawes thought.

Maybe it is.

That isn't nitroglycerin.

It can't be. She handles it like water, she treats it with all the disdain she'd give to water, she wouldn't be so damn careless with it if it were capable of exploding.

It isn't nitroglycerin.

Now wait a minute, he told himself, let's just wait a minute, let's not rationalize a desire into a fact.

I want desperately for the liquid in that bottle to be water. I want it because for the second time in my life I am ready to knock a woman silly. I am ready to cross this room and, gun be damned, knock her flat on her ass and keep hitting her until she is senseless. That is the way I feel right now, and chivalry can go to Hell because that is the way I feel. I know it's not particularly nice to go around slugging women, but Virginia Dodge has become something less than woman, or perhaps something more than woman, she has become something inhuman and I no more consider her a woman than I would apply gender to a telephone or a pair of shoes.

She is Virginia Dodge.

And I hate her.

And I'm ashamed because I hate so goddamn deeply. I did not think myself capable of such hatred, but she has brought it out in me, she has enabled me to hate deeply and viciously. I hate her, and I hate myself for hating, and this causes me to hate deeper. Virginia Dodge has reduced me to an animal, a blind animal responding to a pain that is being inflicted. And the curious thing is that the pain is not my own. Oh, the cheek, I've been hit harder before, the cheek doesn't matter. But what she did to Miscolo, and what she did to that Puerto Rican girl, and what she did to Meyer, these are things I cannot excuse, rationally or emotionally. These are pains inflicted on humans who have never done a blessed solitary thing to the non-human called Virginia Dodge. They were simply here and, being here, she used them, she somehow reduced them to meaningless ciphers.

And this is why I hate.

I hate because I . . . I and every other man in this room . . . have allowed her to reduce humans to ciphers. She has robbed them of humanity, and by allowing her to rob one man of humanity, by allowing her to strip a single human being of all his godly dignity, I have allowed her to reduce *all* men to a pile of rubbish.

So here I am, Virginia Dodge.

Cotton Hawes is my name, and I am a one-hundred-percent white Protestant American raised by God-fearing parents who instilled in me a sense of right and wrong, and who taught me that women are to be treated with courtesy and chivalry—and you have turned me into a jungle animal ready to kill you, hating you for what you've done, ready to kill you.

The liquid in that bottle is *not* nitroglycerin.

This is what I believe, Virginia Dodge.

Or at least, this is what I am on the road to believing. I do not yet fully believe it. I'm working on it, Virginia. I'm working on it damn hard.

I don't have to work on the hatred. The hatred is there, and it's building all the time and God help you, Virginia Dodge, when I'm convinced, when I've convinced myself that your bottle of nitroglycerin is a big phony.

God help you, Virginia, because I'll kill you.

"Where is he?" she said, and looked up at the clock. "It's almost seven-thirty. Isn't he supposed to report back here?"

"Yes," Byrnes said.

"Then where the hell is he?" She slammed her left fist down on the desk top. Hawes watched. The bottle of nitro, jarred, did not explode.

It's water, Hawes thought. Goddamnit, it's *water*!

"Have you ever had to wait for anything, Marcia?" Virginia said to Teddy. "I feel as if I've been in this squadroom all my life."

Teddy watched the woman, expressionless.

"You ro'n bitch," Angelica Gomez said. "You should wait in *Hell*, you dirtee bitch."

"She's angry," Virginia said, smiling. "The Spanish onion is angry. Take it easy, Chiquita. Just think, your name'll be in the newspapers tomorrow."

"An' your name, too," Angelica said. "An' maybe it be in the *dead* columns."

"I doubt that," Virginia said, and all humor left her face and her eyes. "The newspapers will . . ." She stopped. "The newspapers," she said, and this time she said the words with the tone of discovery. Hawes watched the discovery claim her face, watched as she stirred her memory. Her eyes were beginning to narrow.

233

"I remember reading a story about Carella," she said. "In one of the newspapers. The time he got shot. It mentioned that his wife . . ." She paused. "His wife was a deaf mute!" she said, and she turned glaring eyes on Teddy. "What about it, Marcia Franklin? What about it?"

Teddy did not move.

"What are you doing here?" Virginia said. She had begun rising. "Are you Marcia Franklin, come to report a burglary? Or are you Mrs. Steve Carella? Which? Answer me!"

Again Teddy shook her head.

Virginia was standing now, her attention riveted to Teddy. Slowly, she came around the desk, sliding along its edge, ignoring the bottle on its top completely. It was as if, having found someone she believed to be related to Carella, her wait was nearing an end. It was as if—should this woman be Carella's wife—she could now truly begin to vent her spleen. Her decision showed on her face. The hours of waiting, the impatience of the ordeal, the necessity for having to deal with other people while her real quarry delayed his entrance showed in the gleam of her eyes and the hard set of her mouth. As she approached Teddy Carella, Hawes knew instinctively that she would inflict upon her the same—if not worse—punishment that Meyer Meyer had suffered.

"Answer me!" Virginia screamed, and she left the desk completely now, the bottle of nitro behind her, advanced to Teddy, and stood before her, a dark solemn judge and jury.

She snatched Teddy's purse from her arm, and snapped it open. Byrnes, Kling, Willis, stood to the right of Teddy, near the coat rack. Miscolo was unconscious on the floor behind Virginia, near the filing cabinets. Only Meyer and Hawes were to her right and slightly behind her—and Meyer was limp, his head resting on his folded arms.

Quickly, deftly, Virginia rifled through the purse. She found what she was looking for almost immediately. Immediately, she read it aloud.

"Mrs. Stephen Carella, 837 Dartmouth Road, Riverhead. In case of emergency, call . . ." She stopped. "Mrs. Stephen Carella," she said. "Well, well, Mrs. Stephen Carella." She took a step closer to Teddy, and Hawes watched, hatred boiling inside him, and he thought, *It isn't nitro, it isn't nitro, it isn't nitro . . .*

"Aren't you the pretty one, though?" Virginia said. "Aren't you the well-fed, well-groomed beauty? You've had your man, haven't you? You've had your man, and you've still got your good looks, haven't you? Pretty, you bitch, look at me! Look at me!"

I'll jump her, Teddy thought. Now. While she's away from the nitro. I'll jump her now, and she'll fire, and the rest will grab her, and it will be all over. Now. Now.

But she did not jump.

Hypnotized as if by a snake, she watched the naked hatred on Virginia Dodge's face.

"I was pretty once," Virginia said, "before they sent Frank away. Do you know how old I am? I'm thirty-two. That's young. That's young, and I look like a hag, don't I, like death one of them said. Me, me, I look like death because your husband robbed me of *my* Frank. *Your* husband, you bitch. Oh, I could rip that face of yours apart! I could rip it, rip it for what he's done to me! Do you hear me, you little bitch!"

She stepped closer, and Hawes knew the gun would flash upward in the next moment.

He told himself for the last time, *There's no nitro in that bottle*, and then he shouted, "Hold it!"

Virginia Dodge turned to face him, moving closer to the desk and the bottle on it, blocking Byrnes and the others from it.

"Get away from her," Hawes said.

"What!" Virginia's tone was one of complete disbelief.

"You heard me. Get away from her. Don't lay a hand on her."

"Are you giving me orders?"

"Yes!" Hawes shouted. "Yes, I am giving you orders! Now how about that, Mrs. Dodge? How about it? *I* am giving *you* orders! One of the crawly little humans is daring to give God orders. Keep away from that girl. You touch her and . . ."

"And what?" Virginia said. There was a sneer in her voice, supreme confidence in her stance—but the gun in her hand was trembling violently.

"I'll kill you, Mrs. Dodge," Hawes said quietly. "That's what, Mrs. Dodge. I'll kill you."

He took a step toward her.

"Stand where you are!" Virginia yelled.

"No, Mrs. Dodge," Hawes said. "You know something? I'm not afraid of your wedge any more, your little bottle. You know why? Because there's nothing but water in it, Mrs. Dodge, and I'm not afraid of water. I *drink* water! By the gallon, I drink it!"

"Cotton," Byrnes said, "don't be a . . ."

"Don't take another step!" Virginia said desperately, the gun shaking.

"Why not? You going to shoot me? Okay, damnit, shoot me!

235

But shoot me a lot because one bullet isn't going to do it! Shoot me twice and then keep shooting me because I'm coming right at you, Mrs. Dodge, and I'm going to take that gun away from you with any strength that's left in my hands, and I'm going to stuff it right down your throat! I'm coming, Mrs. Dodge, you hear me?"

"Stop! Stop where you are!" she screamed. "The nitro . . ."

"There *is* no nitro!" Hawes said, and he began his advance in earnest, and Virginia turned to face him fully now. To her left, Byrnes gestured to Teddy, who began moving slowly toward the men who stood just inside the gate. Virginia did not seem to notice. Her hand was shaking erratically as she watched Hawes.

"I'm coming, Mrs. Dodge," Hawes said, "so you'd better shoot now if you're going to because . . ."

And Virginia fired.

The shot stopped Hawes. But only momentarily, and only in the way any sudden sharp noise will stop anyone. Because the bullet had missed him by a mile, and he began his advance again, moving across the room toward her, watching Byrnes slip Teddy past the railing and practically shove her down the corridor. The others did not move. Shut off from the bottle of nitro, they nonetheless stood rooted in the room, facing an imminent explosion.

"What's the matter?" Hawes said. "Too nervous to shoot straight? Your hand trembling too much?"

Virginia backed toward the desk. This time, he *knew* she was going to fire. He sidestepped an instant before she squeezed the trigger, and again the slug missed him, and he grinned and shouted, "That does it, Mrs. Dodge! You'll have every cop in the city up here now!"

"The nitro . . ." she said, backing toward the desk.

"What nitro? There *is* no nitro!"

"I'll knock it to the . . ."

And Hawes leaped.

The gun went off as he jumped, and this time he heard the rushing *whoosh* of the bullet as it tore past his head, missing him. He caught at Virginia's right hand as she swung it toward the desk and the bottle of nitroglycerin. He clung to her wrist tightly because there was animal strength in her arm as she flailed wildly at the bottle, reaching for it.

He pulled her arm up over her head and then slammed it down on the desk top, trying to knock the gun loose, and the bottle slid towards the edge of the desk.

He slammed her hand down again, and again the bottle moved, closer to the edge as Virginia's fingers opened and the gun dropped to the floor.

And then she twisted violently in his arms and flung herself headlong across the desk in a last desperate lunge at the bottle standing not two inches from its edge. She slipped through his grip, and he caught at her waist and then yanked her back with all the power of his shoulders and arms, pulling her upright off the desk, and then clenching his fist into the front of her dress, and drawing his free hand back for a blow that would have broken her neck.

His hand hesitated in mid-air.

And then he lowered it, unable to hit her. He shoved her across the room and said only, "You bitch!" and then stooped to pick up the gun.

Meyer Meyer lifted his battered head. "What . . . what happened?" he said.

"It's over," Hawes answered.

Byrnes had moved to the telephone. "Dave," he said, "get me the Bomb Squad! Right away!"

"The Bom . . ."

"You heard me."

"Yes, sir!" Murchison said.

The call from the hospital came at 7:53, after the men from the Bomb Squad had gingerly removed the suspect bottle from the room. Byrnes took the call.

"Eighty-seventh Squad," he said. "Lieutenant Byrnes."

"This is Dr. Nelson at General. I was asked to call about the condition of this stabbing victim? José Dorena?"

"Yes," Byrnes said.

"He'll live. The blade missed the jugular by about a quarter of an inch. He won't be out of here for a while, but he'll be out alive." Nelson paused. "Anything else you want to know?"

"No. Thank you."

"Not at all," Nelson said, and he hung up.

Byrnes turned to Angelica. "You're lucky," he said. "Kassim'll live. You're a lucky girl."

And Angelica turned sad wise eyes toward the lieutenant and said, "Am I?"

Murchison walked over to her. "Come on, sweetie," he said, "we've got a room for you downstairs." He pulled her out of the chair, and then went to where Virginia Dodge was handcuffed to the radiator. "So you're the troublemaker, huh?" he said to her.

"Drop dead," Virginia told him.

"You got a key for this cuff, Pete?" Murchison said, and shook his head. "Jesus, Pete, why didn't you guys say something? I mean, I was sitting down there all this time. I mean . . ." He stopped as Byrnes handed him the key. "Hey, is that what you meant by 'Forthwith'?"

Byrnes nodded tiredly. "That is what I meant by 'Forthwith,'" he said.

"Yeah," Murchison said. "I'll be damned." Roughly, he pulled Virginia Dodge from the chair. "Come on, prize package," he said, and he led both women from the squadroom, passing Kling in the corridor.

"Well, we got Miscolo off okay," Kling said. "The rest is in the lap of the gods. We sent Meyer along for the ride. The intern seemed to think that face needed treatment. It's over, huh, Pete?"

"It's over," Byrnes said.

There was noise in the corridor outside. Steve Carella pushed a man through the slatted-rail divider and said, "Sit down, Scott. Over there. Hello, Pete. Cotton. Here's our boy. Strangled his own . . . Teddy! Honey, I forgot all about you. Have you been waiting lo—"

He shut his mouth because Teddy rushed into his arms with such fervor that she almost knocked him over.

"We've all been sort of waiting for you," Byrnes said.

"Yeah? Well, that's nice. Absence makes the heart grow fonder." He held Teddy at arm's length and said, "I'm sorry I'm late, baby. But all at once the thing began to jell. Let me type my report and away we go. Pete, I'm taking my wife to dinner, and I dare you to say no. We're going to have a baby!"

"Congratulations," Byrnes said wearily.

"Boy, what enthusiasm. Honey, I'm so starved I could eat a horse. Pete, we book this guy for homicide. Where's a typewriter? Anything interesting happen while I was . . . ?"

The phone rang.

"I've got it," Carella said. He lifted the receiver. "Eighty-seventh Squad, Carella."

"Carella, this is Levy down the Bomb Squad."

"Yeah, hi, Levy, how are you?"

"Fine. And you?"

"Fine. What's up?"

"I got a report on that bottle."

"What bottle?"

"We picked up a bottle there."

"Oh, yeah? Well, what about it?"

Carella listened, inserting a few "Uh-huhs" and "Yeses" into the conversation. Then he said, "Okay, Levy, thanks for the dope," and hung up. He pulled up a chair, ripped three D.D. sheets from the desk drawer, inserted carbon between them, and then swung a typewriter into place.

"That was Levy," he said. "The Bomb Squad. Somebody here give him a bottle?"

"Yeah," Hawes said.

"Well, he was calling to report on it."

Hawes rose and walked to Carella. "What did he say?"

"He said it was."

"It was?"

"That's what the man said. They exploded it downtown. Powerful enough to have blown up City Hall."

"It was," Hawes said tonelessly.

"Yeah." Carella inserted the report forms into the typewriter. "Was *what*?" he asked absently.

"Nitro," Hawes said, and he sank into a chair near the desk, and he had on his face the stunned expression of a man who's been hit by a diesel locomotive.

"Boy," Carella said, "what a day *this* was!"

Furiously, he began typing.

Killer's Wedge, 1958

239

THE FAT LADY

From where the two patrolmen sat in the patrol car parked at the curb, it seemed evident that the priest was winning the fight. They had no desire to get out of the car and break up the fight, not with it being so cold out there, and especially since the priest seemed to be winning. Besides, they were sort of enjoying the way the priest was mopping up the street with his little spic opponent.

Up here in the Eight-Seven, you sometimes couldn't tell the spics (*Hispanics*, you were supposed to say in your reports) from the whites because some of them had high Spanish blood in them and looked the same as your ordinary citizen. For all the patrolmen knew, the *priest* was a spic, too, but he had a very white complexion, and he was bigger than most of the cockroach-kickers up here. The two patrolmen sat in the heated comfort of the car and guessed aloud that he was maybe six-three, six-four, something like that, maybe weighing in at two hundred and forty pounds or thereabouts. They couldn't figure which church he belonged to. None of the neighborhood churches had priests who dressed the way this one was dressed, but maybe he was visiting from someplace in

243

California—they dressed that way in California, didn't they, at those missions they had out there in the Napa Valley? The priest was wearing a brown woolen robe, and his head was shaved like a monk's head, its bald crown glistening above the tonsure that encircled it like a wreath. One of the patrolmen in the car asked the other one what you called that brown thing the priest was wearing, that thing like a·dress, you know? The other patrolman told him it was called a *hassock*, stupid, and the first patrolman said, "Oh yeah, right." They were both rookies who had been working out of the Eight-Seven for only the past two weeks, otherwise they'd have known that the priest wasn't a priest at all, even though he was known in the precinct as Brother Anthony.

Clearly, Brother Anthony was in fact beating the man to a pulp. The man was a little Puerto Rican pool shark who'd made the enormous mistake of trying to hustle him. Brother Anthony had dragged the little punk out of the pool hall and first had picked him up and hurled him against the brick wall of the tenement next door, just to stun him, you know, and then had swung a pool cue at his kneecaps, hoping to break them but breaking only the pool cue instead, and now was battering him senseless with his hamlike fists as the two patrolmen watched from the snug comfort of the patrol car. Brother Anthony weighed a lot, but he had lifted weights in prison, and there wasn't an ounce of fat on his body. He sometimes asked people to hit him as hard as they could in the belly, and laughed with pleasure whenever anyone told him how hard and strong he was. All year round, even in the hot summer months, he wore the brown woolen cassock. During the summer months, he wore nothing at all under it. He would lift the hem of the cassock and show his sandals to the neighborhood hookers. "See?" he would say. "That's all I got on under this thing." The hookers would oooh and ahhh and try to lift the cassock higher, making believe they didn't think he was really naked under it. Brother Anthony was very graceful for such a big man; he would laugh and dance away from them, dance away.

In the winter, he wore army combat boots instead of the sandals. He was using those boots now to stomp the little Puerto Rican pool hustler into the icy sidewalk. In the patrol car, the two cops debated whether they should get out and break this thing up before the little spic got his brains squashed all over the sidewalk. They were spared having to make any decision because their radio erupted with a 10-10, and they radioed back that they were rolling on it. They pulled away from the curb just as Brother Anthony leaned over the prostrate and unconscious hustler to take his wallet from his pocket. Only ten dollars of the money in that wallet had been hustled from Brother Anthony, but he figured he might as well take *all* of it because of all the trouble the little punk had put him to. He was cleaning out the wallet when Emma came around the corner.

Emma was known in the neighborhood as the Fat Lady, and most of the people in the precinct tried to steer very clear of her because she was known to possess a short temper and a straightedge razor. She carried the razor in her shoulder bag, hanging from the left shoulder, so that she could reach in there with her right hand, and whip open the razor in a flash, and lop off any dude's ear, or slash his face or his hands, or sometimes go for the money, open the man's windpipe and his jugular with one and the same stroke. Nobody liked to mess with the Fat Lady, which was perhaps why the crowd began to disperse the moment she came around the corner. On the other hand, the crowd might have dispersed anyway, now that the action had ended; nobody liked to stand around doing nothing on a cold day, especially in *this* neighborhood, where somehow it always seemed colder than anyplace else in the city. This neighborhood could have been Moscow. The park bordering this neighborhood could have been Gorky Park. Maybe it was. Or vice versa.

"Hello, bro," the Fat Lady said.

"Hello, Emma," he said, looking up from where he was crouched over the unconscious hustler. He had stomped the man real good. A thin trickle of blood was beginning to congeal on the ice beneath the stupid punk's head. His face looked very blue. Brother Anthony tossed the empty wallet over his shoulder, stood up to his full height, and tucked the five-hundred-odd dollars into the pouchlike pocket at the front of the cassock. He began walking, and Emma fell into step beside him.

Emma was perhaps thirty-two or thirty-three years old, in any event a good six or seven years older than Brother Anthony. Her full name was Emma Forbes, which had been her name when she was still married to a black man named Jimmy Forbes, since deceased, the unfortunate victim of a shoot-out in a bank he'd been trying to hold up. The man who'd shot and killed Emma's husband was a bank guard who'd been sixty-three years old at the time, a retired patrolman out of the 28th

245

Precinct downtown. He'd never lived to be sixty-*four* because Emma sought him out a month after her husband's funeral, and slit his throat from ear to ear one fine April night when the forsythias were just starting to bud. Emma did not like people who deprived her or her loved ones of anything they wanted or needed. Emma was fond of saying, "The opera ain't over till the fat lady sings," an expression she used to justify her frequent vengeful attacks. It was uncertain whether the expression had preceded the nickname, or vice versa. When someone was five feet six inches tall and weighed a hundred and seventy pounds, it was reasonable to expect—especially in *this* neighborhood, where street names were as common as legal names—that sooner or later someone would begin calling her the Fat Lady, even without having heard her operatic reference.

Brother Anthony was one of the very few people who knew that the name on her mailbox was Emma Forbes, and that she had been born Emma Goldberg, not to be confused with the anarchist Emma Goldman, who'd been around long before Emma Goldberg was even born. Brother Anthony was also one of the very few people who called her Emma, the rest preferring to call her either Lady (not daring to use the adjective in her presence) or nothing at all, lest she suddenly take offense at an inflection and whip out that razor of hers. Brother Anthony was the only person in the precinct, and perhaps the entire world, who thought Emma Goldberg Forbes a.k.a. the Fat Lady was exceptionally beautiful and extraordinarily sexy besides.

"Listen, there's no accounting for taste," a former acquaintance once said to Brother Anthony immediately after he'd mentioned how beautiful and sexy he thought Emma was. The man's thoughtless comment was uttered a moment before Brother Anthony plucked him off his stool and hurled him through the plate-glass mirror behind the bar at which they'd been sitting. Brother Anthony did not like people who belittled the way he felt about Emma. Brother Anthony saw her quite differently than most people saw her. Most people saw a dumpy little bleached blond in a black cloth coat and black cotton stockings and blue track shoes and a black shoulder bag in which there was a straightedge razor with a bone handle. Brother Anthony—despite empirical knowledge to the contrary—saw a natural blond with curly ringlets that framed a Madonna-like face and beautiful blue eyes; Brother Anthony saw breasts like watermelons and a behind like a brewer's horse; Brother Anthony saw thick white thighs and acres and acres of billowy flesh; Brother Anthony saw a shy, retiring,

246

timid, vulnerable darling dumpling caught in the whirlwind of a hostile society, someone to cuddle and cherish and console.

Just walking beside her, Brother Anthony had an erection, but perhaps that was due to the supreme satisfaction of having beaten that pool hustler to within an inch of his life; it was sometimes difficult to separate and categorize emotions, especially when it was so cold outside. He took Emma's elbow and led her onto Mason Avenue toward a bar in the middle of a particularly sordid stretch of real estate that ran north and south for a total of three blocks. There was a time when the Street (as the three-block stretch was familiarly defined) was called the Hussy Hole by the Irish immigrants and later Foxy Way by the blacks. With the Puerto Rican influx, the street had changed its language—but not its major source of income. The Puerto Ricans referred to it as La Vía de Putas. The cops used to call it Whore Street before the word *hooker* became fashionable. They now referred to it as Hooker Heaven. In any language, you paid your money, and you took your choice.

Not too long a time ago, the madams who ran the sex emporiums called themselves Mama-this or Mama-that. In those days, Mama Teresa's was the best-known joint on the street. Mama Carmen's was the filthiest. Mama Luz's had been raided most often by the cops because of the somewhat exotic things that went on behind its crumbling brick façade. Those days were gone forever. The brothel, as such, was a thing of the past, a quaint memory. Nowadays, the hookers operated out of the massage parlors and bars that lined the street, and turned their tricks in the hot-bed hotels that blinked their eyeless neon to the night. The bar Brother Anthony chose was a hooker hangout named Sandy's, but at two in the afternoon most of the neighborhood working girls were still sleeping off Friday night's meaningless exercise. Only a black girl wearing a blond wig was sitting at the bar.

"Hello, Brother Anthony," she said. "Hello, Lady."

"*Dominus vobiscum*," Brother Anthony said, cleaving the air with the edge of his right hand in a downward stroke, and then passing the hand horizontally across the first invisible stroke to form the sign of the cross. He had no idea what the Latin words meant. He knew only that they added to the image he had consciously created for himself. "All is image," he liked to tell Emma, the words rolling mellifluously off his tongue, his voice deep and resonant, "all is illusion."

"What'll it be?" the bartender asked.

"A little red wine, please," Brother Anthony said. "Emma?"

"Gin on the rocks, a twist," Emma said.

"See what the other lady will have," Brother Anthony said, indicating the black-and-blond hooker. He was feeling flush. His encounter with the ambitious pool hustler had netted him a five-hundred-dollar profit. He asked the bartender for some change, went to the jukebox, and selected an assortment of rock'n'roll tunes. He loved rock'n'roll. He especially loved rock'n'roll groups that dressed up on stage so you couldn't recognize them later on the street. The black-and-blond hooker was telling the bartender she wanted another scotch and soda. As Brother Anthony went back to his stool at the other end of the bar, she said, "Thanks, Brother Anthony."

The bartender, who was also the Sandy who owned the place, wasn't too happy, to see Brother Anthony in here. He did not like having to replace plate-glass mirrors every time Brother Anthony took it in his head to get insulted by something somebody said. Luckily, the only other person in here today, besides Brother Anthony and his fat broad, was the peroxided nigger at the end of the bar, and Brother Anthony had just bought *her* a drink, so maybe there'd be no trouble this afternoon. Sandy hoped so. This was Saturday. There'd be plenty of trouble here tonight, whether Sandy wanted it or not.

In this neighborhood, and especially on this street, Saturday night was never the loneliest night of the week, no matter *what* the song said. In this neighborhood, and especially on this street, nobody had to go lonely on a Saturday night, not if he had yesterday's paycheck in his pocket. Along about ten tonight, there'd be more hookers cruising this bar than there'd be rats rummaging in the empty lot next door, black hookers and white ones, blonds and brunettes and redheads, even some with pink hair or lavender hair, males and females and some who were AC/DC. Two by two they came, it took all kinds to make a world, into the ark they came, your garden-variety scaly-legged twenty-dollar-a-blowjob beasts or your slinky racehorses who thought they should be working downtown at a C-note an hour, it took all kinds to make a pleasant family neighborhood bar. Two by two they came and were welcomed by Sandy, who recognized that all those men drinking at the bar were here to sample the flesh and not the spirits, and who was anyway getting a piece of the action from each of the nocturnal ladies who were allowed to cruise here, his recompense (or so he told them) for having to pay off the cops on the beat and also their sergeant who dropped in every now and again. Actually, Sandy was ahead of the game, except when the weekend trouble assumed larger proportions than it normally did. He dreaded weekends, even though it was the weekends that made it possible for the bar to remain open on weekdays.

"This is on the house," he said to Brother Anthony, hoping the bribe would keep him away from here tonight, and then suddenly panicking when he realized Brother Anthony might *like* the hospitality and might decide to return for more of it later.

"I pay for my own drinks," Brother Anthony said, and fetched the roll of bills from the pouchlike pocket running across the front of his cassock, and peeled off one of the pool hustler's tens, and put it on the bar.

"Even so . . ." Sandy started, but Brother Anthony silently made the sign of the cross on the air, and Sandy figured who was he to argue with a messenger of God? He picked up the ten-spot, rang up the sale, and then put Brother Anthony's change on the bar in front of him. At the end of the bar, the black hooker in the frizzy blond wig lifted her glass and said, "Cheers, Brother Anthony."

"*Dominus vobiscum*," Brother Anthony said, lifting his own glass.

Emma put her fleshy hand on his knee.

"Did you hear anything else?" she whispered.

"No," he said, shaking his head. "Did you?"

"Only that he had eleven bills in his wallet when he caught it."

"Eleven bills," Brother Anthony whispered.

"And also, it was a .38. The gun."

"Who told you that?"

"I heard two cops talking in the diner."

"A .38," Brother Anthony said. "Eleven bills."

"That's the kind of bread I'm talking about," Emma said. "That's *cocaine* bread, my dear."

Brother Anthony let his eyes slide sidelong down the bar, just to make sure neither the bartender nor the black hooker were tuning in. The bartender was leaning over the bar, in deep and whispered conversation with the hooker. His fingertips roamed the yoke front of her dress, brushing the cleft her cushiony breasts formed. Brother Anthony smiled.

"The death of that little *schwanz* has left a gap," Emma said.

"Indeed," Brother Anthony said.

"There are customers adrift in the night," Emma said.

"Indeed," Brother Anthony said again.

"It would be nice if we could *fill* that gap," Emma said.

"Inherit the trade, so to speak. Find out who the man was servicing, become their *new* candyman and candylady."

"There's people who might not like that," Brother Anthony said.

"I don't agree with you. I don't think the little pisher was killed for his trade. No, my dear, I definitely disagree with you."

"Then why?"

"Was he killed? My educated guess?"

"Please," Brother Anthony said.

"Because he was a stupid little man who probably got stingy with one of his customers. That's my guess, bro. But, ah, my dear, when *we* begin selling the nose dust it'll be a different story. We will be sugar-sweet to everybody; we will be Mr. and Mrs. Nice."

"How do we get the stuff to sell?" Brother Anthony asked.

"First things first," Emma said. *"First* we get the customers, *then* we get the candy."

"How many customers do you think he had?" Brother Anthony asked.

"Hundreds," Emma said. "Maybe thousands. We are going to get rich, my dear. We are going to thank God every day of the week that somebody killed Paco Lopez."

"Dominus vobiscum," Brother Anthony said, and made the sign of the cross.

For some people, it was still St. Valentine's Day.

Many people do not believe a day ends at midnight. It is still the same day until they go to sleep. When they wake up in the morning, it is the next day. Two people who thought it was still St. Valentine's Day were Brother Anthony and the Fat Lady. Even though it was 1:00 A.M. on the morning of February 15, they thought of it as still being a day for lovers, especially since they had learned the name of Paco Lopez's girlfriend. Actually, they had learned her name when it *was* still St. Valentine's Day, which they considered a good omen. But it was not until 1:00 A.M. that Brother Anthony knocked on the door of Judite Quadrado's apartment.

In this neighborhood, a knock on the door at 1:00 A.M. meant only trouble. It meant either the police coming around to ask about a crime that had been committed in the building, or it meant a friend or neighbor coming to tell you that a loved one had either hurt someone or *been* hurt by someone. Either way, it meant bad news. The people in this neighborhood knew that

250

a knock on the door at 1:00 A.M. did not mean a burglar or an armed robber. Thieves did not knock on doors unless it was going to be a shove-in and in this neighborhood most thieves knew that doors were double-locked and often reinforced as well with a Fox lock, the steel bar hooked into the door and wedged into a floor plate. Brother Anthony knew that someone awakened at one in the morning would be frightened; that was why he and Emma had waited until that time, even though they'd had their information at 10:00 P.M.

From behind the door, Judite said, "Who is it?"

"Friends," Brother Anthony said.

"Friends? Who? What friends?"

"Please open the door," he said.

"Go away," Judite said.

"It's important that we speak to you," Emma said.

"Who are you?"

"Open the door just a little," Emma said, "and you'll see for yourself."

They heard lock tumblers falling. One lock, then another. The door opened just a crack, held by a night chain. In the wedge of the open door, they saw a woman's pale face. A kitchen light burned behind her.

"*Dominus vobiscum*," Brother Anthony said.

"We have money for you," Emma said.

"Money?"

"From Paco."

"Paco?"

"He said to make sure we gave it to you if anything happened to him."

"Paco?" Judite said again. She had not seen Paco for at least two months before he was killed. It was Paco who had scarred her breasts, the rotten bastard. Who was this priest in the hallway? Who was this fat woman claiming they had money for her? Money from Paco? Impossible.

"Go away," she said again.

Emma took a sheaf of bills from her pocketbook, the money remaining from what Brother Anthony had taken from the pool hustler. In the dim hallway light, she saw Judite's eyes widen.

"For you," Emma said. "Open the door."

"If it's for me, hand it to me," Judite said. "I don't need to open the door."

"Never mind," Brother Anthony said, and put his hand on Emma's arm. "She doesn't want the money."

"How much money is it?" Judite asked.

251

"Four hundred dollars," Emma said.

"And Paco said he wanted *me* to have it?"

"For what he did to you," Emma said, lowering her voice and her eyes.

"Just a minute," Judite said.

The door closed. They heard nothing. Brother Anthony shrugged. Emma returned the shrug. Had their information been wrong? The man who'd told them about Judite was her cousin. He said she'd been living with Paco Lopez before he was killed. He said Paco had burned her breasts with cigarettes. Which was one of the reasons Brother Anthony had suggested they call on her at one in the morning. It was Brother Anthony's opinion that no woman allowed herself to be treated brutally unless she was a very frightened woman. One o'clock in the morning should make her even more frightened. But where was she? Where had she gone? They waited. They heard the night chain being removed. The door opened wide. Judite Quadrado stood in the open doorway with a pistol in her fist.

"Come in," she said, and gestured with the pistol.

Brother Anthony had not expected the pistol. He looked at Emma. Emma said, *"No hay necesidad de la pistola,"* which Brother Anthony did not understand. Until that moment, in fact, he hadn't known Emma could speak Spanish.

"Hasta que yo sepa quien es usted," Judite said, and again gestured with the gun.

"All right," Emma answered in English. "But *only* until you know who we are. I don't like doing favors for a woman with a gun in her hand."

They went into the apartment. Judite closed and locked the door behind them. They were in a small kitchen. A refrigerator, sink, and stove were on one wall, below a small window that opened onto an areaway. The window was closed and rimed with ice. A table covered with white oilcloth was against the right-angled wall. Two wooden chairs were at the table.

Brother Anthony did not like the look on Judite's face. She did not look like a frightened woman. She looked like a woman very much in command of the situation. He was thinking they'd made a mistake coming up here. He was thinking they'd lose what was left of the money he'd taken from the pool hustler. He was thinking maybe the ideas he and Emma hatched weren't always so hot. Judite was perhaps five feet six inches tall, a slender, dark-haired, brown-eyed girl with a nose just a trifle too large for her narrow face. She was wearing a dark blue robe; Brother Anthony figured that was why she'd left them waiting in the hall so long. So she could go put on the robe. And get the gun from wherever she kept it. He did not like the look of the gun. It was steady in her hand. She had used a gun before; he sensed that intuitively. She would not hesitate to use it now. The situation looked extremely bad.

"So," she said. "Who are you?"

"I'm Brother Anthony," he said.

"Emma Forbes," Emma said.

"How did you know Paco?"

"A shame what happened to him," Emma said.

"How did you know him?" Judite said again.

"We were friends for a long time," Brother Anthony said. It kept bothering him that she held the gun so steady in her hand. The gun didn't look like any of the Saturday-night specials he had seen in the neighborhood. This one was at *least* a .38. This one could put a very nice hole in his cassock.

"If you're his friends, how come *I* don't know you?" Judite said.

"We've been away," Emma said.

"Then how did you get the money, if you've been away?"

"Paco left it for us. At the apartment."

"What apartment?"

"Where we live."

"He left it for *me*?"

"He left it for you," Emma said. "With a note."

"Where's the note?"

"Where's the note, bro?" Emma said.

"At the apartment," Brother Anthony said, assuming an attitude of annoyance. "I didn't know we'd need a *note*. I didn't know you needed a *note* when you came to deliver four hundred dollars to—"

"Give it to me then," Judite said, and extended her left hand.

"Put away the gun," Emma said.

"No. First give me the money."

"Give her the money," Brother Anthony said. "It's hers. Paco wanted her to have it."

Their eyes met. Judite did not notice the glance that passed between them. Emma went to the table and spread the bills in a fan on the oilcloth. Judite turned to pick up the bills and Brother Anthony stepped into her at the same moment, smashing his bunched fist into her nose. Her nose had not looked particularly lovely beforehand, but now it began spouting blood. Brother Anthony had read somewhere that hitting a person in the nose was very painful and also highly effective.

The nose bled easily, and blood frightened people. The blood pouring from Judite's nose caused her to forget all about the pistol in her hand. Brother Anthony seized her wrist, twisted her arm behind her back, and yanked the pistol away from her.

"Okay," he said.

Judite was holding her hand to her nose. Blood poured from her nose onto her fingers. Emma took a dish towel from where it was lying on the counter and tossed it to her.

"Wipe yourself," she said.

Judite was whimpering.

"And stop crying. Nobody's going to hurt you."

Judite didn't exactly believe this. She had *already* been hurt. She had made a mistake, opening the door at one in the morning, even *with* the gun. Now the gun was in the priest's hand, and the fat woman was picking up the money on the table and stuffing it back into her shoulder bag.

"Wh . . . what do you want?" Judite said. She was holding the towel to her nose now. The towel was turning red. Her nose hurt; she suspected the priest had broken it.

"Sit down," Brother Anthony said. He was smiling now that the situation was in his own capable hands.

"Sit down," Emma repeated.

Judite sat at the table.

"Get me some ice," she said. "You broke my nose."

"Get her some ice," Brother Anthony said.

Emma went to the refrigerator. She took out an ice tray and cracked it open into the sink. Judite handed her the blood-stained towel, and Emma wrapped it around a handful of cubes.

"You broke my nose," Judite said again, and accepted the towel and pressed the ice pack to her nose. On the street outside, she could hear the rise and fall of an ambulance siren. She wondered if she would need an ambulance.

"Who were his customers?" Brother Anthony asked.

"What?" She didn't know who he meant at first. And then it occurred to her that he was talking about Paco.

"His *customers*," Emma said. "Who was he *selling* to?"

"Paco, do you mean?"

"You know who we mean," Brother Anthony said. He tucked the gun into the pouchlike pocket at the front of his robe, and gestured to the fat woman. The fat woman reached into her bag again. For a dizzying moment, Judite thought they were going to let her go. The priest had put the gun away, and now the fat woman was reaching into her bag again. They were going to give her the money, after all. They were going to let her go. But when the fat woman's hand came out of the bag, there was something long and narrow in it. The fat woman's thumb moved, and a straight razor snapped open out of its case, catching tiny dancing pinpricks of light. Judite was more afraid of the razor than she had been of the gun. She had never in her life been shot, but she'd been cut many, many times, once even by Paco. She bore the scar on her shoulder. It was a less hideous scar than the ones he had burned onto her breasts.

"Who were his customers?" Brother Anthony asked again.

"I hardly even knew him," Judite said.

"You were living with him," Emma said.

"That doesn't mean I knew him," Judite said, which, in a way, was an awesome truth.

She did not want to tell them who Paco's customers had been because *his* customers were now *her* customers, or at least *would* be as soon as she got her act together. She had reconstructed from memory a list of an even dozen users, enough to keep her living in a style she thought would be luxurious. Enough to have caused her to buy a gun before she embarked on her enterprise; there were too many bastards like Paco in the world. But the gun was now in the priest's pocket, and the fat woman was turning the razor slowly in her hand, so that its edge caught glints of light. Judite thought, and this in itself was an awesome truth, that life had a peculiar way of repeating itself. Remembering what Paco had done to her breasts, she pulled the robe instinctively closed over her nightgown, using her free hand. Brother Anthony caught the motion.

"Who were his customers?" Emma said.

"I don't know. *What* customers?"

"For the nose candy," Emma said, and moved closer to her with the razor.

"I don't know what that means, nose candy," Judite said.

"What you *sniff*, my dear," Emma said, and brought the razor close to her face. "Through your *nose*, my dear. Through the nose you won't *have* in a minute if you don't tell us who they were."

"No, not her face," Brother Anthony said, almost in a whisper. "Not her face."

He smiled at Judite. For another dizzying moment, Judite thought he was the one who would let her go. The woman seemed menacing, but surely the priest—

"Take off the robe," he said.

255

"What for?" she asked, and clutched the robe closed tighter across her chest.

"Take it off," Brother Anthony said.

She hesitated. She pulled the towel away from her nose. The flow of blood seemed to be tapering. She put the towel back again. Even the pain seemed to be ebbing now. Perhaps this would not be so bad, after all. Perhaps, if she just went along with them, played along with them—surely the fat woman wasn't *serious* about cutting off her nose? Were the names of Paco's customers really that important to them? Would they risk so much for so little? Anyway, they were *her* customers now, damn it! She would give them whatever else they wanted, but not the names that were her ticket to what she imagined as freedom. She did not know what kind of freedom. Just freedom. She would never give them the names.

"Why do you want me to take off the robe?" she asked. "What is it you want from me?"

"The customers," Emma said.

"Do you want to see my body?" she asked. "Is that it?"

"The customers," Emma said.

"You want me to blow you?" she asked Brother Anthony.

"Take off the robe," Brother Anthony said.

"Because if you want me to—"

"The robe," he said.

She looked at him. She tried to read his eyes. Paco had told her she gave better head than most of the hookers he knew. If she could reach the priest—

"Can I stand up?" she asked.

"Stand up," Emma said, and retreated several steps. The open razor was still in her hand.

Judite put down the towel. Her nose had stopped bleeding entirely. She took off the robe and draped it over the back of the chair. She was wearing only a pale baby-doll nightgown. The nightgown ended just an inch below her crotch. She was not wearing the panties that had come with the nightgown when she'd bought it. The nightgown and panties had cost her twenty-six dollars. Money she could easily get back from her new cocaine trade. She saw where the priest's eyes went.

"So what do you say?" she asked, arching one eyebrow and trying a smile.

"I say take off the nightgown," Brother Anthony said.

"It's cold in here," Judite said, hugging herself. "The heat goes off at ten." She was being seductive and bantering, she thought. She had captured the priest's eye—they were all supposed to be celibate, some joke—and now she thought she'd make it a bit more interesting and spicy, tease him along a little, make a big production out of taking off the nightgown. The fat woman would go along with whatever the priest decided; Judite knew women, and that's the way it was.

"Just take it off," Brother Anthony said.

"What for?" Judite said, the same light tone in her voice. "You can *see* what you're getting, can't you? I'm practically naked here, you can practically see right through this thing, so why do I have to take it off?"

"Take off the fucking nightgown!" Emma said, and all at once Judite thought she'd made a big error in judgment. The fat woman was moving closer to her again, the razor flashing.

"All right, don't . . . just don't get . . . I'll take it off, okay? Just . . . take it easy, okay? But, really, I don't know what you're talking about, Paco's customers, I swear to God I don't know what you mean by—"

"You know what we're talking about," Brother Anthony said.

She pulled the gown up over her waist, lifted it over her breasts and shoulders, and without turning placed it on the seat of the wooden chair. Goose flesh erupted immediately on her arms and across her chest and shoulders. She stood naked and trembling in the center of the kitchen, her bare feet on the cold linoleum, the ice-rimed window behind her. She was quite well formed, Brother Anthony thought. Her shoulders were narrow and delicately turned, and there was a gently rounded swell to her belly, and a ripe flare to her hips. Her breasts, too, were large and firm, quite beautiful except for the angry brown burn scars on their sloping tops. Very well formed, he thought. Not as opulent a woman as Emma, but very well formed indeed. He noticed that there was a small knife scar on her left shoulder. She was a woman who'd been abused before, perhaps regularly, a very frightened woman.

"Cut her," he said.

The thrust of the razor came so swiftly that for a moment Judite didn't even realize she'd been cut. The slash drew a thin line of blood across her belly, not as frightening as the blood pouring from her nose had been, really just a narrow line of blood oozing from the flesh, nothing so terribly scary. Even the searing aftermath of the razor slash was less painful than the blow to her nose had been. She looked down at her belly in amazement. But somehow, she was less frightened now than she'd been a moment earlier. If this was what it would be like, if this was the *worst* they would do to her—

"We don't want to hurt you," the priest said, and she knew this meant they *did* want to hurt her, would in *fact* hurt her more than they already had if she did not give them the names they wanted. Her mind worked quickly, frantically searching for a way to protect her own interests, give them the names of the customers, why not, but withhold the name of the ounce dealer—you could always find new customers if you knew where to get the stuff. Hiding her secret, hiding her fear as well, she calmly gave them all the names they wanted, all of the twelve she had memorized, writing them down at their request, scribbling the names and addresses on a sheet of paper, trying to conceal the shaking of her fist as she wrote. And then, after she had given them all the names, and had even clarified the spelling of some of them, after she thought it was all over, thought they had what they wanted from her now, and would leave her alone with her broken nose and the bleeding slash across her belly, she was surprised to hear the priest ask, "Where did he get the stuff?" and she hesitated before answering, and realized all at once that her hesitation had been another mistake, her hesitation had informed them that she knew the source of Paco's supply, knew the name of his ounce dealer and wanted it from her now.

"I don't know where," she said.

Her teeth were beginning to chatter. She kept looking at the razor in the fat woman's hand.

"Cut off her nipple," the priest said, and her hands went instinctively to her scarred breasts as the fat woman approached with the razor again, and suddenly she was more frightened than she'd ever been in her life, and she heard herself telling them the name, heard herself giving away her secret and her freedom, saying the name over and over again, babbling the name, and thought that would truly be the end of it, and was astonished to see the razor flashing out again, shocked beyond belief when she saw blood spurting from the tip of her right breast and knew, *Oh dear Jesus*, that they were going to hurt her anyway, *Oh sweet Mary*, maybe kill her, *Oh sweet mother of God*, the razor glinting and slashing again and again and again until at last she fainted.

Brother Anthony and Emma were smoking dope and drinking wine and going over the list of names and addresses Judite Quadrado had given them two days ago. A kerosene heater was going in one corner of the room, but the radiators were only lukewarm, and the windows were nonetheless rimed with ice.

Brother Anthony and Emma were sitting very close to the kerosene heater, even though both of them insisted that cold weather never bothered them. They were both in their underwear.

They had smoked a little pot an hour ago, before making love in the king-sized bed in Brother Anthony's bedroom. Afterward they had each and separately pulled on their underwear and walked out into the living room to open a bottle of wine and to light two more joints before sitting down again with the list of potential customers. Brother Anthony was wearing striped boxer shorts. Emma was wearing black bikini panties. Brother Anthony thought she looked radiantly lovely after sex.

"So what it looks like to me," Emma said, "is that he had a dozen people he was servicing."

"That's not so many," Brother Anthony said. "I was hoping for something bigger, Em, I'll tell you the truth. Twelve rotten names sounds like very small potatoes for all the trouble we went to." He looked at the list again. "Especially in such small quantities. Look at the quantities, Em."

"Do you know the joke?" she asked him, grinning.

"No. What joke?" He loved it when she told jokes. He also loved it when she went down on him. Looking at her huge breasts, he was beginning to feel the faintest stirrings of renewed desire, and he began thinking that maybe he would let her tell her joke and then they would forget all about Lopez's small-time list and go make love again. That sounded like a very good thing to do on a cold day like today.

"This lady is staying at a Miami Beach hotel, you know?" Emma said, still grinning.

"I wish *I* was staying at a Miami Beach hotel," Brother Anthony said.

"You want to hear this joke or not?"

"Tell it," he said.

"So she eats a couple of meals in the dining room, and then she goes to the front desk and starts complaining to the manager."

"What about?" Brother Anthony said.

"Will you let me tell it, please?"

"Tell it, tell it."

"She tells the manager the food in the dining room is absolute poison. The *eggs* are poison, the *beef* is poison, the *potatoes* are poison, the *salads* are poison, the *coffee* is poison, everything is poison, poison, poison, she says. And you know what *else*?"

"What else?" Brother Anthony asked.

"The *portions* are so small!" Emma said, and burst out laughing.

"I don't get it," Brother Anthony said.

"The lady is complaining the food is *poison* . . ."

"Yeah?"

"But she's *also* complaining the portions are too small."

"So what?"

"If it's *poison*, why does she want bigger portions?"

"Maybe she's crazy," Brother Anthony said.

"No, she's not crazy," Emma said. "She's complaining about the food, but she's *also* telling the manager the portions—"

"I understand," Brother Anthony said, "but I still don't get it. Why don't we go in the other room again?"

"You're not ready yet," Emma said, glancing at his lap.

"You can make me ready."

"I know I can. But I like it better when you're ready *before* I make you ready."

"Sweet mouth," Brother Anthony said, lowering his voice.

"Mmm," Emma said.

"So what do you say?"

"I say business before pleasure," Emma said.

"Anyway, what made you even *think* of that joke?" he asked.

"You said something about the small quantities."

"They *are* small," Brother Anthony said. "Look at them," he said and handed the list to her. "Two or three grams a week, most of them. We ain't gonna get rich on two, three grams a week."

"We don't have to get rich all at once, bro," Emma said. "We'll take things slow and easy at first, start with these people who used to be Lopez's customers, build from there."

"How?"

"Maybe the lady can put us onto some other customers."

"What lady? The one eating poison?"

"The one who was supplying Lopez. His ounce dealer."

"Why would she want to help us that way?"

"Why not? There has to be a chain of supply, bro. An ounce dealer needs gram dealers, a gram dealer needs users. The lady puts us onto some users, we buy our goods from her, and everybody's happy."

"I think you're dreaming," Brother Anthony said.

"Would it hurt to ask?" Emma said.

"She'll tell us to get lost."

"Who knows? Anyway, first things first. First we have to let her know we've taken over from Lopez and would like to continue doing business with her. That's the first thing."

"That's the first thing, for sure."

"So what I think you should do," Emma said, "is get dressed and go pay this Sally Anderson a little visit."

"Later," Brother Anthony said, and took her in his arms.

"Mmm," Emma said, and cuddled closer to him, and licked her lips.

Emma and Brother Anthony were celebrating in advance.

He had bought a bottle of expensive four-dollar wine, and they now sat drinking to their good fortune. Emma had read the letter, and had come to the same conclusion he had: the man who'd written that letter to Sally Anderson was the man who was supplying her with cocaine. The letter made that entirely clear.

"He buys eight keys of cocaine," Brother Anthony said, "gives it a full hit, gets twice what he paid for it."

"Time it gets on the street," Emma said, "who knows *what* it'd be worth?"

"You got to figure they step on it all the way down the line. Time your user gets it, it'll only be ten, fifteen percent pure. The eight keys this guy bought . . . he sounds like an amateur, don't he? I mean, going in *alone*? With four hundred grand in *cash*?"

"Strictly," Emma said.

"Well, so are we, in a way," Brother Anthony said.

"You're very generous," Emma said, and smiled.

"Anyway, those eight keys, time they hit the street up here, they've already been whacked so hard you're talking maybe thirty-*two* keys for sale. Your average user buying coke doesn't know *what* he's getting. Half the rush he feels is from thinking he paid so *much* for his gram."

Emma looked at the letter again. "'The first thing I want to do is celebrate,'" she read. "'There's a new restaurant on top of the Freemont Building, and I'd like to go there Saturday night. Very elegant, very continental. No panties, Sally. I want you to look very elegant and demure, but no panties, okay? Like the time we ate at Mario's down in the Quarter, do you remember? Then, when we get home . . .'" Emma shrugged. "Lovey-dovey stuff," she said.

"Girl had more panties than a lingerie shop," Brother Anthony said. "Whole *drawer*ful of panties."

"So he asks her not to *wear* any!" Emma said, and shook her head.

"I'm gonna buy you one of those little things ballet dancers wear," Brother Anthony said.

"Thank you, sir," Emma said, and made a little curtsy.

"Why you think she saved that letter?" Brother Anthony asked.

"'Cause it's a love letter," Emma said.

"Then why'd she hide it in the collar of her jacket?"

"Maybe she was married."

"No, no."

"Or had another boyfriend."

"I think it was in case she wanted to turn the screws on him," Brother Anthony said. "I think the letter was her insurance. Proof that he bought eight keys of coke. Dumb amateur," he said, and shook his head.

"Try him again," Emma said.

"Yeah, I better," Brother Anthony said. He rose ponderously, walked to the telephone, picked up the scrap of paper on which he'd scribbled the number he'd found in the directory, and then dialed.

Emma watched him.

"It's ringing," he said.

She kept watching him.

"Hello?" a voice on the other end said, and Brother Anthony immediately hung up.

"He's home," he said.

"Good," she said.

He closed the suitcase.

So, he thought.

He looked around the apartment.

That's it, he thought.

He picked up the suitcase, walked out of the bedroom, and out of the apartment, and down the steps to the street.

She was waiting for him in the small dark entrance lobby downstairs.

He frowned and started to walk past her, taking her for a crazy bag lady or something, this city was full of lunatics, surprised when he saw the open straight razor in her hand, shocked when he realized she was coming at him with the razor, terrified when he saw his own blood pouring from the open wound in his throat.

She said only, "The opera ain't over."

Ice, 1983